Henry James

Society the Redeemed Form of Man

and the earnest of God's omnipctence in human nature - affirmed in letters to a

friend

Henry James

Society the Redeemed Form of Man
and the earnest of God's omnipotence in human nature - affirmed in letters to a friend

ISBN/EAN: 9783337368753

Printed in Europe, USA, Canada, Australia, Japan

Cover: Foto ©Andreas Hilbeck / pixelio.de

More available books at **www.hansebooks.com**

SOCIETY

THE REDEEMED FORM OF MAN,

AND

THE EARNEST OF GOD'S OMNIPOTENCE
IN HUMAN NATURE:

AFFIRMED IN

LETTERS TO A FRIEND

By HENRY JAMES.

"Man during his earthly life induces a form in the purest substances of his interiors, so that he may be said to form his own soul, or give it quality; and according to the form or quality of soul he thus gives himself will be his subsequen. receptivity to the Lord's inflowing life: which is *a life of love to the whole human race.*"

BOSTON:
HOUGHTON, OSGOOD AND COMPANY.
The Riverside Press, Cambridge.
1879.

ELECTROTYPED AND PRINTED AT THE UNIVERSITY PRESS,
CAMBRIDGE.

CONTENTS.

LETTER V.

LETTER VI.

LETTER VII.

LETTER VIII.

LETTER IX.

LETTER X.

LETTER XIV.

LETTER XV.

LETTER XVI.

LETTER XVII.

LETTER XVIII.

LETTER XIX.

LETTER XX.

LETTER XXIII.

LETTER XXIV.

LETTER XXVII.

LETTER XXVIII.

LETTER I.

MY DEAR FRIEND:—You know that I am not in good health. Ever since my illness of last May, now more than a year ago, my nerves are easily unstrung by protracted labor, and I am consequently not very sure beforehand that I can meet the demands of your recent letter as well as I should like to. Still I am persuaded that even for weary nerves there is no sedative so sovereign as the reconciling truths we are going to consider, and I hope therefore that our conference will not, on the whole, prove tedious or enervating to either of us.

I will quote a few lines of your letter in order that by my comment upon them I may pitch the tune of our subsequent discussion, or indicate the harmonic issues to which I would have it lead. You say: "I cannot bear to think with any purpose of my private regeneration after having so long committed all my Godward hopes to the destiny of my

race. Least of all should I be likely to entertain
that question just now, when the labors of Messrs.
Moody and Sankey, and the rhetoric of Rev. Joseph
Cook, seem providentially intended to show us the
vulgar egotism and the blatant unbelief in the
Divine name, with which it is almost sure to be
associated.''

Now I have as little respect for Messrs. Moody
and Sankey, and for their flashy, histrionic colleague,
as you can desire, and think our daily papers might
easily furnish better food to their readers than the
puerile stuff they give us as reports of these men's
sensational sermons and lectures. But what interests
me chiefly in the extract from your letter is the
general sentiment of preference you exhibit for a
fixed life of relation to God over one of a *free*
and spiritual character: that is, for a life of passive
submission to your race-destiny, over one of active
private regeneration. You have always one great
merit, that of knowing well your own mind. But
I take the liberty of offering you a few considerations in regard to this sentiment of preference you
express, which perhaps you have not done justice
to, and which may therefore lead you in the present case to an improved knowledge of your own
mind.

Let me ask you then, in the first place, what good

our race-destiny is going to do *us* individually? Our race-destiny is thoroughly incapable, I am happy to say, of furnishing a destiny for the individual man. We are not the race, but individuals embraced in it; and though there is beyond doubt a race-destiny for man, there is no such thing as an individual destiny. Human individuality is constituted by freedom and rationality; and if therefore a certain destiny were imposed upon it to fulfil, either by deity or demon, it would immediately collapse. If I am really *destined* to undergo a certain mental development, ending in my spiritual manhood, just as I am destined to undergo a certain physical growth ending in my natural manhood, it must be because I have no self-hood — that is, no freedom and rationality — wherewith to work out my spiritual manhood. In short, to have a fixed "destiny" is not to be a free and rational subject, and therefore to be without individuality; and to be without individuality is to be destitute of spiritual possibilities, and claim only natural.

I repeat, then, that the human race alone, and not any individual subject of it, claims a Divine "destiny," because the race has only an indefinite or universal personality, and of itself therefore is only fit to minister to a defined or individual one. But the individual man, because he is by creation free and rational, is *ipso facto* the arbiter of his own spiritual life and character: that is, he either remains what he already is by derivation from his past ancestry, and the circumstances of his own position, or else he becomes a new and regenerate form of life, according to his own pleasure.

Thus your and my private regeneration is not an outcome of *destiny* in any sense of the word. No doubt, we may picture the heart of God as very much interested in every man's private or spiritual regeneration. But then at the same time we must take extreme good care not to represent Him as interested in it to the extent of "destining" any of us for it, as the sect of Universalists holds; or what is the same thing, imposing it upon any of us contrary to his own good will and pleasure; because obviously that would be to represent Him as violating the express means He has appointed for bringing it about, and so defeating the realization of it. For what does our spiritual regeneration mean? It means — our new birth, or our getting a new heart and mind: that is, a different one from that we are actually born to, or inherit from our forefathers. As this old heart and mind take place in us without our own privity or consent previously asked, so our new birth signalizes its own superior lustre or more intimate nearness to us, by conditioning itself upon our private freedom and rationality, or accommodating itself to our secret hearts' demands, derived from culture.

This is what to every man, spiritually exercised, makes his private regeneration a question of such vital moment, namely: that *his deepest instincts of manhood are met by it, and by it alone.* For example, my inherited personality is full of stain or frailty derived from some or other of my progenitors, so that I find myself, when tempted, not only liable but sure to succumb to theft, false witness, adultery, or murder. Now in this state of things it is evident that unless there be some Divine revelation *in our nature and history* making me aware of this tendency to evil in me, and prompting me to combat it, I am as good as gone to all eternity. For I have no intuitive conscience of the difference between good and evil, but only an empirical or acquired one. As far as my personal intuitions go I unhesitatingly deem good evil and evil good. Our moral conscience is a Divine endowment of *our nature* exclusively, utterly beyond the sphere of our personal intuitions; and we come into the experience of it accordingly only through the intercourse of our kind. It is notorious to every man of thoroughly educated experience, that when he is tempted to bear false witness, to steal, to commit adultery, or murder,

the whole pressure of the temptation lies in the fact
that these damnable things seem ravishingly good
to him and not evil. Other men, interested in pre-
venting me doing them may denounce them as evil.
But I in my secret heart, when tempted by these
unhandsome things, cannot help pronouncing them
good, the most intimate and exquisite good I know,
in fact; and I inwardly renounce the doing of them
only out of deference to the Divine law forbid-
ding me to do them under penalty of death.

I repeat then, that it is this strictly redemptive
effort of God in *our nature*, which alone qualifies
me to realize my deepest human instincts, or learn
in what consists my true freedom and rationality.
Before being inwardly born — before being spiritually quickened — I have no misgiving as to my
appetites and passions forming in me only a conditional or limited good. They seem so much my
nearest good, that I feel no higher exercise of freedom or selfhood possible to me, than to obey them
unreservedly, or whenever they demand satisfaction.
And I have no sort of a suspicion, until I receive
my information from others, that I am then meanwhile, in spite of my apparent selfhood or freedom,
the wretched *slave of my personal organization*. It
seems at this period so like free action to give way
to my appetites and passions regardless of any

higher law, and my nascent unripe sense of self-hood or personality is so fostered by it, that I cannot help yielding for a while to the deceptive seeming: but it is wholly a seeming, destitute of the least vital truth. Sooner or later this *felt* freedom —this *apparent* rationality of mine—confess themselves a burdensome and abject servitude, from which there is no release but in the fetterless air of the spiritual world. In fact, dear friend, our inherited self-hood or freedom — the selfhood that comes to us from birth, or is derived to us from our special ancestry — is a mere provisional base for a Divinely-given selfhood or personality, which comes to us through the natural redemption wrought in us by the Lord Jesus Christ: and it is literally next to nothing, if it refuse to operate as such base.

Admitting then that we have to the fullest extent a "destined" or unfree life of God in our race: I ask afresh how does that supply the wants of our free spiritual or highest culture? And can a man really be so false to the instincts of his proper manhood as deliberately to prefer a "destined" life, even at the Divine hands, to one of freedom? I know my good friend Emerson has long been singing us songs set to this indolent tune, and that many feebler warblers reflect his inspiration. And I know besides, that our orthodox churches give

out so decrepid a doctrine of the Divine name, and
our Unitarian or rationalistic pulpits in their turn
reply to it in so scant and penurious a strain,
that the common mind has grown altogether tired
of the senseless jangle, and prefers to take its very
unexacting religion and philosophy at the hands of a
poet, and that too a pantheistic one. But you don't
belong to the common or scientific crowd of men,
shut up like so many gregarious sheep to the pens
of sense. You are a person first of all of sincere,
original *thought*, taking nothing on trust from other
men, despising the servile limits of sensuous observation by which their intellect is bound, and thinking out your own conclusions according to the free
range of sympathy and intelligence God has given
you. And you accordingly can never permanently
consent to sell your Divine birthright of freedom,
for the paltry mess of pottage these respectable senti-
mentalists offer you under the name of "destiny."
Besides, so active an intellect as yours ought by this
time to know that we can have no positive but only
a negative action upon this destined life of our race,
because our race interests belong exclusively to God,
and He is absolute over them. We have no power
to promote our race destiny, but by our spiritual
regeneration. *Every man who becomes regenerate by*
abstaining from the commission of evils, in virtue

purely of their contrariety to the Divine name, does indirectly promote his race-evolution, because he ceases any longer actively to obstruct and retard it. Our natural evolution, or our race-destiny, is to put on Divine form and order; and this form and order undeniably consist in each man seeking supremely the good of the whole, and in all men seeking supremely the good of each. It is manifest then that the regenerate person does indirectly promote this race-evolution, inasmuch as he alone freely abstains from conflict with his fellowman. But this is all he does towards it, and *à fortiori* all and more than all that any one else does towards it. The man who lives in practically selfish relations with his kind, seeking himself first and his neighbor last, does absolutely nothing for his race or nature but retard its due and orderly evolution. And when it is evolved, he will do nothing spiritually to promote its well-being, because although he will then be inhibited from any *moral* conflict with his fellows, he will cultivate no spiritual sympathy with them.

What then? Do I urge you to cherish an intellectual indifference to your race-destiny? God forbid! I should in so doing be utterly faithless to my own best inspiration. I find it unspeakably blessed to believe that there is a Divine-*natural destiny* for man slowly but surely working out, which no spiritual wickedness in high places, nor any personal stupidity and egotism on our part, can seriously compromise. Why? Because this benign conviction gives me the indispensable stay or guarantee which my meagre individual faith and hope in God demand as a basis. I could of course have no spiritual or private hope for myself in God, unless it were built upon His natural or public mercy to my race: for how shall any man this side of hell ever deem himself a fitter object of the Divine complacency than any other man, especially than *all* men? My moral freedom — my freedom to be good or evil at my pleasure, subject only to what is due to other men — is full of the divinest benignity to my nature, because the development of that nature in all Divine form and order is conditioned upon it. The actual distinction of heaven and hell, in fact, is conditioned upon it; which distinction is no less vital to spiritual order. So that the interests of both worlds, natural and spiritual alike, may be said to demand it. But my moral freedom is but a *quasi* freedom after all, and therefore however it may condition my true or spiritual freedom, is heaven-wide of constituting it. My moral freedom consists in my ability, under the pressure of any mercenary motive, to abstain from false-witness, theft, adultery, and murder. My spiritual freedom endows me with a totally new motive of action, which is the love of God and my neighbor, or the power of immortal life; and so not only enables me to abstain with disgust from these unholy things, but to do with relish the exact opposite. The element of will or choice is everything in the moral life, and the fussy votaries of it accordingly are absurdly tenacious of their personal merit. But this element of will or choice scarcely enters appreciably into the spiritual life, unless into the lowest forms of it; and in all the higher or celestial forms it is unknown.

I rejoice then with unspeakable joy in this ordering of our natural destiny at God's hands — this final and decisive adjustment of men's outward and warring relations — because in the first place it authenticates every deepest breath of man's regenerate hope and aspiration towards God, and in the second place forever exempts men from the temptation again to seek their own welfare by the methods of vice and crime. But apart from these considerations — apart, in other words, from its power to illustrate the Divine name — I have no thought nor care about our natural destiny. Especially when invited to regard it, as so many men at this day do, in the light of a full satisfaction to men's faith and hope in God, it seems to me inexpressibly revolting. For after all is said that can be said, it is a mere reduction to order of man's natural or constitutional life, with the·spiritual, functional, or infinite side of his being left out. And are men content to deem themselves cattle, that they expect no higher boon at the hands of the DIVINE NATURAL HUMANITY but an unexampled provision for their board and lodging?

Understand me then, and understand my books. *I strongly affirm a Divine destiny — a Divine-natural order — for mankind, but I affirm it in the interest of the Divine name alone,* which the church obscures, by practically cutting off men's secular hope towards God, unless it claims a sanctimonious basis. In short I have no interest in maintaining this truth of a Divinely appointed destiny for the race, but the interest of Divine justice or righteousness. Of course no one can deny that it is infinitely pleasanter to think of men living together in outward harmony, than living like pigs in a sty, where every one is bent upon grabbing as much as he can from his neighbor, or pushing away his unfortunate neighbor from the trough altogether. But the outward order of human life is, after all, supremely pleasant to me, because it discloses an eternal Divine rest and refreshment for the inward man, or indicates at least the method by which the individual conscience attains to spiritual peace in God. If our natural evolution did nothing to reveal and guarantee our inward and immortal joy in God, I for one should be obdurately indifferent to it. If my life is to be spiritually snuffed out at last, I should very much prefer to have beforehand no natural glimpse of peace and order, arising from the Divine subjugation of heaven and hell, to mislead me into making false inferences.

I have now said nearly enough to make my meaning on this subject clearly intelligible to you. I am not, you perceive, the least indisposed to believe that I am "destined" by the Divine providence — either in my own person or the persons of my descendants — to the possible enjoyment of health, wealth, and all manner of outward prosperity, in the evolution of a final natural order for man on the earth, or the development of a united race-personality. But I am utterly averse to believing *that "destiny" has any the least hand in, or power over, my inward relations to infinite goodness and truth, or my instinct of spiritual freedom.* Every such sentiment indeed I trample under foot with a resolute and hearty good will, for it aims to obscure the very central glory and most dazzling effulgence of the creative name. Let me here say besides, very briefly, though the theme well deserves a Letter to itself, that if I could feel that I had been "*destined*" to love goodness and truth in spite of the preternatural sweetness to my heart of evil and falsity, the sentiment of an inmost freedom and rationality which now qualifies my manhood, would instantly wither at its source, and even my nature disown its proper life or selfhood. For my nature derives its total power to function from the spiritual world, and if you exhaust that world — the world of man's substantial freedom or individuality — of its hold upon my affection and faith, you *à fortiori* reduce my natural life to inanition, and relegate me, its conscious subject, to instant unconsciousness.

LETTER II.

BUT our difference, according to your own showing, is far more vital, intellectually, than any we have yet apprehended, belonging rather to the realm of *thought* than that of sentiment. You say, for example: "I am told on every hand that you believe in Jesus Christ as the only God. If this be true I cannot help expressing my disappointment." And then, after saying that you have not so understood my books, you continue in words following: "You mean by Christ more than any one human personality. You don't identify God with any *person* whatever, but with *all* human nature. I never should suspect you of the narrowness here imputed to you. But how can I feel sure that I am right about your belief, when all your readers with whom I am acquainted feel sure that I am wrong?"

My books are too small a thing to excite controversy, but at least let me express my mortification that to a reader of your perspicacity they should have borne an uncertain sound on the point in question. This comes in part perhaps of your overlooking the sharp discrimination I habitually make between *nature* and *person*, or between what is *real* and what is merely *phenomenal* in human existence; but I must confess that on the whole your criticism is damaging to my self-love. Let me then try again to expose to you the philosophic ground of my convictions on this subject, and to this end indulge me with a brief backward glance at the history of the human mind, by way of getting a starting-point comprehensive enough to show in the sequel where the philosophic truth comes in.

Since time began two races have struggled for precedence in the womb of humanity, one of which we may call the child of bondage, the other the child of freedom; one embodying the interests of man's outward or conscious life, the other those of his inward or unconscious life; one representing his natural or race-force, the other his spiritual or personal force. In history this antagonism in human thought and life has been variously symbolized: now as the actual or old Jerusalem in contrast with a new Jerusalem which is yet to come; now as a legal Divine economy in opposition to a gracious one; now as a visible or figurative order of human life in opposition to an invisible or real order; finally and in brief, as *the world* and *the church*.

"The world" and "the church," then, have been *symbols of thought* to man, growing out of the fundamental needs of his intellect: what precise intellectual needs do these opposing symbols attest or stand for?

"The world" represents the interests of human universality — say human *nature* in short; "the church" represents the interests of human individuality — say human *regeneration*, in short. Thus we may say that *the world* stands for the fatal side of human life, those interests of man which relate him willy-nilly to his fellowman, and therefore place him more or less in the voluntary category, or under the rule of duty, of force, of necessity, of destiny. And *the church* on the other hand symbolizes the *free* side of human life, those interests of man which relate him primarily to his infinite source, and which exalt him therefore into the category of spontaneity, or express — all duty done and all destiny achieved — the reign thenceforth of taste, of culture, of inward attraction or delight, of immortal life in short. Human regeneration is doubtless the sole spiritual end of God's creative providence; as the human race is its sole incidental natural end. And as the highest Divine blessing for the regenerate man is freedom, so the highest Divine blessing for the race is, incidentally, an order competent to secure such freedom. But I repeat that we cannot be too particular in denying "the world" and "the church" any final validity, and restricting them to a purely symbolic virtue. In their material or technical aspect they are plainly irrelevant to the grand ideas they symbolize: what calls itself "the church," for example, being notoriously so devoted to the pretence of order, as to carry it to the pitch of ritualism or superstition; and what calls itself "the world" so devoted to the pretence of freedom as to run it into radicalism, so contemning the order which alone saves freedom from license. Nevertheless in their symbolic character they have been of incalculable succulence to the intellect, as without the vital contrast and oppugnancy which they have always represented to human thought, human progress would have proved abortive, or perished in its cradle.

And now having secured our needful starting-point in the brief historic generalization here given, it only remains to inquire further in this connection why this sharp discrimination between nature and spirit, or between the universal and individual interest in human life, should have been so vital to the mind, as to make all history resound with it?

To tell the great truth in one very brief word:

it is because man is the *creature of God*, and is essentially therefore a *divided* personality: one aspect of it relating him to his own nature or his fellow-man, so giving him conscious or finite and phenomenal existence; the other aspect of it relating him to God or his spiritual source, so giving him real or unconscious and infinite being. Understand me. If man be in truth a creature of God, then two things become at once necessary: 1. That he possess real or unconscious being only in God; and 2. That he possess conscious or phenomenal existence exclusively in himself. Because if his real or unconscious being were not in God but in himself, then he himself would *instantly cease to exist* or *appear;* and if his conscious or phenomenal existence were not in himself but in God, then he would himself *instantly cease to be.* In the one case he would forfeit natural existence; in the other he would forfeit spiritual being.

This fact, then, of man's creatureship — that is, the bare fact that his real being lies in the Divine perfection, and that he only claims in himself phenomenal or unreal existence — requires that his history present that duality of movement which exhibits him now as a spiritual or individual force, now as a natural or universal one. Accordingly it is sheerly impossible to deal with man intelligently or intelligibly

upon any other logical basis than this of his creatureship: that is to say, upon the basis of his referring his true or spiritual being infinitely away from
himself, namely: to God; and claiming to himself
instead a mere natural, phenomenal, or shadowy existence.   At all events this is the view which I find
myself forced to take of man's being and history,
that is, of his spiritual origin and his natural destiny; and it is especially the view which I shall
try to enforce throughout the present letters.

Very well then: so far at least there is no room
for misunderstanding.   No one can deny that history demonstrates a divided empire in man.   Every
man of experience or observation knows that man
is subject to a double law, one outward, natural, constitutional, so to speak, relating him whether he will
or not to his fellow-man; the other inward, spiritual, creative, so to speak, relating him freely to God.
The first of these laws has respect to man as a whole,
or in a universal aspect, obeying the empire of necessity.   The second has respect to him only in his individual capacity, obeying the inspiration of freedom.
I repeat then: so far there is no ground for misunderstanding between us.

But now I am going to say something which perhaps neither experience nor observation has made
plain to you, and which may therefore give rise to

misunderstanding, if I do not very fully explain myself. You know that I have traced the fact of man's
divided existence to the truth of his creatureship,
which requires on the one hand that he possess spiritual or invisible being in his Creator, and on the
other natural or visible existence in himself. Because
if man possessed only spiritual being in his Creator,
he would be without any ground of consciousness in
himself, and hence without any recognition of the difference between him and God. And if he possessed
only natural or visible existence in himself, he would
manifestly be uncreated. At all events he would
then have no pretension, as now, to deem himself
the creature of an infinite power. I do not hesitate
to say therefore that his peculiar creatureship implies
this double bond of spiritual or infinite being, and of
natural or finite existence.

But if such be the implication of man's creatureship, the phenomenon must of course attribute itself
to something in the creative perfection. There is obviously nothing in the creature which has not its sole
raison d'être in the greatness of the Creator; and if
we would ascertain accordingly why it is that man
has always worn a divided aspect — here exalting
himself above the neighbor, there subjecting himself
to the neighbor — we must seek our answer only in
the excellence of the creative name. Let us ask

therefore, to what essential excellence of the creative name it is owing, that man, its creature, should inevitably wear to himself a finite and phenomenal aspect, or feel a conscience of limitary relations with God and his fellow-man?

It is owing very obviously to nothing else than the *infinitude* of the creative Love: which requires that the Creator in creating or imparting life to His creatures should first of all endow them with selfhood, or subjective consciousness, in order that such consciousness in giving them *quasi* or phenomenal projection from Himself, may ever after serve them as an infallible negative basis or mirror of all positive Divine knowledge. And selfhood, or subjective consciousness, being contingent as it is upon the perception of a controlling object, in relation to which alone it is either good or evil, we have the entire moral history of the race provided in this antagonism of inward and outward, subject and object, man and nature, which is incidental to the very idea of creation.

But here you will ask me to be more explicit. You will ask me to explain to you in a less cursory manner than I have done in the last paragraph, why the infinitude of the Creator requires Him, as I have said, to endow His creature with selfhood, or subjective life? To answer this we must take a

new Letter.   Permit me, however, meanwhile to say,
that after the frank exposition already given you
can have no longer any excuse for doubting that
I at least, whatever others may do, not only value
human freedom in its higher aspect, as the culminat-
ing miracle of the spiritual creation, or what alone
renders the creative name eternally adorable; but
regard it also, in its practical aspect, as the highest
blessing capable of being bestowed by God upon
man: as that blessing indeed which alone keeps every
other blessing from becoming nauseous.   Not moral
or finite freedom — not a mere freedom of choice
between good and evil, though this is of inestimable
value as a basis of the other — but a positive or infinite freedom, which is without any ratio or limit,
being identical with God's own presence in the
created nature, and is felt in the created bosom
therefore, as the spontaneous prompting of its own
spirit.

LETTER III.

MY DEAR FRIEND:—To our natural, uneducated apprehension of Divine things, a proper inference from God's spiritual infinitude or perfection would be, that He might at once bestow what life He listed upon His creatures: if need were, a real and imperishable one. But an enlightened reason teaches us that every such judgment is superstitious or profane, springing from grossly sensuous notions of the Divine infinitude. We naturally think of God as the power of an outward life, and measure His good-will by his readiness to bestow all manner of outward prosperity upon His favorites. But He is in truth and pre-eminently the power of an inward life in man: that is to say, a life so little accentuated to the senses as to seem more innocent than infancy: and where there is no susceptibility in man to this inward life, His power of outward benefaction is thwarted. It is these sensuous prejudices of ours with respect to the Divine power which lead us to put such an exaggerated estimate as we do upon the gift of self-hood, as the sum of all God's outward bounty to the race; when the gift in question is without any objective reality, being one of pure subjective seem-ing. We want to know accordingly what precise exigency of the creative infinitude or perfection it is, which thus prevents the omnipotent Creator from fully authenticating the selfhood of man, or making him (in himself) anything but a mere form of sub-jective or seeming life. In other words our present business is to consider the creative infinitude, in order to ascertain the ground of its signal incapacity to con-fer upon its creatures (in themselves) any other than a subjective, personal, finite, or phenomenal conscious-ness.

We are in the habit of saying that God the Cre-ator is infinite Love, but I doubt whether we are as prompt to understand all that is implied either in the qualifying adjective or the qualified noun. We say, indeed, that the Creator is Love, because He manifestly communicates life or being to other existences, who can have no manner of claim upon Him but what they derive from His own bountiful nature. But when we say His love is infinite, do we do so only by way of characterizing its pure quality, as being unalloyed by any fibre of self-love;

that is to say, by any sentiment of conflict between Himself and others? Obviously there can be no essential or substantial conflict to the creative intelligence between Himself and His creatures, since He furnishes their sole and total being or substance. And any conflict which does ensue between them, therefore, must be purely formal or phenomenal, existing to the created apprehension alone, and involving no compromise of the creative infinitude. This is accordingly the only ground of our ascribing infinitude or perfection to the creative Love: that it is ineffably pure love, or love so wholly unlike ours, as to be absolutely free from any set-off or drawback of self-love, or even of transient self-regard. We say a thing is *infinite*, which has no *subjective* limitation, no limitation *ab intra*. And we say it is *absolute*, as having no *objective* limitation, no limitation *ab extra*. Now the Creator is *in se*, or *essentially*, both infinite, as being void of subjective relations; and absolute, as being void of objective relations; and it is only in His existential relations to the finite understanding of His own creatures, that we apply these terms to Him, in order to express our approximate sense of His perfect being, and so, in the best way we know how, differentiate Him from ourselves.

Now this infinitude of the Creator constituting

Him (in Himself) the all of being that exists, stamps the creature (*in himself*) a mere appearance or image of being, an abject phenomenal form or semblance of being, without a particle more reality in itself than the shadow which your or my person projects upon the ground, has in itself: that is, no philosophic, but a mere sensible or scientific reality. The creature exists sensibly to himself no doubt, and therefore claims to himself a scientific reality; but this existence, at best, is a strictly phenomenal or contingent existence, requiring an objective base or background to give it projection, or render it conscious. The creature is rendered self-conscious by virtue of his subjection to his own body, or the outlying world inherent in his bodily senses; and so far of course is an authentic *datum* of science. But the inferiority of science to sense as a basis of *spiritual* culture is signally evinced by the fact, that the testimony of sense is indisputable, while that of science is nothing if not disputable. Sense gives us all the existence we know; science deals with the inferences or judgments which such existence renders probable, and hence presents an every way unstable or perilous, not to say impossible, base to men's spiritual culture. For if spiritual truth is built, not upon the solid rock of natural fact, but upon the shifting sands of men's opinion, it would be absurd for us to attempt cultivating or even cherishing it, as it could never get body enough to become recognized by us, let alone loved.

In spite, then, of the scientific authentication it claims — rather, let me say, in virtue of such authentication — created existence must be of a purely contingent, phenomenal, conscious character ; that is to say, can never be thought to include in itself its own being or substance. To make it include its own being or substance would be to pronounce it uncreated, in which case it would no longer be a product of infinite power but would itself possess infinitude. Creature would become converted into creator, in short : than which nothing more needs be said to demonstrate the logical absurdity of the position. The exact infirmity of science, regarded as a final or proper intellectual discipline of man, is that it is bound by its own limitation to ignore creation, or make no account of the distinctively Divine implication in existence. This must forever establish its essential inferiority to philosophy as an intellectual *cultus*. For the precise and characteristic research of philosophy is just that spiritual or creative element in all existence which science is bound by the interests of self-preservation to overlook. Philosophy is nothing but a pursuit of the essential ends and causes that underlie and explain phenomena.

Science confines herself only to phenomena and their relations, that is, to what is strictly verifiable in some sort by sense; and so stigmatizes the pursuit of being or substance as fatal to her fundamental principles. Philosophy, in short, is the pursuit of Truth, super-sensuous truth, recognizable only by the heart of the race, or if by its intellect, still only through a life and power derived from the heart. / Science has no eye for truth, but only for Fact, which is the appearance that truth puts on to the senses, and is therefore intrinsically second-hand, or shallow and reflective. To derive one's chief intellectual nurture from science, consequently, would be as unwise as to seek to know a man through a persistent study of his old clothes. It is, accordingly, a truth no way surprising to Philosophy that the creature, *quâ* a creature, must be absolute nought *in se*, and become both conscious and cognizable only by virtue of the creative being or substance dwelling in him as *himself*: that is, in spiritually despised, rejected and crucified form. For the Creator in order to communicate His own wealth of being to the creature, is first obliged to give the creature a *quasi* or supposititious standing before Him, by making him at least *self*-conscious, or phenomenal to himself; and then by gradually revealing to him the abysmal death that is incident to this *quasi* or finite existence, win him

to that hearty disgust of himself which is the inex-
pugnable condition of his knowledge of — and sincere relish for — Divine things.

I have shown you then that the creative power
is inhibited by its own strict infinitude or perfection, from allowing its creature any life more real
than that of selfhood, or mere subjective seeming:
because to do this would be to disjoin its creature
from itself, or render him independent of his sole
source of life.   I confess I do not see how, if you
acknowledge the truth of creation at all, but especially acknowledge it to be spiritual or living, you
can help agreeing with what I have said.   And if
you agree with me that man — being a creature —
is not, and in the very nature of things, can never
be, his own spiritual being or substance: then, as
it strikes me, the main obstacle will be removed to
our general agreement in the fundamental postulate
of Christianity, which is the sole Divinity of Christ's
Humanity.   That is to say, we shall both alike be
able to perceive, that as all men like you and me
naturally feel that personal or egoistic substance
(being the least material or most vitalized substance
they know) is veritable Divine substance, and does
really constitute their own deeply recognized and
highly prized Divine being: so the most urgent obligation which this natural hallucination of the created

intelligence imposes upon the Creator, is eventually to redeem His creature from the overpowering bondage of self, and the utter spiritual blight it engenders, by fully incarnating His own perfection in the *nature* of the creature, and from that "coign of 'vantage" gradually glorifying the consciousness of the latter out of personal into race dimensions; out of selfish into social form and order.

Now I shall not affront your self-respect by affecting to demonstrate the truth of God's NATURAL humanity scientifically: in the first place, because it is not a fact of sense, and therefore escapes the supervision of science; and in the second place, because in all this correspondence, I am anxious to conciliate your heart primarily, while your head is quite a subordinate aim. I cannot tell you a single reason, unprompted by the heart, why I myself believe the truth in question, or any other truth for that matter; and so far as my own pleasure is concerned, accordingly, I would not give a fig for your acknowledgment of it, if the acknowledgment did not betray a like cordial source. In fact, I believe it simply because I love it, or it seems adorably good to me; and once having learned to love it, I could not do without it. It would in truth kill me, intellectually, to doubt it. So you see I am at least disinterested in my advocacy of the truth. I recom-

mend it to you for its own sake exclusively, and not
at all for yours. It may indeed, for aught I know,
prove as odious to you as it is precious to me; and
God forbid that I should take it upon me to say
you nay, whatever way your heart inclines you. To
my experience this is the only thing that in the long
run authenticates truth to the intellect — *the heart's
sincere craving for it.* I find that truth unloved is
always at bottom truth unbelieved, however much it
may be "professed." In short, I am persuaded
that there is no more galling bondage known to the
intellect, than that of truth unsanctioned and unsoft-
ened by affection; and I don't the least wonder at
Swedenborg — when describing men in a freer world
than this, however — saying that they willingly
plunge into the depths of hell to be rid of it.

LETTER IV.

FREE your mind, then, at once and utterly, so far as I am concerned, of all apprehension of being *reasoned* into truth, or having your understanding coerced against your heart's consent. Ratiocination is doubtless an honest pastime, or it would not be so much in vogue as a means of acquiring truth. But the truth we are elucidating is Divine, and therefore is great enough to authenticate itself, or furnish its own evidence. Divine truth, to be sure, must always be unpopular or out of fashion, so long as God is the simply merciful or magnanimous being He is. But if it had to be acquired at the same cost to mind and body that scientific truth exacts, — if the result involved an equally wide field of sensible induction, an equally studious observation of particulars, the same painstaking investigation of evidence, and the same power to formulate a just conclusion, — there would be still fewer persons to pursue it, and com-

paratively few of these again would feel very secure
of their results.

But the case is widely different. Divine truth,
simply because it is Divine, has first to create the
intelligence that recognizes it, and therefore releases
its votaries from that costly and toilsome research
which is demanded by science. It takes nature or
the senses for granted, and the will and understanding in man: but that is the sum of its exactions.
For it propagates itself by the method of Revelation
exclusively: that is, by gradually unveiling to human
intelligence the spiritual sense or meaning which is
latent in all natural symbols: and hence desiderates
no preparation in its disciples but a modest and
docile intelligence. Its entire aim is to lay a foundation for men's spiritual life, by first disabusing
them of their sensuous prejudices, and the selfish,
untender science which is begotten of these; and
consequently it makes no direct appeal to their conceited intelligence, but seeks to cure their spiritual
disability by first purifying their hearts of the evil
loves which engender it.

Thus the sole disciplinary apparatus of Divine
Truth is detergent or purgative, being fully embodied
in the ten commandments. He would very grossly
mistake the purpose of "the moral law," as we
term it, which is the basis of our existing civili-

zation, who should fail to discern its intensely spiritual *animus,* as intended above all things *to bring
about a change of heart in the votary.* By the irresistible bent of their finite nature the affections of
men are obdurately set upon perishing things, and
the main design of the law therefore is to convince
them of this death-bearing nature they carry about
in themselves, and fix their attention upon a great
natural deliverance to be accomplished for them in
the fulness of time by the infinite Divine mercy.
Thus in the sacred or symbolic Hebrew Scriptures,
the law is always prefaced by the assertion of a great
figurative redemption Divinely wrought. "And God
spake all these words, saying: *I, the Lord thy God,
have brought thee out of the land of Egypt, out of the
house of bondage.*" This is the law's supreme sanction, and its invariable challenge to the imagination
of its votary, that the spiritual Creator of men — He
who is their true but unseen being — is their natural Redeemer as well, giving them deliverance first
from the infirmities and corruptions incident to their
finite generation, as the indispensable condition of
their truly fulfilling it. Then in strict accordance
with this majestic proem, the letter of the law goes
on to indicate to its intelligent subject, first, those
dispositions of heart and mind which befit this great
deliverance: namely, a sentiment of tender awe and

reverence for his adorable Divine Redeemer, of
deference to his natural elders and superiors, and
of brotherhood or impartial fellowship to his natural equals : and, secondly, sums up and stigmatizes
to his eternal abhorrence the four or five generic
forms of evil action which alone perpetuate the sway
of his old nature, and therefore vitiate his experience
of the regenerate life. And now mark what the
comment of the New Testament upon this Old Testament legal Divine administration is, namely : that
every subject of the law—who so far failed to sym-
pathize with its spiritual scope as a discipline of the
heart in man in including *all* men without exception under sin, as nevertheless to make a boast of its
letter in giving *some* men a conscience of righteousness — was Divinely rejected.

Of course we no longer live under a literal administration of Divine things, but an overtly spiritual
one. But our ecclesiastical leaders are apparently
blind to this patent fact, being determined to eter-
nize this inveterate Jewish itch after a carnal righteousness, such as may distinguish Christians outwardly no less than inwardly from other men. The
skulking and beggarly way they take to gratify this
evil concupiscence, is by reorganizing the law —
considered as the unchanged and indefeasible ground
of man's justification — under the specious mask of

a Christian "profession," or the duty which believers owe their faith "to profess Christ" before the world, and so mortify the secular spirit within them. And we may frankly appeal accordingly to any of the more flagrant types of the Christian "profession" among us, to confirm and illustrate the New Testament affirmation of the profound spiritual death and damnation that inhere in every attempt to compass a literal or personal holiness at the Divine hands.

I will not cite the frequent testimony of our newspapers to show how common an instinct of the public mind it is to feel, that a man's practical morality invites close scrutiny the moment he becomes any way conspicuous as claiming a *professional* sanctity. And it is in fact growing a ludicrous spectacle, to see how an almost fatal Divine *nemesis* pursues those who abound in the ways of the current self-righteousness, or achieve a place of honor in the ranks of technical piety, until they turn out very often an actual stench in men's nostrils for their grossly immoral practices. But I prefer to shut my eyes to these catastrophes in the moral or subjective sphere, in order to look behind them at what may be regarded as their root. The moral experience of man has been hitherto completely subservient to the needs of his spiritual freedom, or his growth in humility and tender reverence for the

Divine name; and now that this freedom is inflowing into the human mind in unexampled measure, it is not to be wondered at that those who are insensible and indifferent to the Divine substance should be equally insensible and indifferent to the genuine morality which has been its human type. But, bad as these moral obliquities are, I am persuaded that the interests of spiritual religion are far more deeply compromised in the world by those of its "professors" who are not practically immoral, but contrive on the contrary to enjoy the esteem of their friends while they live, and to die — when they die — in the odor of a corrupt conventional sanctity.

The only danger to the spirit of religion (and this is a danger that besets *every* inward grace of manhood) comes from the effort of the soul to assume and cherish a devout *self*-consciousness ; or so to *abound* in a religious sense, as to incur the imputation of religiosity or superstition. This is the inalienable vice of professional religion, the only sincere fruit it is capable of bringing forth. The evil spirit which religion is primarily intended to exorcise in us is the spirit of selfhood, based upon a most inadequate apprehension of its strictly *provisional* uses to our spiritual nurture. The gradual conquest or slaying of this unholy spirit of self in man is the sole function which religion proposes to itself during his natural

life; and without taxing our co-operation too se-
verely, it yet gives us enough to do before its benignant mission is fully wrought out. Such being
the invariable office of the religious instinct, *professional* religion steps in to simulate its sway, and with
an air all the while of even canting deference, proceeds to build again the things which were destroyed,
by reorganizing man's selfhood on a more specious
or consecrated basis, and so authenticating all its
unslain lusts in a way of devotion to the conventicle,
at least, if not to the open, undisguised world.

Professional religion thus stamps itself the devil's
subtlest device for keeping the human soul in bondage. Religion says death — *inward or spiritual
death* — to the selfhood in man. Professional religion says: "Nay, not death, above all not inward or
spiritual —because this would be *living*—death, and
obviously the selfhood must live in order to be vivified of God. By no means therefore let us say an
inward or *living* death to selfhood, but an outward
or *quasi* death, *professionally or ritually enacted*, and
so operating a change of base for the selfhood. Selfhood doubtless has been hitherto based upon a most
unrighteous enmity on the part of the world to God,
and has of itself shared the enmity. Let man then
only acknowledge, professionally or ritually, this
wicked enmity of the world to God, and he may

keep his selfhood unimpaired and unchallenged, to
expand and flourish *in secula seculorum.*"

Professional religion, I repeat, is the devil's mas-
terpiece for ensnaring silly, selfish men. The ugly
beast has two heads : one called Ritualism, intended
to devour a finer and fastidious style of men, men of
sentiment and decorum, cherishing scrupulously moderate views of the difference between man and God ;
the other called Revivalism, with a great red mouth
intended to gobble up a coarser sort of men, men
for the most part of a fierce carnality, of ungovern-
able appetite and passion, susceptible at best only
of the most selfish hopes, and the most selfish fears,
towards God. I must say, we are not greatly dev-
astated here in Boston — though occasionally vexed
— by either head of the beast ; on the contrary, it
is amusing enough to observe how afraid the great
beast himself is of being pecked to pieces on our
streets by a little indigenous bantam-cock which calls
itself Radicalism, and which struts, and crows, and
scratches gravel in a manner so bumptious and per-
emptory, that I defy any ordinary barnyard chanti-
cleer to imitate it.

But I am forgetting to answer your doubt in
relation to the Christian truth, which is the wholly
spiritual truth of God's NATURAL humanity.

LETTER V.

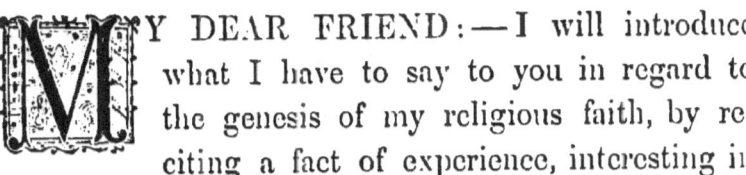Y DEAR FRIEND:—I will introduce what I have to say to you in regard to the genesis of my religious faith, by reciting a fact of experience, interesting in itself no doubt in a psychological point of view, but particularly interesting to my imagination as marking the interval between my merely rationalistic interest in Divine things, and the subsequent struggle of my heart after a more intimate and living knowledge of them.

In the spring of 1844 I was living with my family in the neighborhood of Windsor, England, much absorbed in the study of the Scriptures. Two or three years before this period I had made an important discovery, as I fancied, namely: that the book of Genesis was not intended to throw a direct light upon our natural or race history, but was an altogether mystical or symbolic record of the laws of God's *spiritual* creation and providence. I wrote a course of lectures in exposition of this idea, and delivered them to good audiences in New York. The preparation of these lectures, while it did much to confirm me in the impression that I had made an interesting discovery, and one which would extensively modify theology, convinced me, however, that a much more close and studious application of my idea than I had yet given to the illustration of the details of the sacred letter was imperatively needed. During my residence abroad, accordingly, I never tired in my devotion to this aim, and my success seemed so flattering at length that I hoped to be finally qualified to contribute a not insignificant mite to the sum of man's highest knowledge. I remember I felt especially hopeful in the prosecution of my task all the time I was at Windsor; my health was good, my spirits cheerful, and the pleasant scenery of the Great Park and its neighborhood furnished us a constant temptation to long walks and drives.

One day, however, towards the close of May, having eaten a comfortable dinner, I remained sitting at the table after the family had dispersed, idly gazing at the embers in the grate, thinking of nothing, and feeling only the exhilaration incident to a good digestion, when suddenly — in a lightning-flash as it were — "fear came upon me, and trembling, which made all my bones to shake." To all appearance it was a perfectly insane and abject terror, without ostensible cause, and only to be accounted for, to my perplexed imagination, by some damnèd shape squatting invisible to me within the precincts of the room, and raying out from his fetid personality influences fatal to life. The thing had not lasted ten seconds before I felt myself a wreck, that is, reduced from a state of firm, vigorous, joyful manhood to one of almost helpless infancy. The only self-control I was capable of exerting was to keep my seat. I felt the greatest desire to run incontinently to the foot of the stairs and shout for help to my wife, — to run to the roadside even, and appeal to the public to protect me; but by an immense effort I controlled these frenzied impulses, and determined not to budge from my chair till I had recovered my lost self-possession. This purpose I held to for a good long hour, as I reckoned time, beat upon meanwhile by an ever-growing tempest of doubt, anxiety, and despair, with absolutely no relief from any truth I had ever encountered save a most pale and distant glimmer of the Divine existence, — when I resolved to abandon the vain struggle, and communicate without more ado what seemed my sudden burden of inmost, implacable unrest to my wife.

Now, to make a long story short, this ghastly condition of mind continued with me, with gradually lengthening intervals of relief, for two years, and even longer. I consulted eminent physicians, who told me that I had doubtless overworked my brain, an evil for which no remedy existed in medicine, but only in time, and patience, and growth into improved physical conditions. They all recommended by way of hygiene a resort to the water-cure treatment, a life in the open air, cheerful company, and so forth, and thus quietly and skilfully dismissed me to my own spiritual medication. At first, when I began to feel a half-hour's respite from acute mental anguish, the bottomless mystery of my disease completely fascinated me. The more, however, I worried myself with speculations about the cause of it, the more the mystery deepened, and the deeper also grew my instinct of resentment at what seemed so needless an interference with my personal liberty. I went to a famous water-cure, which did nothing towards curing my malady but enrich my memory with a few morbid specimens of English insularity and prejudice, but it did much to alleviate it by familiarizing my senses with the exquisite and endless charm of English landscape, and giving me my first full rational relish of what may be called England's pastoral beauty. To be sure

I had spent a few days in Devonshire when I was young, but my delight then was simple enthusiasm, was helpless æsthetic intoxication in fact. The "cure" was situated in a much less lovely but still beautiful country, on the borders of a famous park, to both of which, moreover, it gave you unlimited right of possession and enjoyment. At least this was the way it always struck my imagination. The thoroughly disinterested way the English have of looking at their own hills and vales, — the indifferent, contemptuous, and as it were *disowning* mood they habitually put on towards the most ravishing pastoral loveliness man's sun anywhere shines upon, — gave me always the sense of being a discoverer of these things, and of a consequent right to enter upon their undisputed possession. At all events the rich light and shade of English landscape, the gorgeous cloud-pictures that forever dimple and diversify her fragrant and palpitating bosom, have awakened a tenderer chord in me than I have ever felt at home almost ; and time and again while living at this dismal water-cure, and listening to its endless "strife of tongues" about diet, and regimen, and disease, and politics, and parties, and persons, I have said to myself: *The curse of mankind, that which keeps our manhood so little and so depraved, is its sense of selfhood, and the absurd abominable opinionativeness it engenders. How sweet it would be to find oneself no longer man, but one of those innocent and ignorant sheep pasturing upon that placid hillside, and drinking in eternal dew and freshness from nature's lavish bosom!*

But let me hasten to the proper upshot of this incident. My stay at the water-cure, unpromising as it was in point of physical results, made me conscious erelong of a most important change operating in the sphere of my will and understanding. It struck me as very odd, soon after my breakdown, that I should feel no longing to resume the work which had been interrupted by it; and from that day to this — nearly thirty-five years — I have never once cast a retrospective glance, even of curiosity, at the immense piles of manuscript which had erewhile so absorbed me. I suppose if any one had designated me previous to that event as an earnest seeker after truth, I should myself have seen nothing unbecoming in the appellation. But now — within two or three months of my catastrophe — I felt sure I had never caught a glimpse of truth. My present consciousness was exactly that of an utter and plenary destitution of truth. Indeed an ugly suspicion had more than once forced itself upon me, that I had never really wished the truth, but only to ventilate my own ability in discovering it. I was getting sick to death in fact with a sense of my downright intellectual poverty and dishonesty. My studious mental activity had served manifestly to base a mere "castle in the air," and the castle had vanished in a brief bitter moment of time, leaving not a wrack behind. I never felt again the most passing impulse, even, to look where it stood, having done with it forever. Truth indeed! How should a beggar like me be expected to discover it? How should any man of woman born pretend to such ability? Truth must *reveal itself* if it would be known, and even then how imperfectly known at best! For truth is God, the omniscient and omnipotent God, and who shall pretend to comprehend that great and adorable perfection? And yet who that aspires to the name of man, would not cheerfully barter all he knows of life for a bare glimpse of the hem of its garment?

I was calling one day upon a friend (since deceased) who lived in the vicinity of the water-cure — a lady of rare qualities of heart and mind, and of singular personal loveliness as well — who desired to know what had brought me to the water-cure. After I had done telling her in substance what I have told you, she replied : "It is, then, very much as I had ventured from two or three previous things you have said, to suspect : you are undergoing what Swedenborg calls a *vastation;* and though, naturally

enough, you yourself are despondent or even despair-
ing about the issue, I cannot help taking an altogether
hopeful view of your prospects." In expressing my
thanks for her encouraging words, I remarked that I
was not at all familiar with the Swedenborgian tech-
nics, and that I should be extremely happy if she
would follow up her flattering judgment of my condition by turning into plain English the contents of
the very handsome Latin word she had used. To
this she again modestly replied that she only read
Swedenborg as an *amateur*, and was ill-qualified to
expound his philosophy, but there could be no doubt
about its fundamental postulate, which was, that a new
birth for man, both in the individual and the universal realm, is the secret of the Divine creation and
providence: that the other world, according to Swedenborg, furnishes the true sphere of man's spiritual
or individual being, the real and immortal being he
has in God; and he represents *this* world, consequently, as furnishing only a preliminary theatre of
his natural formation or existence in subordination
thereto; so making the question of human regeneration, both in grand and in little, the capital problem
of philosophy: that, without pretending to dogmatize, she had been struck with the philosophic
interest of my narrative in this point of view, and
had used the word *raslation* to characterize one of

the stages of the regenerative process, as she had found it described by Swedenborg. And then, finally, my excellent friend went on to outline for me, in a very interesting manner, her conception of Swedenborg's entire doctrine on the subject.

Her account of it, as I found on a subsequent study of Swedenborg, was neither quite as exact nor quite as comprehensive as the facts required; but at all events I was glad to discover that any human being had so much even as proposed to shed the light of positive knowledge upon the soul's history, or bring into rational relief the alternate dark and bright — or infernal and celestial — phases of its finite constitution. For I had an immediate hope, amounting to an almost prophetic instinct, of finding in the attempt, however rash, some diversion to my cares, and I determined instantly to run up to London and procure a couple of Swedenborg's volumes, of which, if I should not be allowed on sanitary grounds absolutely to read them, I might at any rate turn over the leaves, and so catch a satisfying savor, or at least an appetizing flavor, of the possible relief they might in some better day afford to my poignant need. From the huge mass of tomes placed by the bookseller on the counter before me, I selected two of the least in bulk — the treatise on the *Divine Love and Wisdom*, and that on the *Divine Providence*.

I gave them, after I brought them home, many a random but eager glance, but at last my interest in them grew so frantic under this tantalizing process of reading that I resolved, in spite of the doctors, that, instead of standing any longer shivering on the brink, I would boldly plunge into the stream, and ascertain, once for all, to what undiscovered sea its waters might bear me.

LETTER VI.

Y DEAR FRIEND :— I read from the first with palpitating interest. My heart divined, even before my intelligence was prepared to do justice to the books, the unequalled amount of truth to be found in them. Imagine a fever patient, sufficiently restored of his malady to be able to think of something beside himself, suddenly transported where the free airs of heaven blow upon him, and the sound of running waters refreshes his jaded senses, and you have a feeble image of my delight in reading. Or, better still, imagine a subject of some petty despotism condemned to die, and with — what is more and worse — a sentiment of death pervading all his consciousness, lifted by a sudden miracle into felt harmony with universal man, and filled to the brim with the sentiment of indestructible life instead, and you will have a true picture of my emancipated condition. For while these remarkable books familiarized me

with the angelic conception of the Divine being and
providence, they gave me at the same time the
amplest *rationale* I could have desired of my own
particular suffering, as inherent in the profound unconscious death I bore about in my *proprium* or selfhood.

— Here let me interpose a few words of caution.
I have not the least ambition to set myself up as
Swedenborg's personal attorney or solicitor. Swedenborg himself is not the least a fascinating personality to my regard, and if I were able by skilful
palaver to reason you out of an unfavorable into
a favorable estimate of his personal genius and
worth, I should prefer not to do it ;/because just in
proportion as you concede any personal authority
to a writer you are unlikely to be spiritually helped
by him. / You are sure, in fact, to be spiritually
enfeebled by him. Besides, I am persuaded that,
notwithstanding Swedenborg's personal limitations as
measured by the taste of our day, his amazing books
will suffer by no man's neglect, were he the most
considerable man of his time in religion, in science,
and in philosophy. And I should think myself very
ill employed, therefore, in drumming up a regiment
of raw recruits to dim their patient lustre, or degrade
it to the glitter of the gutters. His books invite the
most opposite appreciation, for they have all the

breadth and variety of nature in their aspect — now smiling with celestial peace, now grim with infernal storm and wrath. But they have always a light above nature, that is to say, not only above this realm of *mixed* good and evil which we call the natural world, but also above that realm of *divided* good and evil to which we give the name of the spiritual world; and in this Divine light we may discern, if we are attentive, an objective reconciliation of infinite and finite, which shall finally blot all memory, either of a mixed or a divided good and evil, forever out of mind.

At the moment I am speaking of — the moment of my first encounter with Swedenborg's writings — my intellect had been so completely vastated of every semblance of truth inherited from the past, and my soul consequently was in a state of such sheer and abject famine with respect to Divine things, that I doubt not I should have welcomed "the father of lies" to my embrace, nor ever have cared to scrutinize his credentials, had he presented himself bearing the priceless testimony which these books bear to the loveliness and grandeur of the Divine name. Nor should I counsel any one, who is not similarly dilapidated in his intellectual foundations — any one who is still at rest in his hereditary bed of doctrine, orthodox or heterodox — to pay the least attention

to them. For on the surface they repel delight.
They would seem to have been mercifully constructed
on the plan of barring out idle acquaintance, and
disgusting a voluptuous literary curiosity. But to
the aching heart and the void mind — the heart and
mind which, being sensibly famished upon those
gross husks of religious doctrine whether Orthodox
or Unitarian, upon which nevertheless our veriest
swine are contentedly fed, are secretly pining for
their Father's house where there is bread enough
and to spare — they will be sure, I think, to bring
infinite balm and contentment. I am confident that
no such readers will ever care to discuss any question which is properly personal to Swedenborg.

I disdain to argue, then, with you or anybody
else, in regard to Swedenborg, on general or *à priori*
principles. Think what you will, and say what you
will, of his dogmatic pretensions — make him out
if it please you, in the abundance of your self-satisfaction, either a knave or a fool or both — the judgment it is true may give out a strong subjective
flavor, but I have something better to do than to
argue it on its objective merits. Besides, I take it
that no man is eager to argue a question about which
he himself has not at least some secret misgiving.
And I have no more misgiving, either secret or open,
in regard to Swedenborg's teaching, than the new-

born babe has in regard to its mother's milk. He
has moreover so effectually vulgarized to my mind
the inmost significance of heaven and hell by expos-
ing their purely *provisional* character and contents,
that I should feel myself wanting both in proper
self-respect and proper homage to the Divine name,
if I continued to cherish anything but a strictly
scientific curiosity with regard to angel or devil;
or viewed it as the consummation of my being to
be eternally associated with the one and eternally
separated from the other.

In thus avowing my free conviction of the immortal services Swedenborg has rendered to the
mind, I confess I should be greatly mortified if you
looked upon this avowal as a " profession of faith " in
him, or as an ascription on my part of any more
dogmatic authority to him than I should ascribe
in their various measure to Socrates or John Mill.
He reports himself as interviewing, by special Divine
appointment, spirits and angels and devils in respect to what they could attest each in their degree,
whether consciously or unconsciously, of the principles of the world's administration. Thus he is
at best a mere informer or reporter, though an
egregiously intelligent one, in the interest of a new
evolution of the human mind, speculative and practical; and his testimony, therefore, to the spiritual

truth of the case, however much it may attract your confidence both in respect to its general competence and its palpable veracity, is not for an instant to be regarded as a revelation, or confounded with living Divine truth. The sphere of Revelation is the sphere of life exclusively, and its truth is addressed not to the reflective understanding of men, but to their living perception. (Truth, to every soul that has ever felt its inward breathing, disowns all outward authority,)— disowns, if need be, all outward *probability* or attestation of Fact. The only witness it craves, and this witness it depends upon, is that of good in the heart; and it allows no lower or less decisive attestation. Swedenborg, at all events, is incapable of the effrontery thus imputed to him. Nothing could have awakened a blush of deeper resentment on his innocent brow, if he could have foreseen the outrage, than the base spirit of sect, which in the face of his honest denunciations of it ventures to renew its unhallowed empire by clothing him with Divine authority.

The pretension to authority in intellectual things belongs exclusively to the Romish Church; and it has of late grown so reckless and wanton even in that hysterical suburb, as to show that it has no longer any faith in itself, but is clung to only as a desperate commercial speculation. If, accordingly, any taint of this spiritual dry-rot attached to these transparent books, I should advise you to send author and books, both alike, into the land of forgetfulness. It is not conceivable that the Divine providence should deliberately endow a quack to further his wise designs towards the intellect of the race. And every man in this day of restored spiritual liberty, and with the doomed papacy before him, who yet apes its blasphemy, so far as to claim either for himself or another a delegated Divine authority over the reason and conscience of men, must be a double-distilled quack ; that is, knave and fool both ; though he may not have perspicacity enough to suspect himself of either obliquity. Indeed, none but a truly wise man ever suspects himself of being a fool, and none but a truly good man has courage to avow himself a knave; so that if the world could once get fairly defecated of its unconscious knaves and fools, we should have only good men and wise left behind.

At all events, Swedenborg is conspicuously free of this vulgarity. His own faith is vowed unaffectedly and exclusively to the one sole and consummate revelation of the Divine name, made in the gospel of Jesus Christ; and he is not such a silly and vicious he-goat, accordingly, as to go about peddling a rival revelation. His sole intellectual pretension is to emphasize the eternal lustre of the gospel to men's regard, by disclosing its interior or spiritual and philosophic contents, as they became known to him through the opening of his spiritual senses. Take particular notice, therefore : what any honest mind goes to these sincere books for is, not to find any Divine warrant there either for his faith or his practice, for every man's own heart alone is competent to that question; much less to discover in them any new deodorizing substance which will disguise the stale fetor of ecclesiasticism or sacerdotalism, and so commend it anew to men's revolted nostrils; but all simply to find light upon the philosophy of the gospel, or ascertain what its internal or universal and impersonal contents are, of the truth of which contents he himself is all the while his own sole and divinely empowered arbiter.

And here a proper caution must be used, lest one run headlong into an exaggerated or superstitious estimate of Swedenborg's books, even from their own point of view. For it is past all dispute that Swedenborg himself had at best only a most general and obscure notion of the benefit which was to accrue to the mind of man, on earth and in heaven, from the last Judgment whose operation in the world of spirits he so minutely describes. The immediate chaotic or revolutionary effects of the Judgment apparently so absorbed his attention as to leave him neither leisure nor inclination, even if he had had the power, to prognosticate its redeeming virtue upon the progress of the human mind. But he had no such prophetic faculty, even in reference to the events he was daily witnessing in the world of spirits, much less, therefore, in reference to the contingencies of God's order in this lower or universal world. Indeed, he tells us that when he asked the angels what *their* judgment was, as to the specific effects which would follow upon earth from the events occurring in the world of spirits, they were completely unable to satisfy his curiosity in that behalf. They replied, in effect, that *they* knew just as little of the specific future as he did —future events being present only to the Divine mind — and that all they felt sure of *in general* was, that the old spiritual tyranny under which the human mind had been so helplessly stifled, being now at last effectually dissipated by the breaking up of the ecclesiastical heavens, Popish and Protestant alike, freethinking in religious things would be henceforth the divinely guaranteed basis of the Church on earth. And if freethinking or scepticism in religious things — the things of the intellect — be henceforth the normal attitude of the natural mind as a consequence of the last Judgment, surely nothing could have well seemed more preposterous to Swedenborg than to think of ever again elevating the discredited banner of Authority.

Conceive of Swedenborg then, personally, as you will, and welcome. What alone I care about is not to interest your intelligence in anything that is personal to the devout and estimable old seer, but in his performances. I feel, indeed, a perfect indifference to all his private claims upon attention. But my gratitude and admiration are immense for what he has done to flood the human mind with light out of inscrutable darkness, upon the question of our human origin and destiny; upon every question, in fact, involved in a true cosmology, or permanent science of the relations which exist between the world of thought and the world of substance. But then, remember, there is no access to this light but through honest research, guided by the felt needs of your intellect, and not by any idle literary curiosity, or mere silly ambition to know what other people know, and to be able to talk about what they talk about. Above all, let me counsel you to avoid, as you would avoid a fog, every flippant jackanapes who is ecclesiastically ordained (or unordained by the holy Ghost) to minister truth to you. The ecclesiastical spirit, and the civic spirit bred of it, are now the only evil spirits upon earth, and they are no longer compatible with any living knowledge of truth. Indeed, no man can outwardly communicate truth to his neighbor, much less any whose profession it is to do so,

however skilled he may be to communicate scientific
information. For truth is living, spiritual, Divine,
being shaped to every one's intelligence only by what
he has of celestial love in his heart. Thus Swedenborg will doubtless give you any amount of interesting and enlightening information about the spiritual world, and its principles of administration. And
this knowledge taken into your memory, or mental
stomach, will constitute so much nutritive material
to be intellectually assimilated by you, when the
living truth itself has begun to germinate and sprout
in your heart. But as to actually communicating
the truth to you — or making it literally over to
your understanding — Swedenborg is of course just
as flatly incompetent to that function as every other
man of woman born, and even more incapable morally, if that be possible, than he was intellectually,
of making any such blasphemous claim.

LETTER VII.

MY DEAR FRIEND:— I have not lost sight of my subject, as you doubtless by this time suspect, and we shall soon return to it. But, as I told you in my first letter, my nervous force is very much abated at present, and I am obliged to write not exactly as I would, but as my defective energy permits me. Besides, even if my nerves were unimpaired, it would be within the strict logic of my theme to hold a little discourse with you about Swedenborg and the relation of my thought to his books, since he is the only man, as it seems to me, in human history who has shed any commanding or decisive light on the physiology of the soul. That is to say, his books set before you, as no other books have the least pretension to do, *certain* FACTS *of spiritual observation and experience* which must, if you read them with interested attention, very soon convince you that you, like all other men, have hitherto utterly misconceived the function of selfhood

in man, and hence have attributed an original or caus-
ative influence, instead of a purely ancillary or ministerial one, to morality in human affairs. Observe
what I say. *It is exclusively these facts of spiritual
observation and experience*, recounted by Swedenborg,
which produce the effect in question, and not the least
any reasoning of his own in regard to the facts. For
this is what Swedenborg never does, namely, reason
about the things he professes to have learned from
angels and spirits. It may betoken great wisdom or
great imbecility in him to your mind that he does
not; but such, nevertheless, is the fact. He never
once, so far as I have observed, has attempted to throw
a persuasive light upon the things he professes to
have heard and seen among his angelic acquaintance.

Indeed, his own intellectual relation to the facts is
left altogether undetermined in his books. There can
be no doubt that the things he learned diffused an
atmosphere of great peace and sweetness in his breast,
and this makes his books the most heavenly reading I
know; but there is no sign extant, that I can see, of
any intellectual quickening being produced by them,
on his part, in regard to the history or the prospects
of the race. I am not going to be so dull, therefore,
as to promise you the very same intellectual results
that I get from Swedenborg's books, even if you yourself actually have recourse to them. Indeed, multi-

tudes of people are said to read his books and bring
away almost no intellectual result, — multitudes who
resort to them with great apparent complacency, and
get, no doubt, much incidental entertainment and
instruction from them, and yet are quite blind to
their proper intellectual significance, to the extent, I
am told, many of them, of seeming acutely hostile to
it when it is brought before them.   All this, of course,
because of the more or less vacant mind they bring
to the reading of him; or rather, their more or less
unsympathetic hearts.   Most of them come to the
banquet of facts and observations Swedenborg spreads
before them with an obvious gross hankering after
ecclesiastical righteousness, and make the most, accordingly, of every crumb they can pick up adapted to
gratify that unmanly and dyspeptic relish.   But if
you bring human sympathies to the banquet in question, I can assure you, you will find no speck of that
base, unworthy nutriment.   For it cannot be too
much insisted on, that no books address the reader's
intellect so much through the heart as these of Swedenborg do, all in confining themselves to giving him
spiritual information merely.

This is no doubt an endless stumbling-block to the
mass of readers, who regard Swedenborg as a sort of
intellectual tailor, whose shop they have only to enter,
to find whatsoever spiritual garments their particular

nakedness craves, all made to hand. And when they find, as every one among them is sure to do who has any faculty of spiritual discernment, that there are absolutely no garments made up, but only an immense sound of the shearing of sheep and the carding of wool and the whirling of wheels and the rattling of looms and the flying of spindles, and that every forlorn wight who would be spiritually clad must actually turn to and become his own wool-grower, weaver, and tailor, the great majority of course go away disgusted, and only those remain whose vocation for Truth is so genuine as to make any labor incurred in her service welcome if not pleasant. The case of course is far more hopeless when one goes in with absolutely no conscious nakedness to cover, but only to satisfy a vague outside curiosity about intellectual novelties, and make, perchance, a handsome addition to an already luxurious literary wardrobe. But Swedenborg is not now, and probably never will be, so much the mode as greatly to attract this style of customer.

In fact, the whole existing conception of the man and his aims is a mistake. He is not at all the intellectual craftsman or quack the world takes him for. He is no way remarkable as a man of original thought, or even as a reasoner, unless it be negatively so, while as a man of experience, or a seer, his worth is of the very highest grade, as imposing no kind of obligation upon your belief. His judgments doubtless in regard to this world's affairs were those of his day and generation, and strike one as grown very antiquated ; but there is almost no fact of spiritual observation and experience he recounts which does not seem of really priceless worth to my imagination, *as illustrating and enforcing a new mind in man.* If his books seem interesting to you also in this point of view, if they tend to enlighten you upon very many things which have puzzled you in your own mental pathway, or in respect to our race-origin and destiny, well and good ; no doubt you too are bound to an ultimate profitable commerce with them. And in this event you will find it unquestionably true that their main advantage to the intellect is, that they furnish it with truths which really nourish and quicken it, or irresistibly compel it to function for itself, and independently of foreign stimulus. His books, in fact, amount to nothing so much as to an intellectual wheat-field, of no use to any one who does not enter in to gather and bind his own golden sheaves, and then proceed to thresh and grind his grain, to bolt his flour, to mix his bread, to build it up and bake it in such shapely and succulent loaves as his own intellectual bread-pan alone determines.

But *revenons à nos moutons.* I have said that the

main philosophic obligation we owe to Swedenborg lies in his clearly identifying the evil principle in existence with selfhood. The Christian truth somewhat prepares us for this; but the church theology so overlays and systematically falsifies the truth, that we practically get little good of it. This theology, for example, identifies evil with a person called the *Devil* and *Satan*, outside the pale of human nature, but intimately conversant with its secret springs, and both able and disposed to use his knowledge with the malign purpose of corrupting all its subjects. Of course this conception was originally due to a very immature scientific condition of the mind, when men had not the least idea of good and evil as having an exclusively spiritual or subjective source. It befits, in fact, a strictly mechanical or material conception of the soul's relation to God, and only deepens the mystery it attempts to explain; for if the good and evil of human life acknowledge no inward root, but betray a purely moral, voluntary, or personal genesis, it can only be because the creative relation to man is primarily in fault, being the power of an external, not an internal, life. And if God were the power primarily of an external life in man, and *not altogether mediately through an internal one*, neither creature nor creator would ever invite, as they assuredly would never reward, the homage of an intellectual appreciation.

LETTER VIII.

MY DEAR FRIEND:—Without doubt I had suffered intellectually from the same or similar unworthy views of the creative relation to man, as those I adverted to in my last letter. I had always, from childhood, conceived of the Creator as bearing this outside relation to the creature, and had attributed to the latter consequently the power of provoking His unmeasured hostility. Although these crude traditional views had been much modified by subsequent reflection, I had nevertheless on the whole been in the habit of ascribing to the Creator, so far as my own life and actions were concerned, an outside discernment of the most jealous scrutiny, and had accordingly put the greatest possible alertness into His service and worship, until my will, as you have seen — thoroughly fagged out as it were with the formal, heartless, endless task of conciliating a stony-hearted Deity — actually collapsed. This was a catastrophe far more tragic to my feeling, and far more revolutionary in its intellectual results, than the actual violation of any mere precept of the moral law could be. It was the practical abrogation of the law itself, through the unexpected moral inertness of the subject. It was to my feeling not only an absolute decease of my moral or voluntary power, but a shuddering recoil from my conscious activity in that line. It was an actual acute loathing of the moral pretension itself as so much downright charlatanry. No idiot was ever more incompetent, practically, to the conduct of life than I, at that trying period, felt myself to be. It cost me, in fact, as much effort to go out for a walk, or to sleep in a strange bed, as it would an ordinary man to plan a campaign or write an epic poem. I have told you how, in looking out of my window at the time at a flock of silly sheep which happened to be grazing in the Green Park opposite, I used to envy them their blissful stupid ignorance of any law higher than their nature, their deep unconsciousness of self, their innocence of all private personality and purpose, their intense moral incapacity, in short, and indifference. I would freely, nay, gladly have bartered the world at the moment for one breath of the spiritual innocence which the benign creatures outwardly pictured, or stood for to my imagination ; and all the virtue, or moral righteousness, consequently, that ever illustrated our specific human personality, seemed simply foul and leprous in comparison with the deep Divine possibilities and promise of our common nature, as these stood symbolized to my spiritual sight in all the gentler human types of the merely animate world. There seemed, for instance — lustrously represented to my inward sense — a far more heavenly sweetness in the soul of a patient overdriven cab-horse, or misused cadger's donkey, than in all the voluminous calendar of Romish and Protestant hagiology, which, sooth to say, seemed to me, in contrast with it, nothing short of infernal.

You may easily imagine, then, with what relish my heart opened to the doctrine I found in these most remarkable books, *of the sheer and abject phenomenality of selfhood in man ;* and with what instant alacrity my intellect shook its canvas free to catch every breeze of that virgin unexplored sea of being, to which this doctrine, for the first time, furnished me the clew. Up to this very period I had lived in the cheerful faith, nor ever felt the slightest shadow of misgiving about it — any more, I venture to say, than you at this moment feel a shadow of similar misgiving in your own mind — that my being or substance lay absolutely in myself, was in fact identical with the various limitations implied in that most fallacious but still unsuspected quantity. To be sure, I had no doubt that this being or self of mine (whether actually burdened, or not burdened, with its limitations, I did not stop to inquire, but unquestionably with a capacity of any amount of burdensome limitation) came originally as a gift from the hand of God; but I had just as little doubt that the moment the gift had left God's hand, or fell into my conscious possession, it became as essentially independent of Him in all spiritual or subjective regards as the soul of a child is of its earthly father; however much in material or objective regards it might be expedient for me still to submit to His external police. My moral conscience, too, lent its influence to the same profound illusion; for all the precepts of the moral law being objectively so good and real, and intended in the view of an unenlightened conscience to make men righteous in the sight of God, I could never have supposed, even had I been tempted on independent grounds to doubt my own spiritual or subjective reality, that so palpably Divine a law contemplated, or even tolerated, a wholly infirm and fallacious subject; much less that it was, in fact, altogether devised for the reproof, condemnation, and humiliation of such a subject. I had no misgiving, therefore, as to the manifest purpose of the Law. The Divine intent of it at least was as clear to me as

it ever had been to the Jew, namely, to serve as a
ministry of plain moral life or actual righteousness
among men, so constructing an everlasting heaven
out of men's warring and divided personalities : and
not at all, as the apostles taught, a ministry of death,
to convince those who stood approved by it of SIN,
thereby shutting up all men, good and evil alike, but
especially the good, to unlimited dependence upon
the sheer and mere mercy of God.

It was impossible for me, after what I have told you,
to hold this audacious faith in selfhood any longer.
When I sat down to dinner on that memorable chilly
afternoon in Windsor, I held it serene and unweak-
ened by the faintest breath of doubt. Before I rose
from table it had inwardly shrivelled to a cinder.
One moment I devoutly thanked God for the inappreciable boon of selfhood ; the next that inappreciable boon seemed to me the one thing damnable on
earth, seemed a literal nest of hell within my own
entrails. Whatever difficulties then stood in the way
of a better faith, they were infinitely milder and more
placable than those inherent in the old one. In fact
the old faith was itself the only obstacle in the path
of the new. Take the one away, and the other be-
comes inevitable. | If you admit the intrinsic or essen-
tial phenomenality of selfhood — its utter unreality
or non-existence out of consciousness — you are logi-

cally forced upon the truth of the creative incarnation in the created nature — or the Divine Natural Humanity — as the sole possible method of creation, as the only truth capable of explaining nature and history. When I say *forced*, I take for granted that you have some rational interest in the subject; I take for granted that you deem nature and history worthy to be explained, and are not a mere sensualist so intent upon your own pleasure as to feel no capacity for inward satisfactions. In that case, I repeat, the only existing obstacle to your belief in the necessary incarnation of the Creator in the created nature in order to the redemption and salvation of the human race from the empire of evil and falsity, will be dissipated by your coming to acknowledge the pure phenomenality of consciousness, or to disbelieve in the spiritual reality of selfhood. Nothing hinders one believing in spiritual truth but the limitary influence of falsity. And so, conversely, nothing hinders a man succumbing to spiritual falsity but the liberating influence of truth. So that the only possible way for men to arrive at the spiritual or living knowledge of truth, is by unliving their natural prejudices and prejudices of education. Now the deepest and most universal of these prejudices is that which makes selfhood the greatest of realities, and consequently inflates the heart of man with all manner of spiritual pride,

avarice, and cruelty. And it is accordingly the conquest of this fundamental prejudice which best promotes our spiritual rectitude, or living conjunction
with God.

We are now at the very focus of our difference,
and let me utter no word that shall not be clearly
understood. Nothing can be farther from my desire
than to weaken the authority of the moral law, considered as the literal aspect of all true spiritual fellowship between man and man. When the *spirit* of
fellowship or equality between men is absent, then it
behooves them, as they love their manhood and prize
its salvation, to make much in their intercourse with
one another of a strict conformity to the *letter* of the
law. The spirit of human fellowship or equality is
mutual love, and mutual love prompts only the most
accordant action between all its subjects. But where
mutual love does not as yet exist among men, but self-
love only and love of the world, and positively accordant or harmonious action is therefore not to be expected
from them, it becomes all-important to provide some
natural symbol of these spontaneous manners — some
purely negative and formal reminder of these ethics
of the skies — whereby a faint perfume of the heavenly
life may be kept up among men, and men thereby be
prepared, in their turn, to recognize the Divine substance itself when it is finally ready to come.

Now this precise propædeutic function is exquisitely served by the letter of the law. For the subject of this letter — out of sincere outward or formal reverence for the Divine name — is taught by it freely to abstain from false witness, theft, adultery, murder, and covetousness, since a reverential abstinence from these evils is the only practicable moral equivalent or ultimate of the highest spiritual goodness. *To refrain when tempted from doing evil because evil is contrary to the will of God*, is the only outward rule of human conduct at all commensurate with inward love to God ; since it is the only rule which provides a formal basis for that spiritual humility in man, which is the sole Divine end of the law for righteousness. Abstinence from evil, then, is a necessary condition of the spiritual or inward life in man ; but it profits a man only in so far as it is reverential, or prompted by a formal and paramount regard for the Divine will. A great many persons fulfil the law formally or outwardly, because it is reputable so to do, and promotes their civic advantage ; and no doubt our infirm civilization is very much indebted to these people, of an insincere religious character, who yet do all, and even more than all, that the spiritual man does in the way of promoting men's outward fellowship. Many persons also, who are not actuated by worldly motives, unaffectedly mistake the purpose of the law. They have no idea that its purpose is spiritual, being addressed to making its subjects humble, or giving them a conscience of death *in themselves*, but suppose that it was intended to confer actual life or righteousness upon them, by entitling all who obey it to permanent Divine honor, and all who disobey it to permanent Divine reproach. They have no perception that the law is essentially ministerial to the gospel revelation of the Divine love, being intended to soften the hard heart of its votary — to knead and supple it outwardly — to inward Divine issues when they come. They conceive, on the contrary, that the law is its own end, being rather magisterial to the gospel than ministerial, since they regard the latter as being essentially substitutionary to the former, or view it in the light of a mere tardy Divine concession to men's weakness, after the former had sufficiently demonstrated their absolute want of strength. In short, their idea of the law is, not that it is purely provisional and educative, in order to prepare men for becoming spiritual out of natural, but that it is a Divine finality, addressed to the making men morally or actually righteous. And hence they value its formal moral letter infinitely above its inward or living spirit, contenting themselves with a mere actual abstinence from the evils it denounces, but caring very little about the temper of mind from which the abstinence comes.

Acquit me then, I pray you, of any desire to diminish the prestige of the moral law, considered as ministering to the only true Divine righteousness in man, by helping to bring about a spirit of unaffected, unostentatious humility in his bosom. For this is the whole spiritual scope of the law, the only thing that for a moment sanctifies it, or makes it holy, to the recognition of the human heart : to conjoin the worshipper with God by freeing his heart from the evil spirits that hinder such conjunction ; and every man therefore who is not a spiritual sot, or whose heart is not dead to all Divine inspiration, gives it in this point of view his unqualified homage.

But there comes a time when the moral law no longer ministers to the Divine life in man ; when it most distinctly does *not* produce a spirit of humility in its subject, but a spirit of pride and self-inflation. The law is now wrenched from its commanding spiritual uses, which are all summed up in making the individual man think small things of himself, and employed by men as an instrument of their own material aggrandizement. When the law is thus wrested from its only proper Divine to purely human uses, from its exclusively spiritual to an exclusively material function, it becomes no longer an instru-

ment of mutual peace and unity among men, but of
mutual self-seeking and warfare. Then the law from
being confessedly Divine becomes the most undivine
thing beneath the skies; for then it ministers — as
nothing else on earth has power to do — by its
usurped Divine authority, to the inmost spirit of hell
in man, to a spirit of pride and self-assertion and
intolerance and lust and cruelty and revenge. It
was originally given by God only to humble the pride
of selfhood in man, *that so the neighbor might become
exalted in his regard.* It is most undivinely used by
man only as a cunning instrument *for suppressing the
neighbor,* or subjecting him to one's boundless cupidity
and avarice. It is no longer Divine, then, but out
and out diabolic, confessing itself spiritually the only
fortress of evil known to the human bosom. This is
what secretly nauseates all good men with our legal
righteousness, fills them with an inward loathing of
our conventional respectability, sickens them to death
with our technical "Church" and its flatulent senti-
mentality, with our technical "State" and its dishonest morality. This is what makes them inwardly
hate our existing civilization as, spiritually, a thing
of infamy, as the only thing which stands in the way
of the Divine kingdom on earth; and they would,
themselves, gladly beat the drum and blow the trum-
pet for its final burial out of human sight.

LETTER IX.

MY DEAR FRIEND : — Don't imagine that my reference to the law in my last letter was intended merely or chiefly to illustrate what Paul says of the legal economy under which the Jew lived, namely : *that it was designed only to give its subject a knowledge of sin.* Doubtless this was an argument of great weight to the Jew, for he was the actual subject of a Divine kingdom, and if the law of that kingdom in its practical scope could be shown to be designedly subversive of the national hope towards God, his main opposition to the gospel considered as dishonoring the law would of course fall to the ground. But this argument has no similar pertinence to us, who have never been subjects of a literal Divine regimen, and whose law consequently has always claimed a more or less strictly spiritual administration. To be sure, we have certain portentous Jewish phantoms of our own to contend with — certain very orthodox Christian enemies of the Divine Spirit — in the persons of our Popish and Protestant ritualists, or high churchmen. But no one is in any danger of mistaking these worthless pretenders for authentic Divine persons, nor of gravely combating their ecclesiastical fopperies and gross covert disloyalty to the human ideal. They are not natural Jews, but only spiritual or spurious ones: only simulated or imitative ones. They are not the pure gold of the sanctuary, once famous but now vanished from earth forever: they are a mere counterfeit and pinchbeck image of it, with a view to impose upon simple and credulous imaginations. Their ecclesiastical pretension is in itself an inversion of the most fundamental principle of spiritual order, which is, that the natural in every case descend from the spiritual: while they, on the contrary, are the direct spiritual progeny of a very ugly and sordid natural parentage. Thus, they are by no means actually living under a specific Divine regimen, but only " making believe" that they are. They have not so much even as a *quasi* Divine obligation on their consciences to do what they do; they only act *as if* they had. This, you perceive, makes all the difference in the world between the honest natural Jew and our own dishonest spiritual ones, and shows moreover the admirable reason why Christ called these latter, in the persons of their representative types at his day, " hypocrites," that is, ACTORS,

unconsciously playing a part to which they are noway
Divinely summoned. We may then safely leave all
our spectacular prodigies in this line to Christ's con-
cise characterization of them, assured that nothing
of harm can ensue to any serious interest of the world
from so strictly histrionic an activity.

But the apostles had to deal with a much less
effeminate and contemptible class of zealots, whose
superstitious regard for their own law threatened,
indeed, to stop the world's progress, so hearty and
malignant was their opposition to that gospel which
the apostles proclaimed, and whose sole burden was
that Jesus of Nazareth was the Christ. They esteemed
their own law a living Divine one already as to the
minutest jot or tittle of its letter, and this purported
to bless them exclusively as children of Abraham.
How could they conceive, then, that the law had,
as the apostles taught, a far more living, or inward
and Divine SPIRIT, purporting to bless them only as
they renounced their Jewish selves, and identified
their interests with those of the Gentile world? In
fact, this tiresome and frivolous letter of their law
inspired them with so frenzied and fanatical a regard
as having a purely Jewish end, that it at last left
them in all intellectual respects hopelessly blind and
imbecile. It was a timely office in Paul, therefore, to
remind his unenlightened countrymen of the deadly

animus of their law towards every one who boasted
of its literal friendship. Even natural death, he ar-
gued, would be harmless if it were not for the law.
"The sting of death is doubtless *sin :* but then it is
only the law that gives us a conscience of sin. The
sole strength of sin is the law; and every subject of
the law, therefore, who sees its intention to be to
give men a knowledge of sin and not of righteousness,
will bless God that it was never a final dispensation,
but at best a preparatory one for the gospel we now
proclaim. The law may be best viewed, in fact,
under the similitude of a respectable pedagogue, in
charge of a school of turbulent urchins, whom if he
can make even tolerably sensible of their own vast
deficiencies in point of culture, he will deem his duty
done towards them, and contentedly leave them to the
chances of their future manhood."

This, I repeat, was a very important truth to those
to whom it was addressed, a typical "outside" people,
subjects of an external Divine law, who were di-
rected to an external Divine Saviour as the veritable
end of their law for righteousness. In short, the Jew
was notoriously a frivolous subject — as near to worthless as a people could well be that still wore the
human form — and cultivating only such base ideas
of the Divine righteousness as stood in a mere "outside cleansing of the cup and platter, while inwardly

they were full of extortion and excess." But it ought, I repeat, to be particularly and frankly noted that this apostolic reasoning has no special relevancy to us at this day, who have always lived not under a literal but an exclusively spiritual Divine dispensation. Our forefathers, in the revolution they accomplished, simply designed to free themselves and their descendants from political vassalage to England. But in the form they subsequently impressed upon their work they builded greatly better than they designed, or even than they themselves suspected. For in disowning, as they resolutely did, an authoritative Church and a consecrated State, they managed quite unconsciously to swing clear, not only of political and ecclesiastical England, but of literal Christendom as well: *which derives its form or quality from those two disowned institutions exclusively.* The result is that we, their descendants, are denizens henceforth of spiritual Christendom only. For so far as we confess ourselves their legitimate children, logically approving of and identified with their acts, we frankly acknowledge ourselves with respect to the rest of the world a new or spiritual people, sifted from the nations as wheat is sifted from chaff; amenable only to a living or inward and imprescriptible Divine Law in our own bosoms — that of our growing humanitary affections and thoughts; perfectly atheistic therefore, if need be, in so far as our faith is due to any merely instituted Deity, that is, any Deity outside of our own nature; perfectly irresponsible and immoral, if need be, so far as our obedience is due to any merely putative, or arbitrary and established, Divine order: that is to say, any order not strictly conformed to the recognized principles of human nature.

If you will pardon me a slight digression here, I would like to observe that what I have just said explains the reason why the spiritual world — the world of heaven and hell — has undergone such dire eclipse, or fallen so completely under the shadow of the natural world, that men no longer scruple to claim a direct commerce with God, even in the flesh, and therefore not only reject all so-called "spiritual" authority as obsolete or impertinent, but are fast growing indifferent even to their once highly prized civic righteousness.*   It is impossible to watch the fatal demoralization which of late years has been creeping

* This of course outside the technical church. The state of things within the church is strictly and strikingly parallel to that witnessed at its founder's first or carnal coming. That is to say, the Jew vindicated his legal or formal orthodoxy at whatever cost of shame and suffering to the person of him who alone constituted its prophetic scope or substance. And the professing Christian church avouches its fidelity to the *person* of Christ, by reviling, evil-entreating, and persecuting every interest, Divine and human, which makes his person spiritually venerable or memorable.

over men in positions of public and private trust, and
still believe that citizenship is estimated as it once
was, or that men in general still retain their respect
for any merely *instituted* sanctity or decency under
heaven. Freedom, and no longer force, has become
the acknowledged ethics of the Divine administration,
to the consequent enfeebling of the obligations of
outward law; and this enlarged consciousness on our
part brings with it a new and wholly spiritual conception of creative power. It enforces in us such a
growing sense of harmony between the Divine and
human natures, as must erelong thoroughly foreclose
the old controversy of flesh and spirit — the church
and the world — and reduce ritual religion itself to
a mere code of good manners.

I have no desire and no right to confirm what I
say by reference to my own personal history; but
I cannot help confessing, by way of illustration, that
I myself have found few things for the last thirty or
forty years more fatiguing to my regenerate inward
sense — less accommodated to my growing conviction
of God's NATURAL humanity — than our current ecclesiastical culture. Nothing could be pleasanter than
" going to church" upon certain holidays — every
holiday in fact — and losing oneself in the great con-
gregation, if the worship were only sincere and innocent. But no worship can be sincere or innocent

which is not first of all disinterested or spontaneous.
If any gain however small is hoped to be realized from
observing it, if any loss however small is feared to be
incurred from neglecting it, the worship confesses
itself mercenary; and surely nothing can be more
remote from spiritual innocence than a mercenary
habit of mind in Divine things. All living or acceptable worship is free, unforced, spontaneous, as expressing a heart and mind unaffectedly reconciled to
God; and who shall pretend to be at peace with
God that has yet anything to ask or expect at the
Divine hands?

Nothing, it appears to me, can be more utterly
worthless and even degrading, in a spiritual estimation, both to oneself and to society, than a life passed
in ritual devotion, or the exercises of formal piety.
It is an insult to God and man to dignify so sodden
a routine with the sacred name of life; call it rather
death and damnation to every soul of man *that finds
it life.* I wonder above all how any one who reverences even the letter alone of the New Testament,
and remembers the terrible warnings and objurga-
tions it denounces upon a mere conventional or legal
hope towards God, can dare to associate his spiritual
fortunes with our modern ecclesiastical Judaism.
The visible Church seems to me in a spiritual or
philosophic point of view to be " the abomination

of desolation"; a refuge and embodiment of the frankest spiritual egotism and the rankest spiritual cupidity. Its pharisaic airs and temper provoke one to alternate smiles and tears: smiles, to see such transparent spiritual pride simulating the aspect and language of humility; tears, to see so many well-to-do worldly-wise people inwardly hardening themselves against the access and solicitation of God's tenderest and most timely pity in our *nature*.

How blasphemous, then, to talk of God's life at this time of day in any such self-righteous precinct! How inevitable, one might say, its encounter almost everywhere else, especially where there is no pretension to anything but a secular temper. I can hardly flatter myself that the frankly chaotic or *a*-cosmical aspect of our ordinary street-car has altogether escaped your enlightened notice in your visits to the city; and it will perhaps surprise you, therefore, to learn that I nevertheless continually witness so much mutual forbearance on the part of its *habitués;* so much spotless acquiescence under the rudest personal jostling and inconvenience; such a cheerful renunciation of one's strict right; such an amused deference, oftentimes, to one's invasive neighbor: in short, and as a general thing, such a heavenly self-shrinkage in order that "the neighbor," handsome or unhandsome, wholesome or unwholesome, may sit or stand at ease: that

I not seldom find myself inwardly exclaiming with the patriarch : *How dreadful is this place ! It is none other than the house of God, and the gate of heaven.* Undeniably on its material or sensuous side the vehicle has no claim to designation as a Bethel ; but at such times on its spiritual or supersensuous side it seems to my devout sense far more alert with the holy Ghost, far more radiant and palpitating with the infinite comity and loveliness, than any the most gorgeous and brutal ecclesiastical fane that ever gloomed and stained the light of heaven.

But I only allege this familiar experience as a sample of the way in which, to our quickened or regenerate perception, persons and places and things that have been hitherto conventionally most sacred, are ready and eager to confess themselves profane, to confess themselves in fact sheer spiritual rubbish ; while things and persons and places hitherto reputed especially forlorn and commonplace are becoming spiritually hallowed, becoming inwardly vivid and picturesque with God's revealed modesty, truth, and mercy.

And now that this digression is ended, let me return to my subject, and say that my purpose in referring to Paul's famous contention about the spiritual import of the law is quite different from his, though doubtless it lies in the same philosophic direction. Paul was content to show that the law being spiritual, could not but be fatal to the claim of a moral or actual righteousness among men: that it condemned those only of its subjects who stood literally justified by it, and justified those only who confessed themselves literally condemned by it: because the former, in arrogating merit to themselves and ascribing blame to others, violated the spirit of the law, which was charity, or neighborly love; and because the latter gave evidence of that humility of spirit which is the only and inseparable basis of charity, or neighborly love.

But this does not content me. I admire the apostle's profound critical insight, it is true, and applaud the lesson conveyed by it with all my heart; but I cannot help going on to say that if such be the one unflinching spirit of all Divine law upon earth, namely, to reveal the evil which is latent in all men by nature, and so lay an eternal basis for a spirit of charity or good neighborhood in the human breast, why then it becomes at once grandly evident that the estimate formed by God of every man of woman born — the morally good no less than the morally evil man — differs infinitely, or in kind, from the estimate formed by man himself.

It is evident, for example, that whereas the latter, for lack of spiritual apprehension of the Divine law,

regards the moral differences of men as final or absolute, the former regards all men — the morally good
and the morally evil man both alike — as blent in
one and the same community of evil so long as they
are *disaffected to the spirit of the law,* which is one
of charity, or mutual love.

But much more than this is evident. For it is evident that while man attributes to himself alone the
source and the consequent responsibility of his evil
moral acts, the Divine mind stigmatizes this sentiment as false, or sets the individual evil doer free by
charging his shortcomings to the common stock of
human nature.

But even this is a very small part of what is evident.
For if the Divine wisdom imputes no guilt to the
individual man, but charges all the evil done by men
to the account of their common nature, why then it
is evident that inasmuch as no man can feel himself
responsible for his natural but only for his personal
limitations, so he is bound to look to God alone for
the final reconstitution of human nature in harmony
with His own infinite goodness.

Now this Divine RESUSCITATION OF OUR NATURE,
OR COMPLETE UNITION OF IT WITH THE INEFFABLE
DIVINE PERFECTION, is precisely the work which Swe-
denborg ascribes to Jesus Christ.

LETTER X.

MY DEAR FRIEND : — When I began writing these letters I imagined myself able to say all I wanted to say within the compass of ten short letters, at most : and this after making a generous allowance to the weakness of my nerves. But the allowance apparently was not generous enough, and the consequence is that I find myself, at the opening of my tenth letter, only fairly abreast of the great truth of the Incarnation, to which nevertheless everything else I have said was meant to be strictly subordinate. My nerves, in fact, are like a spirited horse, out of whom you may coax a good deal of service if you use patient and persuasive methods, but who violently resents and resists the coercion of whip and spur. What then remains to be done? Shall I, like a vicious horse, leave my work unfinished? Or shall I go on to bring it still to such orderly close as my infirmities will permit? I choose the latter course, although the bulk of my

scribble be unduly augmented thereby, simply because
I hate to leave entirely unreported certain *explicanda*
in relation to the great truth of the Incarnation, which
may be of use in softening if not altogether obviating
your prejudices against it. I know that these prejudices are due mainly to the very dense ignorance we
all of us cherish with respect to spiritual life and
order. And if I may only say some word which shall
induce you to have recourse to Swedenborg's books,
where the amplest information of the sort needed is
supplied, and where all one's intellectual unrest and
perturbation of every kind find themselves tenderly
soothed and placated, I shall be happy.

I had best, perhaps, state first of all what the
apotheosis of our nature in the person of Jesus
Christ, as reported in Swedenborg's pages, practically amounts to ; and then make such comments
upon it in detail as may be needful to commend the
truth to your awakened attention.

The truth, then, as I find it in Swedenborg, practically amounts to this, namely : *an alleged redemption
of human nature* — from what ? — *from the spiritual
limitations and disabilities imposed upon it by heaven
and hell;* and the consequent unlimited purification
of that nature into harmony with the Divine perfection.

Mind well what I say here. I say that the redemp-

tion of human nature means its redemption from
certain evils which are by no means incident to it in
virtue of its own quality, but are imposed upon it
through the influence of the spiritual world — meaning thereby the realm of heaven and hell — upon
the individual subjects of the nature.

But here you will ask me: "What is the necessity
for what you call the spiritual world, or the divided
realm of heaven and hell, in the scheme of creation?"
To which I might as briefly answer: "The spiritual
world, or its division into heaven and hell, is a necessary incident of the cleansing of human nature from
evil, and its consequent complete impletion or unition
with the Divine perfection."

But here again a new question confronts me:
Whence then this liability to evil in human *nature?*
What, in other words, is the origin of spiritual evil in
men, or the evil which attaches to them by nature?
For one rightly reasons that if the spiritual world by
unduly influencing individual minds on earth ends
by vitiating or corrupting human nature itself, it is
important to know how so malign an influence ever
becomes exerted by the spiritual world. We can
perfectly understand how *physical* evil, or the evil
which man *suffers*, originates: namely, in a want of
harmony between himself and his own body. One
knows too very well how *moral* evil, or the evil which

man *does,* comes about: namely, from a want of free harmonic adjustment in the relations of man to man. But here is an evil incomparably deeper than both of these, because it is, in fact, their very and exclusive root: not the paltry and passing evil under which man is passive, as *pain;* nor yet the still more superficial and remediable evil in which he is active, as *vice* and *crime:* but spiritual evil, or the evil which he *is,* an evil which characterizes him in relation to his own vital consciousness, and if not removed therefore must utterly palsy his consciousness considered as a means of development to his nature.

This gigantic and hopeless evil in man, then, springs from no defect of his physical nor of his moral make, but wholly from the limitation and infirmity of his finite or personal consciousness, which is a most rigid SELF-consciousness, excluding any other than a subjective basis; whereas it has manifestly no warrant in the creative infinitude, which is the infinitude of Love, to have any but an objective basis, that is, to be anything but a social consciousness, embracing the neighbor along with the self, or involving a public and private element quite equally. But you will ask why the creature of God is thus shut up in his beginnings to a conscious or phenomenal existence in himself, instead of being endowed outright with his creator's vital substance or being? It is that God, by the

necessity of his perfection, cannot permit any other
than a phenomenal or conscious existence to his creature, so long as the latter remains wholly inexpert,
or untried and undisciplined, in the utter spiritual
death or nothingness which he bears about in himself as finitely constituted, and which whilst the inex-
perience lasts makes it impossible to commit the
Divine substance or being to him.   The creator
himself is of course the only real or natural life of
the creature — as is implied in the very terms of the
proposition : but how is the creature ever livingly
to learn this great truth?   His creator is not the
least a denizen of space and time; is not the least
a visible or outward existence, so that his senses will
afford him at best but a reflected or lifeless knowledge of Him.   Evidently then the creature demands
some other avenue to Divine knowledge than sense —
some *inward* avenue, since the creator is not to be
found outside of him — and this inward avenue is
supplied by consciousness, or *self*-knowledge.   In
proportion as I come truly to know myself in all
the compass of my physical, moral, and spiritual disability, do I come to a living or hearty apprehension
of God's infinitude.   *And in no other way.*   All the
bibles, all the churches, all the sacraments, all the
rites and ceremonies, all the priesthoods in the land,
are totally impotent to confer upon me one fibre of

this living knowledge of God which is given by my life or consciousness alone; however much I doubt not they may instruct my intellect in things pertaining and subsidiary to such knowledge. Thus until the creature's own life or consciousness be so tried, disciplined, or purified as readily to yield him this living lore : until he be inwardly or SELF-taught, in other words, to discern the ineffable holiness which underlies and transfigures his own boundless cupidity and cruelty : he will necessarily refuse to receive or reproduce that only real or unconscious life which is God, and must accordingly be content for a time to put up with the unreal or seeming and fallacious life of selfhood. This beggarly life will doubtless seem to the creature, while he is still unconscious of any inner or higher and better life, most real and stupendous; and it will indeed in the miraculous providence of God, and through all his blindness however fatuous, serve as an admirable basis of experience to him, slowly but surely promoting the final evolution of his real or natural life; but in itself, or absolutely, the personal or conscious life — this life of selfhood — is not merely worthless, but ruinous, and Schopenhauer and the rest of our purblind modern Buddhists, from their unchristian point of view, do every way well to execrate it.

And now, having answered your doubt, I return to

my subject. The ineradicable imperfection of created existence, *as such*, or the origin of spiritual evil in the creature, consists, as we have seen, in his attributing to himself a rigidly personal or finite consciousness, and so perverting the creative energy and influx in him to purely selfish or unsocial issues. The creature is of course perfectly unaware of this evil, and is as innocent of any intention to bring it about as the child unborn. He is himself as yet the spiritually unborn child of God — a mere embryo of still undeveloped Divine possibilities in his nature — and one does n't expect to find any divinely normal or natural results in himself or his surroundings. It seems indeed inevitable to any Divine creation — and this simply because it *is* Divine or infinite — that it should always exhibit soil or taint upon its subjective side, or present spiritually the strongest possible antagonism to its creator. At least I myself do not see how, otherwise, the creative perfection or infinitude *as the bringer of good out of evil*, is ever going to be vindicated by it. The creature as we have seen can never come to the conception of the creative infinitude through the senses, because the senses themselves are a grossly limitary power, or witness exclusively to the finite. He must come to it then only from within, or livingly, that is to say: as that infinitude makes itself manifest to him *through consciousness* or *the*

development of his own nature. If the divine infinitude be, as it undeniably is, a purely inward one —
if it attach to the creative name or character, and not
to His works, thus to what He is in himself, or essentially, and not to what He is in his creature, or existentially — then the sole worthy judgment we can
form of it must necessarily reflect in the first place
our experience of our *finite* selves, or express above
all things our essential difference *in kind* from the
Creator. It must be a judgment in fact confessing
all creatureship to be a state of otherness or alienation to the Creator, and as such otherness or alienation
finite or imperfect. In other words — for I confess
the living sentiment is not easily put into adequate
form — our only spiritual or living acknowledgment
of the creative infinitude, is an internal or worshipful
acknowledgment, implying our own inward self-efface-
ment, our own free or spontaneous death to ourselves.
Thus it is a homage of the heart which the Creator
covets in the first instance from the creature, and only
by remote derivation thence of the intellect : and this
not with any absurd view of course to aggrandize
Himself by the puny homage of the creature, but
only with a view to its softening the latter's sense of
otherness or alienation to Himself, so rendering him
accessible to all those Divine traits of tenderness,
gentleness, and pity infinite, whereby he is destined

one day to live: for heart-homage, as we know from
our own secular experience even, is full of profound
humility on the subject's part, being convertible indeed in every case into a confession of sin; and you
know with what reluctance the intellect reverberates
any such confession.

Almost obviously then we may say — may we not,
my dear friend? — that all spiritual or subjective
creation, as expressing the infinite love, or inmost
heart, of the Creator, is *ex vi terminorum* or by virtue
of such infinitude, miraculous.   For it is no outward or material result that is aimed at by such a
process, but a purely inward or conscious one, and it
involves therefore spiritually the humiliation of creative substance to created form, and suspends its own
actual achievement upon the Creator showing himself able by means of such spiritual humiliation to
lead captivity captive, or rise triumphant over death
and hell, by exalting the created nature into complete unison with his perfection.   At all events, we
may say with entire certainty, that the creative energy in the actual creation — and simply because it
is creative, having therefore no other vent for itself,
or field of manifestation, than its creature's consciousness — is not only fairly shut up to that finite abode
such as it is, or whatever be its intrinsic limitations,
but freely engages itself precisely THERE to avouch

and make intelligible its own majestic infinitude, by permanently rescuing the created nature from the keeping of the created subject, and enlarging or glorifying it into Divine proportions.

—I have a vague sense of having said very nearly what I wanted to say in this letter, and yet on reflection I am not sure about it. I feel such a mental impotence in regard to the ineffable theme, such a sense of silent and amazed and abashed truth in relation to it, that, say what I may, I can hardly feel sure of having said anything to the purpose. This comes, I suppose, from the creative truth appealing for reception so exclusively to the heart in the first place, and disposing one rather to mute adoring wonder than to voluble appreciation. I confess for my part that this truth of the spiritual creation, or of God's NATURAL humanity, is in itself so grand and unexpected as utterly to beggar my imagination at the start, and make me more abjectly thankful for positive knowledge about it, such as I find in Swedenborg's books, than I have ever been for my daily bread. And precisely the most fundamental point of that knowledge is what I have been trying to make plain to you, namely: that creation is a subjective or living and spiritual achievment of Divine love and wisdom within the strictest precincts of human nature, and that it accordingly neither appeals to nor admits any other attestation in us than that of consciousness, which is the strict or true organ of our nature.

You, unless I greatly err, have not been in the habit of viewing creation in this light nor of assigning to consciousness so distinctive and important a *rôle* in the evolution of our nature. You have been wont, that is, to regard creation in its mere legendary aspect, as primarily a material and objective work of God, wrought within the proper precincts of space and time, and only secondarily or reflectively spiritual and subjective, as effected within the sphere of men's affection and thought. And you have been wont consequently to regard consciousness not as the organ of men's proper nature, attesting only what is unitary and universal in their experience, but rather as a mere authentication and badge of their private personality, attesting what is but individual or trivial and differential in their annals.

But these distinctions are obviously too large a theme to be approached at the close of a letter; and we shall do them more justice after getting a little more insight into the philosophy of creation generally, and particularly into the doctrine of nature as rigidly incidental thereto, as in fact its inevitable *point d'appui.*

LETTER XI.

MY DEAR FRIEND:—It is sometimes hotly contended among professing Christians whether there be few or many saved. The gospel itself sheds no light upon the dreary problem either way, and what it does say renders this and every similar idle question from a human point of view altogether superfluous and tiresome. For it testifies that a certain man called Jesus the Christ, who was conceived and born of a virgin mother (and was therefore presumably free from limitation on the psychical or paternal side) was eventually able by the things which he suffered and did, to unite his human nature to the Godhead, and invest that hitherto undefined and unknown force with the perfectly clear lineaments of a glorified flesh-and-blood man. In face of this testimony all our breathless theologic and scientific disputes sink into the insignificant prattle of childhood, and one wholly forgets to consider whether in fact

the number of saved be absolutely few or many.
For if a man be sure that his nature is enlarged to
the compass of infinitude, it can signify very little
to him what afterwards becomes of his very uninteresting person. To be sure one cannot very well
doubt that in that case his person will fare much
beyond its proper deserts: for if the nature of man
become divinized it is hard to see how his person,
which is a strict phenomenon of his nature, can
escape reflecting a proportionate enlargement: but all
I want to say is that provided the gospel be true,
a man can perfectly well afford to dismiss all anxiety
upon the score of his private or personal fortunes at
God's hands.

"Aye," you reply, "*provided the gospel is true!*
But I have serious doubts of this. That is to say,
I have lately taken counsel of certain distinguished
scientific teachers, and they have so discredited miracle to me as a factor in human affairs, that I even
hesitate to admit any truth however little 'scientific,'
which like that of the gospel seems necessarily to
involve it."

Miracle no doubt is very properly disowned by
science as a true cause of phenomena, because if men
attempt to account for physical facts by the allegation
of metaphysical causes, or causes extrinsic to the physical realm, they must end by denying physics an order

of their own, and so disqualify science. But because miracle is disowned by science as an answer to her physical interrogations, we are not justified, nor ever shall be, in excluding it from philosophic recognition, as in truth the most efficient factor in the history of human nature. For philosophy unlike science has no interest in physics as a literal fact, but only as a spiritual symbol, and is no way disconcerted therefore when you deny miracle a place and function in physical order. She has never been disposed to assign it such place and function, but on the contrary has expressly relegated it to spiritual or metaphysical uses. No man of philosophic genius, that is, no lover of truth for truth's own sake, has ever dreamt of finding a place or function for miracle in reference to physics, or the fixed statics of the mind, and has allowed it at most in reference to history, or its living dynamics and outcome. Every such man unfeignedly reverences miracle under this reserve, because in the long spiritual night of the mind when all knowledge of Divine things was obscured under the pall of men's mental and material penury, it alone shone as a feeble but prophetic day-star from on high to lift men's faith and hope out of an every way lifeless and ignominious present, and fix them on a living and radiant future big with God's unimaginable mercy. Thus miracle has always spoken to the free or spontaneous mind of

man, which recognizes in itself a higher life than that
of organic nature, and has always nurtured it to immortal issues.   It has alone in fact kept this mind
alive in men, when science, or their servile intelligence, being as absolutely tethered to physics as
an imprisoned bird to its cage, would otherwise
have willingly immersed it in the mere mud of
sense.

It ought to be confessed moreover that science
has never taken cognizance but of strictly objective
facts, facts of man's physical or outside experience,
facts, every one of them, susceptible in a more or
less subtle fashion of a sensible verification.   So
that it is only by breaking her own tether, the
tether that binds her to existence, and leaping the
petty fences that shut her out from the free domain
of the human mind, that science comes to know anything more about facts of life or consciousness, facts
of man's interior or subjective experience, than a
blind mole knows of astronomy.   Yet these are the
express *data* of philosophy, or things given in her
very existence, without which accordingly she has no
foothold upon earth.   For philosophy has but one
end, the research of being, and confines herself consequently to the only field where she finds any
echo or revelation of such being, namely: the field
of man's phenomenal life or consciousness.   Life or

consciousness unites what sense or science divides, and it is this unitary point of knowledge in man that philosophy takes for granted in all her appeals, while she bestows a very fitful and subordinate glance at the lifeless or divided testimony of sense or science.

Now science is self-excluded — excluded, that is, by the necessity of self-preservation — from the research of being, i. e., what gives spiritual or invisible unity to things, and devotes herself instead to ascertaining the constitution of existence, that is, to the discovery of the strictly material bond or tenure of existence which this magnificent framework of nature exhibits. In spite however of these purist or pedantic airs of science the craving of man after higher knowledge has been so inveterate as to force science herself upon the effort to supply it, by formulating a strictly ontological theory of existence, making sense final and absolute, so at all events barring out the conception of a spiritual creation, with all the ghostly interests and imaginations incident thereto. This is a clever dodge, for although it is no more warranted by science than by philosophy, it still enables the scientific man by winking hard to exclude from his mental horizon a vast array of intrusive questions of exceeding interest to the average mind, which yet bring nothing but perplexity and dismay to a wilfully narrower intelli-

gence.   No one of a philosophic turn of mind, I
am persuaded, grudges science any temporary relief
it secures to itself in this crafty way; but when
scientific men, not content with this good-humored
concession, attempt disingenuously to foist in upon
other minds those purely negative and authoritative
conclusions of theirs, they should be made clearly to
understand that they are guilty of a very impudent
interference with human freedom.   An ontologic or
absolute scheme of universal existence may be freely
tolerated to them personally, as summarily saving
them much precious time which they would devote
to minor pursuits.   But it is nothing short of ludicrous to suppose that the great unsophisticated
spiritual instincts of mankind are ever going to
acquiesce in any such piddling scheme of things,
did it even claim to its support all and sundry the
cumbrous *personnel* of science fifty times multiplied.
For my own part I laugh to utter scorn this sottish
and grovelling notion of an ontologic basis to existence, and hold the *dicta* of any of our more flagrant
scientific popes thereupon to be quite as contemptible rationally, and not near so honest morally, as
those of their deposed and degraded ecclesiastical
rivals.   The first duty of a scientific teacher is to
bring definite conceptions before the mind; and
what has a spurious theology to offer more stupid

and depraved intellectually than this ontologic explication of creation, wherein existence frankly confesses
to constituting her own absolute being, and the cart
meekly acknowledges its long misunderstood duty of
drawing the horse.

> "Now in the name of all the gods at once,
> Upon what meat doth this our 'science' feed,
> That she is grown so great"

as to convert the abject limitations of her own servile intelligence into a law of the human mind, or
sink heaven-born wisdom itself into a mere synonym
of learning?   It seems in fact to be a modern
instance of Æsop's fabulous old fox, who was so
annoyed by an accident to his hinder dimensions
which compelled him always to maintain a sitting
posture, that he found thenceforth no solace in life
but in persuading his brethren to undergo a like
physical mutilation.

It strikes me then that the cavil you urge against
the Christian truth, as involving a miraculous basis,
is simply captious, or disowns even a scientific warrant, let alone a philosophic one.   For the only objection which science (short of self-stultification) can
offer to miracle is, when it is postulated as a physical
cause.   And the miracle in question, which is the
birth of Christ from a virgin, so far from being
adduced to characterize any fact whatever of physical

genesis or order, expressly confines itself to signaliz-
ing a new beginning of human history, that is, a
fact exclusively of metaphysical genesis or spiritual
order. Science to be sure may deny if she pleases
that there is any metaphysical genesis to human history, or that physical fact is a mere witness to the
activity of spiritual order: but we are no way bound
to listen to her. She may in short deny any dis-
crete difference between physics and history, or run
the mind of man into his own entrails; but she does
so only at the risk of degrading her utterances to the
level of a goose's cackle, and disqualifying herself for
men's respect.

— But now after all let me say that I really stand
in a much more free and uncommitted relation to
miracle than you do, or any mere scientific dogmatist.
For while you are vehemently impelled to reject both
its actual and its possible truth, I value it as an
unquestionable race-tradition simply, or deliverance of
the common mind, and am as little concerned therefore about its literal truth or falsity in a scientific
point of view, as I am about the truth or falsity of the
multiplication table, which I learned by heart in my
uncritical infancy, and the truth of which I have never
challenged nor suspected since. Were I indeed as
wise as Sir Isaac Newton I should not know how
to set about increasing my faith in it; or as acute

as Professor Huxley, I should be at an utter loss to
imagine the means of weakening it. For it lies entirely back of my intellect, being in fact and in part
its indispensable mother's-milk, or constituting that
basis of fixed or positive knowledge which is requisite to give my intellect *body;* so that to argue with
me about its truth or falsity is to destroy my mental
personality, or at the least put its foundations in doubt,
and leave me consequently at most a mere reasoning
or gabbling idiot. It is one of those rich gratuitous
gifts of my race-intelligence to me which are necessary to constitute my own intellect, or endow me
consciously for my subsequent intellectual unity and
fellowship with mankind. And to attribute to me
therefore a shadow of ability to turn round upon it
and scrutinize it with a view either to my private
acceptance or rejection of it, is in my opinion flatly
to deny my sheer intellectual dependence upon my
race.

Just so with this beneficent race-tradition of miracle : it quite antedates men's turbid scientific judgments of Divine things, and constitutes a revelation
to their devout believing hearts of the truth of God's
sole spiritual existence and activity in the realm of
man's nature and history, long before their intellect
is educated to discern it. In the infancy of the race,
as in that of the individual, the heart in its worship-

ping innocency is far more impressible to the Divine presence in nature than the understanding; and often as in the case before us accepts a truth which the slower and more timorous intellect takes centuries to interpret. Especially at that early day there was no such thing possible as a scientific judgment of the mind upon the pretension of Jesus Christ to constitute a final revelation of the creative name in humanity. Nor, if there had been, do I suppose that the great bulk of mankind would have been less obdurately indifferent to it, than they are to similar judgments in our own day. For, remember, that the pretension of Jesus Christ imported no such transparent quackery as a reform in men's moral relations: for a mere moral reform of mankind could not be effected of course save with the privity and concurrence of every one interested in the result: but was tantamount to the spiritual recreation or renewing of their common nature, and appealed therefore for its truth to the competency of no individual judgment, but to the verdict of the great race or nature itself, when its personality should be definitely constituted. Especially was the gospel clear of tolerating, much more of inviting, any ratification at the hands of the philosopher, or the scientific man, or the religious man, *as such*, but at most it summoned to its ranks every bruised and tattered outcast of humanity, through whose dilapidated private personality the great race-consciousness of mankind might vindicate its sole and sovereign truth.   Thus these precious facts of revelation, whether they fall within the sphere of my understanding or my affections, quite transcend the grasp of my critical faculty, and impose themselves upon my heart as an unmixed good, which I am just as incapable of measuring in terms of the analytic intellect, or reducing to the contrast of the true and the false, as I am of demonstrating to a blind man the pleasure of a gorgeous sunset, or reasoning a man without a palate into the savor of sugar.

Doubtless it is not important, dear friend, that every specific atom of the human race should in his own history vividly reflect this superiority of the sacred and tender heart to the comparatively commonplace and misleading intellect; because the fortunes of no individual mind are of much account in the development of our natural history.   But it is vitally important to the race's integral evolution that this hierarchical supremacy of heart to head should be clearly acknowledged and maintained.   For our race-evolution constitutes the distinctive and exclusive line of Divine revelation, and we, blind and selfish egotists that we are, should be little enlightened by a revelation that gave truth the supremacy of good in human life.   Hence the value to the human mind

of the race's unreasoned traditions, for they alone
through the utter darkness, and in a crude but
effectual way, have kept alive the faith of men in
God's unbroken spiritual providence and government.
We at this late day, who have lost the interior or
spiritual perception of Divine truth, cannot help to
be sure cavilling at the credulity of earlier ages, and
insisting for our own part that we shall believe only
what is level to our senses. We have an unquestionable Divine right thus to cheapen truth if we
like; but we must bear the inevitable penalty: which
takes place in a like unquestionable cheapening or
lowering of our faculty of spiritual insight. I for
one am not aware of being able to exert the least
voluntary or personal control over the things of my
religious life. For religion above all things is what
identifies me consciously with the life of my kind;
and I should accordingly feel it nothing short of
sacrilege to attempt legislating for myself in a matter
where the race alone was competent. Least of all
should my scientific conscience empower me so to do;
for inasmuch as my scientific conscience is my sole
legitimate citadel and armory of self-defence against
unauthorized aggression, I can never have occasion
to appeal to it against my race, whence alone comes all
my intellectual nutriment and succor, but only against
chance individual dogmatism and false pretension.

Understand me then : I do not care a fig whether any of the incidental facts or even the total scope of Divine revelation, be regarded as a literal verity or not. For if so they contravene no scientific fact, or fact of physical order, because they profess on their face to be facts of a spiritual or metaphysical order, and therefore leave every ordinary fact as well as the total course of nature uncontradicted and unimpaired. And if they are without literal truth they yet claim an infinitely higher — which is a living or spiritual — truth, affirmed by consciousness alone. They are a truth in other words of man's vital or associated consciousness, and science is entirely unqualified either to affirm or deny it. Science has no power to penetrate the living consciousness of man; because her observation invariably restricts itself to phenomena capable in the last resort of being sensibly apprehended, or reporting themselves to other persons than the proper subject of them. Her activity is limited to the deceased or reflective consciousness, to consciousness considered as a spent force, in short, but leaving some footprints of its former life on the lower sands of sense. Unless therefore we are fully prepared to accept Comte's judgment of science, and look upon it not as an essentially servile sphere of the mind, which it is, but as the end or final cause of all its precedent stages of progress, we may dis-

miss it from our further regard as having any legitimate title either to revise or reorganize our past
historic evolution, or predict that which is still future.
I doubt not there are as many foolish scientific men,
in proportion to the whole number of the adherents
of science, as there are foolish religious men. And
we must expect all such accordingly, under the
prompting of a silly ambition or covetousness, now
and then to transgress their own territorial limits,
and sit in presumptuous judgment on the concerns
of their neighbors. Their religious neighbor at least
has no call to complain of this, for he himself has
long set the vicious example. But the one pretension
is just as disorderly as the other, and I think that the
better class of scientific men, who have no mercenary
aims, are perfectly persuaded of this.

But a truce to this polemic. Science has to do
only with specific facts, or experiences of sense, ignoring universals or experiences of the mind; and she
has a perfect right therefore, indeed it is her proper
business, to ontologize on a physical basis, or account
for species upon rigid time and space principles. But
existence is spiritual before it is material; belongs to
the mind before it comes down to the senses; is universal or dynamical before it is specific or fixed; and
Philosophy accordingly, which is the science of Man,
and deals directly therefore only with mental expe-

riences, has an equal and indeed prior right to take up these logical universals, these dynamics of the mind, and account for them on strictly metaphysical — that is to say, spiritual — principles.

And now let us get back to our starting-point, which is the conception Swedenborg entertains of creation. But before proceeding directly to canvass his ideas upon that subject, and as apropos to the attitude of the purely scientific mind, I desire to quote you a few pages of criticism from his books, bearing on the great disadvantages which result to the intellect from wantonly rejecting the race-continuity, or violently disallowing the absoluteness of knowledge in its own sphere.

"I will show you briefly," he says, "what the difference practically amounts to, between an inclination to truth and an inclination to good. Those who are inclined to truth primarily stick in the letter of things, or inquire among themselves *whether the thing affirmed really exist or not,* and *whether or not it exist thus and so;* and only when they have aired their doubts sufficiently as to these preliminary matters, are they prepared to take up and discuss the character of the actual thing itself. Thus they plant themselves obstinately upon the threshold of the temple of wisdom, and refuse to enter in until all their habitual doubts have been dealt with and overcome.

"On the other hand those who are primarily well-affected towards good, and have no regard for truth but as its minister or servant, have no perplexity in regard to the existence of things, but know and perceive them to exist not by virtue of their racionative intellect, but by virtue of the affirmative power of good in their heart; and thus they dwell not upon the threshold but in the inner chambers of the temple. Suppose some one to say for example that it is true wisdom *to love your neighbor not for his own sake, but for the sake of the good manifest in him.* Those who are in the first instance in the affection of truth, that is, in a critical or sceptical state of mind, begin at once to speculate whether or not the proposition be true, and then stop; while those who are in an affirmative state of mind, as loving good first and truth subordinately, admit the proposition at once, and discern, by virtue of the good they are in, who is most truly the neighbor, and in what degree he is such, and that all men are neighbors in different degrees. In fact these latter perceive ineffable things in truth, while the former admitting no higher inspiration than truth itself, discern comparatively nothing. So also in regard to this allied truth: that *he who loves his neighbor for the good attaching to him, loves the Lord:* they who value truth more than good speculate whether such be the actual fact of the case or not.

And if they are told that it must be so, because he who loves good in the neighbor more than the neighbor himself, loves good itself (which good itself the Lord alone is) and therefore loves the Lord : they again begin to speculate *whether it is really so*, and *what good is*, and *whether good be really more divine than truth*, and all the rest of it ; and so long as they stick to such speculations, they do not catch even the most remote glimpse of wisdom.*

"It is notorious that much of our disputative skill at this day goes no further than to put the existence of things in doubt. But as long as this habit continues, and men are content to debate *whether things be or not*, and *whether they be as alleged or not*, it is impossible to make any progress in wisdom. For wisdom grows and thrives only upon the numberless *particulars* which are embraced in the thing whose existence is put in doubt; and as long as this scepticism on the main point, or as to the certainty of knowledge, endures, all these particulars must remain unknown and inoperative. Our current erudition is almost wholly taken up in inquiring whether things exist or not, or whether they exist in such or such a manner, and the consequence is that it has no intelligence of truth. It is surprising how wise people of this sort conceive themselves to be in comparison with

* *Arcana Celestia,* 2718.

others; and how they measure their wisdom by their skill in argument, and especially by their ability to determine it to negative conclusions.   But men of simple good hearts, whom these high-flyers despise, perceive at a glance, without debate or learned controversy, both the existence of the thing put in doubt, and also its quality.   These unsophisticated people possess that common-sense perception of truth, which the former have extinguished in themselves by their inveterate habit of growing disputatious about the foundations of knowledge, or the existence of truth.*

"I have sometimes spoken with angels about heavenly dwelling-houses, and said to them that hardly any one upon earth believes that angels have need of such accommodation; some because they have no sensible proof of the fact; others because they do not know that angels are men; others still because they believe that the angelic heaven is the visible vault overhead; and inasmuch as this vault appears empty, and they suppose angels to be ethereal creatures, they conclude that angels live in the ether.   Besides, as they are ignorant of everything spiritual, they have no conception how such things can exist in the spiritual world as exist in the natural.   The angels replied that this was no news to them, but that it was never-

---

* *Arcana Celestia*, 3428.

theless matter of surprise to them that such ignorance existed chiefly in the church, and rather among the intelligent than among those whom these latter call *the simple*. They replied moreover that if these ignorant churchmen would only take the testimony of the Scriptures they profess to follow on the subject, they would see that angels were only human beings, and as such requiring houses; and that although they are spiritual men they are not therefore mere ethereal forms as some people ignorantly and insanely suppose. They thought moreover that men would think of angels truly if they would obey the dictate of common sense, which flows in from heaven and tells us that angels are human beings; but the moment they put this inward impression in doubt, and take to speculating first *whether the fact really be so*, they annihilate the influx which has no longer anything to fall into. This occurs among the learned mainly who by leaning unduly to their own understanding, shut out heaven from themselves, and the approach of light thence. So also every one instinctively believes in immortal life, and when he does not think of the subject from what learned men have had to say about it, has no difficulty in believing; but when he reverts to learned hypotheses concerning the soul and the doctrine of the body's reunion with it, and asks of himself *whether immortal life be really true or not,* of course his instinctive belief is dissipated." *

— I have cited these pregnant passages not so much for their own sake, as exemplifying the exquisite inwardness so to speak of Swedenborg's thought — the infinite delicacy and devoutness of mind which were habitual to him — as with a view to illustrate how profoundly dissident his intellectual method is with the whole scope of our modern scientific research. Happily for us the ontological questions which occupy our current scientific speculation — questions as to whether "things are or are not," which result for the most part in a negative conviction, as that everything runs into everything else with such good-will that at bottom all things are identical, with only an evanescent individuality or difference attaching to anything—did not occupy him, and we have consequently one positive intellect surviving — and long destined to survive, as I think — the craziest revolutions of our modern thought. The reason why these ontological temptations did not assail him, nor in any wise bewitch or bedevil his clear understanding, is that he viewed creation as exclusively a function of the Divine life, and hence looked upon nature as a covert spiritual dynamics, or sheer involution of the spiritual world, not only requiring no being in

* *De Cœlo et Inferno,* 183.

itself, but actually abjuring it as the right exclusively of a higher power. Thus he had no shred of a tendency to Idealism, but was a realist of the first water, a realist of absolutely no *nuance* whatever, having just as unfeigned a reverence for the senses in their sphere as for the soul in its sphere, and practically therefore just as incapable of confounding the two spheres as any carman you may meet upon the street.

LETTER XII.

MY DEAR FRIEND: — Creation with Swedenborg is the alpha and the omega of Philosophy. But then be very sure to understand that the creation he thus regards as the fundamental postulate of philosophy is not the least a mechanical exhibition of Divine power, consisting in giving the creature finite or phenomenal existence, but, on the contrary, an altogether living or spiritual achievement, *whereby God communicates Himself to the creature, in the plenitude of His infinite and eternal being.* He views creation as a spontaneous work of God, that is, a work of delight; because God, being infinite love — which means love without any drawback or limitation of *self*-love — lives only by communicating Himself to whatsoever is not Himself. And men commonly, you know, conceive of creation as a voluntary work of God, effected in time and space, whereby He makes all things out of stark nought, and which therefore He might, had it so pleased Him, have altogether forborne to accomplish. Swedenborg then stamps this conception of creative power as utterly sensuous and puerile, inasmuch as space and time with all their contents possess no reality save to an infirm or imperfect intelligence. There never was a space, according to him, where creation was not, nor a time when it was not. In other words, space and time fall exclusively *within* the created intelligence, and constitute the broadest or most common form of the natural mind. There is no such *thing*, that is, no such objective existence, as space or time, save to our sensuous judgment. We, by nature, are densely ignorant of the spiritual links that bind the universe of existence together, and our flickering reason, following the dictate of sense, substitutes for these the obvious *liaisons* of space and time. Thus they are both of them mere terms of relation supplied by our infirm intelligence between the various objects of our senses, and the various events of history. They constitute a mental background, as I have said, the one to our perception of existence, the other to our perception of life; the one being fundamental to our conception of *things*, the other to our conception of *events*. They neither of them have any positive force, space signifying nothing but the absence to our perception of limitation (or the finite), and time the absence of eventuality (or the relative).*

But if space and time bear no semblance of reality to creative thought, and possess at best but a bare semblance of it even to man's spiritual intelligence, then of course we must expect Swedenborg to deny all reality to Nature, for nature is conditioned in space and time, being the sum total of the limitations of the one and the vicissitudes of the other. And this is

---

* In fact, they are negative witnesses to the mind of the infinity and eternity which are alone competent to the explanation of existence. Space, whenever I affirm it, and in so far forth as it is affirmed, means, neither more nor less, the absence to my perception of sensible limitation, and time the absence of eventuality. Thus the space of a mile upon the earth's surface is an explicit denial within that interval of any limitation, and to that extent of course an implicit affirmation of the infinitude which subtends all existence. And the time of an hour or a day or a year of the earth's history means the denial within that interval of any eventuality to my perception, and hence an affirmation by implication of the eternity which subtends all our experience. In short, space, being the logical background of existence to our perception — being the necessary fulcrum or purchase which our intelligence exacts in order to its discernment of finite existence — must needs constitute a negative or inverse attestation to the essential infinitude which underlies all the phenomena of nature, simply because there is no logical negation of infinitude but sensible limitation. And time, being in like manner only the logical background of eventuality to our perception — being the necessary shadow exacted by our imperfect intelligence in order to its discernment of relative existence — is an inverse or negative remembrancer of the essential eternity which underlies and animates all the phenomena of history.

what in truth he actually does. He systematically denies a natural creation, and limits the creative activity in nature to a purely redemptive significance and efficacy. Thus nature has no existence to Swedenborg but what is conferred upon it by our most obscure and unveracious intelligence in spiritual or Divine things. It is but the dense mask which the spiritual creation puts on to the sensuous intelligence, the understanding limited and dominated by sense. There is no such entity or thing as nature to the spiritual apprehension ; for to that apprehension the mental generalization to which we give the name of nature and thence postulate as real, is merely a sign of our crude inadequate thought, and implies nought beyond that. The various forms of our sensible experience, mineral, vegetable, and animal, exist to the spiritual intelligence much more vividly than to ours, but the mental attribution which we make of all these forms to some unitary or universal substance called Nature, it utterly refuses to make, because the only unitary or universal substance it recognizes as underlying nature's forms, is not nature but Man. In fact, our term Nature expresses only the indolent mental judgment which we in our ignorance of spiritual laws instinctively frame to account for the origin of existence. We have an intuitive apprehension of the generic or universal identity which underlies and binds together the objects

of our senses, notwithstanding their specific diversity;
but we are intellectually incompetent to refer this
identity to its true source, which is the human mind,
and postulate for it meanwhile the supposititious substance which we term Nature, and which means nothing more after all than the mental sum or aggregate
of our impressions of space and time. Everything
embraced in sense exists in a particular place and at
a particular time, and by abstracting these particulars,
or universalizing their contents, we fancy ourselves
arrived at a most real or objective existence, instead
of a purely apparitional or subjective one, and unhesitatingly name it Nature, venerable mother of all
living.

We cannot, then, dear friend, too clearly make up
our minds that Nature does not exist in herself, or
absolutely, but only as an hallucination of our rudi-
mentary intelligence, Divinely permitted, and indeed
engineered, in the interest of our eventual spiritual
sanity. What we call by the familiar name of Nature, and find our chief imaginative activity in *personi-
fying*, is not so much as a thing even, but all simply
a most strict process or functioning of the Divine love
and wisdom towards our spiritual manhood. It is
nothing more nor less than the living method which
the creative energy adopts in order to spiritual pro-
lification. Spiritual existence, you know, cannot be

directly propagated. The bare conception of such a thing is nugatory, since the existence so propagated would be without natural or conscious projection from its creative source; while the fundamental postulate of spiritual existence is that it be both conscious and spontaneous. But it can be propagated indirectly: i. e. by the ministry of what we call Nature; for nature has a *quasi* existence or selfhood to our intelligence, upon which the Divine may subsequently and to any extent mould His own more real and perfect communication. *Omne vivum ex ovo.* That is to say, there is no form possible to our apprehension without its appropriate substance; nothing exists to our understanding except from some previous ground of existence. No farmer expects next year's crop unless he sow this year's wheat. No man can become a father without the mediation of a wife. Could the father beget offspring, and the farmer produce a crop directly from themselves, the product in both cases would manifestly be visionary, since there could be no basis of discrimination in either case between product and producer. In like manner precisely the architect of the spiritual creation accomplishes His work, not by the exhibition of magical or irrational power, not by any idle and pompous incantation addressed to empty air, but solely by the inward fecundation of natural germs *existing in our sensuous intelligence,* and the consequent development of a spiritual progeny every way commensurate with His own perfection.

— Anyhow, right or wrong, the fact is precisely what I have stated: Swedenborg makes nature the realm of *uncreation:* and by that unexpected word sends a breath of health to the deepest heart of hell. It is what neither *is* nor *exists* in itself, but only *seems* to be and exist to a subject intelligence.   But its use as such seeming is incomparably great.   For it educates the mind, by giving a logical background to existence, or enabling the creature to distinguish what is real or generic in things from what is merely phenomenal and specific, so furnishing a basis for the subsequent development of his spiritual intelligence, or his living perception of the Divine name.   Thus in Swedenborg's doctrine of creation nature plays the precise part which " nothing " is made to play in the ordinary theory.   For, as I have said, creation is vulgarly conceived to be a strictly magical * or irrational

---

* Magic is the power of instantaneous creation : the art of producing things irrationally, or without the use of means, thus by sheer force of will, and without any aid of the understanding.   It is the pretension to produce offspring without maternity, form without substance, soul without body, spirit without flesh, life without existence. So that if God should create spiritual existence, as we commonly suppose Him to have done — i. e. directly or without nature's intervention — not only would He confess Himself a mere flashy showman or conjurer, but the existence so created would turn out a monstrous im-

procedure of God, whereby He evokes all things *out of nothing*. The common people hold so unscrupulously to this idea, that persons among them of very good intelligence have no doubt that the magic which creates might again, if it pleased, reduce what is created to its primeval " nothing "-ness. Now it is easy to see the part which " nothing " is made to play in this popular hypothesis of creation. It serves precisely to emphasize or underscore existence, to give it that

---

posture utterly devoid of rational depth or character: for manifestly the stream cannot transcend its source, and if the creator be a charlatan, the creature must *à fortiori* be a deception. Our theologies, of course, intend no dishonor to the creative name but the contrary when they represent the spiritual creation as devoid of natural substance, or as being the instantaneous product of God's unlimited will. But nevertheless magical or irrational power is the only power they implicitly ascribe to God's perfection. I know of no pulpit which does not habitually interpret the Divine omnipotence into a faculty of unlimited *hocus pocus*, or irrational and immediate creation from Himself: thus into a power of purely arbitrary or capricious — which is essentially mad — action; a power of doing as he wills, without regard either to the beneficent ends His infinite love conceives in endowing his creatures with life, or to the exquisite means His infinite wisdom provides in order to carry those ends out. They thus in effect make God's glory to lie in His really being what every low juggler in the land only makes believe to be, namely: a maker of something out of nothing; and hence they fix their votaries in an attitude of such insincere worship towards the most High, as to vindicate even to a cursory intelligence the foresight of Christ, when he predicted that the professional religion of his own nominal followers would prove the chief obstacle to his second or spiritual advent.

logical relief, background, or mother-substance which it needs in order to be recognized by our intelligence, and which in Swedenborg's more philosophic view is supplied by nature.

Thus the popular mind cuts itself off from any just insight into the philosophy of creation, because it holds to nature as *created,* and consequently is obliged to resort to "nothing," or non-existence, as the only conceivable mother-substance out of which it could be fashioned. To show the fallacy of the church cosmogony, accordingly, nothing more is needed than to deny its fundamental principle, which is, the existence of "nothing," or the reality of non-existence. Nothing does not exist *in rerum naturâ.* Things and persons, or objective and subjective existences, divide the entire realm of nature between them; and to claim that "nothing" *exists,* nevertheless, *in some preposterous limbo beyond the realm of nature,* and constitutes that unthinkable substance out of which nature was educed, is a denial of the spiritual world, and convicts the claimant of gross philosophic fatuity. For if "nothing" exists beyond nature, spirit or life has no existence. In fact "nothing," in this depraved cosmologic sense of it, is a term invented to cover or eke out men's infirm conception of being. Men conceive of being not as inwardly or logically — but as outwardly or ontologically — generated ; that is to say, as constituted or made up of mere existence in space and time. The tree before my window apparently exists in space and time, and this appearance is enough to give the tree *being* to the popular imagination. Cut the tree down accordingly, and you have a corresponding dearth of being, which men express by saying that "nothing" really exists in the tree's place. In short, they regard specific existence as the presence of being, and specific non-existence as the absence of it; and hence, as I have already said, they regard being as ontologically constituted, that is, as made up of existence in time and space. Whereas the very most you are entitled to say in the premises is, that being is *apparently* manifested by existence, and manifested, moreover, to a style of intelligence which is entirely unacquainted with what being is in truth. Your image in a looking-glass is an apparent manifestation of your existence, or even of your *being* as thus ontologically conceived: but surely you would never allow that your being or your existence was in any way constituted by such appearance.

To the ordinary apprehension the creator is a *person*, and exists, as a person necessarily must exist, in space and time; and creation to the same apprehension is a *thing*, also existing or projected from Him in space and time, but involving infinitely less than He does of these ontological elements. The creature of

Divine power is doubtless popularly held to be infinitely inferior to the creator in other respects also, as
in love, in wisdom, and in power; but the difference
between them which dominates every other is this
brutal personal difference, arising from the assumed
infinitude of the one in time and space, and the
obvious finiteness of the other in those regards. It is
this low carnal estimate of the creative truth which
turns all our sectarian theology into rank intellectual
poison, and renders it exquisitely nauseous to every
heart and mind at all emancipated from sense. It
takes for granted that the creature is his own spiritual
or real being as well as his own natural or phenomenal form, and hence exhibits the creator, who is thus
excluded from any internal relation to the creature,
as restricted to a purely external activity towards him,
or an interference with his freedom so very wanton
and malignant as ends by filling the world with every
sinister apprehension of the Divine name. It is the
same superstitious conception of creation which is embodied in the letter of revelation. Swedenborg no
doubt justifies it in its own place, that is, in accommodation to the early or uninstructed scientific intelligence of the race, while as yet the sciences of observation had not come to fill that intelligence out, or
give it body, by interpreting Nature into Man. He
regards it both as in itself a very gross and misleading

effigy of the creative idea, and at the same time practically as an altogether invaluable one, because it was so eminently fitted to be lodged in the servile memory or devout imagination of the race, until such time as men's intelligence should have become quickened to discern the living and spiritual truth of the case. Thus it all the while bears to his imagination, in this crude literal form, just as inverse a resemblance to the eternal truth of things, as an egg bears to the chicken which is eventually to be hatched from it, or as the squalid sand of the sea bears to the gorgeous temples and palaces of living art which are yet to be wrought from its dismal wastes.

We see, then, dear friend, that in Swedenborg's view, no intellectual interest attaches to the creative problem *in so far as it is scientific merely*, or contemplates creation itself not as a spiritual, living, or regenerate result exclusively, but only as a *quasi*-living, natural, or generate one. A universe of animals might furnish an agreeable spectacle to the human intelligence, and even awaken in it admiration of the creative power; only there would be then no human intelligence present, no intelligence capable of enjoying the spectacle, or recognizing the power displayed in it to be Divine. The human intellect is not bred of any observation of the order of nature, or capacity of adaptation between it and the mind; it is originally quickened and born of man's adoring heart, or of his perception that nature manifests a power superior to itself to which all his moral and rational allegiance is due. And this power he recognizes as Divine only because it is miraculous, that is, able to originate a free or spontaneous style of life capable of immortal fellowship with Himself. The highest and best intellect of man grows out of his worshipful heart; and his heart's worship, whenever real, is energized by the conviction that God's perfection is most distinctively *human,* or without personal ends; in other words, that God is great enough in absolutely rejecting every man's personal or interested homage, to care solely and above all things for every man's spiritual or living sympathy and fellowship.

With these hints you will not be likely to do injustice to Swedenborg's comprehensive treatment of creation in shutting it up to the sphere of consciousness. I have tried to bring out the motherly character of his teaching, the incomparably tender and succulent aspect which it bears to the guileless, unmercenary heart of man. The difference, in fact, between his teaching and that of all our laborious philosophic journeymen from Descartes down to the modern scientific school of thought, is the difference between mother's milk and a Strasburg *paté:* the former teaching being addressed exclusively to

the needs of a nascent and most tender spiritual intelligence in man, the latter to the wants of a debauched
and worn-out intellectual digestion, living only upon
stimulants.   Swedenborg's primary demand upon his
reader is a heart attuned to goodness ; and he leaves
what subsequent truth he reports to his intellect
fearlessly and without argument to the heart's sole
arbitrament.   And every man who sincerely loves the
neighbor, or whose zeal for the human race is at
least equal to the zeal he is in the habit of expending
on his own account, is bound eventually to stumble
on his unostentatious books, and reap the abundant
stores of nutriment there and nowhere else provided for the intellect.   Swedenborg never betrays by
any chance the least of an intellectual self-consciousness, and yet, if intellectual power is to be measured
by the measure of truth possessed, it would seem unaffectedly ludicrous, to any one acquainted with his
writings, that any other person in the intellectual
history of the race should " be named," as they say,
"in the same day with him."   For even the Divine
creation itself, being a spiritual or living truth, is not
the least with him an outward or objective event, but
falls with all its miraculous machinery of space and
time, or all the vaunted life of nature, so-called, *clean
within the compass of the human understanding;* and is
a truth therefore of our growing human consciousness

exclusively, coming home to the business and bosoms
of the race as no other truth begins to do.   For what
in brief *is* creation spiritually pronounced?   *It is the*
evolution of man's nature in exact harmony with the
Divine perfection, or its plenary redemption out of
selfish into social form and order.   It does not contemplate, save by implication, either our unconscious
physical genesis, or our conscious moral exodus, but
addresses itself directly and exclusively to the spiritual-
ization of our nature.   *It is life eternal to know God;*
and hence creation in any wise estimation can only
mean the purification of our natural knowledge, the
exaltation of our flesh-and-blood consciousness, until
it compasses infinitude.   It can only mean, in other
words, giving the creature universal spiritual or social
form, never particular moral or physical substance.
The creator, of course, takes these lower things for
granted : physical substance being implied in moral
form, and moral substance in social or spiritual form,
just as the foundation of the house is implied in the
house, or earth in heaven, effect in cause, stream in
fountain.   So Swedenborg shows all lower things to
be *involved* in higher, physical in moral, and moral in
spiritual, existence, but never confounds the two.   By
thus planting the creative problem on higher ground
than it has ever before occupied, or carrying it back
to the infinite heart of God, he has anticipated every

really intellectual obstacle to the acknowledgment of creation : since these obstacles all pivot upon the difficulty of accounting for finite existence, or reconciling the creature's identity with the infinitude of the creator.

LETTER XIII.

MY DEAR FRIEND:—It is popularly conceived that the world is administered on positive and not on negative principles; in an active and not in a passive manner; in a way for example to promote the ease, honor, and emolument of the administrator, and not to cause him shame, confusion, and anguish. The Creator is universally supposed to occupy a position of the grossest sensible objectivity to the creature, a position fruitful on occasion of the greatest conceivable tyranny and oppression; and the creature a position of the subtlest spiritual subjectivity to the Creator, a position susceptible on occasion of the greatest conceivable dread, horror, and aversion.

Now this reputed relation between God and man in the first instance, and man and God in the second, is in the point of view of Philosophy an immense illusion; because Philosophy identifies the subjective element in the creative equation exclusively with the

Creator, and the objective element exclusively with the creature. That is to say: Philosophy regards creation not as a material or mechanical, but as a purely spiritual or LIVING operation of God in the created *nature;* and hence cannot help looking upon the Creator alone as the proper subject of the operation, and upon the creature alone as its proper object. For creation, being spiritual or living, consists, *first,* in a communication on the Creator's part of His own life or being to the creature; and evidently this communication stamps the Creator as essentially subjective to His creature, that is, essentially passive or suffering in his behalf; and, *secondly,* in a reaction or receptivity on the creature's part to such communication: and this reaction or receptivity evidently stamps the creature as essentially objective to the Creator; that is, essentially active or joyous. In other words creation spiritually regarded makes the Creator the sole and total subjective life of the creature, and the creature in his turn the sole and total objective life of the Creator. The vulgar misconception of it, accordingly, by which man is made God's submissive subject, and God is made man's controlling object, is grossly illusory to Philosophy; but it is an illusion, nevertheless, which is strictly incidental to the creature's unripe intelligence, and hence claims above all things to be understood, not denounced.

It is logically in fact the very essence of the creative idea, that creation is practically a marriage of
Creator and creature, whereby the creature alone spiritually *is*, or becomes infinited *in the Creator*, while
the Creator alone naturally *exists*, or becomes finite,
in the creature : so that the creature has at most only
a seeming or phenomenal existence *in himself*, even
while he has at the same time a most real or absolute and unqualified being *in his Creator*. It is true
enough no doubt that the creature — through his
bottomless ignorance on one hand of the truth that
creation is a purely spiritual work of God in the
created *nature*, and through his bottomless conceit
on the other that it is an altogether shabby natural
work of God effected in the creature's petty self —
egregiously misinterprets this fundamental logic, or
attributes to himself and not to the Creator his natural or finite personality, while he remains persistently
blind and deaf to the spiritual and infinite being he
and all his kind have in God. But the spiritual
truth of the case is not a whit inwardly altered or
even prejudiced by this mistake; it is only outwardly
obscured or deadened. What alone happens is that
the spiritual or creative truth is obliged to lower
itself to the creature's sensuous and grovelling imagination, by masking itself in moral lineaments, or
taking the creature at his own stupid estimate of

himself, and addressing him as if he were in truth
his own natural substance, and God himself consequently his mere outward and moral or regulative
law.   And this is literally *all* that happens.   Creation becomes converted in men's infirm understanding from a spiritual, or infinite and eternal, Divine
life in the *unconscious nature* of the creature, which
has therefore strictly public or universal issues in
humanity, into a mere legal or moral administration
of Divine power in the *conscious person* of the creature, having at best therefore strictly private or particular issues.

Let creation, then, in the sole and exclusive spiritual truth of the word, remain perfectly intact, dear
friend, to our particular faith, whether all the world
say us nay or yea.   Let it be to us both forever
nothing else than an inmost and inseparable life of
God within the strictest limits of our nature, whereby that nature — gladly responsive to such an un-
precedented subject! — becomes freely redeemed out
of its otherwise inveterate personal or selfish lineaments, into the imperishable image and likeness of
God most High, that is, into grandly social form
and order.   Neither you nor I have ever had, have
now, or ever shall have, any particle of just or rational hope towards God which is based either
upon any possible personal difference in us to other

men, or any possible personal difference in us to ourselves in past time, but solely and wholly upon His own reconciling spirit or temper in universal man, whereby we and all men become gradually softened and refined out of our natural egotism and savagery, by being lifted out of our petty egotistic moral consciousness, and becoming gradually invested with social or race-consciousness. This is what creation, spiritually regarded, means, and all it means, not any stupid and brutal event in space and time, transcending human nature and antedating human history, but a most real and authentic life of God identical with human nature and consubstantiate with human history: beginning with that history, animating all its movements, keeping steadfast pace with it through all its marvellous vicissitudes and revolutions, and bringing it at length to its grand triumphant climax in the coming splendors of the mystical city of God. Thus our spiritual creation is only the truer or philosophic name for our distinctively NATURAL REDEMPTION: since nothing short of this redemptive work can establish the Divine claim to be a universal creator. I know, for my own part at least, very well, that it must prove a "scandal" to our imitative modern Judaism, and "foolishness" to our simulated modern Hellenism, but I cannot help saying all the same,

nor rejoicing as I say it, that I look upon the fast-
approaching close of our corrupt civilization in the
New Jerusalem — which is the Gospel symbol for
the evolution of a free society, fellowship, or equality of all men with each and each with all on earth
and in heaven — as the veritable apotheosis of our
nature, since it will reveal and vindicate to eternal
years, not the truth of God's spiritual or essential
manhood, for that has been long acknowledged, but
to us the infinitely more momentous because infinitely more prolific, truth of His NATURAL or *adventitious* manhood : a manhood forced upon Him,
so to speak, in the interest of the strictly universal
— which are the lowest corporeal and sensual —
needs of His creature.

But what precisely do we mean by the created
nature ?

" Nature," then, when used abstractly means the
realm of the undefined or relative in knowledge ;
means that vast potentiality of existence which perpetually allures and at the same time baffles the
grasp of science, inasmuch as it is always *becoming*, yet never *is* definitively known. It signifies
what is generic, impersonal, or universal in existence, in contradistinction to what is specific, personal,
or particular. It is not of course what *creates*, that
is, gives invisible being or substance to things ; but

only what *constitutes* them, that is, gives them visible form or existence. It is the maternal principle in existence, thus what produces all things or gives them body, in opposition to the paternal principle which begets them, or gives them soul. In short, Nature is what all men instinctively believe in, yet what no man has ever had sensible contact with. We cannot help believing in it, because we see it revealed as we think in its endlessly varied phenomena or productions; but we have and can have no *direct* acquaintance with it, because it is not the least a fact of sense, but at most a probable truth of science. From the necessity of the case, or in the interest of science itself, it must always remain a merely probable — that is, a strictly *undemonstrated* — truth: for if Nature, or the universe of our scientific faith, could once be grasped by observation, and so be forced to confess itself Thing instead of Thought, science would *ipso facto* lose her whole intellectual capital, would forfeit in fact her sole *raison d'être*, and be obliged to tumble incontinently back into the arms of sense. To be sure we talk very glibly of "the laws of Nature"; and where "laws" are of recognized obligation, it should be presumable at least that the lawgiver is very distinctly known. But these so-called "laws of nature" are laws of human thought exclusively, and laws of nature only in so far as nature itself is taken for a symbol of the mind. That is to say, they are only so many scientific generalizations on our part based upon sensible observation, whereby the mind moved by a profound instinct of its spiritual origin and destiny, *seeks unconsciously to universalize itself*, and so wrest from "Nature" the provisional or educative and superstitious homage it has so long enjoyed.

Nature in short, thus abstractly viewed, is the only purely subjective existence we are acquainted with, inasmuch as it never falls under the cognizance of our senses, but invariably posits itself as the attribute of a subject, and utterly refuses to be cogitated apart from such subjectivity. It is true that some one may object to regarding nature as this strictly subjective or metaphysical quantity, on the ground that we are in the habit of applying the term to the external world, which is made up of sensibly objective existences. But it is a sufficient answer to this objection to say that we always apply the term to the world as *a whole*, or by way of discriminating what is generic or universal in the sphere of sense, even, from what is specific or particular; and universals claim no physical but a purely logical or metaphysic subsistence. The world or universe is not a thing of sense, but a pure thought of the mind; and when we designate it accordingly by the name of nature, the effect is not to degrade nature into a physical substance, but to elevate the world itself, regarded as a universe or whole, into a metaphysic substance. Whatsoever exists to sense is practically or at bottom nothing else than a concrete or specific form of the logical or metaphysic *not-me ;* and outward nature, consequently, regarded as the universal term in which alone all our sense perceptions are supposed to cohere, is in its turn but the abstract or generic form of this negative judgment on our part.

Then too it ought to be noted, in reply to the objection just made, that when the word Nature is applied to the external world, or the phenomena of sense, it is used just as much to signify the field of the subjective and relative which we find there: only the relations existing between minerals, plants, and animals are *outward* or *objective* relations exclusively, which are wholly unknown to and unperceived by the minerals, plants, and animals themselves, and which consequently presuppose and address our commanding subjectivity alone. The animal for example has no science of the relations of agreement or difference which bind him to his own and other species, although he instinctively obeys them doubtless ; for they *exist* only to another eye than his own. And all that the observant eye of our science cares to signalize in these relations is that they characterize the animal *nature* apart from any visible or objective subject of it.

All the concrete uses of the word betray the same universalizing or undefining scope and tendency. What we call the nature of a horse, of a dog, of a bull, is not what belongs primarily to any particular animal so-named, but to the entire horse, dog, or bull species or kind; although the particular animals in question may be at the same · time exceptionably favorable specimens of their race. And so throughout the whole compass of the word's concrete application: the nature of a particular mineral, vegetable, or animal, is in every case strictly what universalizes, or equalizes, or identifies it with its species or kind, and so far forth of course individualizes it from all other kinds. But it confers no private individuality upon it, that is, no spiritual or subjective discrimination with its own kind. We say to be sure that one man has a *good* nature, and another an *evil* nature: meaning by that phrase, that the one is sensitive and the other indifferent to his legal obligations. But all we are really *entitled* to say in the premises is, not that the men are of a different nature, but that human nature itself is of so universal a range or quality as to

embrace a relatively high and a relatively low element, or exhibit in itself the sheer neutrality, indifference, or equilibrium of good and evil: so that
any particular subject of it may be morally good,
and any other particular subject morally evil, without the slightest strain or compromise, on either
side, of their common nature. For human nature is
distinctively social in form, being the unity of self-
love and neighborly love — thus of what is widest
or most universal in affection and thought, and what
is narrowest or most particular — and the morally
good man accordingly is one in whom the higher
element practically rules, while the morally evil man
is one in whom that element is made practically to
serve. In short they are men of a strictly identical
nature, and their moral divergence is due to the
fact that until human nature shall have attained to
its destined sabbath in the permanent social evolution of the race, the greatest possible antagonism,
consistent with providential order, must necessarily
prevail between its component factors — to the extent even of organizing the entire spiritual world
into the divided spheres of heaven and hell.

Understand then, dear friend, that there is no such
thing, or congeries of things, as what we call nature,
or universal existence. All real existence is specific
or particular, so that natural, generic, or universal

existence is never physical but metaphysical, discernible therefore not by sense, but exclusively by life or consciousness. It is realizable to thought, but not to sight, and herein differs from specific existence which is realizable to sight, but not to thought. The earth really exists in space, and plant and animal really exist upon it clothing it with life and beauty. But strive as we may, we cannot *think* these existences; cannot for the life of us think either earth or plant or animal; and for the very good reason that they all of them anticipate and supersede thought, being already given to us in sense. We can recall them to memory whenever we list; but we cannot possibly think them as we think *God* and *man*, or *goodness* and *truth*, *grace* and *beauty*, *holiness* and *peace*, *justice* and *mercy*, simply because they rigidly forestall our intelligence, or what is the same thing, because unlike spiritual existence they have no inward or living but a purely outward and sensible objectivity to us. It is no way true of course to say that the objects of sense into which we are born, spiritually *create* our intelligence or give it soul; but it is perfectly true to say that they materially *constitute* it, or give it body, cradling and nursing it indeed upon the chaste breasts of their maternity, until such time as it is fit to be weaned from sense, and fed upon truth alone. But we do unquestionably think *nature* or *universal* existence, and can do no more than *think* it; because it is not the least given us in sense, but is on the contrary a most strict projection of the spiritual world, or the associated human mind, upon our private and personal thought. We do not see nature or the universe; neither do we hear it, nor smell it, nor taste it, nor touch it. And being thus wholly inaccessible to our senses, it can never fall within the conditions of our memory even; for we can remember nothing and imagine nothing which is wholly divorced from sense. But we *think* nature or universal existence day and night; and we think nothing else. Our living intellect — which is heart and mind in actual unison — broods upon it, feeds upon it, waxes fat upon it, vehemently denies itself at last either anchorage or sustenance apart from it. We love and cherish it, we confide in it, we adore it, we aspire to it, we associate our eternal fortunes with it — do everything in short but pretend outwardly or sensibly to know it.

But what we want just now is to discover the exact intellectual significance of *human* nature, that we may be able to assign its due philosophic weight and function in the evolution of the spiritual creation. Let us accordingly address ourselves forthwith to this latter interest.

As by the nature of a thing we always mean to

express what to the eye of science gives the thing objective relation with other things, so too. by human nature we mean to express the sphere exclusively of the *relative* in human life, only the relations which connect man with man are not such as can be scientifically discerned. They are not, like the other, external relations which address the sense; they are internal relations, which appeal for their truth only to consciousness. This establishes a great discrepancy between human and brute life. The relations which exist between man and man, and which reflect their characteristically *human* nature, are not, like those of the animal, outward and organic. Man to be sure has these outward and organic relations also to his fellow-man, but it is only in so far as he is yet undivorced from animal, or uneducated into man. The relations which bind the partakers of human nature together, as such, are intensely living and conscious, or inward and æsthetic, instead of outward and organic. They are relations, not of appetite and passion, controlled by necessity and duty, but of taste or attraction, governed exclusively by the freedom or spontaneity of the parties; and consequently, as the saying is, they never leave any bad taste in the mouth behind them. The contrary is well known to be the case when men identify themselves with the animal nature, and cherish its lower delights: for in so doing they only reap disgust, degradation, and frequent despair. This sharp discrepancy of the human nature with the brute nature is owing of course to the truth of the spiritual creation, and is one of its most constant attestations. Man's nature, whatever the splendors of Divine power incident to it, is after all nothing but a vehicle of transcendent spiritual blessing to the man himself; whereas the brute nature knows no such spiritual subserviency. And when accordingly the subject of the higher nature persistently identifies himself with the lower, he is sure to find in his way every sharp regret and bitter humiliation which may tend to frighten him back into his place. Otherwise he would be like a noble house ruined by bad drainage.

And now, dear friend, I think you and I have attained to a pretty definite notion of what constitutes human nature. Human nature is the field exclusively of man's *subjective* relations to his kind, and constitutes therefore the realm of *identity* among men, the realm in which all men, whatever may be their individual or spiritual differences to their own eye, are one and undistinguishable to God. And being such it is the appanage or attribute of course of a *conscious* or *living* subject, whose existence it therefore presupposes, just as the work of a statuary presupposes the existence of the marble. I say *of course*, for this field of relationship between man and man, being intensely subjective, that is, free, spontaneous, inorganic, living, never falls by any chance within sense, like the relations of the animal, but exclusively within consciousness. It is the whole virtue and efficacy of sense to antagonize one thing with another, to concentrate and inflame points of discord and difference between things. And if men accordingly were not endowed with a deeper life than that of sense, namely, consciousness : or the faculty of discerning the free or subjective unity which exists among them, in spite of their superficial or obvious and outward personal disjunction : they would always have remained the inveterate animals they were aboriginally born, nor ever have dreamt consequently of the infinite possibilities which had been squandered in their own ineffectual human form.

Understand then, dear friend, that human nature has no existence *in se*, but is invariably the attribute of a *conscious subject*, whose existence is presupposed by it. It is almost superfluous to say that this natural subject must be an exclusively *conscious* subject, because human nature has two constitutive and extremely different elements, a finite and an infinite one, or a creator and creature, and these two can coexist only in the integral unity of consciousness. But this much cannot be too emphatically said, namely: the natural subject cannot be a mere personal subject, cannot be what we are apt to call a mere individual subject, because in that case he would practically exclude the race-element. You yourself know quite as well as I do, that your own and my style of personal· subjectivity is much too finite to do any sort of justice to the generic quality of our manhood, or what especially stamps it *natural:* our personalities are so far from doing our nature justice in fact, that they leave it, in our own spiritual estimation at least, an every way futile, petty, egotistic, ignominious thing. And what is spiritually true of our natural subjectivities is true no doubt of all the world's. Accordingly, the only adequate exponent of human nature must be able to interiorate his object to himself, and not, like us, merely exteriorate it. He must be a man broad enough in other words to embrace his nature, and spiritually reproduce it in his own subjectivity. In short, he must be both universal and individual, both generic and specific, both natural and spiritual, or comprehend within his own undefined and equatorial personality, both poles of the nature he claims to make his own — infinite and finite, Divine and human: or else incontinently avouch himself an unworthy exponent and illustration of the nature.

But I must bring this long letter to a close. It is evident then from what has gone before, that — *pace* Messrs. Darwin and Spencer — man's natural genesis is not at all physical, but on the contrary strictly metaphysical, involving as it does his transformation or development out of a selfish being into a social one. For humanity is not a material fact discernible to the outward eye; it is a spiritual truth, discernible solely to the inward eye, an eye rendered clear by love. It is a SOCIETY, not a *herd* of men, and claims a distinctly qualitative not a quantitative unity. On his animal side man is doubtless physical enough, his origin connecting him not only with the animal tribes, but with the vegetable and mineral kingdoms as well. But when we speak of human *nature*, we speak of what logically belongs to man alone, and therefore disconnects him with all lower existence. This metaphysical nature of ours involves physics as its necessary basis of manifestation, just as the house involves its foundation, the tree its bark, the gem its matrix. For the house which towers to heaven to lay permanent hold upon sun and air, descends first into the bowels of the earth to compel the damp and darkness of the latter sphere into its own higher vassalage. So precisely our natural evolution, which serves as a matrix for our subsequent spiritual or individual conjunction with infinite goodness and truth, familiarizes us first with the death and hell latent in ourselves, latent in our finite or personal consciousness, in order to reduce them ever after to its eternal subserviency. Man's spiritual destiny is so sublime, it is so vivified and empowered by the intimate Divine fellowship, as to call for this preliminary wealth of mineral, vegetable, and animal existence, in order to furnish him the alphabet of *self*-knowledge, and in that knowledge the sure pledge and guarantee of his ultimate free or spiritual acknowledgment of God. A finite consciousness can only recognize good by the previous contrast of evil, truth by the previous contrast of error ; so man by the experience of the wretched death-in-life wrapped up in his proper person, learns truly to know and heartily to aspire to the only real and true life. It is the only rational and satisfactory explanation of our moral experience to look upon physics as this necessary involution of our natural evolution : our moral experience being given us only to signalize the transition — only to bridge the interval, and make the passage practicable — between our finite organic or physical *persons*, and our undefined, inorganic, impersonal, metaphysic *nature :* which it does by releasing us from the bondage of animal instinct, and opening our interiors to spiritual Divine influx.

Such I do not hesitate to say is the literally awful grandeur of human nature, as being the sole link or *liaison* between creator and creature, between the infinitude of God and the finiteness of man! And such the so long inscrutable secret of its incompressibility into any merely organic or finite physical dimensions! It involves — lodged or masked in our vicious, obdurate personalities — a fossil infinitude or chronic Divine element, and insists upon this element being fairly reckoned with or put into fluid diffusible form, before it will permit the least righteous judgment of itself to be formulated. And there is no nature properly speaking but human nature. There is any amount of specific mineral, vegetable, and animal form, but there is no nature corresponding to it, because there is no universal mineral, vegetable, and animal substance except man, and his nature infinitely transcends their wants. His nature is not theirs, any more than their form is his. The former contingency is gainsaid by the circumstance that his nature is a universal one while theirs is partial; and the latter by the circumstance that their form is specific or gregarious, while his is strictly individual. Every man claims to be estimated by himself alone, every animal by its species. Thus there is a universal human substance called selfhood, not a material substance, not an organic substance, but a strictly immaterial or inorganic one confined to consciousness, and hence incapable of scientific scrutiny. And human nature consequently is alone entitled to the designation of Nature, and to absorb in itself, as so many subject provinces merely, mineral, vegetable, and animal existence. I do not in the least mean to deny of course that besides this generic difference which I exhibit to all lower existence, and which puts an eternal gulf between us, I also exhibit many specific resemblances to it: being innocent with the dove, subtle with the serpent, gentle with the lamb, fierce with the tiger; and so forth. These are not generic traits of humanity, but only and at most specific traits, characterizing us not as *homines*, but as *viri*: not as we stand substantially knit together, all and each, each and all, in one immortal bond of unity called society, but only as we stand superficially differenced each from every other in our petty selves, and so become distributed by an adorable providential wisdom into two great classes of men — respectively celestial and infernal — in which the finiting or specific principle, the principle of endless variation and conflict, and the infiniting or generic principle, the principle of permanent unity and peace, are severally represented or embodied, and held in enforced mutual equilibrium.

The adorable use of this arrangement in the Divine

economy above adverted to, is our natural or race-development. For the race of man, or human nature, is not the least numerically or materially constituted, is not, as we are apt to conceive it, the mere uncouth lumping or hideous agglomeration of our acrid, frivolous, and uncompromising *selves*. It is on the contrary altogether qualitatively or spiritually constituted, being an exquisite Divine distillation of our foul and perishable natural selfhood, and a subsequent sublimation or rectification of it into an ineffable unitary form and order called society. For obviously if selfhood be the mere adventitious base out of which human nature or the race-consciousness of man becomes divinely fashioned, it can have no show of pretension to enter into the finished superstructure itself, save at most as coloring matter, or perpetually vanishing reminiscence.

Thus there is no way open to us philosophically of accounting for selfhood in the human bosom, save upon the postulate of its being the mask of an *infinite spiritual substance now imprisoned, but eventually to be set free, in our nature:* a substance whose proper energy consists in its incessantly going out of itself, or communicating itself to what is not itself, to what indeed is infinitely alien and repugnant to itself, and *dwelling there infinitely and eternally as in its very self.* That is to say, the Divine being or substance is Love, love without any the least set-off or limitation of self-love, infinite or creative love in short; and it communicates itself to the creature accordingly in no voluntary or finite but in purely spontaneous or infinite measure, in a way so to speak of overwhelming *passion:* so that we practically encounter no limit to our faculty of appropriating it, but on the contrary sensibly and exquisitely feel it to be our own indisputable being, feel it to be in fact our inmost, most vital and inseparable *self*, and unhesitatingly call it *me* and *mine, you* and *yours,* cleaving to it as inmost bone of our bone, and veritable flesh of our flesh, and incontinently renouncing all things for it.

LETTER XIV.

MY DEAR FRIEND:—We have seen that the sphere of human nature is the relative or associated sphere of human life, the sphere of men's free, spontaneous fellowship, each with all and all with each, in contradistinction to that of their felt or personal absoluteness, which is the sphere of their voluntary, interested, selfish disjunction of each with every other: so that society is of necessity the Divinely unitary *form* of human nature.

But now what is the bearing of the definition of human nature I gave in my last letter, upon the doctrine of creation regarded as the regeneration of that nature? Why, as I conceive, it most clearly brings out the purely spiritual character of creation; brings it out indeed with an emphasis sufficient to arrest and exalt even the simplest intelligence. If human nature, as we have seen, possess neither moral nor physical quality, save by implication, that is, be

neither person nor thing: if on the contrary it be
nothing else than a most powerful but invisible *Divine bond of relationship between man individual and
man universal;* a bond moreover so free and elastic
as safely to permit the appropriation of a private
selfhood to man, and the subsequent expansion of
that selfhood even to diabolic proportions: then the
only philosophic obstacle to the recognition of creation as a living or spiritual work of God disappears.
That is to say: the only philosophic hindrance to
men's believing in God as a creator, is their inability to believe in *themselves* as created. Self-consciousness, the sentiment of personality, the feeling
I have of life in myself, absolute and underived
from any other save in a natural way, is so subtly
and powerfully atheistic, that no matter how loyally
I may be taught to insist upon creation as a mere
traditional or legendary fact, I never feel inclined
personally to believe in it, save as the fruit of some
profound intellectual humiliation, or hopeless inward
vexation of spirit. My inward *afflatus* from this
cause is so great, I am conscious of such super-
abounding personal life, that I am satisfied, for my
own part at least, that my sense of selfhood must
in some subtle exquisite way find itself wounded to
death — find itself *become death* in fact, *the only
death I am capable of believing in* — before any

genuine spiritual resuscitation is at all practicable for me.

I don't say, mind, that church authority is not sufficient to make us ritually acknowledge, or acknowledge with the lips, creation in space and time. But creation in space and time is intellectually absurd or preposterous, and this is all that our ritual acknowledgments are good for in the long run, to make some absurd or incredible thing tolerable to us. We are talking here of a very different creation, that is, of the living or spiritual creation; and what I say is that the sole effectual hindrance to our acknowledgment of this is the unhappy conviction to which we are ecclesiastically born and bred, of our natural realism, of our being by nature veritable existences. Remember what spiritual creation involves. It involves the giving things phenomenal existence as well as, or in order to, real being; natural substance as well as, or in order to, spiritual form. In other words, the creator of men is their maker also. He not only gives his creatures *soul*, or *spiritual life*, which forever individualizes them from all other things, but He alone it is who out of His own spiritual substance gives them *body* as well, that is, *natural existence*, which forever identifies them with all other things. He does this, because He, HIMSELF, constitutes the true

and *quasi*-vital mother-substance of things, or furnishes, *Himself*, the natural material out of which
they are fashioned. This is the adorable difference
of creative to created art. No artist or inventor
amongst us ever finds the mother-substance or material of his work exclusively within himself, or
supplied by his own spiritual resources. He finds
it already provided to his hand by nature, and all
he has to do consequently is to apply ordinary skill
and judgment to the manipulation of this material,
in order that his work may duly appear. So that
unless the artist or inventor had first some natural
community with these lower or artificial things he
makes — his statue, his poem, his picture, his clock,
his house, his steam-engine, his what-not, and were
himself, to begin with, the fruit of a most spiritual
Divine art, even as these lower things are a fruit
of his own natural art, he would never be able to
conceive them even, let alone execute them. Now
the creator of man has, to begin with, no such community of nature with his creature as this. He is
not a subject of being, but its unalterable source,
nor is He capable of naturally or subjectively existing save in his creature. All natural or subjective existence derives from Him accordingly, being
nothing else but that instinctive and unconscious
appropriation and imprisonment of His most holy

substance, which is involved in our spiritual consciousness, and is necessary to constitute it. And
what we call "the universe of nature," which to our
unspiritual imaginations is the outward sum or objective truth of such existence, is merely an artifice
of our innocent puerile intelligence to hide from our
own eyes our dense ignorance of the fact, and so
maintain a good conceit of ourselves.

Besides, all physical existence that we know of is
plainly specific : how therefore should we ever feel
ourselves authorized to infer that there was some
unknown *universal* substance that constituted the
invisible generic unity, or source, of all these in-
numerable visible species ? And by what magic
above all were we ever taught to divine that the
only proper name to bestow upon this universal
substance was the indefinite term : Nature ? There
is no universal mineral, nor vegetable, nor animal
substance, genus, or nature answering to any of
these specific mineral, vegetable, or animal forms
our eyes are familiar with ; and there is even express
provision made in the moral law, as we shall see bye
and bye, that no moral subject especially shall ever
suggest the possibility of such universality. And yet
men have always had this profoundly philosophic
instinct of the underlying unity which binds together
all the endlessly different and hostile forms of exist-

ence that fall within the compass of sense; and have moreover always characterized it by this profoundly philosophic because purely undefined and prophetic designation — Nature. Whence then this marvellous intellectual instinct? And whence this equally marvellous and just expression of it?

Simply from the infinite craving which the creator of man has for the spiritual sympathy and fellowship of His creatures; they themselves being both alike a providential impulsion within the unconscious soul of the creature to bring about that Divine end. For this end requires for its own fulfilment a preliminary process of purgation in the created nature: requires that all the forms of evil and falsity to which the created nature is subject, by reason of its inherent alienation from, or otherness to, the infinite creator, should first have been thoroughly eliminated or sloughed off. And it is evident that these abstract evils and falses cannot be sloughed off until they have been concentrated, or become concrete and actual in the *personality*, so to speak, of the created nature: that is, in the experience of the various persons who derive from the nature. The original sin of the creature — his πρωτον ψευδος from which all his evils and falses flow — is that he feels himself to exist *absolutely*; and this is a sin he may well be unconscious of, since the boundless love of his creator is at the bottom of it. At least if God gave himself to his creature in a finite manner, there could be no danger of the sin being committed. But He gives himself to the creature without stint, in *infinite* measure; and the creature cannot help feeling therefore that he is life in himself. So profoundly unconscious is he of falsifying the spiritual truth of things by this vicious estimate of himself, that here after six thousand years of experience scarcely any one has yet attained to right ideas upon the subject. Above all, the people who preserve the outward or formal revelation of the church's long fatuity in regard to it, and bestow upon that revelation the most abundant honor, are the most densely and devoutly blind to its spiritual significance: and one would sooner expect a true acknowledgment of God from the stones in the street than from them.   '

But though man starts with this feeling of his own absoluteness, or of his being life in himself, he is by no means left without a divine witness in his own bosom to the profound untruth of the feeling. For he feels, at the same time that he feels his existence, *that there is nothing in himself to warrant or justify such existence.* Let him start then never so gayly in the career of existence, he nevertheless starts with a threatening bombshell in his very vitals, which is ready to explode and lay him waste every moment that he remains unreconciled to the essential truth of things; or, what is the same thing, unenlightened as to the essential emptiness, imbecility, and charlatanry he carries about with him under the name of selfhood. Now the only possible way of his becoming reconciled to the absolute truth of things is, to give over this fallacious feeling of his constituting his own life or substance, of his constituting even his own existence or selfhood, inasmuch as this fallacious feeling itself is a sheer effect of spiritual causes, all of which have their being in God most High, and are contingent upon His vast designs of mercy towards the race. And in order that his reconciliation may be complete or perfect, the nature or quality of the being which all spiritual existence has in God most High, becomes reflected to his experience by a law he finds within his bosom called conscience, the whole drift, spirit, or purport of which is that he love his neighbor as himself. For only in this way, namely: by his coming to learn, and his agreeing to act upon, the maxim, that the being which alone vitalizes his existence is spiritual, not material, and that its nature is Love: is the portentous bombshell which he bears about in himself rendered gradually, and at last perfectly, inexplosive and harmless.

Now manifestly the inward or spiritual disciplining of the creature to this divine height, demands in order to base it, in order to illustrate and enforce it, some answering outward or natural experience on his part; demands in fact the literal verification of his own nature. The essential freedom and rationality which he has in God utterly disqualify him in the long run for receiving truth on authority, and so render it imperative that all nutriment intended for his spiritual growth be capable of scientific authentication — that is, of ultimating itself outwardly or to his senses — before he can assimilate it. In short his inward or spiritual creation and culture exact a strictly empirical, conscious, or phenomenal realm of existence on the creature's part, to endow him with true self-knowledge, that is, to correct the conceit and ignorance and vanity that are incident to his private or finite generation, and so inoculate him in time with the chastening and otherwise unattainable knowledge and love of God. We may say then that God's creative purposes towards the human race necessarily involve a long preliminary wrestle or tussle on the part of the individual or self-conscious man *with himself:* a long, toilsome, most bitter, and vexatious conflict on his part with his own puny, crooked, insincere and ineffectual ways: before he can attain to that steadfast peace in God, which shall eventually leave him profoundly disinterested, indifferent, and actively inert in his own behalf.

And now, my friend, I wish you to take most particular notice: that this provisional, or ancillary and pedagogic sphere of human life — in which man is thus left to make his own acquaintance, and to become for a while apparently his own exclusive guardian and providence, with a view to his ultimate and intimate spiritual disenchantment with himself — is *the world of our actual historic consciousness, the world of our daily experience which subjects us to a fixed existence in space and time.* It may astonish you to find any definite philosophic rationale assigned to this crazy world of ours, as much as it did M. Jourdain in the play to learn that he had been talking prose all his life without knowing it; but that this and nothing else is its proper function, there can be no doubt. This most outward and lowest of all worlds, in which space and time have a fixed and not a fluid character as they have in the spiritual world, is necessary to the development and training of our finite consciousness; and it is the gradual enlargement of this consciousness of ours out of the contemptible personal limitations in which it begins, into the largest social dimensions in which it ends, that constitutes the sole veritable stuff of human history. When that history has attained its apogee, accordingly, and not before, we may expect to begin the realization of our spiritual creation. But the reason of my asking you to take particular notice of the fact here stated, was that I might by means of your so doing the better impress upon you another truth, which is : *that what we call human history is at bottom nothing else than a theatre of* DIVINE REVELATION; the precise historic form which the revelation takes being a display of the Divine dealings in relation to human nature. The initial acts of the drama reveal God in a state of apparently complete prostration to the created nature, so passively subject to it, as to be blasphemed, humiliated, and done to death in the daily chaos of its selfish and malignant passions : so that the Divine name sinks at last into a mere formula of execration among men, while its inherent merciful quality is almost wholly forgotten. But the later scenes of the astounding drama, and its final *dénoument*, show Him spontaneously rising again from the death and hell to which He has thus been consigned in the persons of the created nature, and exalting the nature itself — henceforth discharged of personal limitations, or made forever social and unitary — into the intimate fellowship of His own eternal being.

The truth to which I here call your attention is of the gravest rational import. The professing Christian church is too baldly avaricious in a material sense, and is moreover too instinct spiritually with rival personal ambitions, and rival sectarian emulations, to give any heed to it, or to any other broadly human question. And the thin scum of so-called liberal or radical religionists which it is continually throwing off, seem even more superficial than the church itself in their intellectual tendencies, for they apparently crave no deeper satisfaction to their peculiar religious perplexities than science deigns to minister. Above all, men of science — such of them especially as make their science into a vehicle and instrument of philosophizing — are apt quietly to ignore the truth of a spiritual creation. So I forewarn you that you will not find yourself in a crowded company, if you consent to cultivate the truth. Perhaps, however, for the first time in your life, you will feel yourself able *en révanche* to breathe to the full compass of your freed intellectual lungs. But I beg of you, if you have any dealing with this truth of the rigidly apocalyptic character of the world in which we live, to deal with it in the most literal unsentimental manner. I mean exactly what I say. The whole use of the actual world is to mirror or reflect Divine realities to us, as much so as the whole use of your looking-glass is to mirror or reflect your physical person to your own eye. And it mirrors or reflects these realities to us in connection strictly with our own nature in contradistinction from our proper persons, which are only and at best a factitious and perishable sem-

blance or phenomenon of the nature. So that the
total spiritual or philosophic meaning of this revelation is to declare God a MAN in the completest sense
of the word : not merely a spiritual or internal man,
infinite in love and wisdom, but much more a natural
man, experienced in all our appetites and passions,
and able therefore to subjugate every densest hell of
personality in our nature to the broadest human use.
The machinery, spiritual and material, by which this
great revelation becomes possible and effectual, is explained with great industry and iteration by Swedenborg, in all his books more or less. But I confess
I have been content to abide in the full spiritual light
of the revelation itself, without taking an undue or
pedantic interest in the comparatively dull and tedious
recital he gives of the methods of its evolution.

Cease then to conceive of our physical and moral
existence as directly implicated either in our spiritual
Divine creation or our natural Divine redemption.
They are only indirectly implicated therein as furnishing us that secular and outside knowledge of the Divine ways which is necessary to base or induct our
inward or spiritual recognition and appreciation of
both one and the other. Our spiritual creation and
our natural redemption are, both alike, a purely Divine and miraculous work, transacted within the unconscious depths of our nature; so that neither our

physical existence nor our moral history reflects the least original light upon them, their only active function being servilely to symbolize them to our intelligence. How absurd then to expect any new light from the physical sciences, now so much cultivated, upon the questions of human origin and human destiny! Neither the physical nor the moral world constitutes the true sphere of our life or being, but only of our factitious seeming or appearance; and the more satisfied we are with the knowledge they impart to us, the more hopelessly remote are we from spiritual insight or perception. This phenomenal world in which we live is the world not of Divine reality, but of Divine revelation; and he whose knowledge of it is greatest vindicates his superiority to his brethren only in boasting a larger familiarity with shadows. I am surprised that a person of your intellectual pith should be so easily duped by the airs of our scientific scepticism. Do you think it fair to deny the Divine being and existence, because science can discover no trace of them throughout the wide realm of physics? If so, it can only be because you are speculatively blind to any higher realm of being than that of physics. At all events your need to believe in God is vastly less sensitive than mine. For my part I should unfeignedly thank science for its negative discovery, simply because it brought the Divine existence nearer to my own nature, or approximately humanized Him. I confess I should have an involuntary or inveterate shrinking from science, if it found any direct attestation of God in mineral, vegetable, or animal existence, much more any unmistakable traces of His habitat in the mechanism of the celestial spaces. For I should find it hard to persuade myself that a being who had any direct sympathy with either of those low and servile fields of existence could be possessed of any intimate human quality.

All this will remind you of the intellectual value I attribute to miracle in the evolution of our race-history. For in the absence of it, there would have been nothing to suggest or authenticate to the universal heart and mind of the race the infinite and adorable name of God, nor consequently any power to resist the incessant scientific debasement of our individual intelligence to mere nature-worship at most. For miracle is only a brute affirmation or attestation of the creative infinitude to men's brute or undeveloped spiritual intelligence, and has been full therefore of the tenderest and most timely Divine pity. That we happen to have outgrown its need at this day, and can intellectually dispense with it, has been owing to no diminution of the creative benignity, but rather to a practical enlargement of its scope, in widening the sphere of man's freedom and rationality to such an extent, as effectually to deliver him henceforth from the dominion of great names, or of routine and authority, in scientific as well as in spiritual or sacred things, and thus make him over at long last to the inspiration of the unimpeded Divine GOOD in the form of our own glorified flesh and bones. We may say in fact that without miracles as a perpetual reminder of a supersensuous life in us, the intellect must have lost its highest Divine charm which is that of freedom, or inward inspiration, and have incontinently succumbed to the limitations of science which forever enchain it to sense. Every intellect the least spiritualized is now free to assert its just insubordination to the senses, or claim to be wholly uninspired by science. And I maintain that it owes this freedom solely to the long respect entertained among men for miracle as a distinctively Divine mode of action. For without miracle to serve as a symbol of the otherwise unrecognized creative infinitude to us until such time as the intellect itself should revolt from the worthless symbol in the interest of its own living Divine substance, men would never have dreamt of ascribing a present reality to creation, but have been content to regard it as a past, or outward historic fact merely, intrinsically incapable therefore of arousing any deeper intellectual homage in us than that of our servile and dead memory.

LETTER XV.

MY DEAR FRIEND:—We have dwelt long enough on general principles: it is time we begin to make some particular application of them.

We have seen in recent letters that human nature is not the least physical, but on the contrary strictly metaphysical, involving physics simply as its organic or material base, in order to fix it, or give it anchorage. And you, yourself, doubtless, will be as prompt as I am to infer hereupon, that we men—in whom this organic or finite base of existence almost completely controls its distinctly natural and infinite possibilities—have small claim to be considered in our own right apt specimens of human nature. Thus far, in fact, I think we may be said to furnish only good negative specimens of it; that is, to furnish much better evidence of what the nature is not, than of what it is. We constitute hardly anything more as yet than the underground phenomenal basement

floor of the majestic human house God is uprearing
in our nature — a basement floor dug deep in mineral, vegetable, and animal substance — and he would
sadly err, accordingly, who should look upon us as
the celestial superstructure itself.   And being but
this material base of our nature, we have no more
pretension of course to constitute its living or spiritual personality, than the metals which enter into the
material structure of a watch have to constitute the
functional power so named.   I have already shown
you, indeed, that human nature — being bipolar,
having two factors, one creative or infinite, the other
created or finite — involves a hopeless contradiction,
an inextricable puzzle, for every one born subject to
it, and can only be integrally constituted therefore
in a perfectly unitary personality, or one which shall
do exact and equal justice to both of its extreme
factors.   In short, human nature is normally constituted only in the person of GOD-MAN.

Thus if Jesus Christ had never actually lived, the
necessities of our thought would have driven us to
invent him.   At the same time I don't wonder that
so many people at this day, who seem to me more
or less tinctured with his spirit, are grievously perplexed to connect that spirit with the aims lent by
professing Christians to the Christian name.   The
Christian spirit, as represented by those who make

a formal or visible profession of it, is at most and altogether a *personal* spirit. It may have incidentally, to be sure, more or less benignant issues to human life associated with it, but these issues are purely incidental : the main or direct tendency of this pseudo-Christian spirit is to deepen the sense of personality in men, and modify it in the way of rendering it more and more consonant with the Divine will. The theory of the church seems to be that God's purpose in creation is : *not*, all simply, to form a heaven out of the human race, and make history infallibly conduce to that supreme end in becoming ever more and more a grand school of discipline for humanity, in which men, taught by a profound experience of the evils of self-love and love of the world, may at last become *naturally* or spontaneously roused to react against these evils, and freely incline instead to the promotion and culture of a race-sentiment in humanity, which has no practical admixture of evil and falsity in it to betray and defeat their devotion : but to form *both a heaven and a hell out of the human race*, leaving it strictly optional with every individual to determine himself to either of these opposite poles, but allowing him no chance, when once his choice is made, of ever after correcting it. The revolting hideousness of ascribing such a purpose to the merciful Creator of helpless, dependent men,

you are as quick to discern as I am, and I need
not dwell upon it.   But I want you clearly to understand that these diabolic audacities and blasphemies
which men theoretically allow themselves with reference to the Divine name, *essentially inhere in our insane habit of regarding human life as* PERSONALLY
and not as SOCIALLY *constituted*, and attest the necessarily perverse interpretation which that insane habit
leads us to impose upon every form of Divine truth.

   Dear friend, if men could but once livingly swing
free of these *personal* implications in their thoughts
and aspirations towards God : that is to say, if they
could, even for a moment, spiritually feel themselves
as no longer visible or cognizable to God in their
atomic individualities, but only as so many social
units, *each* embracing and enveloping *all* in affection and thought : the work would be forever done,
as it seems to me.   Heaven would be begun on
earth, and the very nature of man reflect or reproduce at last the lineaments of Divine good.   But
what hope of this is there within the precincts of
the Church at all events, where men are expressly
taught that the only imaginable theory of Christ's
office is to save men in their individual persons,
or their piddling private capacities, and not at all
as a nature or race ; and consequently that *their*
only chance of salvation at his hands lies in their

diligently and impudently ' "*appropriating*" him, every one to his worthless and insignificant little self. As if Christ could be in any sense a *personal* possession of men, to be made theirs by some cheap and odious methodistic mouthing of his name, and afterwards to be paraded as an ornament on their sleeve to dazzle the eyes of harmless worldlings who still have modesty and grace enough left thoroughly to *dis*own him! If these thoughtless Christian sectaries of ours could once be led to suspect that "our Lord," as they vulgarly call him, is the veritable and only great God almighty himself in men's natural lineaments — the spiritual father therefore of all mankind, especially of those who in their own conceit are hopelessly remote from Him, I wonder whether the discovery would arouse them at last to a sense of spiritual awe and reverence, or whether all spiritual possibilities are not effectively drowned out for them under this rubbish of ritual righteousness with which they affect to be clad. The inmost life and sanity of my own faith in God depend upon my feeling myself incapable of any personal or outside relation to Him, because the bare thought of such a relation as possible between us is the menace of death to my soul. And this is the reason why I cling with even a passionate intellectual gratitude to the revelation of the Divine name

in Jesus Christ, because he alone in history shows
me the Divine infinitude or perfection actually blent
or identified, in his dying and risen person, with
human nature — my own nature as man — and so
forever disenthralls me to my own consciousness
from the pungent damnation wrapped up in my own
odious and imbecile selfhood.

Swedenborg's books throw a flood of light upon
the method of this ineffable Divine achievement in
our history, and you are so blessedly free of ecclesiastical biases that I see no reason why you should
not read them with a profit and pleasure equal to my
own. There may be some reason, unknown to me,
blinding you to the honest intellectual charm of the
books; perhaps, like many others, you have been
prejudiced against them by the obvious fact that they
have been hitherto engineered, not in the interest
of mankind, but exclusively in that of a low sectarian
ambition, or lust of ecclesiastical self-righteousness.
But surely after the many lessons the Christian ecclesiasticisms have taught us, of the inevitable deprava-
tion Christ's spirit is bound to undergo whenever the
attempt is made to reproduce it in corporate form,
you would not hold the upright old Swedenborg himself answerable for this helpless betrayal of *his* truth
on the part of his professed followers, would you?
If any obvious prejudice of this sort really threaten

to cut you off from the immense benefit Swedenborg's
books bring to the intellect, let me briefly assure you
that they themselves are infinitely remote from suggesting to an unperverted mind any of these shallow
— and, as we may say at this day, profligate — ecclesiastical conceptions.   Swedenborg indeed of good
set purpose finds very much to say of the church
both "old" and "new," and he says it all without
a shadow of reticence or apology, as if he never
doubted that every one who came to his books would
be thoroughly vastated of sectarian aspirations, and
incapable therefore of supposing him such an ass as
to represent God almighty solicitous only to establish
under the name of "new" church a more baldly
vicious and contemptible ecclesiasticism than any
that had ever yet cursed the burdened and patient
earth.   What then *is* his general doctrine of the
constitution of the church, as shadowed forth in
sacred or symbolic history?

This doctrine cannot be at all understood, unless
we previously take into consideration the state of
things in which it is grounded, namely : that *the
world in which the church exists,* and for whose benefit it is a spiritual provision, *is essentially a sphere
of Divine revelation :* while at the same time it is
profoundly ignored by the world, or those who in-
habit it, that it is charged with any such universal

function. The world has indeed no faintest suspicion of the truth, that it exists for nothing else but to constitute an orderly revelation of God's spiritual infinitude or perfection; but stupidly settles down to the far more flattering conviction, that it constitutes on the contrary a most real and permanent Divine work, a work of true and finished creation, and this in spite of its being destitute of every spiritual Divine mark. Now the church was intended to be a standing witness or memorial of God amidst this prevalent ignorance of men concerning Him. It is a candle irradiating by its feeble but honest glimmer the otherwise unmixed and hopeless darkness. Swedenborg accordingly views the church throughout its entire history *in the light of a Divine drama, prefiguring to the reflective understanding of men* — who are inwardly callous to the most tender and spiritual Divine substance latent in their own coarse souls and bodies, and outwardly therefore unobservant of it — *in certain symbolic or representative persons and peoples, the entire and signally miraculous truth upon the subject of man's Divine nature and destiny.* About the prehistoric beginnings of the church indeed he is naturally able to give us very little information, since the greatest amount of such information could only conduce to the satisfaction of a purely idle curiosity. But he shows that it grew out of a very

tender and infantile spiritual intelligence in man,
scarce weaned as yet from Nature's maternal bosom;
and that this intelligence accordingly was wholly
made up of a perception of the interior correspondence that obtains between spirit and nature, that is,
between celestial goods and their derivative terrestrial
truths. That the peculiar quality of this intelligence,
however, was very exalted, being inspired by the
heart, appears from all he specifically says of it,
and especially from a brief but pregnant incidental
glimpse he gives of its broadly human genius and
sympathies, in a remark he makes about the church
called Adam, with which our sacred or symbolic
scripture opens, and of which he saw the spiritual
or heavenly state. He says : "Those who belonged
to the most ancient church, designated by the name
of Man or Adam, are above the head in the Maxi-
mus Homo, and dwell together in the utmost happiness. They told me that it is seldom others come
to them, except *such occasionally as come, not from
this earth but*, as they phrased it, *from the universe*." *
The men of this church in fact "were internal men,
delighted only with internal things," which are the
things of Love and Wisdom, "and viewing external
things only with their eyes, while they reflected upon
the spiritual goods and truths they represented. Thus

---

* *Arcana Cælestia*, 1115.

external things were held of no intellectual account by them, save as leading them to reflect on internal things, and these in their turn to reflect on celestial things, and these again on the Lord, who to them was all in all." *

It is very difficult, I admit, to do any justice with our inspissated spiritual faculty to Swedenborg's descriptions of this early or internal development of the church in man. They suggest to our coarser intellectual fibre a very much feebler grasp upon life than our own, and it even disconcerts us to imagine the truth otherwise. To the cultivated or regenerate heart, however, this intellectual judgment of ours, no doubt, seems very profane or sensuous; very much as, to the common heart, a judgment which should affirm the superior sweetness of the adult man to the infant child would appear little short of sacrilegious. Anyhow the state of things here described was very incongruous with the Divine designs in humanity, for man then, as Swedenborg says, was more like a *spirit* than a man, and the Divine design could be fulfilled only by making him *flesh*. "For in this way only could celestial and spiritual life be adjoined to *man's proper nature*, that they might be as one." †

Swedenborg accordingly proceeds to represent the

* *Arcana Cælestia*, 54.

† *Ibid.* 160.

descendants of the church, thus styled Adam or Man,
as inclining to selfhood: that is, desiring to become
instead of an internal man an external one. But
he does not fail to characterize this change of genius
in it, though relatively unfortunate of course, since
everything deteriorates in proportion as it becomes
remote from its source, yet as by no means absolutely
so; inasmuch as selfhood, though regarded in itself
or absolutely it is unmixed evil, is yet the indispensable condition of man's natural development, or
race-evolution, and consequently of that redemptive
achievement in our nature which constitutes God's
true or eternal spiritual glory in creation. This
rising inclination to selfhood is the inevitable dawn
of the natural or race-mind in us, and as such of
course is noway evil, though *viewed apart from that
subordination* it is the fountain of all the evil known
to the universe. We don't get angry with the infant,
although we feel bound in the interests of his own
maturity to correct him, when we see him instinctively exhibiting the traits of his future natural manhood; on the contrary we are secretly diverted by
his arch and graceful ways of self-assertion, because
as yet they are full of innocence or innocuous. Exactly so we may say there is no ground for moral
disapprobation in these nascent or unconscious egotistic inclinations on the part of the early church,

because to the wiser mind they simply foretell the advent in the fulness of time of the Divine natural humanity, and are themselves meanwhile full of infantile ignorance and innocence.

Indeed Swedenborg always draws a wide distinction between the *natural* love of self and the world, and an absolute or unnatural love of them, that is, a love of them for their own sakes; calling the former a wise love, and the latter a stupid or insane one. He says for example in his profoundly clear and beautiful Essay upon the Divine Love and Wisdom, of which Lippincott published an extremely good translation by Mr. Foster eight or ten years ago, and which, if you are interested in what I say, I recommend you to get: "The loves of self and of the world are *by creation heavenly loves*, because they are loves of the *natural man subservient to spiritual loves*, in the same way that foundations are subservient to houses. These natural loves guarantee a man's wishing well to his own body, desiring food, raiment, and shelter, consulting the welfare of his family, seeking after useful occupation, and even after honors proportionate to the worth of the public trusts he fulfils, and the extent of the fulfilment he renders them; and guarantee moreover his enjoying worldly pleasures, and finding delight and refreshment in them: but now mind! our natural loves guarantee all these things, not at all for any absolute or unconditional worth to be found in them, for there is no such worth, but for a certain end of use which they promote in rendering a man fit to serve the Lord and serve the neighbor. But where this use is not promoted, as in the case of a man who has no relish for serving the Lord or his neighbor, but only for serving himself by means of the world, then his natural self-love ceases to be heavenly and becomes infernal, because it cuts the man off from delighting in his nature or kind, and shuts him up, spiritually, to his own selfhood, which is wholly evil." *

Swedenborg goes on to give his readers a detailed mention of the specific churches that succeeded to this Adamic one, with the several characteristics that made each of them noticeably distinct from its predecessors. These details are excessively tedious and uninteresting at this day, though to future inquirers into our distinctively race - genesis they may prove perhaps exhilarating; and I have not the least intention of dwelling upon them. They were churches still in the gristle, unclad as yet with natural flesh and bone, and devoid therefore of proper historic interest, so far at least as indicating any constructive providential purpose in human nature; being based every one of them upon some mere diver-

---

* *Divine Love and Wisdom.* See also *Ath. Creed*, 43.

gent relation in the personal genius of its founders
with respect to every other that preceded it, and destined like them to be engulfed in some more general
form which should round them all off into visible
unity. I suppose it is all very exact church-physi-
ology, but I confess I feel little or no interest in the
very unhandsome pre-natal physiological development
of the church, while it was still an immature and unborn providential embryo in the earth, peopling it too
with every uncouth, unclean, and monstrous form of
life below the human. And even after it has attained
to fully formed consciousness of itself as man, and
separates itself from whatsoever is not-man, it awak-
ens no philosophic interest save as it tends, by unconscious copulation with the world, to generate what
men subsequently recognize as *human nature*. Accordingly I shall only attempt to give you a con-
densed philosophic *aperçu* of the ever-growing corruption of the early churches, until that corruption finally
culminated, or became a momentous historic phenomenon, in the gross fanatical lineaments of the Jewish
theocracy : certainly from a spiritual point of view the
most complete and comprehensive embodiment of ungodliness ever Divinely consecrated in human annals.
But the only result of this philosophic glimpse will
be, I hope, to suggest afresh to your mind what an
adorable wonder-worker we have in Him who thus

utilizes, or turns to the advantage of human nature, the inmost and most implacable evil of its individual bosoms, making it indeed the fertile womb of infinite and otherwise inconceivable Divine and human good.

LETTER XVI.

MY DEAR FRIEND : — To say as Swedenborg says : *that this early church called Adam or man inclined to selfhood, or from internal tended to become external :* is manifestly equivalent to saying that it lost sight of the only reason it had for existing, namely : *the service it might do the world in keeping it mindful of God :* and began to value itself on its own account, as if it had existed *ab origine* for its own sake, and were itself an absolute Divine good in the earth.

The original bias to evil in the human heart, or what separates it from God, is constituted by self-love and love of the world. But these loves are not in themselves evil, but innocent and heavenly, because they are purely instinctive or organic loves in man serviceable to spiritual loves, just as foundations are serviceable to houses. "For from these loves," say Swedenborg, "man wishes well to his body, desires to be fed, clad, lodged, to consult

the comfort of his family, to seek after useful em-
ployment, yes, to be honored for the worth of the
services he thus renders to society, and also to be
delighted and recreated by the pleasures of the
world : but all these for a certain spiritual end,
which ought to be use, for by these loves thus exercised and refreshed he is fitted to serve the Lord
and the neighbor.   But when these loves refuse to
become subservient to more universal loves, as Divine and neighborly love, they then become infernal, because they then immerse a man's mind and
soul in *selfhood*, WHICH IN ITSELF IS ALL EVIL."*
In course of time then these wholesome impersonal loves are sure to lose their innocence or become personal by being made to minister to *selfhood* in man, or promote the interests of his fallacious individuality as against those of his common
nature.   In other words all men in time become
selfish and worldly, that is, *unduly* addicted to the
love of themselves and the love of the world.   This
natural degeneracy of mankind is not fatal by any
means, but it calls aloud for God's redemptive
power in human nature to save the race from premature blight.   Neither selfishness nor worldliness
will ever be considered obsolete forms of human
nature, but they will always be considered more

---

* *Arcana Cælestia*, 396.   See also *Ath. Creed*, 43.

and more disreputable or unworthy forms of it.
They will always drive men of spiritual culture to
desire to realize their nature in social or Divinely-
redeemed form, but they will never have power
actually to deprive any one of hope towards God.
As long indeed as animals and vegetables continue
to exist man will scarcely be robbed of his God-
ward faith and hope by any amount of selfishness
or worldliness, for the animal is a very innocent
and unconscious type of the former love, and the
vegetable of the latter. Until God sends an utter
blight upon the life of the animal and vegetable
kingdoms therefore we shall feel no misgivings
about His intimate dealings with our own nature.
What is worldliness at bottom? We all know well
enough what it is in a literal or moral aspect — as
separating between man and man; for we all love
the world too much, and sometimes sacrifice our
neighbor's esteem, and our own peace of mind, to
its tempting pleasures, honors, or emoluments. But
what does worldliness mean in a spiritual rather
than a moral aspect, that is, as separating no longer
between man and man, but between man and God?
It means to esteem and love the world as a finality, to be satisfied with it as a fulfilment of our
hopes and aspirations towards God: thus it means
at bottom to ignore God, to ignore His spiritual

perfection, or His essential infinity and eternity, and acknowledge Him at the most as a physical and moral power, the creator and maker of this realm of finite personal existence. When the worldling acknowledges God at all, this is the extreme limit of the homage he renders Him: he considers Him as the author of the very pleasant life that now is, the giver of every good and perfect gift to his senses. To be sure there is nothing very exhilarating to the Divine mind in this degree of homage, provided it is anyway sincere, which is extremely problematical at least: but just as surely there can be nothing revolting in it, nor even displeasing, to that mind: so that if the creator had but destined His creature to remain an innocent animal merely, without any capacity of spiritual life or enjoyment, He would, I dare say, have been highly satisfied with it.

Selfishness to be sure is a much more potent, stubborn, and profound evil than worldliness, and far more hostile practically to human society or fellowship; and Swedenborg in order to show the superior malignity of the former love to the latter as an element of human life, characterizes the hells which grow out of it as *diabolic*, whereas he always gives the hells of worldliness the milder designation of *Satanic*. But selfishness, although a less super-

ficial evil than worldliness, accommodates itself in
some sort equally well to the Divine administration
in human affairs : as is shown by what Swedenborg says of the hells to which it is ministerial.
The devil and Satan would be very discreditable
products of the creative love, provided they owed
their original existence to it.   But they do not in
the slightest degree.   Satan and the devil (by
which terms respectively of course one would be
understood to mean not any individual existences
but the whole mass of human kind in whom either
the love of the world or the love of self characteristically predominates) owe their origin to a vital
misconception they are both alike under in regard
to human freedom, deeming it absolute instead of
moral, contingent, relative.   This misconception on
their part is very unfortunate no doubt, because, as
it leads to all manner of practical injustice and untruth, it requires them to be separated from the
orderly mass of their brethren, and shut up for a
long while in work-houses where they are compelled under pain of forfeiting their daily bread,
and of even worse punishments, to work, and refrain from bad manners.   But they are never *in the
slightest degree* objects of God's contempt, let alone
abhorrence, but equally with heavenly existences attract His unswerving mercy or compassion.

And thus you are prepared for what I have next got to say. It is a very intelligible proposition in itself, but it may perhaps encounter some prejudice in your understanding. The proposition is this: that while we owe our milder or moral evils, those, namely, which separate us outwardly from our fellow-man, to the inspiration of the world-spirit, the spirit which reigns in every man by virtue of his natural birth, the inspiring cause of our deeper spiritual evils, those which separate us inwardly from God, our life-source, and call for our natural redemption at His hands, is exclusively the church-spirit in humanity, the spirit that leads every man that has it to think himself nearer to God than other men.

This proposition, I repeat, may meet with a slow reception at your hands. Let me then above all things make sure that you perfectly understand what I mean by it.

What I call the deeper spiritual evils which attach to men, separating them from their creative source, are those of confirmed selfhood or self-righteousness. Do I mean you to understand me, then, as saying that the church-spirit in humanity is the source of all our spiritual unrighteousness? This is literally what I mean to say, and what I would be understood as saying: that the church-spirit is *par excellence* the evil-spirit in humanity, source of all its profounder and irremediable woes. Don't, I beg of you, interpret me to your own thought as saying that the church stimulates any of man's actual or moral evils. I say no such stupid thing. For it is notorious that the church studiously fosters the sentiment of moral worth or dignity in its disciples, the sentiment of distinction or difference between them and other men. It is only by so doing indeed that she *fixes* or hardens them in that tendency to *proprium* or selfhood to which they are naturally inclined, and thus delivers them over bound hand and foot to spiritual pride, pride of character, in short a *self*-righteous spirit, which is the only form of evil, the only form of sin or blasphemy, fundamentally at variance with man's spiritual existence. But this latter evil is undeniably a church development in our nature. The church is the actual parent or protagonist of all the spiritual evil latent or possible in human nature — evil of selfhood or self-righteousness ; and by focusing it in her own haughty personality gives God at length his opportunity — in allowing the church to become the mere mendicant and impotent existence it now is in the earth — to crush out in every spiritual highplace, or most recondite corner of human nature itself, the otherwise inaccessible and flagitious evil which it represents. God has no power to combat spiritual evil, save as it ultimates itself in natural or outward form. And the church pretension in humanity is the ultimate natural or outward form of all man's spiritual profligacy. For human nature has no existence *in se*, and comes to light only through men's consciousness: not their individual or private consciousness, but their associated or public one: and the church and the world are as yet the only recognized forms of this latter consciousness.

I mean then that the church-spirit in humanity is the expression of all man's patent or latent *spiritual* evil, and reduces his mere moral evil to comparative insignificance, for the latter is curable, and the former not. However selfish or worldly a man may be, these are good honest natural evils, and you have only to apply a motive sufficiently stimulating in either case and you will induce the subject to forbear them. But spiritual evil is inward evil exclusively, pertaining to the selfhood of the man, or livingly appropriated by him as his own, and cannot therefore become known to him save in the form of an outward natural representation; for it is not like moral evil mere oppugnancy to good, but it is the actual and deadly profanation of good, or the lavish acknowledgment of it with a view of subordinating it to personal, or selfish and worldly, ends. It is the only truly formidable evil known to God's providence, being that of *self*-righteousness, and hence the only evil which essentially threatens to undermine the foundations of God's throne. It is that evil of unconscious hypocrisy or making believe which alone Christ is represented in the New Testament as having spiritually stigmatized to men's eternal abhorrence, and which Swedenborg says he was able to overcome only by subjugating the influence of all the heavens and all the hells to his own spotless love of mankind, so utterly elim-inating from our nature or history in its Godward relations the vicious and thoroughly damnable ele-ment of privacy or *proprium* — that is, of private or personal pretension among men, of individual char-acter, or finite independent selfhood.

This all seems plain enough, but now you will ask me : How the church comes to be representa-tively identified with this capital evil of selfhood or self-righteousness in man.

I will answer your question in as few words as possible, though I am not without a fear that they will not be so few as I could wish. But I will at all events do my best, in the limited space that the plan of these letters allows me, to make the point clear. God knows that I have not the least idea of making my answer acceptable to you, except through your own goodness of heart, or love of mankind. What I want to do then is to convince you that the church is alone chargeable with the production of actual *proprium*, character, differential selfhood, among men; and that in so doing it has representatively brought to a head the fundamental evil of the created nature, that which spiritually vivifies all its other evils moral and physical: so that absolutely nothing remains between us and the full fruition of God's spiritual kingdom on earth, but the hearty recognition of the visible church as once a living but now an entirely fossil representative element of human nature.

To begin then: Suppose for a moment that selfishness and worldliness were our only vices. Suppose that man and the world alone existed to men's senses and intelligence, just as they do to the senses and intelligence of the animals; and that the influence of these things was entirely uncomplicated by any influence derived from the church as an institution. It is easy enough to see that selfishness and worldliness in this hypothetical state of things would be no vices at all, but simple instincts of men's natural life leading them to the fullest possible enjoyment of the goods about them, and begetting in them meanwhile of course the utmost possible indifference to God and their neighbor:

but there stopping. For these things are vices only
as they tend to selfhood, or lead us into practical
conflict with our spiritual destiny; only as they tend
to interest us supremely in a lower order of life
than that which our nature fits us to enjoy: and
palpably in the case supposed these spiritual limitations would be wholly lacking. It is to the church
primarily that the world is indebted for its every
gleam of spiritual knowledge; and without the
church therefore the world would never have learned
to condemn either selfishness or worldliness. A man
here and there by obeying a greedy or covetous
spirit might paralyze the life of his senses, or bring
practical ruin upon his organization; but however
unfortunate his particular excesses might prove him,
he never by any possibility could deem them either
sinful, as reflecting a certain inward or spiritual turpitude on himself, or even *evil,* as reflecting a certain outward or moral opprobrium upon his conduct.
So far indeed from anything of this sort being possible to the man, we have only got to invest him
with a capacity of reflection in order to see that
he would necessarily under the circumstances deem
his selfishness and worldliness, or his lust and covetousness, his highest law or duty.

But in point of fact a man of that simple spirit-
less make could have no capacity of reflection, and

consequently no conscience of law or duty. Conscience presupposes in all its subjects a personal development, or sense of selfhood, as its necessary ground; and personality in every case is a resultant of two forces, a conventionally good and evil one, belonging to the unconscious nature of the subject, and yet so exquisitely adjusted to each other, or so evenly balanced, as to make him feel without the least misgiving that he is absolutely a free and rational individuality, the essential arbiter of his own actions. In short the existence of conscience in men presupposes the existence of the church and the world as extreme representative factors of human nature, while the perfect equilibrium or mutual adjustment of these factors in their practical operation upon the subject argues a really Divine or infinite purpose and providence in humanity. You see then that it would be the height of absurdity to attribute to a man whose very nature is representatively expressed by the church and the world anything short of a highly composite genesis.

It is thus exclusively the alliance of the church and the world in our nature that stamps it human, and so gives men their original consciousness of evil being, in being either selfish or worldly. And it is specifically the influence of the church in our nature that brings about this result. It is a grand providential work for the church to do, for it would never have got into the mind of man that to live for self and the world was not the highest ideal of human life, the supreme law of human destiny, unless the church had put it there. And since human history is only a conflict between the claims of our private selfhood and the claims of our Divine-natural manhood upon our allegiance, we may say that the church in stigmatizing selfishness and worldliness to men's opinion, laid the foundation stone of human history.

But now do you not see at a glance that the practical effect of the church's initiative in this matter could only be to originate a broad division of men into two classes : one *good*, as painfully abstaining from selfish and worldly lusts, the other *evil*, as freely indulging them ? The church, so far forth as it is a *visible* institution in the earth, and claims a Divine warrant corporately to exist and function, looks upon all men without exception as naturally bound to the pursuit of happiness. For bare existence is a happiness to man, stimulating as it does every variety of passional desire and activity in his bosom, and by a necessary instinct he seeks to promote, enlarge, and intensify this happiness. Now the church authoritatively bids the man pause in this enticing career, saying to him that happiness is *not* the supreme law of his activity, at all events is not its first law ; that he is first of all a creature of God, gifted with freedom and intelligence, and bound therefore to acquaint himself with his creator's will, in order to see that his private pursuit of happiness involve him in no practical contrariety with that will. The man either listens, or does not listen. If he listens, he forthwith enrolls himself in the church ranks, and separates himself from a world conventionally supposed to be lying in wickedness. If he does not listen to the church's testimony, but rejects it as against himself, he identifies himself with the profane world, and cuts himself off from the church's blessing.

Hence, as I say, the inevitable division of mankind into two classes, a good and an evil class, or a sacred and a profane class, the one professing to observe the Divine will, or what is reputed to be such in all things, the other following its own will supremely, without making any profession one way or the other. Now however necessary and providential a work this may have been on the part of the church to effect, let me remark first of all that it was an exceedingly rude work at the very least; a very unskilful carrying out of the Divine design. Undoubtedly the Divine design in giving the church a visible institution was to establish a witness of

Himself in the earth of men's carnal memory, which might always serve to base and authenticate their interior or spiritual apprehensions of Him as a power actively latent in human nature and human affairs. But it was, to say the very least, an exceedingly rude and crude memorial of the Divine name, to identify it not with the spiritual revelation exclusively of that name or quality, but with the literal and objective discrimination of certain perfectly petty and squalid persons into a celestial and infernal class, the one full of righteous or just hope in God's favor, the other consigned to righteous despair.

I say " at the very least." But the work which this early church thus did in the earth was very much worse than coarse and unskilful. It spiritually falsified the sacred name it was intended to keep the world in remembrance of; and it has assiduously perpetuated the falsification — through its long and dreary *sequela* of lineally descended churches — even down to the present day. For the distinction of men into good and evil, however fundamental a datum it be to our natural intelligence, does not really or spiritually exist to the Divine mind save in accommodation to the needs of that most nascent and infirm intelligence. That is to say: it is no absolute distinction, as the church holds, characterizing men spiritually or as they exist in themselves, but only as they stand differentially related by their phenomenal action to a great objective work of righteousness to be accomplished by God in the fulness of time in human nature itself: by which all men, notwithstanding their relative or subjective differences in regard to it, will be brought into complete formal or objective harmony with the Divine will.

—But as I dimly foresaw, my friend, I shall be obliged to interrupt my writing here that I may try to impress you anew with the extreme intellectual importance of rightly conceiving the work I am endeavoring to elucidate in this place: *a work of spiritual creation, purporting to be wrought by God within the precincts,* by no means of men's phenomenal personality, *but of their common substance or nature.* This is our one theme, and we must perpetually bear it in mind under all our discussion of incidental topics. I have undoubtedly been remiss in not sufficiently enforcing this necessity upon you. And I am persuaded that I cannot do better now, awkward and tardy proceeding though it be, than to interpose an intercalary letter or two just here, defining what I mean by spiritual creation much more fully than I have hitherto done: leaving the interrupted thread of my discourse in regard to church history to be resumed afterwards.

LETTER XVII.

MY DEAR FRIEND:—A spiritual or living creation, which consists in giving its creature life or being, must of necessity on the part of the creator confess itself a purely subjective or miraculous one, attesting at most His indwelling infinitude in the created nature. "From the uncreate, infinite Being itself and Life itself," says Swedenborg, "no being can be immediately created, because the Divine is one and indivisible. *But from created and finite substances, so formed that the Divine may be in them,* beings may be created. Since men and angels are such beings, they are only recipients of life; wherefore if any suffers himself to be so far misled as to think that he is not a recipient of life but life itself, nothing can hinder him thinking himself a God."* Again: "Divine Love cannot create any one immediately from itself, for in that case the creature would be love in

---

* *Divine Love and Wisdom*, 4.

its essence, or the Lord himself; but it can create beings from substances so formed as to be capable of receiving its love and wisdom. Comparatively as the mundane sun is unable by all its heat and light to make the earth germinate, when nevertheless it can produce germination from earthy substances," such as seeds, " in which it may be present by its heat and light, causing vegetation." * So he says elsewhere, to the same effect : " Life viewed in itself, which is God, cannot create another being that shall be life itself : for the life which is God is uncreate, continuous, and indivisible; hence it is that God is one. But the life which is God can create, out of substances which are not life, *forms in which it can exist, giving these forms to seem as if they themselves lived.* Now men are such forms, which as being only receptacles of life, could not in the first creation, or originally, be anything but images and likenesses of God : for life and its recipients adapt themselves each to the other like active and passive, but in no wise mix together. Hence human forms, being but recipient forms of life, do not live from themselves but from God who alone is life." † " It seems to man as if he lived from himself, but this is a fallacy. The reason why it seems as if life were in man is, that it enters by influx from the Lord into his *inmost forms,*

---

* *Divine Love and Wisdom,* 5.   † *Ath. Creed,* 25.

which are remote from the sight of his thought, and so
are unperceived. Further, the principal cause which
is life, and the instrumental cause which is recipient
of it, act together as one cause and this action is felt
in the latter, or in Man, as if it were in himself.
Still another reason why life appears to be in man
himself, is that the Divine love is of such an infinite
quality that it desires to communicate to man " (or
have in common with him) " what belongs to itself." *
As is said in another place : " It is the essence of
love not to love itself but others, and to be joined
in unity with them by love. It is also essential to
it to be beloved by those others, since thereby conjunction is effected. The essence of all love consists in
conjunction : yea the life of it, what we call its enjoyment, pleasantness, delight, sweetness, beatitude,
happiness, felicity. Love consists in willing what is
our own to be another's, and *feeling that other's private delight as our own.* This it is to love. But for a
man to feel his own delight in another, and not the
other's delight in himself, — this is *not* to love ; for
in this case he loves himself, but in the other his
neighbor. These two loves, self-love and neighborly
love, are diametrical opposites ; for in proportion as
any one loves another from self-love, he afterwards
hates him. Hence it is evident that the Divine love

---

* *Ath. Creed,* 26.

cannot help being and existing in *other* beings and existences whom it loves and by whom it is beloved. For when such a quality exists in all love, it is bound to exist in the amplest measure, that is, *infinitely* or without drawback, in Love itself." * And Swedenborg goes on to say, that if infinite love existed in others, by creation, they would be Love itself, and God consequently would be self-love, whereof not the least conceivable fibre is possible to Him, being totally opposed to His being. " This reciprocation of love must take place between God and other beings in whose selfhood there is nothing of the Divine."

This objective middle-ground however, which all spiritual creation implies between creature and creator, and makes common to them both, is objective only to the creature's imperfect intelligence, while it is in truth a necessary element of his subjectivity, being requisite to define the spiritual creation to his limited perception, or give it anchorage and embodiment to his experience. It no way enters as such objective middle-ground into the creative idea, but confesses itself a mere latent, still unrecognized, constitutional factor or law of the created subjectivity. Thus in the actual creation nature is the objective middle-ground between creature and creator ; the

---

* *Divine Love and Wisdom,* 47, 48, 49.

mother-substance which to the created intelligence
gives creation sensible background, or is necessary to
constitute it, and make it visible. But this natural
mother-substance has no independent existence to the
creative intelligence ; but exists only as an implication
or involution of the created or finite selfhood, to which
fallacious quantity it affords all the while the only real
or universal and *quasi*-spiritual pretext and justification, and hence in every way invites and secures to it
self the tenderest Divine concession or accommodation.
Nature indeed offers to the universal heart of man
the nearest possible symbol — that is, pledge or realization — of the Divine infinitude it is any way capable of acknowledging; and it is freely worn therefore
by God as a temporary mask or visor, under cover
of which He pursues, and finally legitimates to the
created intelligence, His stupendous spiritual ends.

It is plain to see, then, that creation, in the only
sense in which it is capable of being rationally
apprehended, that is, as a purely spiritual or living
work, is bound by virtue of the creator's infinitude to
determine itself to objective natural form ; or, to use a
compact and convenient expression of Swedenborg, is
bound to *ultimate itself* naturally or objectively to the
creature's experience, in order to reflect or reproduce
to his finite consciousness the infinite life or being he
has in God. "By creation is meant," says Sweden-

borg, " what is Divine from inmost to outermost, or first to last. Everything which proceeds from the Divine begins from Himself, and progresses according to order even to the ultimate end : thus through the heavens into the world, and there rests as in its ultimate " or home; " for the ultimate of Divine order is in the nature of the world. What is of such a quality is properly said to be created." * So, in another place, he says : " Scientific things " — by which he means, well-established facts as disengaged from the personal or superstitious fancies of men — " which belong to the sphere of man's natural intelligence, are the ultimates of order there ; and things prior, that is, spiritual things, must be in ultimates that they may exist and appear in the natural sphere. All prior or spiritual things, moreover, tend to ultimates as to their own boundaries or limits, and exist in those boundaries or limits as causes in their effects, or as superior things exist in inferior, as in their proper vehicles or vessels. Hence it is that the spiritual world terminates in man's natural mind, in which mind accordingly the things of the spiritual world are exhibited *representatively*," as in a glass, or picture. " Unless spiritual things " — which, remember, are always living affections of goodness and

---

* *Arcana Cœlestia*, 10634. See also *Ath. Creed*, 29.

truth — "were representatively reproduced by such things as are in the world, they would not be at all rationally apprehended." *

" Divine order never stops in a middle-point (as the angel or heaven) and there forms a thing without its ultimate, for then it would not be in a full and perfect state; but goes straight on to its ultimate, and when it is in its ultimate, it then forms, and also by mediums there brought together, it redintegrates itself and produces ulterior things by procreations: whence the ultimate is called the seminary or seed-place of heaven." †   " The ultimate of Divine order is in man, and because he is the ultimate of Divine order, he is also its basis and foundation. Heaven without the human race would be like a house wanting its foundation." ‡   " The end of creation, which is that all things may return to the creator, and that conjunction may be effected, exists in its ultimates." §
" That all ultimate ends become anew first ends, is evident from the fact that there is nothing so inert and dead but has some efficiency in it; even sand exhales somewhat which contributes assistance in producing and therefore in effecting something." ||
" The ultimate, *when order is perfect*, is holy above

---

* *Arc. Cæl.* 5373.

† *Heaven and Hell*, 315.

‡ *Ibid.*, 304.

§ *Divine Love and Wisdom*, 171.

|| *Ibid*, 172.

interior things, for the holiness of interior things is there complete." *

It is this implication of the created *nature*, accordingly, in the spiritual creation, which alone gives that creation its truly miraculous quality, and saves it from being what otherwise it must always have appeared to be, a mere magical product, or work of enchantment. Magic is the power of gratuitous or ostentatious productivity; the power to produce something out of nothing, consequently without labor-pains : thus a something which has no inward ground of being, and therefore exists surreptitiously or by virtue of a deception practised upon the senses of those who acknowledge it. It is a power which used to flourish, in very high places too, upon the earth; but is happily now confined to the hells, save in so far as the hells themselves are vainly trying to compass an unsuspected lodgment in the human mind in the guise of an absurd doctrine called Spiritualism. But the power of all the hells put together would be impotent at this day to persuade any man of average spiritual intelligence that magic, however specious its performances, is anything but a gross mockery of creative power, or ever succeeds in demonstrating anything but its own unlikeness to it. It is the characteristic of power truly creative to be able to

---

* *Arcana Cœlestia*, 9824. See also 5077, 9360, 9212, 9216.

endow its creature with a miraculous mother-substance, or natural basis, and by that means reproduce as in a glass all its own spiritual effects, so verifying or authenticating them to the creature's understanding. And it is the unfailing attribute of natural existence to be a form of *use* to something higher than itself, thus the mineral to the vegetable, the vegetable to the animal, and the animal to man ; so that whatsoever has not either potentially or actually this soul of use within it, does not honestly belong to nature, but confesses itself a mere sensational effect produced upon the individual intelligence.*

---

* " Hence," says Swedenborg, " you may discern how sensually — that is, from the inspiration of the bodily senses, and the darkness which they cast over spiritual things — they think who deem that nature is self-originated. These men think from the eye and not from the understanding. People of this sort are able to think nothing of what being and existing is in itself, namely : that it is eternal, uncreate, and infinite. Nor are they able to think of Life in itself, but as of some volatile thing, passing off into nothing ; nor yet of Love and Wisdom, being totally incapable of discerning that all things of nature derive thence their existence. And indeed it cannot be seen by any one that all things of nature exist thence, *unless nature herself be thought of as an orderly series of uses*, and not estimated *from some of her outward forms* merely, which are only visual objects. For the uses of nature proceed only from life, and their series and order from wisdom and love. But her visible forms are mere *continents* of these uses, so that if they alone or primarily be regarded, nothing of life can be seen in nature, much less anything of love and wisdom, and consequently nothing of God." — *Divine Love and Wisdom*, 46.

Creative power in truth has at this day no fitter expression than that which is furnished it by the modern doctrine of Evolution: understood, to be sure, somewhat more largely than that doctrine is by its current scientific adherents. For to men of science generally the doctrine of evolution imports merely the development of one natural species or kind out of other pre-existing species or kinds; whereas a true or philosophic doctrine of evolution implies the conversion of natural (or lower) substance into spiritual (or higher) form. There is no doubt that man, in so far as his very inferior animality is concerned, is a strict product of the animal kingdom: but there is therefore no reason to hold him to be an evolution of it, unless indeed evolution means devolution, or a process from more to less, from strength to weakness. He is, doubtless, so far forth as his animal nature is concerned, identical with all other animals, only less highly gifted than they with aggressive and persistent force; and so far accordingly there is more ground to pronounce him an involution of the animal kingdom than an evolution of it. But man is not essentially animal. He is animal at most on his organic side, and it is only by remorselessly slumping his distinctively inorganic or human attributes in his animal or organic ones, that any pretext is found for making his existence a product of evolution from lower forms. In so far as he is animal, he does not require any doctrine of evolution to explain his advent unless it be one which explains at the same time the advent of the whole animal kingdom of which he forms a part. And so far as he is distinctively human and inorganic — that is, unembraced in the animal kingdom — his own particular animality stands between him and the rest of that kingdom, stamping itself the only ground or earth of involution he can possibly need, for the subsequent uses of his spiritual or characteristic evolution.

My subjective existence, physical and moral, is involved in my spiritual being, just as the shell is involved in the oyster, the egg in the chicken, the husk in the wheat, the matrix in the gem, the parent in the child : that is, as giving it not substance but surface, not being but background, not centre but circumference, not inward reality but outward apparition, not soul but body. My subjective existence in short is the worthless, perishable ground of my immortal spiritual being. Thus involution is anything else than evolution. It is the direct logical opposite of Evolution. It is indeed a literal and strict inversion of it, just as the root of a plant is an inversion of its stem, or its seed an inversion of its fruit. Involution is logically proportionate and precedent to Evolution, as earth is logically proportionate and precedent to heaven; and no hypothesis of evolution will ever be competent to furnish a pedigree of existence, unless it start from a previous philosophy of involution. Thus if, as many self-constituted partisans of science are prone to believe, monkey *evolves* man, it can only be by virtue of man first *involving* monkey. And to account for man therefore on monkey principles, near or remote, without first accounting for monkey on distinctively human principles, would be to leave our poor ancestral monkey himself unaccounted for: that is, it would practically be to deify him. It would be to explain being by existence, the absolute by the contingent, substance by accident, church by steeple, ship by sails, house by cellar. Whatever is really involved in any existence is merely and at most *constitutional* to it, as conditioning its apparition, and is not the least *essential* to it, as conferring its being. My various *viscera* are no doubt a condition of my physical statics; but that they in the least degree explain my moral dynamics, can only be affirmed as it seems to me by wilful fatuity. They are involved in my physical existence, which is itself involved in my moral consciousness; so that you will never be able to account for them, until you first account for *me*, independently of them.

For, *per contra*, whatsoever is evolved by any existing form, is itself rigidly *creative* of such form; that is, causes it to exist *in natura rerum.* So that to attempt explaining evolution by involution, man by monkey, is a palpable logical dodge or quibble, whose whole force consists in confounding two essentially discrepant and reciprocally inverse things, namely : creation and constitution, being and existence, substance and surface, cause and condition, spirit and flesh. Involution is to evolution precisely what shell is to oyster, what husk is to wheat, what matrix is to gem, what parent is to child ; and to explain evolution by involution, therefore, is to make the oyster cradle its shell, the wheat nourish its husk, the gem protect its matrix, the child support its parent ; all which to the eye of philosophy constitutes a downright witches' sabbath of science ; but a sabbath nevertheless which Mr. Herbert Spencer and the so-called positivists generally are content and proud to sanctify.   To think of our most eminent *religiosi* being frightened by these vagaries of our modern scientific thought !   What does their alarm prove ?   Certainly little or nothing with respect to the object of it, but very much with respect to its subjects.   For it proves not that Positivism, or any subtler form of meditative Atheism, is any way dangerous to any properly human interest, but only that our existing religious faith is every way insecure, being founded not upon the rock of Truth, but upon the shifting sands of authorized opinion.

Thus, as I have said, evolution is an every way fitting doctrine wherewith to express the truth of spiritual creation, provided we give the phenomenal basis of involution which it claims a strictly subject position ; or make Evolution a regenerate spiritual flower, and Involution its natural earthly stem. This is precisely what the scientific men fail to do. They invariably put the cart before the horse, in making the stem account for the flower, and not the flower for the stem, which is the true philosophic order. They make the earth explain heaven, and not heaven the earth, the body explain the soul, and not the soul the body, physics explain morals, and not morals physics, and thus practically outrage all the deeper and finer instincts of humanity, dogmatically sundering that exquisite thread of tradition which in the absence of positive knowledge has hitherto bound men in intellectual and *quasi*-spiritual unity. The obvious philosophic objection to recent scientific speculations is not that they practically tend to invalidate the current religious dogmas in regard to creation, which they cannot do half forcibly enough ; but that they substitute in their place a scientific dogmatism which is not half so respectable in itself, to begin with, and which if it should ever become established in popular regard would be fatal to the very conception of creation, and hence to the spiritual dignity of human nature.

Science has a notable function in the world, but as I have already said it is an intensely humble not a commanding one; an abjectly servile not a leading function. Its name is Esau, not Jacob, being born of the bond woman not of the free. That is to say, science reflects the heart still in bondage to the intellect, while philosophy alone expresses the intellect inspired by the heart. The function of science is to observe and connote the actual facts of existence, in order to determine the mental relation of unity which binds them all together; not in the least to dogmatize, or build up a philosophic *credo*, either upon the physical facts themselves, or the logical unity with which the mind invests them. In short, *fact and the relations affirmed by the mind amongst facts*, is the field of science. Thus it is scientifically competent to Newton to prove that the elliptical movement of the earth around the sun as demonstrated by Kepler, is due to the attraction exerted by the sun upon the earth. For what Newton thus does is simply to establish by Kepler's aid a hitherto unrecognized law of planetary life or intercourse. And it is perfectly competent moreover to Mr. Darwin, in the point of view of science, to collect and colligate, under any generic law of unity he pleases — say Natural Selection, Sexual Selection, or both together — whatsoever actual facts of transmutation he may have observed in

existing animal and vegetable species. For what he
thus does is simply to establish and announce a certain spiritual or living unity, with which the mind
by an instinct of its own underlying infinitude, insists
upon filling up all the crevices of nature, and accounting for all its changes. Mr. Darwin may, to be sure,
have been faithless to fact, or faithless to the mind :
that is to say, his observation may be imperfect, or his
generalization premature : but at all events his method
is thus far irreproachable. But when any one, under
cover of Mr. Darwin's name, quietly "slips over," as
Aristotle says, "into another kind," and making a
fulcrum of his induction in regard to the existing or
fossil variations in the same species, applies his lever to
the disclosure of the *origination* of species, he at once
casts off the honest livery of science, and converts
himself all unconsciously into an ambitious dogmatist. Mr. Darwin makes it scientifically very probable that natural and sexual selection account for all
the varieties observable within our existing species.
But to reason hereupon that these two principles are
sufficient to account for the origin of existing species
themselves, is *not* to reason scientifically, because the
reasoning admits of absolutely no verification in fact.
My tailor yields a sufficient scientific explanation of the
differences between my clothes and those of other people ; but when you seek a philosophic justification of

clothing itself, you must go beyond the tailor. It is good science to say : the sartorial art originated more or less all the varieties we observe in the costume of men ; certainly all those variations which simply imply advance : for here we have any amount of well-attested fact to sustain us. But it is complete recreancy to science to say hereupon " the sartorial art also originates clothing itself among men " : for here we have absolutely no historic fact to keep us in countenance.

Just so with the scientific evolutionist. The basis of his speculation here is not fact at all, but pure fancy. He says in effect : " I conclude that natural and sexual selection have operated all the changes we observe within our extant species of existence, and between some of these species again and certain allied species of which we have only a few fossil remainders ; because a great store of well-attested facts in natural history warrant this conclusion " ; and this is good science. But now he proceeds : " I take another step, and conclude, from the adequacy of these laws to account for specific changes in existence, that they are adequate also to account for the origination, which is the creation of existence." And this is spurious science. Why ? Simply because it is obviously incapable of verification by any fact of nature or of history, and depends for its justification upon a certain bias or prejudice of the man's own intellect, and upon this exclusively.

Nature gives us absolutely no hint, much less any distinct affirmation, in respect either to the origin or destiny of any of her forms or species. All that we see in nature is a foreground of change upon a background of stability, thus fixity in universals, mutation in particulars. But nothing originates and nothing ends in nature. Why? Because nature is not being nor even existence, but only, and at most, appearance. Hence all of nature's forms or species are purely relative or phenomenal ; that is to say, they presuppose an intelligence which is capable of comprehending them, and to which alone they exist. And the scientific evolutionist consequently, in so far forth as he invents a natural origin even for the larvæ of our existing marine ascidians, let alone for the mind of man itself, proceeds upon a total misunderstanding of what nature means, and so turns the actual truth of things upside down. In fact he discharges the mind of all freedom or life ; for he makes nature no longer the obedient mirror of truth, but its absolute source and arbiter.

LETTER XVIII.

Y DEAR FRIEND : — Let me say again, in simple justice to myself, that I have no shadow of objection to the new scientific dogma, in so far as it is purely negative; that is, bears upon the stagnant religious faiths of the world. Doubt or denial is the legitimate weapon of scientific advance. And our present science is, I apprehend, only an indispensable John the Baptist blindly preparing the way, and proclaiming the advent, of a new, or a spiritual and living faith: which it does by vastating the active intellect of men of its dead faiths. Accordingly in so far as our recent bellicose science goes to discredit an historic or literal creation, I have no quarrel with it. For I see in it only the augury of a new faith, based upon a profounder acknowledgment of creation, as being no preposterous physical exploit of God accomplished in the realms of space and time, but a wholly spiritual operation of His power in the realms of human affection and thought.

Thus it is altogether in their positive aspect that I pretend to any quarrel with our recent scientific dogmatics. When science, disdaining the humble but honorable office of ministering to a new intellectual faith and a new spiritual life in man, assumes itself to constitute or even forecast such faith and life, she is no longer amiable nor respectable, and invites as it seems to me a just disclaimer on the part of the outraged common sense of mankind.

The forte of science, be it always remembered, is reflection, or reasoned observation; and these things are plainly possible to man only in so far as his feet are planted in a fixed physical or organic world existing objectively or outwardly to his senses. Now reflection being the proper *forte* of science, or the mode of industry whereby she thrives, I hope it will be allowed me to ask what is her consequent *foible*, or the mode of activity by which she dwindles? The foible of science, then, reflection being her forte, is perception, or spiritual insight; which is possible to man only in so far as his head dwells in a free, inorganic, ethereal, or metaphysical world existing inwardly or subjectively to his affections. Now, such being the forte, and such the foible, of science, it follows naturally enough to the eye of philosophy, that the *punctum saliens* both of her reflective strength and her perceptive weakness should be, as I have before alleged, a certain ontological illusion which she shares with the mass of uninstructed men, in regard to the natural constitution of things: or all simply the constitution of nature. Accordingly let us look into this.

We give the designation of Nature to the outlying universe, or world of things existing to sense. Now what is the earliest and deepest intellectual lesson we derive from this world of sense? It is that everything embraced in it exists really in a composite manner, however much it may seem to exist in a simple or absolute one. The reason of this discrepancy between the rational truth and the sensible fact of the case is, doubtless, the infirmity of the created intelligence: *we the dependents of nature*, who get our highest knowledge exclusively from the gradual revelation she gives of the Divine goodness and truth, *bring to her observation and study first of all a simple, and then a composite faculty of attention;* and she miraculously adjusts herself to our need. Thus we first apprehend nature by sense, and only afterwards learn to apprehend it by the understanding. The exigency of our senses imposes upon everything that exists an apparently *absolute*, that is, a fixed or finite, quality, which the thing is thought to possess in itself, or quite irrespectively of all other things. But our reason or understanding subsequently enables us to convert this absolute or fixed quality of existence, which it apparently possesses in itself, into a *relative*, unfixed, or contingent quality which it possesses only in relation to other things. That is to say, we first apprehend the thing as a purely *physical* existence, and afterwards rise to the conception of it as a *natural* existence. The first or sensuous aspect of the world presents us everything in a purely selfish, personal, or phenomenal point of view; the second or rational aspect of it alone exhibits everything as existing in a purely relative, or associated, and harmonious light. A horse, for example, happens at this moment to be tied before my door. This horse, I repeat, is an absolute or fixed fact of sense, entirely distinct from all other facts; so fixed or absolute, that to dispute or deny it would be equivalent to disputing or denying the competence of my senses in their own sphere. But notwithstanding that the horse is this absolute or fixed fact to my senses, you yourself will agree with me that he has no existence to my reason out of relation to all other horses. That is to say: while he apparently exists in himself alone, or as an individual horse, he in very truth exists only in solidarity with his kind. And so with all other things in the realm of sense.

Now what I want hereupon to point out to your attention in the first place, is a truth which perhaps you never have thought of before, namely; that this *relative* existence of things — the existence they have in relation to all other things — alone stamps them *natural;* while their absolute or individual existence — the apparent existence they have in themselves — is a grossly fallacious or unreal thing, in total contradiction to the constitution of nature. To be sure it is only a judgment of our infirm or imperfect sense that things have this absolute or fixed individuality. Nothing claims it but man; but because he, inspired by sense and uncontrolled by reason, affects selfhood, he does not hesitate to bestow it also in modified form upon all other existence. All other things utterly disclaim it in fact; and it is only the profound hallucination which he cherishes in regard to himself as involving his own being and existence, that ever leads him to invest them also in their degree with selfhood, reckoning their innocent persons in fact good and evil, and subjecting them to reward and punishment, as they stand affected to his dubious and very wilful supremacy.

I said just now that this absolute or individual aspect of things, the aspect they have of existing in themselves, and irrespectively of other things, was grossly unnatural: "in total contradiction to the constitution of nature." Nature, to our conception, is a composite existence made up of an objective and

subjective unity. That is to say, it is the strict unity
in all its subjects of a public and a private, or a common and a proper, force. It embraces two elements,
one universal the other particular, one statical the
other dynamical, one material, in short, the other
spiritual; and these two elements moreover are most
distinctly one or united, so that however easily we
may divorce them in thought or reflectively, they are
never separable in fact. A really absolute, finite, or
independent existence, save as a fallacy of the human
mind, is disavowed by the nature of things, and we
may safely dismiss it from rational regard therefore.
There is no such existence out of our infirm understanding, and no subjective pretension to it outside of
hell, which fairly lives and grows fat upon the hallu-
cinations bred of it. But I admit that nature *outwardly viewed* does wear the appearance of being
almost wholly made up of these absolute or finite
and independent existences. *But what business have
we, as philosophers, to be caught looking at nature outwardly?* This in fact is just my complaint in the
premises, that we should be so long philosophically
content to view nature as an outward thing, or as she
stands revealed to sense, when she herself prays to be
regarded inwardly alone, or as she reveals herself to
our understanding : that is, to be regarded no more
as mineral, vegetable, and animal, but as exclusively

human. It is only an inveterate sensuous fatuity on our part which leads us to mistake the mere sensible or physical appearances of things for their fundamental natural or rational realities. And there is no way of correcting the mistake but by outgrowing this fatal intellectual fatuity ; that is, by at once manfully deposing sense from the governing or inspiring relation it now bears to the intellect, and remanding it forthwith to a wholly ministerial or subordinate place.

Believe me, my friend, it is nothing but this subtle and insinuating serpent of sense (rightly so named in sacred or symbolic writ) which — appealing to the woman in us, that is, the still latent or unrecognized spiritual Divine force in our nature — has ever had power so to falsify and otherwise bedevil our intelligence as to make us look upon creation as a material or sensibly objective work of God, detached from Him by the laws of space and time, instead of a purely spiritual or inwardly subjective one, intimately blent with His eternal Love and Wisdom through the laws of our own nature or the life of our affection and thought. It is simply this stultifying pressure of sense upon the intellect that has always until now rendered it intellectually impossible for us to identify our own honest natural manhood, let alone our Divine natural one. Have you not under the guidance of sense always looked upon your natural manhood as at bottom physically engendered? That is to say, as engendered out of the various limitations you derive from your mineral, vegetable, and animal organization? You have never thought — have you? — that your natural manhood was what forever lifted you out of mineral, vegetable, and animal relationship, and rendered you eternally *solidaire* with mankind. Much more, if you have ever considered the truth of a Divine natural manhood at all, you have thought — have you not? — that it was altogether *personally* constituted : that is, constituted by a person of another nature to ours, acting in fact in total aloofness from, and independence of, your and mine and all men's common nature, instead of identifying himself exclusively with that nature, and glorifying it to Divine dimensions. Personality has never been anything else than a mark which we stupid men have required to assure us of our natural difference from mineral, vegetable, and animal, although we ourselves have none the less always contrived stupidly to interpret it into a providential signal of the natural relation of disunion or inequality we were under to our fellow-men. Accordingly when the Divine natural humanity condescends to reveal itself in personal form, we may be sure that it is for no purpose of living to that form but only of dying to it, in order that men may cease any longer to find their life in

what merely differences them from lower natures, and
seek it henceforth in all that identifies them with their
own nature, now become Divine.

But I am forgetting my purpose, which was to
show a certain ontologic craze on the part of science,
which rendering her view of nature hopelessly infirm
or inadequate except for isoteric or shop purposes,
utterly defeats her educational competence.

This craze consists all simply in looking upon
nature as a fixed or finite existence, thus as materially
constituted, as being in short a strict phenomenon of
space and time. It is all very well, mind, nay, it
is a matter of stern necessity, to regard nature as
materially or outwardly constituted *to our senses*. For
inasmuch as nature is a purely metaphysic quantity,
it is evident that she can only be reflected to our understanding through the obedient mirror of physics.
Her existence then to our recognition must be conditioned upon fixed or sensibly objective relations
between mineral, vegetable, and animal substance ;
otherwise it will be impossible for us ever to apprehend her, ever to catch even a glimpse of her living
and glorified presence. But this is not what science,
at least in the person of her more renowned modern
adepts, means. She does not hold that nature is dependent for her intellectual recognition by us on a
certain objective or material imagery addressed pri-

marily to our senses, and through them to our understanding. By no means. She holds that nature is actually identical with this physical imagery, and has neither conceivable being nor existence apart from the unconscious forms which to a more instructed eye simply reveal her perfections. This is why I called this illusion a craze on the part of science. Surely you would think a man out of his wits who should identify himself with his image in a glass. And I in like manner deem science out of her wits when she identifies the mistress she professes to worship with the perishable mirror that reflects her. These objective or material facts, which so gravel and impede the onward march of science, are nothing, as we have seen, but *ultimates* of Divine order, in the sphere of sense; just as bricks and mortar are ultimates in the same sphere of architectural order. You would not rate very high a man's genius who should pretend to deduce the architectural order of the Parthenon from the stone and lime and water which nevertheless gave it its sole material basis? So too you would not feel constrained to put a high estimate upon the conceited science, which — because it is able to lay a profane or familiar hand upon these mere bases, or material ultimates, of Divine order in human nature — irreverently supposes that it has got within its grasp the ineffable spiritual results of that order?

If so, I should feel painfully constrained in my turn not to put a very high estimate upon your philosophic sagacity.

Spiritual creation cannot possibly be understood save in so far as the spiritual or created subject is seen to be invested incidentally with natural constitution. His person must be seen to be naturally constituted, in order to give him conscious projection from God, and make anything, even existence, truly predicable of him. For spiritual creation, you remember, is purely *subjective* creation; that is, the creator gives being to the creature only by giving Himself to him, or endowing him with his own infinite substance. But no mere person, much less all persons, would be equal to this Divine communication, unless it incidentally provided, or involved in itself, a natural or objective development on the part of the creature to give him background or a basis of identity; otherwise it must instantly collapse or turn out a false pretension. There would be no created object at all commensurate with the creative subject and creation consequently, which, to begin with, is a strict equation between creator and creature, would fall through, or confess itself impossible from the start. This is all that Swedenborg means by his doctrine of natural ultimates as incidental to spiritual creation. It is a doctrine which, for the first time in

the philosophic annals of the mind, not only accounts
for Nature, and perfectly accounts for it too, but
brings the dread and formidable spiritual world itself
into our own keeping, as it were, by harnessing it and
taming it down to the phenomena of men's familiar
natural history.   Any other doctrine would turn the
creator into a mere magician, or supreme charlatan,
making everything out of nothing, and so avouching
himself infinitely below not merely any renowned artist, but any honest stone-mason.   For the mason's art
does n't pretend to make bricks without straw, or subjective existence without any objective implication,
but finds *its* ultimation also in things most real and
tangible to our senses, whereby alone it is that we are
never liable to mistake it for a mere creation of the
fata morgana.

Now it would be by no means remarkable if science
should be content to fix her regard exclusively upon
this *constitutive* sphere of things, thus objectively involved in the spiritual or subjective creation.   For
this outwardly objective sphere of things constitutes
the true and legitimate field of her activity, furnishes
her with her sole *raison d'être* in fact ; and within
that sphere accordingly none can gainsay her voice.
But she is not thus content in point of fact.   Some
busy imp from some dusky hell of ambition has bitten
her with an unfortunate desire to dogmatize, or take

captive the realm of faith in man; that is to say, the
field of his interior knowledge as well as his external.
This is the only reason why I have allowed myself to
call her craze an *ontologic* one.   It does not confine
itself to speculating upon existence, but assuming
apparently that natural existence is the same thing
with spiritual being, it undertakes authoritatively to
check or limit what *is* by what sensibly appears to be;
or array natural constitution *against* spiritual creation.
Thus where Swedenborg says that all natural existence
is created by a soul of use behind it — use to other
and higher things — our modern science affirms that
all natural existence is constituted by some primary
natural substance, say protoplasm, and that there is
an end of the matter.   There can be no objection of
course to the scientific man's attempt to reduce if he
can all organized existence to a common basis; but
the objection comes in when he attempts to make any
formula of his on this grossly gratuitous and impertinent subject, of vital concern to philosophy.   For
in doing this he at once betrays his crass ignorance
of what philosophy means, confounding, for example,
every concept that is proper and dear to it with its
exact opposite, *individuality* with identity, *life* with
existence, *form* with substance, *cause* with condition,
creation with constitution.   Philosophy is perfectly indifferent to what naturally *constitutes* existence or

gives it outward body, but reserves all her interest
for what spiritually *creates* it, or gives it inward soul.
To misconceive and misrepresent this, however, is the
inveterate temptation of clever scientific men, and the
infirmity has never been more aptly illustrated than
in the developments of our recent scientific material-
ism. "Pursue," says Professor Huxley, "the nettle
and the oak, the midge and the mammoth, the infant
and the adult, Shakespeare and Caliban, to their common root, and you have protoplasm for your pains.
Beyond this analysis science cannot go; and any
metaphysic of existence consequently which is not
fast tethered to this physical substance, which is not
firmly anchored in protoplasm, is an affront to the
scientific understanding."

Such in substance is Professor Huxley's attitude towards philosophy. Professor Huxley is consciously no
doubt a very independent man, and an uncommonly
able writer; but it seems to me very odd, to say the
least, that any one interested not in the pursuit of
scientific knowledge primarily, but of philosophic
truth, should be at all moved, and especially at all
disconcerted, by his facts: for whether they be scientifically valid or not, they are properly irrelevant to
philosophy. Like Mr. Spencer, M. Taine, and all
the other men who desire not only to make science
the king, but also to invest it with the priesthood

of the mind, Professor Huxley restricts his researches to the principle of *identity* in existence — that point in which all existence becomes essentially chaotic or substantially indistinguishable. The philosopher, on the other hand, who sees science to be not the end but the means of the mind's ultimate enfranchisement, enlarges *his* researches to the principle of individuality in existence, or that comprehensive spiritual unity in which all existence becomes essentially cosmical, or formally differentiated *inter se*. Far be it from me to question Mr. Huxley's statistics, for I know nothing about them ; I only question, nay I am heartily amused by, the extravagant intellectual conclusions he deduces from them. I have no doubt, on his own showing, that the initial fact in all organization is protoplasm. But at the same time I avow myself unable to conceive a fact of less vital significance to philosophy. *Philosophy cheerfully takes that and every similar fact of science for granted.* The initial fact in the edifice of St. Peter's at Rome was a quantity of stone and lime. This fact was assumed by the architect as necessarily included in the *form* of his edifice, about which form alone he was concerned. The identity of his edifice, or what it possessed of common substance with all other buildings, interested him very little ; only its individuality, or what it should possess of differential form from all other

buildings, was what exercised his imagination. To
conceive of Michael Angelo concerning himself mainly
with the rude protoplasm, or mere flesh and bones,
of his building, is at once to reduce him from an
architect to a mason. And, in like manner, to conceive the philosopher intent upon running man's immortal destiny, or spiritual form, into the abject slime
out of which his body germinates, is to reduce him
from a philosopher to a noodle.

Protoplasm means intellectual chaos; means the
resolution of the existing cosmos into absolute form-
lessness or disorder. That is to say: you cannot
arrive at protoplasm experimentally or livingly, except by disowning our present cosmical form and
order, except by eliminating all that you organically
are, with all that is contingent upon your organization, namely: all your experience of life and consciousness, every fact of appetite and emotion, of
reason and imagination, of passion and action, everything, in short, that constitutes you a living person
and so stamps you of the slightest moment to philosophy. Protoplasm, in truth, as an intellectual
symbol, means the extinguishing of the soul or life
or being of things, and the permission of mere bodily
existence to them, without any source either for them
to exist, or go forth, from, but what is essentially inferior to themselves. For no one will pretend that

protoplasm, or the formless unqualified material of
things, is any way comparable in intellectual interest
with the least of its formed or qualified products.
Nevertheless, to such absolute drivel does the man
of science reduce himself when he aspires, *on scientific grounds*, to play the philosopher! And such is
the invariable penalty of violating spiritual bounds.
The realm of Philosophy is invariably soul, or inward
consciousness; the realm of science is, as invariably,
body, or outward sense. And although it is past all
dispute that these two realms stand to each other in
the relation of superstructure and base, it is none the
less but all the more true that while the former is indeed *outwardly conditioned* upon the latter, the latter
is *inwardly created* by the former; and hence that the
higher realm of soul is no more *continuous* with the
lower realm of body, than a house is continuous with
its foundation, or a tree which fills the air with bloom
and fragrance is continuous with its underground
roots. The roots of the tree are a mere involution of
the tree in order to its subsequent evolution, and any
expansion they may attain to is not in the direction
of the tree, but in a contrary or inverse direction, that
of the earth. The foundation of the house in like
manner is so wholly subservient to the house, that
every subsequent enlargement it may chance to undergo in itself, will only enhance such subserviency

by carrying the foundation deeper, that is away from the house rather than towards it.

Notwithstanding all I have said, however, I have not the least doubt that the gospel of physicism is a strictly providential movement in our mental history. I have no doubt that in thus making as it does *tabula rasa*, or a clean sweep, of our sensuous or inherited ontology, it does unwitting good service to the mind in clearing the ground for a new and purely spiritual conception of being or life. Idealism seems in fact a gross but inevitable husk of the mind's spiritual advent. But its rôle is essentially critical : that is, it is not the least rightfully dogmatic. And nothing can be more insane, therefore, than to regard the new dogmatism as constituting the positive boon to the intellect which it ignorantly assumes to do. Our intelligence is built not upon negation but affirmation, and the current scientific idealism is at best but a transition point between the once active but always baseless and now defunct metaphysics of theology, and that philosophic naturalism or realism which is even now looming in our intellectual horizon, and ready to avouch itself the fixed immovable earth of the mind, the adamantine rock of man's spiritual faith and hope.

LETTER XIX.

AND now, my dear friend, we are almost ready to take up the thread of discourse we dropped, in reference to the function of the church in history: almost ready, but not quite. For I think a little further effort should first be made perfectly to familiarize your thought with Swedenborg's philosophy of nature as being a strictly necessary involution of the spiritual creation. Nothing short of clear conceptions on this subject will permanently avail to free the mind from the rubbish of inane and idle ontologic speculation which now threatens to drown it out.

The intellectual formula to which the truth of the spiritual creation with its marvellous implication of nature reduces itself, may be thus expressed: *The created subject, in order to his subjective life or consciousness being perfectly authenticated, requires that it be altogether outwardly or objectively realized, or claim a supremely natural root.* The justification of this intellectual formula, or law of thought, is to be found in the very nature of creation ; which, as being the operation of an infinite power, cut off therefore from all outside resources, is restricted to purely subjective issues ; and hence, in order spiritually to qualify its creature, or redeem him from the sheer and abject phenomenal subjectivity to which as a creature he is doomed, is obliged to endow him thereupon with a career of distinctively natural evolution, which may serve as a true and objective basis of his eventual spiritual enfranchisement. Creation of course is the prerogative of an infinite being ; but we are in the habit of borrowing the word to characterize the products of our own æsthetic genius or free activity. Thus we say Hamlet is a creation of Shakespeare, Dante created the Inferno, the Parthenon divides its creation between Callicrates and Phidias, the artist creates the statue. Now, of course, regarded strictly, it is not a just use of the word to employ it simply in the way of characterizing our unforced or spontaneous activity ; because it is essential to the creative idea that the creator give spiritual or living form to His creature only by Himself first furnishing him with natural or mother-substance. And Shakespeare, Dante, and the rest, may worry themselves out of their meagre wits, before they will ever be able any of them to endow the products of their distinctive genius with anything more than a purely lifeless or imaginative existence ; for with all their genius they can never bestow upon its offspring natural subjectivity or mother-substance.

Still we may get a very good hypothetical illustration out of the word even in this familiar misuse of it. Let us suppose then that the artist were a veritable creator, and had power accordingly to give his statue subjective or conscious life by himself spiritually vivifying the marble from which it comes. In that case one thing would be at once clear, and that is, that the statue would be no longer as now a dead material form, but a conscious or *quasi*-living one, instinct, no doubt, through its vivified mother-substance with all its creator's genius. But another thing would be almost equally clear, and that is, that he would never be able to reproduce that genius in himself. Why not ? Because this ability would presuppose in the statue a certain interior or sympathetic discernment and appreciation of its creator's genius, whereas he is as yet, by the hypothesis of his finite maternal genesis, debarred all interior or sympathetic experience, and made conscious alone of his own material or outward existence. By the necessity of his finite generation he is ignorant not only of his creator's genius or individuality, but also of his creator's name or identity ; ignorant in fact of everything but his mother-substance, and the outward life and sustenance wherewith it fills his veins. It is indeed evident to the least reflection that this self-conscious life of the statue — the self-conscious or *qudsi*-life he derives from the mother — instead of spiritually approximating him to the father, will have the effect in the first instance to render him spiritually remote from the father, or spiritually alienate him from his creative source by filling him with the sentiment and *animus* of independent or unrelated existence. And consequently before he can come into any genuine spiritual or æsthetic sympathy and fellowship with the father, it is necessary that his natural force be abated — that he inwardly die to it in fact as the supreme law of his activity, and so rise again to the experience of an inward and better life.

But how shall we even conceive of any such issue coming about in the case supposed? In the first place when a thing is naturally biased to infirmity, and its nature is yet the only force it obeys or even recognizes, it seems impossible ever to expect it voluntarily to contract a contrary bias. The trite lines of the Roman poet:

> " Facilis descensus Averni,
> Sed revocare gradum, superasque evadere ad auras,
> Hic labor, hoc opus, est ":

easily suggest the smooth and flowery path of dal-

liance that leads downward, and the sharp and
arduous return path. But I very much doubt
whether Virgil himself, or any other poet, Pagan or
Christian, has ever faced the real difficulty. The real
difficulty in the way of a man becoming good out of
evil, or celestial out of infernal, is that good and evil,
heaven and hell, are not outgrowths or accidents of the
human personality by any means, but necessary con-
stituents of human nature itself, by which the nature
becomes freely developed to the recognition of its subjects, and by whose active oppugnancy and contrast
it becomes enabled at last in the person of some
adequate subject gradually to slough off its infirm
mortal lineaments, and ally itself with infinitude.
Good and evil, heaven and hell, are not facts of creative,
but of purely constitutive order. They bear primarily
upon man's natural destiny, and have no relation to
his spiritual freedom save through that. They are the
mere geology of our natural consciousness, and this is
all they are. They have no distinctively supernatural
quality nor efficacy whatever. They have a simply
constitutional relevancy to the earth of man's associated consciousness, and disavow therefore any properly creative or controlling relation to his spiritual
or individual freedom. We have been traditionally
taught that good and evil, heaven and hell, were
objective realities, having an absolute ground of

being in the creative perfection. But this is the
baldest, most bewildering nonsense. They have not
a grain of objective reality in them, and are noway
vitalized by the absolute Divine perfection. They are
purely subjective appearances, vitalized exclusively
by the created imperfection, or the uses they subserve
to our provisional moral and rational consciousness.
When accordingly this consciousness — having more
than fulfilled its legitimate office, and become as it
now is a mere stumbling-block or rock of offence to
the regenerate mind of the race — finally expires in
its own stench, or else frankly allows itself to be
taken up and disappear in our advancing social and
æsthetic consciousness, good and evil, heaven and hell,
will cease to be appearances even. For angel and
devil, saint and sinner, will then find themselves perfectly fused or made over in a new or comprehensive
race-manhood which will laugh to scorn our best
empirical or tentative manhood, that is, our existing
civic and ecclesiastic manhood so-called. Thus, as I
have said somewhere else, I am fully persuaded for
my part, that no objective heaven will ever be found
expanding to our foolish personal hope, nor any objective hell ever be found responsive to our foolish
personal fear. We may be very sure that our true
immortality, that which is energized by the Divine
NATURAL humanity, is far too human and miraculous

to be mechanized on any such preposterously simple basis. No man, not a simpleton in all spiritual regards, will ever acknowledge a heaven of which he himself is not his own sole St. Peter, nor any hell of which he is not his own jealous and exclusive turn-key. Assuredly no heaven could exert the attractive force of a toyshop to a good man's imagination, if it aimed to conciliate his self-love and his love of the world ; and no hell could exert the binding force of a cobweb to an evil man's imagination, if its primary aim were *not* to conciliate those exacting loves.

But we are digressing. If the evil of men then did not refer itself primarily to their nature, as that nature is determined by its spiritual Divine source, but were an outward or physical experience of the subject, asserting itself primarily through his sensations, there could be no manner of difficulty in the evil subject winning himself back to the upper air. For man's veriest life is a sensitive one at the best, and if any serious conflict accordingly should announce itself be-tween the life of his senses and that of his habitual subjective aspirations, it is safe to say that he would very speedily end by renouncing the latter.

But the idea is simply stupid. Evil is not an out-ward thing save to the inexperienced mind. Hell is not objectively constituted save to a juvenile and flimsy imagination. It is on the contrary a purely subjective life in man, being the bloom of that excessive delight he takes in his new-found natural self, and its proper belongings : a delight so *naïve* and sincere at first, and at length so infatuated or magical, as to be capable of making evil seem unadulterate good, and falsity undissembled truth.   So that what you virtually ask of an evil man in expecting him to become heavenly, is literally to turn himself outside in, or dilapidate himself as to his existing carnal structure, and build himself up anew in quite an opposite style of life or consciousness to that which alone seems to him either practicable or savory.   In short, you ask a rigid impossibility of him.   Swedenborg is eminently explicit and satisfactory as to this rigidly natural genesis of evil in man.   He says somewhere — I forget at this moment exactly where, but I am very sure generally that it is in his most interesting little book on the laws of the Divine Providence : but I beseech you not to argue from this amiable scrupulosity of mine in trying to supply you with chapter and verse for all my citations from Swedenborg, that I hold his sayings to be of the slightest conceivable intellectual authority, for I do no such stupid thing ; and indeed if I were *à priori* inclined to any such fatuity, his books would supply the best possible corrective of the inclination, *being the only books I know which inwardly, or of their own proper substance*, abjure such an ungodly pretension : — that he had been, for demonstrative purposes no doubt, let into the life of hell in man ; and he found it to be a life of such abundant and exquisite delight, arising from the immense love of dominion consequent upon the unrestrained love of self in the subject, that all the delights of the world seemed dull in comparison with it. He describes it, I remember, as " a delight *of the whole mind* from its centre to its circumference," though it only reported itself in the body as a certain triumphant swelling of the breast. And this delight moreover would never invite compression, as he says, if it were not for the tendency it has to express itself in unjust and injurious action. Whenever accordingly this inherent tendency ultimates itself outwardly, the evildoer finds his inward freedom, which is the freedom of *willing and thinking* evil, suddenly converted into outward bondage, which is an inability *to do* evil. For hell is a condition of life in which men's outward necessities constrain them to live together in harmony, while they have no inward bent to that style of life. The possibility of their co-existence in this condition depends upon an inflexible law : *that no person shall ever be allowed to harm another with impunity.* This salutary law, which is full of infinite Divine benignity towards them, each and all, and which heavenly-minded people inwardly impose upon themselves every moment, is yet to hellish-minded people an absolute bondage, and constitutes the sole drawback or qualification to their bad blessedness. For what can be more absolutely disgusting to one who delights in *willing* and *thinking* evil towards another, than to be constrained by the righteous fear of punishment from ever *doing* him any evil? There can be no intenser hell known to a selfish man than to have a prudent regard for others thus *enforced* upon him. But Swedenborg always takes pains to apprize his gentle reader that the practical administration of this law, which the evil man finds it so hard, and the good man so easy, to submit to, undergoes all needful mitigation — short, to be sure, of rendering its chastisements ineffectual — through its always taking place under the most watchful and tender angelic supervision or control.*

---

* The broad flood of light which Swedenborg throws upon the intimate Divine dealings with human nature throughout history, ending with its final apotheosis, or actual Divine glorification, is apt to leave his reader disenchanted of any speculative interest he may have felt in regard to the continued existence of hell. I think that a man must have read Swedenborg to little intellectual profit, if his mind is not *hopefully* made up to two things: First, that the antagonism of heaven and hell on moral grounds, or as a tradition of human *nature*, is some day sure to be done away with by the advance of human society or fellowship: Second, that its persistence as a spiritual tradition, or condition of individual experience and culture, may always be counted upon. Still

But we are losing sight of our hypothetical illustrative statue. The statue, then, in accordance with its constitutional limitations, and in spite of its apparent subjective vivification, must remain utterly hopeless of regeneration, or æsthetic life; that is, must forever despair of reproducing in itself the genius which begat it. I say this is in accordance with its constitutional limitations; for its constitutive or mother-substance which gives it body, can do no more for it than give it body; that is, cannot give it soul, or make it inwardly responsive to its creator's genius. And this simply because the constitutive or mother-substance of the statue was originally or in itself independent of the artist's genius, and beyond a certain point therefore refractory to his will. This in truth is the inherent defect of all artistic creation, that the artist is without infinitude, even his genius not being original with him, but inherited or derived

---

I have thought it best to throw together a few brief passages from his books, which may be suggestive of thought to you. His books contain no dogmatic statement of opinion on the subject of the eternity of the hells now so much mooted between the sentimentalist and traditionalist wings of the church; and questions of this magnitude besides can never be settled for us by any the wisest and most erudite head, but only by our own wise and loving hearts. At all events all Swedenborg's utterances on the subject may be looked at without suspicion, as they have no pretension to be anything else than *obiter dicta*, or observations by-the-way. See Appendix A.

from his past ancestry; and hence he is obliged to find
the material or mother-substance of his work exclusively within outward nature, and not, like the Divine
genius, within Himself, or the resources of His own
infinite spirit.   Were the artist infinite like God to
begin with — that is, did he also supply from his
own æsthetic resources natural or mother-substance
to his creations — then *his* creatures, like God's, would
be capable of æsthetic regeneration or spontaneous
life, by virtue of his prior capacity to overcome for
them any latent death-tendency inherent in their
merely constitutional substance.

And thus our supposititious statue perfectly illustrates, in a negative way, the positive truth I wish to
impress upon you, namely : that the spiritual creation
derives all its power to function from the implication
or involution of the created nature.   *The actual* — or
ultimate and phenomenal — *sphere of creative order
is the sole sphere of creative power*, in other words;
and if the power fail here, accordingly, the entire
spiritual creation must instantly come to an end, like
a tale that is told.   If the creative power is unable to
reduce the creative nature to order, and that moreover to an order perfectly consonant with His own
infinitude or perfection, the day must soon come
when the creative name itself will be blotted out
from men's recognition.   But if it is competent —

even infinitely competent to this sublime necessity, then we have only to look forward to the
fast approaching advent of the Divine kingdom on
earth — *the earth, namely, of man's redeemed natural
subjectivity*, mind you, and not at all, save by implication in that superior earth, the mere outside
objective earth of his mineral, vegetable, and animal
existence — and the consequent advent of a heaven
of spiritual peace, felicity, and power in man, every
way unimaginable save upon the basis of that redeemed or Divine-natural earth.

But you ask me not merely to assert this competency of God to our natural redemption, but to
state the method of it. And that statement will
require a complete letter to itself, or perhaps two.

LETTER XX.

MY DEAR FRIEND :— Our almost solitary topic hitherto has been CREATION. And creation is first of all a rigid practical equation between creator and creature, or the creative and created natures. No doubt creator evolves creature, as subject evolves object. But then as involution is always equal to evolution, being its strict logical counterpart or correlative, so if creator evolve creature, or subject object, just as truly on the other hand does creature *in*volve creator or object subject. But if this were all the truth upon the subject, creation would be defeated by its own genesis. For where involution and evolution are thus logically equal, creature and creator, object and subject, practically neutralize each other, and no logical exodus from the difficulty is either possible or conceivable. That is, creator and creature must confess themselves convertible terms, in order to creation becoming living or conscious. Created life or consciousness is

possible only on one condition, which is : that creation exhibit so complete a fusion between its unconscious and conscious factors, as practically to annul
their logical inequality, and so make the resultant life
or consciousness one.   It is impossible that God should
create absolute life or being — that is to say, what
has life or being in itself — for such life or being
is *ex vi termini* uncreated, would in truth be God
himself.   He can only create therefore what has not
life or being in itself, what consequently is merely
relative or associated life or being, and consists in
loving others : and He creates this only by the free
or infinite *communication* to the creature of His own
life or being, that is, of Himself.   It is this infinite
communication which alone makes created life or
consciousness conceivable.   For how shall that which
by the hypothesis of its creatureship is void of life or
consciousness in its own right, ever attain to actual
life or consciousness, but by the free unstinted communication of its creator's life to it as henceforth its
own life ?

We, nevertheless, misled by sense, have had the
fatuity to conceive that creator and creature are
essentially inconvertible terms, sternly repudiating
each the other's practical identification with itself.
We are in the habit of postulating such an essential
oppugnancy between them, as necessarily converts

human life into a sign or witness of their inveterate duality, and so fills the universe of consciousness with pride, blasphemy, and despair. How necessarily we make creation appear the limping, one-horse-concern it does appear, in thus making it include the creature but exclude the creator, or include matter and exclude mind or spirit! As if the creature could ever be given without the logical implication of creator to constitute him! Or the creator ever be given without the logical explication of creature to reveal Him! What wonder is it, under these circumstances, that our men of science should tend so generally to identify God's glory primarily with sun, moon and stars, and only secondarily or derivatively with man? Our traditional creeds to be sure still echo the ancient faith of mankind, that matter and mind, nature and spirit, are inextricably married or interfused ; but this faith has so little vitality left, or has become so completely fossilized by the worldliness of the Church, that very many of our leading scientific men spring eagerly to the conviction, which some of them do not hesitate to avow, that the material universe exists absolutely, or for its own sake exclusively, and betrays no record whatever of a creator,

Such is the intellectual disability which our ignorance and imbecility in regard to the spiritual truth of creation inevitably impose upon us ; and so long as we remain contentedly disabled we must forego our intellectual manhood, and lie supine and inert in spiritual infancy. For manifestly so long as I am content to look upon creation, not as the living fusion, but as the living divorce of the two natures, creator and creature, I must necessarily think the divine nature to be essentially alien or antagonistic to my own. That is to say, I can never think of God as a being of an essentially human quality. And if I cannot think of God in this light, if I do not think of him as essential man, I had better not think of him at all, since I cannot think of him to any good but only to an evil purpose. For if God is my creator, and yet claims a nature essentially alien and antagonistic to my own, I never can really love him, because I can never really know him, inasmuch as I cannot know what my nature does not qualify me to know. In fact I can only hate him, however much my prudence may lead me to dissimulate my hate ; for no rational being can feel himself at the mercy of a power infinitely superior to himself, and at the same time utterly alien and antagonistic to himself, without a righteous hatred to such power. So that if every man is — spiritually or intellectually — only what his idea of God makes him, I may freely say that my idea of God as being of a nature essentially foreign and repugnant to my own, makes all my worship of him superstitious or depraved, and hence fixes me in intellectual night. So long as I admit an essential contrariety between the two natures, which I needs must do when I in thought identify the creative activity primarily with the geometry of the physical universe, and refuse to identify it, save in a very secondary and derivative or indirect way, with the laws of the human mind, I never can rationally acknowledge the Divine existence, nor consequently ever honestly worship it. For human nature claims so divine a quality to my imagination — seems to be so infinitely worthy of my devout love and worship — that I cannot spontaneously recognize any divinity outside of it. And if I yet pretend to recognize such a divinity, and offer Him my servile or interested homage, what am I but a degraded being, sunk in spiritual penury, or intellectual savagery? I may indeed be all unconscious of my degradation, because such multitudes partake it in common with me; but there it unmistakably is, all the while, nevertheless.

In short, DEISM as a philosophic doctrine, that is, as importing an essential difference between the divine and human natures, or God and man, is a philosophic absurdity. There is no God but the Lord, or our glorified NATURAL humanity, and whatsoever other deity we worship, is but a baleful idol of our own spiritual fantasy, whom we superstitiously project into

nature to scourge us into *quasi* or provisional manhood, while as yet we are blind to the spiritual truth.
We ourselves reflect upon the universe the divinity
which dwells latent, and unrecognized — if not crucified, in our souls ; and we see only what we ourselves
give. The untaught rustic may look forever at the
shapeless block of marble, without receiving a hint
from it of its essential subserviency to the uses of Art.
So we might forever contemplate the material world,
without its ever giving us so much as a suggestion of
deity, unless our *inward* instinct of his omnipresence
compelled the suggestion. The animal sees the same
things we see. Why does not he also suspect a latent
divinity ? Simply because he, unlike us, is destitute
of an inward divine genius or nature, and hence has
no power to shed an outward shadow of divinity upon
things below him. No. God is a denizen first of
the microcosm, and only by reflection thence of the
macrocosm. That is to say, he spiritually inhabits
the human mind alone, and what we discern of him
in the mechanism of nature, or the laws of the universe, is but a faint image or reverberation of the
living death, or spiritual infamy, to which we consign Him in our own souls, while as yet we are obdurate to the solicitations of His essential humanity.

Now it strikes me that what I have just been saying is very true in its place, but that this is not its

place; at all events it is not exactly what I set out
to say. What I intended at starting to show you
was that creation, being this undeniable spiritual or
infinite equation of the Divine and human natures
which I have described it to be, would be a very
shallow form of blessing to bestow upon the creature.
If the entire creative bounty consisted in giving the
creature existence, if it involved no deeper, subtler
Divine mercy than this, creation would turn out a
signal curse to man, for it would leave the Divine
being a mere prey to man's devouring and destroying
appetites and passions. By creation alone — that is
to say, creation left undivinized by the creature's
subsequent natural redemption — man is made simply self-conscious, and endowed moreover with selfhood of a marvellously infirm and even infra-bestial
character. For in that case God's creature, unlike
the beasts, would have no instinct to moderate and
mitigate his natural ferocity, but would be an unqualified form of raven and slaughter. Accordingly
I repeat, that if creation resulted only in giving
man conscious existence, or phenomenal selfhood, it
would be a boon altogether unworthy of the creator
to bestow.

Creation, however, is not of this futile pattern. It
does not consist, either wholly or in part, in giving
the creature self-consciousness, or investing him with

phenomenal personality. It merely assumes these things in the creature, or takes them for granted, as the outcome and expression of his essential spiritual imbecility and nothingness. And then it forthwith proceeds to make this negative base or spiritual unconsciousness of the creature the surest possible guarantee of his subsequent spiritual conjunction and fellowship with God. We may say then that creation, viewed as a spiritual or infinite Divine process, necessarily involves to the created intelligence two stages, first: a descending or centrifugal one, in which the creator becomes thoroughly identified with the nature of the creature, in becoming thoroughly alienated from his finite personality; and, secondly: an ascending or centripetal stage, in which the creature becomes exalted in his turn to immortal spiritual conjunction with God, in renouncing the interests of his proper person whenever they conflict with those of his common nature.

How is this natural redemption of the creature practically brought about? We shall be best able to answer this question by keeping clearly in mind what we have seen to be the precise form of evil in the creature to which his finite genesis, or his very nature as a creature, exposes him, and from which it is the true glory of God to deliver him.

The evil then to which, as we have seen, man is

naturally prone, and indeed doomed by his finite generation, is personal consciousness, or the feeling of life in himself as his own life absolutely, or without respect to other men. There is no evil at all comparable with this either for comprehensiveness or intensity, if it be allowed to go uncorrected; for it is altogether fatal to man's spiritual life, which consists in his loving his neighbor as himself. Now the only possible way for a man to do this is to feel that he is *not* self-centred, that his life is *not* his own personally, but belongs to him in strict community with his neighbor; thus that he and his neighbor are both alike dependent at every moment for every breath of life they draw upon one and the same merciful and impartial source. In other words a man loves his neighbor as himself only by virtue of his first loving God above himself, or supremely. And the only way this supreme love becomes developed or educated in him, is through his moral experience, or his obedience to law. Whenever, and so long as, man is tempted to commit false or malicious speaking, theft, adultery, murder, or covetousness, and yet abstains from doing it out of a sincere inward regard for the Divine name, his self-love, so far as it is harmful, is spiritually slain, and the Divine love infallibly replaces it. These formal vices express the whole substantial evil known to the human heart, and when man, therefore, in the

exercise of a felt freedom and rationality deposes them
or any of them from their habitual control over his
action, not because they conflict with his outward
welfare, or expose him to the contempt of men, but
simply because they wound his inward reverence for
the Divine name, he becomes spiritually regenerate or
new-born. Falsehood, theft, adultery, murder, and
covetousness are, in other words, only signs or symbols of a deeper and altogether latent spiritual evil
fatally separating man from God: the evil of a supreme self-love. Grave as these evils unquestionably
are in themselves, or absolutely, they have yet only
a superficial moral quality, that is, grow out of men's
still unreconciled or inharmonic relations *inter se*, or
their frank insubjection to the social sentiment, and
do not by any means necessarily imply any permanent spiritual or individual estrangement between
them and God.

But the evil consciousness which they typify in
men is man's only true and spiritual evil. *The consciousness of a finite existence or selfhood, given outright to every man in strict independence of every other
man:* this is essential death and hell to the human
bosom, and spiritually litters all its abounding moral
corruption. Why? Because it practically gives the
lie to men's spiritual creatureship, or affirms that
they have no natural form and order corresponding to

their inward or spiritual unity in God. Accordingly if man's mind had never been fatally drugged by this stupid conceit of his rightful independence of his neighbor in the Divine sight, he would never have been so suicidal as to dream of coveting the goods, or wounding the honor, or compassing the life of his neighbor. On the contrary he would have been exquisitely sure to defend his neighbor's interests as if they were his own. Thus it is man's very nature as a creature to absorb or appropriate the Divine life or being to his own paltry and fantastic little self; and the Divine name consequently would soon have lapsed from human regard even as a tradition, were the creature not all the while providentially prompted to conceal his flagrant misappropriation of the Divine substance from his own eyes, by assiduously *expropriating* the mere name of God to any worthless or imaginary supernatural candidate who may apply for the distinction : so relegating his creator to an entirely objective or outward relation to himself.

Subjective or personal consciousness, then : the feeling we all of us have that our natural selfhood is our own absolutely, and without reference to any grander natural objectivity, such for example as SOCIETY : is the brimming spiritual death wrapped up in every man by virtue of his finite generation. And now we shall be able to see with all possible clearness with what a mighty hand the Divine providence delivers us from this infernal blight incident to our nature.

The inevitable vice of man's natural subjectivity, or finite selfhood, is, that it *exteriorates* object to subject, or places a man's proper life outside and below the man himself. This is hopelessly contrary to the spiritual order of human life, which *interiorates* object to subject, and places a man's proper life within or above the man himself. In other words, the fundamental infirmity of human nature is that it subjects man primarily to the control of sense, and allows him only so much soul, or spirituality, as consists with that primary requisite. In confirmation of this, we may point to the notorious fact, that the method of man's spiritual or private regeneration has always been defined by the professing church as standing in no frivolous moral change or improvement wrought in the subject, but only in a change of heart: that is, such a complete reversal of the law of his nature as makes him act henceforth from the impulsion of an inward motive or object, instead of an outward one. It is well known, moreover, that the church has always looked upon this reversal of the law of his nature as practically energized by the subject *inwardly constraining himself*, through a most living reverence for the Divine name, to deny his senses whenever they prompt him to selfish or unmanly action.

Do not mistake my present purpose, however, in this reference. We are not now talking of a man's spiritual or private regeneration, which is his individual deliverance from the law of his nature, but of a much grander problem. We are talking in this place of *our poor and abject human nature itself*, and of the peculiar freeing or infiniting it gets at the Divine hands from the bondage imposed upon it by our wretched personalities, both good and evil. For human nature itself is condemned in its turn to inevitable and hopeless limitation or finiteness by all its personal subjects, whether these be relatively to each other celestial or infernal; and is bound therefore by the Divine righteousness to undergo in its turn also a plenary redemption. And the question of immediate interest to us is, to ascertain the method of this transcendent Divine deliverance. This is the problem I am about trying to solve to your understanding. If I only approximately solve it, I shall nevertheless deem myself entitled to claim your patient attention while doing thus much. But if I succeed in perfectly solving it, as I hope to be able to do — and that too without claiming to myself any exceptional ability — I trust that you then, like me, will honestly give the sole praise of my performance to the boundless intellectual inspiration and illumination of the Christian truth.

The characteristic natural evil of man is *subjective consciousness*. Naturally ignorant that his life or being inheres exclusively in God his creator (though he is no way backward to admit that it originally came from Him), he unhesitatingly appropriates it to himself, feeling himself to be good when its issues are orderly, and evil when its issues are disorderly. This I say is the natural and therefore the deepest evil known to the human race. Man no doubt attributes to himself personally many much lesser evils than this, such as murder, adultery, false witness, theft, and covetousness, and thinks if he were once well rid of these outward evils, he would be inwardly or spiritually quit of evil altogether; neither knowing nor dreaming that his moral maladies are only so many visible symptoms of a far deeper invisible disease in his nature to the cure of which God alone is adequate. These moral evils, however grievous they may justly seem in a scientific or police estimate of human life, are of absolutely no consequence in a philosophic estimate, save as revealing that profound and otherwise undiscoverable spiritual evil in man to which alone they owe every fibre of their unhandsome existence. This latter evil is the only deadly evil known to the heart, because it is the only one which directly impugns the Divine sovereignty over His creatures; and in giving man deliverance from its dominion accordingly, the Divine love restores him *ipso facto* to moral purity.

Now the immediate effect, as I have before said, of this fallacious subjective consciousness in man, or of his inwardly appropriating the Divine substance to himself, is to put the creator bodily outside of His creation to the imagination of His creature : to compel Him to occupy at best a merely magisterial or legal and critical relation to His creature ; in short : to relegate the father of our spirits to a purely external and objective intercourse with us. By this misappropriation of the creative life or being to himself, the creature becomes the only subjective consciousness, the only conscious form of selfhood, known to the universe, and by an unerring instinct of that limitary form after thus appropriating to himself the Divine substance, he instantly hastens — as if to hide that ugly transaction from his own eyes — to *expropriate*, as I have before said, the robbed and rifled Divine *name* away from himself, in relegating it to the use of any imaginary supernatural pretender who seems worthy of it, and evinces such worth by consenting to stand in a purely sensible or outward and objective relation to him : that is, consenting to treat him as an absolutely free and rational subject, rightfully praiseworthy and blameworthy on the ground of his own independent merits alone: that is, as a distinctly private and sacred *person* utterly ignoring and disallowing a social, public, or race-consciousness.

Of course this little provisional drama that I have just been describing, enacts itself within, and confines itself to, the limits of the creature's consciousness, and those limits *exclusively*, and does not even project a passing shadow of itself upon the field of his true and intimate yet most unconscious relations to God. But within these limits the most High does tenderly condescend to the part assigned Him by his audacious creature, and unfalteringly play it out moreover to its last gasp of humiliation. For only by the creator consenting to incarnate himself in flesh and blood, and play the part of real object to the creature's fallacious subjectivity, does the drama of human nature and history convert itself out of a stupid and meaningless farce, into a grand, sublime, and tragic revelation of the infinite and eternal perfection. Do you ask me, How? I will gladly proceed to tell you, for this at length is the whole point of my protracted epistolary mission to you.

— But in order to do so fairly and squarely, I shall be obliged to make an addition to the sum of these specifically *intercalary* letters.

LETTER XXI.

MY DEAR FRIEND: — We have seen that the creator, because He gives being to the creature, must always remain the latter's sole and total vital substance. How, in this state of things, shall the creature ever attain to selfhood, or come to feel himself an alien being to God?

Only in a way we may be sure of the strictest illusion, or in consequence of a gross deception imposed on him by his senses.

In the first place the creature is necessarily ignorant of the truth of a spiritual creation, and utterly blind therefore to the intellectual significance of Nature as affording it a necessary basis of evolution. If he has ever at all entertained the idea of creation as an attribute of the Divine perfection, he regards it at most as an explanation of existing things, or as accounting for the production of Nature, which he hence conceives as a work of God taking place in

some pre-existing space and time, and finished at one
or more successive *coups-de-main* of the Divine architect as his sacred traditions report. Thus nature,
instead of being to his intellect the fertile evidence
and argument of God's eternal spiritual activity, is
the practical denial and stoppage of it when it once
existed, interposing so far as the creature's faculties
are concerned a dense wall of partition between him
and God, instead of a transparent medium of communication.

In the second place : being thus ignorant of the
truth of a spiritual creation, and of nature's purely
educative uses in subordination thereto, he is an
every way apt pupil of his senses which stand ready
to impose upon his nascent intelligence two immeasurable and wellnigh inveterate fallacies. The first of
which is : That Nature, or the great realm of unconscious life to which our senses give us our earliest
introduction or initiation, exists ONLY to sense, being
finitely or materially constituted. And the second
follows from this : In that Nature being thus finitely
or materially constituted, every natural thing must be
created in sheer independence of every other natural
thing, and exist therefore on its own substantial basis,
being its own absolute self, without obligation to, or
necessary connection with, any other coexisting thing.

In this way then, or by the mere and sheer docility

of his intellect to his senses, the creature not only attains to the illusion of selfhood, or the feeling of life *in himself* absolutely, and irrespectively of all other men, but he also manages to maintain himself in that illusion, through every casualty and calamity to which an earthly lot engineered upon so shallow and treacherous a basis, necessarily exposes him. And having these sensuous ideas of creation to begin with, the creature instinctively and unwittingly honors the Divine name in making it henceforth sensibly external and objective to the sphere of his own fallacious and fraudulent subjectivity.

What is the effect on the creator of this stupidity on the part of the creature? Does He consent to abandon — as the creature would gladly have Him do — His essential spiritual primacy in all the realm of the created consciousness? Does He consent to forego, at His creature's bidding, His indefeasible spiritual supremacy over the creature?

By no means. On the contrary, He enhances His spiritual hold upon the creature indefinitely, by frankly acquiescing in the banishment which the latter assiduously imposes on Him, and obediently masking or concealing Himself henceforth in the lineaments of the created *nature.* For the creature as finite or conscious subject can have no proper object but his unconscious nature. And if the creator consents to identify Himself with this object, sinking all His spiritual activity in the endeavor to develop it, His spiritual hold upon the creature will only be indefinitely promoted in place of being abated.

Let me make this point very clear to your understanding, and thus do you the greatest philosophic service which one man may do another. In fact we are now arrived at the actual turning-point of dark to bright in the entire field of philosophic truth, and no cloud, if it be not a very passing one, will be able henceforward to obscure our good understanding.

What I have said, then, I now repeat: 1. That the creator in submitting to the misappropriation of His creative being or substance by the creature to his own shallow self, is necessarily — in condescension to His creature's infirm understanding — forced out of an exclusively spiritual or subjective relation to the creature, and obliged to occupy a purely natural or objective and personal relation to him : and 2. That this purely adventitious or limitary manhood into which the creator finds Himself constrained by zeal for the creature's welfare, constitutes His own eternal spiritual glory, inasmuch as it affords Him his only opportunity to come in contact with the sphere of evil in the creature (that is, the sphere of *selfhood*), and hence endows Him with all His ability to deliver the latter from its mortal coil and defilement.

And now before proceeding to give you the *rationale* of this transcendent deliverance, allow me first to state precisely what is meant by the created *nature*, in contradistinction to the *persons* of that nature.

By the abstract nature of a thing, then, we mean the relation of community existing between that thing and all other things embraced in its nature, in spite of their specific differences. So by the created nature I mean the relations of community — that is, of common unity — necessarily existing between each and all creatures. Every creature claims to be *in himself* absolutely other than, or alien to, every other creature. Consequently, the *nature* of the creature imports, that in spite of these alleged personal, subjective, or absolute differences on the part of the creature, they have all a common unity : and is in fact itself the expression and affirmation of such unity. Now, obviously, as all creatures claim to be in themselves, or subjectively, alien to every other, hence without personal unity with each other, this reciprocal natural unity which they exhibit cannot possibly inhere in themselves, and so avouch itself a subjective or substantial unity, but must refer itself altogether to some foreign source, and so confess itself at best a purely formal or objective unity. Let us always remember therefore that the nature of the creature is obligatory upon him, and supremely obligatory. It does not express him,

but he expresses it.   It does not derive from him, but
he derives from it.   He says for himself : "individuality or difference *à outrance*."   It says : "individuality
or difference, to your heart's content indeed, as a finality ; but only in virtue of a previous natural community or identity keeping it eternally fresh and sweet."
In short he is subject to his nature, and his nature is
object or law to him.   One cannot be subject to anything, without the thing being his master, without its
turning out his sole object or supreme law ; nor consequently without his turning out its involuntary servant; that is, its slave.   For in all natural or related
existence it is the object which determines and controls the subject, and not, as the idealists foolishly
hold, the subject which gives law to the object.   It
is indeed the object which altogether *constitutes* the
subject, which makes it self-conscious, or seem to
itself to be ; and never the latter which does this for
the former : for the natural object is always unconscious, or undefined and without selfhood, towards
the natural subject.   To say in one word all that
need be said : it is the object which alone is *mother-
substance* to the subject, or endows it with appreciable
body : so guaranteeing to it a fixed or constant natural identity, whatever surprising enlargements may
subsequently befall its spiritual individuality.

It is plain now, I think, both what we mean when

we speak of the created nature, and what we mean when we speak of the created personality. By the former we express that thing which alone gives spiritual reality or objectivity to the creature, in giving him constitutional or unconscious substance; and we express by the latter that thing which alone stamps the creature with spiritual unreality or phenomenality, in giving him, not constitutional or unconscious substance, but only conscious personal form. I say, to be sure, that thus much is plain, and I would willingly believe it to be so. But I confess I should like to make it much plainer by some fitting illustration derived from our natural experience; which, in showing how invariably and absolutely primary the real or objective element in consciousness is to the phenomenal or subjective element, may also throw some illustrative light upon the great truth of the spiritual creation : the Divine Incarnation.

Take, for example, any familiar fact of knowledge, say a horse. My living knowledge of the horse is direct and absolute, being given in sense. You may, if you like, divide this knowledge, for scientific purposes, into the two constitutional factors which it involves to your logical or reflective understanding, namely : 1. the horse, or object known; 2. the me, or subject knowing. But this scientific practice no-way modifies the living experience in question. It

is obviously a mere logical analysis on your part of
that living experience, by which you attempt reflectively or scientifically to resuscitate the body of
knowledge after its soul has fled. Knowledge—and
by knowledge, mind you, I mean knowledge *in its
true sense*, as altogether actual or living; as it is involved, indeed, in your mental constitution, and so
becomes the basis of your subsequent spiritual or
intellectual manhood; and not any mere beggarly science, or learning, which is not living knowledge at
all, but merely remembered or reflected knowledge,
such as the people by a fine instinct stigmatize under
the name of *book*-knowledge — knowledge, I say, is
within its own precinct the living marriage of object
and subject; and therefore, like all true marriage,
annuls the possibility of their subsequent divorce.
In livingly knowing the horse, for instance, I am
wholly unconscious of, and indifferent to, any logical
relation of object and subject subsisting between us.
The only thing that survives of this merely logical
and pedantic relation to my feeling, *is the horse, or
object known;* while I, the knowing subject, am incontinently licked up and disappear in his overpowering sensible reality. Life or consciousness, in other
words, knows nothing of the relation, which is so
vital to mere science or learning, of subject and
object in existence as given in sense; but indissolu-

bly blends, fuses, or marries them in its own miraculous individuality.

Thus life or consciousness — living knowledge or perception — defies analysis, or laughs it to scorn out of its own glorified personality. And its dissection consequently into object and subject is possible only when it has become a *caput mortuum* in your memory, or mental stomach, and been there reduced to pulp by the gastric juice of your ruminant or logical understanding. When you resolve any living experience into these purely logical constitutional factors, the result is very good logic no doubt, but is no longer life or experience. Just as when you chemically resolve water into oxygen and hydrogen, the issue of your analysis is very good chemistry, but it is no longer water. Oxygen and hydrogen combined in definite proportions constitute the chemistry of water, or give it visible body. But they are a very long way indeed from constituting its characteristic activity, or giving it soul. Water claims both a physical co-existence or identity with all other things ; and a spiritual power or individuality of its own, which differentiates it from all other things, and which all the untamed gases of the universe are unable either to supply or to explain. Oxygen and hydrogen perfectly account for the physical constitution, or statical repose, of water. But they have no shadow of a pretension to account for its dynamic functioning, or the spiritual and life-giving power it specifically exerts over other existence.

So object and subject no doubt constitute a very good logical analysis of any deceased fact of knowledge; but they are heaven-wide of any pretension to constitute the least vital experience itself so-called. Knowledge is direct or miraculous, being given in sense or gratuitously; while logic, or science, or learning is indirect or reflective, being elaborately generated by our reasonings upon the data of sense. You may talk logic and chemistry, consequently, "till all is blue," as the old people say : you are never in so doing talking towards life, but always steadfastly away from it. Philosophy laughs at your logic and your chemistry both alike, as inevitably predestined to come limping along a day after the fair, and spectrally revel upon the stale victuals and drink which have survived the joyous banquet of life. Science is never life. It is at most the moon-lit shadow of life projected upon our logical or reflective understanding; and the method of the one is no less disproportionate to that of the other than earth is disproportionate to heaven. That is to say : in all living or conscious experience the logical or scientific distinction of object and subject is utterly unknown, *both the alleged factors being actually and indistinguishably one*, and having no distinction but to your ruminant or reflective thought. Their unity, moreover, is not a simplistic but a strictly composite one, being fashioned in no foolish legal or voluntary way, but in a rigidly free or spontaneous manner.   In short, the unity they realize is the hierarchical unity of marriage, in which the masculine or objective element is primary, commanding, active; the feminine or subjective element secondary, subordinate, passive.   For example : in the living experience just supposed — called *knowledge* — the subject is vivified exclusively by the object of knowledge : I myself having absolutely no power to know the horse but what is furnished me by the living animal himself.   Of course I might learn a good deal about the horse from books, from pictures, from hearsay ; but no amount of such learning could ever pretend to be convertible with an actual knowledge of the animal. Nothing is more common than for a very learned man to be a very unknowing one; except, perhaps, than for a very knowing man to be a very unlearned one.   If, indeed, learning should ever supersede knowledge or claim identity with it, the world would be in its dotage, and would wag infinitely worse I am persuaded than it has ever done hitherto.   Learning or science is a capital handmaid of knowledge so long as she reveres her mistress, or does n't grow conceited of her own glittering livery.   In that event it is sure to be soon superseded by a more modest article.

But to return to my subject. Horses might exist in any number and in great comfort all unknown to me. But in that case, of course, my existence as knowing subject would be so far curtailed. My existence *as a knowing subject* does not the least date from any so-called faculty of knowledge I am supposed to possess — for, in point of fact, I know absolutely nothing by virtue of such alleged faculty — but exclusively from the objects my senses embrace : so that *I can legitimately be held to know* only in so far as *objects exist to make me know.* Take away, consequently, the object of knowledge (or thing known) as our logicians do when they resolve it into the sensations of the subject (or person knowing), and you *à fortiori* take away the subject : for the subject in existence is logically constituted only by the object for which and to which and by which he lives.

This illustration drawn from our natural knowledge will show you what Nature thinks of the attempt to give the primacy of the object to the subject in any of her processes. For Nature manifestly stamps the objective element in all natural functioning the only real element, and the subjective element altogether unreal or fallacious and misleading independently of that.

But the specific use I wish to make of this illustration is to shed light upon the fundamental method of creation, or the Divine Incarnation in human nature. Accordingly let us now attempt to show that what we have found to be the rule of our natural knowledge is really the rule also of our natural life.

In the first place, then, remember, most distinctly, the topic we are discussing — *human nature :* that is to say, the nature, not of minerals, nor of vegetables, nor of animals, but of men. No doubt the nature of these lower existences, if they have any nature, is included in that of man,* but their nature is anything but human nature. Human nature is a strict sublimation or evolution from all lower physical forms, by virtue of man containing an essential Divine or infinite element, which they do not contain. But then it would be very illogical to argue that because a certain thing was evolved from another thing, it was therefore at all identical with that thing. Its evolu-

---

* By the " nature " of these existences one can only mean their specific possibilities ; inasmuch as the nature of things, strictly speaking, expresses their universal and unitary form, and mineral, vegetable, and animal existences expressly deny and reject the imputation of such a form. They cannot be classed as natural existences, accordingly, save in so far as they are comprehended in human nature, of which they are so many discordant and conflicting types revealed to sense, and furnishing therefore an inestimably precious basis to man's natural knowledge, and through that to his spiritual experience.

tion from it only proves it to have been — not identical with it, but distinctly and totally different from it; as different in fact as heaven is from earth.

And then having thus in the first place remembered that our sole subject is human nature, do me the favor in the second place to bear in mind what I have said about human nature being altogether objectively constituted, or obeying a certain spiritual end. Men commonly hold to .their nature being altogether subjectively constituted : that is, constituted by its proper subjects. In other words, they deny that their nature is vitalized by any spiritual Divine end, and hold that it is a term designed merely to express the total contents of men's actual subjectivities. So that if I were to put the question to a thousand men chosen at random : What does human nature mean ? I doubt not that nine hundred and ninety-nine of them would reply : It means the outcome and aggregate of all men's private personalities, of every man's subjective or limitary experience. But this answer would be wholly unintelligent, for it would allow no discrimination between our undefined nature and our finite personalities. Men's personalities on the one hand are all that they have within them of most finite and particular ; while their nature on the other hand is all that there is within them of most indefinite and universal. There is to be sure any amount of particulars

included in a universal; but no amount of such particulars, were the amount great enough to comprise all
the particulars beneath the sky, would ever avail by
themselves to constitute a universal. For universals
and particulars make two distinctly different *genera*
or kinds, and hence in themselves, or essentially, are
as reciprocally conflicting and inconvertible as truth
and fact, wisdom and knowledge, love and self-
love, heaven and earth, are in themselves. That
is to say: the logical difference between a universal
and its particulars is not a quantitative difference, but
exclusively a qualitative one, being the exact difference of substance and form.* We men undoubtedly
furnish the finite perishable stuff of human nature, or
the material substance which the indwelling Divine
life in us moulds into immortal spiritual form, just as
the marble furnishes the perishable material substance
of the statue. But we have quite as little share in
giving our nature form, as the marble has in giving
ideal form to the statue.

No, the form of our nature, or its distinctive qual-

---

* "Spiritual thought," says Swedenborg (*de Divinâ Sapientia*, No. 5,
in the 6th volume of *Apocalypsis Explicata*), "is altogether unlike
natural thought, so much unlike that spiritual ideas transcend natural
ideas, and cannot be made to coalesce with them save in the way of an
interior rational perception: *this rational perception taking place no
otherwise than by abstracting or removing quantities from qualities.*"

ity — apart from which it has no cognizable existence,
being sunk in the abject slime of our disunited or warring personalities — is wholly derived from its objective element, or the uses it subserves to the evolution
in us of a Divine-natural manhood.   The technical
" church," ending in the life, death, and resurrection
of Jesus Christ, has been throughout history a witness
of this coming glorification of our nature.   But the
church has always misconceived its own mission.   It
has always conceived its mission to lie — not simply
in bearing witness to the miraculous facts of Christ's
career — but much more, in converting these miraculous facts into so many spiritual truths which men are
bound to receive solely upon its own dogmatic authority.   There could not be in the nature of things a
more unfounded and undivine pretension than this.
Men gratefully receive and confide in the church's
testimony in regard to all the literal Christian facts,
whether ordinary or miraculous, but especially the
miraculous ones — because, as I have said before,
miracle is the only evidence and sanction of a Divine
revelation which a carnal or sensuous mind is capable
of receiving.   But when the church assumes now as
of old to be the authorized interpreter of these facts
to the intellect of men, and to impose her authority
upon them as final, she cannot fail to provoke a revolt
whose only issue must be the acknowledgment of her

utter spiritual triviality and imbecility. The Christian facts are of inestimable value to the intellect in furnishing a fixed immovable basis to thought in reference to Divine things, and hence a guide to speculation in reference to the developments of human destiny; and all modest and reasonable minds, as I conceive, will be prompt to bless the church accordingly for the signally pointed and consistent testimony she has always borne to these facts amidst the darkness, indifference, and conflict of men's opinions. But I must say that no independent mind cares a jot for the church's traditional judgment of the Divine and human meaning (that is, the strictly intellectual meaning) which has always been latent in the facts, and so marvellously adapts them to our nascent spiritual intelligence. In fact one would be inclined to rate the judgment of any honest living mind in all that line of inquiry, as of vastly superior worth.

Every one will admit that the church, in thus attesting the integrity of the Christian facts, has played a vitally important part in the education of the human mind; but I maintain, moreover, that this attesting function of the church has furnished her only true claim to men's respect, a claim infinitely transcending that based upon her usurped dogmatic authority. There is no function in life half so honorable or venerable to the heart of man as that of a nursing mother; and this is the exact relation which the church was meant to stand in towards the mind. She had nothing to do but administer the pure milk of the Gospel to her offspring, leaving its spiritual assimilation by them, and its subsequent conversion into good solid intellectual flesh and bone, to the exquisite providence which watched with like assiduity over it and them. When I was a tender babe on my mother's knee, feeling as yet no personal consciousness beyond the cravings of my insatiate little stomach, it would have been an egregious outrage to my intellectual innocence to have put upon me also the providence and preparation of my needful food. Now the intellect, in its infancy, is nothing else than a mental stomach, or ravenous memory, which craves nothing but a fixed motherly lap of knowledge to cradle and nourish its nascent powers, until such time as it is fit to enter for itself upon the administration of its spiritual heritage. How sheerly preposterous, therefore, would it be to expect it — as our twittering "free-religionists" do — to sit in judgment upon the food of succulent knowledge thus presented to it, and critically determine whether it be true or false, fit or unfit, before its small high mightiness deigns to receive it! With precisely equal propriety you might expect the child to sit in judgment on its mother's milk, and decide before receiving it whether it be the distillation of a chaste or an unchaste bosom. What a prodigy of nastiness would you make of the innocent child at his maturity, in the one case! And what an essentially petty and pedantic rôle must you suppose the intellect destined to fulfil at *its* maturity, in the other!

I confess for my part that I should as soon think of spitting upon my mother's grave, or offering any other offence to her stainless memory, as of questioning any of the Gospel facts. And this, not because I regard them as literally or absolutely true — for the whole realm of fact is as far beneath that of truth, as earth is beneath heaven — but simply because they furnish the indispensable WORD, or master-key, to our interpretation of God's majestic revelation of Himself in human nature. When accordingly I am asked whether I believe in the literal facts of Christ's birth from a virgin, his resurrection from death, his ascension into heaven, and so forth, I feel constrained to reply: That I neither believe in them nor disbelieve, because the sphere of fact is the sphere of men's knowledge, exclusively, and therefore invites neither belief nor disbelief; but that I have a most profound, even a heartfelt, conviction of the truth which they, and they alone, reveal, namely, *the truth of God's essentially human perfection, and,* as implied in that, *the amazing truth of His natural or adventitious man-*

hood : which conviction keeps me blessedly indifferent to, and utterly unvexed by, the cheap and frivolous scepticism with which so many of our learned modern pundits assail them. I have not the least reverence nor even respect for the facts in question, save as basing or ultimating this grand creative or spiritual truth ; and while the truth stands to my apprehension, I shall be serenely obdurate to the learned reasonings of any of my contemporaries in regard to the facts, whether *pro* or *con.* I know, to be sure, all that the sceptics know about them, that is, that they have come down to us from apparently honest and intelligent men, who themselves knew, or thought they knew, them to have occurred as they are reported to us. But, unlike the sceptics, I am content and more than content to receive the facts upon the testimony of these simple men, because they appeal so strongly to my heart, or seem to be the homely and harmless anchorage or ultimate of most vital and otherwise unattainable Divine knowledge. If Christ and his apostles had professed the desire and intention to convey mere stupid scientific knowledge to men : that is, *the knowledge that precedes regeneration, and is wholly independent of it :* the great mass of mankind would have remained forever deaf to their teaching, for there is happily no Divine thirst in men after scientific information ; and I for one would cheer-

fully leave them in that case to the tender mercies
of any ambitious scavenger who might enhance his
own reputation with unintelligent people by throwing
scientific mud at them. But as they did n't at all
profess this commonplace ambition, — as their sole
desire was to commend to men a new and living revelation of God, based upon a spiritual creation of man,
i. e. upon affections and thoughts in men deeper than
those which they inherit from their past ancestry,
or derive from the little world of consciousness and
convention about them, I see no reason why we should
not regard the malignant criticism they receive at the
hands of our popular scientific scribes, as a virtual
confession on the part of these latter that they know
nothing of, and are signally incompetent to, the merits
of the question they have undertaken to discuss.

But, in addition to all this, I have no hesitation
in avowing that I for my part am thoroughly sick
and tired of regulating my intellectual life on any
principle of scientific certitude, because this in the
long run is to make sense the arbiter of the mind.
No doubt man is by creation *both* internal and external, and his voluntary or rational mind, which
intervenes between the two discordant spheres and
enables him eventually to harmonize their interests,
may doubtless determine itself towards either interest
in preference to the other. But I am persuaded

that if it determine itself towards science or the
senses, the result to one's spiritual understanding
cannot help being disastrous in the extreme. I am
sure at all events that it would be to the last degree
disastrous in my own case. For science takes no
cognizance but of finite existence. To what exists
infinitely or in itself, and is therefore undiscerned
and unauthenticated by the senses, she is as blind
and deaf as the stone. And consequently if I
should allow my intellectual life to be ruled by
science, I should cease to have any intellectual life
left. For one's intellect is the child of a double
parentage, the offspring of a marriage-union between
goodness and truth. But goodness is essentially
invisible and incognizable to sense, being infinite,
and therefore altogether livingly or spiritually discerned. The only good that the senses recognize
is a finite good, a good limited by evil. And even
truth is never discerned by the senses in direct or
positive, but always in indirect or inverse form.
My intellect accordingly, if it should succumb to
the limitations of science, or deliberately submit
itself to the arbitrament of sense, would virtually
renounce the whole of its characteristic life, which
lies in a heartfelt surrender to infinite goodness and
truth, and is compatible with no other or lesser
instinct. In fact, I should be incapable in that case

of believing in truth at all save under the guise
of a probability. For scientific certainty is never a
certainty of what is infinitely true, i. e. *true in itself*, but only of what is true to our intelligence,
i. e. of what is merely phenomenally true, or probable, and may therefore be denied even all probability to-morrow. What an intolerable bondage
this would be to the intellect, to have the heart's
capacity of belief limited by the grovelling senses!
It would be the blighting of human nature at its
very root, or its reduction to less even than bestial
freedom and innocence! Such, moreover, I am persuaded is the practical attitude at this day of all
genuine men of science. They are none of them
livingly ruled by science, or submit the life of their
intellect to its unwise and impertinent stewardship.
They all — unless they are men of unworthy lives
to begin with, which is a supposition not to be
thought of in reference to any sincere devotee of
science — firmly believe in a good whose existence
science is totally impotent on her own principles
either to affirm or deny, and they none of them
believe even in a truth which the senses by themselves are competent to confirm, or which they do
not become qualified to confirm solely by having
undergone the previous discipline and correction of
the intellect.

The long and the short of the whole matter is that what men call true in science, is not the truth they intellectually or spiritually apprehend. The two orders of truth differ fundamentally, one being based in sensible experience, the experience common to the race, and not worth a jot but as involving it; the other originating in inward perception, and claiming therefore a rigidly individual ground or basis. Thus the law of universal gravitation — the law which imports that all the bodies of the universe attract each other with a force directly proportioned to the mass of matter they contain, and inversely proportioned to the squares of their distances — is a scientific truth, that is, one whose existence depends upon its strict universality, or its involving all things in its grasp whether they know it or not. And the truth of the Divine being and existence — the truth which imports that all men are derivative or created existences, and enjoy therefore a strictly fallacious life *in themselves* — is an intellectual or spiritual truth, but it is a truth which falls wholly within consciousness. That is to say, this truth unlike the other is never the interpretation of men's common or outward experience, but is a result exclusively of their inward culture or refining. No man believes it in virtue of any force of intellect he possesses, still less in virtue of

any degree of natural goodness or gentleness he is
born to. Every man, who believes it at all, — that
is, who believes it not as a mere hereditary tradition,
but with his spirit or life, — believes it as the effect
of a decided inward discipline, or genuine individual
culture, awakening a heart-craving for it, i. e. telling
him that it is supremely *good* to believe it, that for
him indeed eternal death and damnation lie in his
not believing it; and in comparison therefore with this
most excellent knowledge, the science or learning of
all worlds is as the small dust of the balance in his
sight. In other words : every one who believes it
does so with the heart first, and the intellect afterwards : that is, believes it primarily as *good*, and not
as *truth*. This, and this alone, is why I believe any
Divine truth : because my heart fiercely hungers after
it, and stamps every thing false and foul that con-
flicts — or even comes into passing rivalry — with it.
What does it matter to me that some cold-blooded
prig or pedant is able to demonstrate the scientific
untruth of my belief? Have I ever pretended that
it had any scientific basis or justification? Do I not
know in all my bones that the tendency of science,
and the whole current of men's servile opinion, run
directly counter to it? Do you think that I love
it any the less on that account? Do you think
that my fierce relish for it is not all the while

quickened and fomented by this popular and scientific indifference to it? Or that the gainsaying of it by all the world, vulgar and polite, would have any other effect upon me than driving me joyfully to die for it? And I should like to know what man ever went to death for a scientific truth. Galileo, I believe, declined to do so, and for the very good reason no doubt that he did not feel his highest life involved in any truth of science. Otherwise he could have hardly rejected the auspicious opportunity offered him by the church of his day, to assert and signally illustrate that life. "Scientific untruth of my belief," indeed! Words are not able to express my joy that men's belief has no scientific basis, that is, no basis in their sensible experience, because then my heart and mind would depend for their beggarly life upon the heart and mind of other men, and I should have no direct inspiration from Him who now fills me with these fragrant tides of love and joy and worship.

We may say in fact, that nowhere in Christendom, outside the professing Christian church, do we find the human mind backward to admit that its allegiance is due primarily to good, and only derivatively to truth. The revelation in Jesus Christ of God's incarnate perfection may be called the definite inauguration of the heart's sole authority thenceforth in the sphere of belief. His manifestation in Christ as a natural man, even in ultimates or personal form, that is, down to the assumption of flesh and bones, and His consequent exaltation of human nature itself out of limitary into universal dimensions, so making it thenceforth the only true measure of infinitude, appeals for sanction to the heart's deepest instincts of Divine good, and disclaims the superficial homage of the intellect, save in so far as the intellect itself is shaped and enlarged by the experience of the heart. For the heart is what alone universalizes man to the dimensions of his kind, and unites him with it, while the intellect, fed by sense, restricts him to the most meagre personal form, or divides him from it. The heart alone consequently is capable of acknowledging a Divine or universal truth, and the intellect derives all its capacity of similar acknowledgment from it. Now unquestionably human nature embraces all that man is capable of recognizing as Divine good; and Jesus Christ accordingly in revealing to the faith of his disciples the Divine and human unity, that is, the truth of God's intimate and perfect NATURAL humanity, has forever exalted good to the sovereignty of human affection, and relegated truth to a comparatively inferior or subordinate place. Every man of intellect and conscience feels, accordingly, by an indomitable Divine

instinct of the truth, that his own particular nature
is not human nature, but rather a caricature of it;
feels that it is shockingly inhuman in fact, because
its universal element, or what relates him to the
neighbor, is so inactive or poorly developed compared with its personal or individual element, which
relates him to self.   Every man, in other words, of
spiritual or living culture throughout history has
felt his particular nature to be unmixed evil, has
felt in very truth *that he himself was no man*, and
has always appealed to God consequently with tears
of penitence and humiliation, as his only hope and
succor against himself.   Thus Jesus Christ in identifying man's religious aspiration with the redemption
and salvation of human nature from the evils incident to every man's particular nature, and its consequent eternal union with the Divine infinitude,
has exalted religion itself out of a wretched ritual
or ceremonial worship, into the diligent handmaiden
and minister of every man's unadulterate natural
good.

LETTER XXII.

MY DEAR FRIEND:—I have been digressing sadly, and must forthwith return to my thesis. I was saying, when my pen took another direction, that the form of human nature, or its distinctive quality, apart from which it has no real existence, is derived wholly from its objective element, or the uses it subserves to the evolution in the earth of a Divine-natural manhood. And I have certainly no desire to divert your attention from this statement, since all our intellectual accord depends upon your doing full and frank justice to it. For the uses referred to constitute the sole actual presence of God in our nature, being all spiritually fulfilled in the nature coming to form, or, what is the same thing, in the advent of a perfect society, fellowship, or equality of all men with each and of each man with all men, on earth or in heaven. The technical Christian church in simply bearing witness to the gospel facts, has unconsciously but un-

falteringly ministered to these providential uses in
nurturing and giving birth to the Christian state,
which is the initial objective or actual form under
which God's spiritual incarnation in our nature becomes realized.   The rudiment of the State under all
its forms, even the most expanded, is the marriage
institution, engendering the family unity.   For out of
this small unit of the family grows successively the
larger unities of the tribe, or unity of many fami-
lies; of the city, or unity of many tribes; of the
nation, or unity of many cities; and finally of the
republic, or unity of many nations.   These successive
political structures have been only the material scaffolding by means of which God's spiritual edifice in
human nature has gradually worked itself out to
men's recognition; and accordingly, now that the full
daylight of Divine truth is upon us, they only spiritually obscure what they once obediently promoted.
For their pretension is (and in this pretension they
are diligently backed by a mercenary and menda-
cious church) that they do not constitute the mere
provisional scaffolding of God's great edifice in human nature, but the very edifice itself; and they
consequently influence men's minds to every downward base issue, instead of inflaming them to noble
upright endeavors and aspirations.   But, as I have
said, all these political structures attain to their

climax and culmination in the republic, whence
their decline becomes swift and eternal. The reason why the republic is necessarily the final form
of God's institutional or educative providence in
human affairs, is because the republic makes it impossible to realize any larger *literal* order among
men, any more expansive form of merely instituted
or enforced fellowship among them, and so inevitably gives way itself at last to a free spontaneous
society, or a spiritual unforced fellowship of each
and all men, as the supreme development of human
destiny, because such a destiny alone befits man's
human or God-given nature.   And the reason why
the republic makes it impossible to conceive of any
larger literal form of Divine administration on earth,
is that the republic is the government of the people
by chosen representatives of the people, without reference to smaller political or customary divisions.
And surely nothing larger in the way of literal administrative rule can be imagined than a government
whose only sanction is the will of the whole people.

Thus the republic inaugurates a change from a
literal or seeming order to a spiritual or real one in
the Divine administration of human life.   Now what
is the exact distinction here announced?   What is
the exact difference between spirit and letter, between
reality and appearance, between a universal and a

partial order? And what is the necessary ground
of such distinction in the Divine economy? Why
does the Divine housekeeping in our nature admit,
nay prescribe and exact this immense difference in
things? If we come to a good understanding on
this point, we shall be likely to disagree on no other.

The difference in question, then, is the exact difference between a regimen of *good* enforced by the
heart, and one of *truth* enforced by the intellect.
That is to say: it is the difference between inward,
free, spontaneous action on the one hand, and outward, voluntary, prudential, or deliberate action on
the other. If indeed your ear were broken in to
a logical distinction which Swedenborg's necessities
constantly compel him to make, I could more briefly
define the difference by saying that literal order is
motived by a sentiment of *duty* in its subject, and
spiritual order by a sentiment of *delight*. Thus the
exact difference involved is that between our moral
and our æsthetic culture: between the life of obedience to truth in his intellect which a man lives in
preparation for his regeneration, and which is always
a life of more or less painful *death to himself*, and
that which he lives from the inspiration of good in
his heart, *after his regeneration is complete*. Swedenborg found the regeneration of the angels very
incomplete, apparently because the doctrine of the

Lord, that is, of the Divine assumption and glorification of human nature, had so little spiritual recognition among them.   Their regeneration was the fruit of
moral culture, or obedience to law, involving of course
more or less self-denial; whereas the fundamental
idea of Christianity is the redemption of man's nature
to God, or the making him *spontaneously* regenerate,
regenerate *through natural taste or attraction.*   Swedenborg represents the angels, accordingly, as indebted exclusively to the restraining influences of the
Divine power, that they do not rush headlong into
infernal evil.   For in regeneration the evil is never
separated from man, but is only rendered innocuous
or quiescent, so as actually to *appear* annihilated,
when really it is not at all so.   Such is the state of
the angels.   So far as their own knowledge goes,
they do not know but that they are separated from
evil, but in truth they are only providentially restrained from it, which makes their evil quiescent
and apparently annihilates it.   *But this separation is
only an appearance,* which the angels themselves discover upon reflection.*   In short it is Swedenborg's
uniform testimony that the selfhood in angels no less
than in men is altogether false and evil.†   Doubt on
this point, he says, disqualifies a man for heavenly society.   Indeed I might cite any number of passages

---

* *Arcana Cælestia*, 1581.   † *Ibid.*, 633.   See also 681.

from his books in which he profoundly affronts our most inveterate ecclesiastical superstitions, by reporting that the angels of themselves or of their own nature bear a very sinister relation to goodness and truth, just as sinister a one as any of the infernals.

I think this a very serious indictment of the angelic personality, as that personality is ordinarily conceived by us, and well worthy of men's philosophic scrutiny. "There is with man no understanding of truth, nor any will of goodness: but when he becomes a denizen of heaven, *it appears as if he possesses these things*, when nevertheless he knows, acknowledges, and perceives that they are of the Lord alone." These possessions are in fact the positive presence of God in him, constituting all he shall ever really know of God. Never was a doctrine propounded by living man, more revolting to flesh and blood than this. And yet the wise old man was so devoted to it, heart and mind, and brings such an amazing amount of striking experience, observation, and angelic testimony to corroborate it, that it cannot fail some day to attract the attention of philosophic minds. The so-called "Swedenborgians" may be left out of our account altogether: for these preposterous people are so bent upon adding another to the Christian sects by devoutly *playing* " New Church " and " New Jerusalem " every Sun-

day to complacent handfuls of men and women, and
so trying to impose upon the world the fiction that
Swedenborg himself is an accomplice of the stupidity, that they actually do nothing but disgust all
right-minded men with his books.   But how many
fairly honest and competent minds nowadays, think
you, minds freed from sectarian sottishness, and
hating the influence of the sects upon the world as
they hate the jaws of hell, have recourse to these
modest volumes to find a clew out of our gathering
political and social perplexities?   Their number
might almost be counted on the fingers.   Yet I am
fully persuaded that such men will find intellectual
relief nowhere else; and nowhere in Swedenborg
half so readily as in thoroughly mastering the truth
that we are now canvassing, namely: the truth of
man's (and hence the angel's) limited freedom or
selfhood.

I said however just now that no truth could be
more revolting to our "flesh and blood" personality,
or the pride of individuality in us, than this.   Clearly
this effect is owing to the immense natural illusion
we are under in respect to our flesh-and-blood personality.   For a very long while this personality
constitutes literally all we know of life.   The whole
realm of sense is its appanage either as ministering
to our material support, or as serving our varied fac-

ulties of intelligence.   In our ignorance and inex-
perience of any higher or truer life, what wonder is
it then that we should deem ourselves the best result of God's creative power, and look upon life as
absolutely our own?   And yet the whole persuasion
is a downright fallacy.   There is absolutely no such
thing in nature as a finite selfhood or an independent personality.   The conception of such an existence belongs wholly to our own crazy way of en-
visaging creation, that is, regarding it primarily as a
material or quantitative result, rather than a spiritual
or qualitative one.   We are taught to call God infinite to be sure, but only because we have been first
taught to call ourselves finite.   In reality, however,
we deem God the most finite of beings, the most
essentially absolute or independent of beings.   This
is our own ideal of human perfection, or the mode
of existence we most aspire to for ourselves; and it
is not marvellous therefore that we attribute the
full enjoyment of it to God our creator.   Endowing
the creature as we do in imagination with his own
inward life or being, we necessarily relegate God to
an exclusively outward position towards him, and
thus are compelled to finite the creator by all the
breadth of creation.   In short, notwithstanding our
vague and crude ascriptions of a nominal infinitude
to Him, we really or in thought make Him, as I

have said, the most finite or restricted of beings, and rob Him of His rightful infinitude the better to adorn our factitious selves with it. But I do not hesitate for my own part utterly to scout this materialistic hypothesis of the relation between creator and creature as having no ground in the essential truth of the case.

I do not hesitate, for example, to express my conviction that the distinction between creature and creator is not the least a sensible or objective fact, but a purely rational or subjective truth. It is not at all true that man presents any antagonism with the infinite in his outward or public and universal aspect, that is, as an organic subject, or subject of sense; but only in his inward, private, or particular aspect as an inorganic subject, or subject of consciousness. My physical organization which passively unites me with the universal realm of existence, obviously does not disunite me with the creator, since in that case I should cease to live, because I am essentially a created existence; but only my metaphysical or inorganic consciousness by which I am actively isolated or differentiated from all other men. If my divorce from God were real or objective as well as conscious or subjective — if it were a fact of physics as well as a truth of metaphysics — then it would be impossible for me to enjoy a vital sensation; for I have not the presumption to suppose that I myself constitute my sensitive life: that is, that I myself contribute a particle of force to my seeing or hearing or smelling or tasting or touching faculty. I am in truth as passive in all the range of my sensuous experience as the child is in parturition. That is to say, I see, hear, smell, taste, touch, not by virtue of the slightest conceivable exertion of personal power on my part, but by virtue of a marvellous inherited organization which fuses in itself the two conflicting realms of a wide universality and a narrow particularity, and thereby renders me a conscious person. It would not be a whit less silly accordingly in me to take credit to myself for my physical endowments, than it would be in a child to take credit to itself for its own generation. In short my finite or imperfect personality is itself a sheer outbirth and dependency of an organization which combines and expresses in itself the grossest universality and the subtlest individuality; and I consequently realize my personality as finite or imperfect, only because I am persistently blind to the grandeur of that organization as a universal symbol, or look upon it solely as a private or specific and not as a generic or race possession.

Understand, then, that our *alienation from* or *otherness to* our creator is not the least a demonstrable

fact of science, implying a sensible or real estrangement between us.   On the contrary it is a strict
truth of consciousness — a fruit of our purely metaphysical or subjective illusion — implying on our
part doubtless a certain phenomenal projection from
the creator whereby we become *self*-constituted, become *personally* conscious, but arguing no particle
of essential antagonism, or absolute remoteness between us.   In other words our felt finiteness is no
way a law of our spiritual creation, or of the infinite
and eternal being we possess in God, but only and
at most an incident of our natural constitution, or
of the limited and transient existence we possess in
rigid community with all other men.   Thus, all I
mean to say is that the finiting principle in human
life, the evil principle, is invariably that of selfhood
or private personality; while the infiniting principle,
the good principle consequently, is invariably that of
society, or the broadest possible fellowship, equality,
brotherhood, of man and man.   And creation will
never be spiritually or philosophically appreciable to
us until we take to heart this discrimination.

As well as I can remember, in fact, the spring of
all my intellectual activity in the past was to know
for certain whether our felt finiteness was a necessity
of our spiritual creation, or simply an incident of our
natural constitution : whether, for example, it was to

be interpreted as having been arbitrarily imposed upon us by the Divine will, or as inherent merely in the sentiment we so inordinately cherish of personal independence. For in the former case my hope in God necessarily dies out by the practical decease of His infinitude, while in the latter case it is not only left unimpaired but is revived and invigorated. If my felt finiteness be a necessity of my creatureship, that is to say, if the creative perfection necessitate the creature's imperfection in any real and not a simply logical sense; then clearly the creative perfection is only nominal, not real, is only a comparative, not a positive, perfection : and a creator whose perfection is of this finite sort only, may be worthy indeed of a certain respect as addressing my fear, but is so far from attracting my adoring hope and love as to be much more likely to provoke my energetic distrust and aversion. But if on the other hand my felt finiteness be a mere suggestion or affirmation of the natural mind in me, evidencing only the dense ignorance every man is specifically under with respect to the true spirituality of his nature, or its latent divinity, then of course the sentiment I cherish of the creative greatness will become so much the more aggrandized and expansive as I perceive His immortal bounty toward us to suspend itself not upon any foolish and violent castration, so to speak, of our vain and flippant and conceited intelligence, but rather upon such an unlimited impregnation of its ignorance and falsity by His own wholesome and healing truth as cannot fail in the end to make us naturally wise with His infinite and eternal wisdom.

Here, in fact, was the veritable secret source of all my intellectual unrest. During all my early intellectual existence I was haunted by so keen a sense of God's *natural* incongruity with me — of his *natural* and therefore invincible alienation, otherness, externality, distance, remoteness to me — as to breed in my bosom oftentimes a wholly unspeakable heartsickness or homesickness. The sentiment to be sure masked its ineffable malignity from my perception under the guise of an alleged *super*natural limitation on God's part; but it none the less filled my soul with the tremor and pallor of death. I have no doubt indeed that if it had not been for my excessive "animal spirits" as we say, or the extreme good-will I felt towards sensuous pleasure of every sort, which alternated my morbid conscientiousness and foiled its corrosive force, I should have turned out a flagrant case of arrested intellectual development. I could have borne very well, mind you, a conviction of God's *personal* antipathy to me carried to any pitch you please; for my person does

not go with my nature as man, and a personal condemnation therefore which should not cut me off
from a natural resurrection, would not deprive me
of hope toward God.   But my conviction of God's
personal alienation had been hopelessly saddled,
through the incompetency of my theologic sponsors,
with the senseless tradition of His inveterate estrangement also from *human nature*.   Thus unhappily although my person did not go with human
nature they made human nature to go with my
person, or managed so perfectly to confound the two
things to my unpractised sense, that whenever I felt
a superficial or intrinsically evanescent pang of mere
personal remorse, it was sure to pass by a quick diabolical chemistry into a sense of the deadliest *natural*
hostility between me and the source of my life.

It is in fact this venomous tradition of a natural
as well as a personal disproportion between man and
his maker — speciously cloaked as it is under the
ascription of a *super*natural being and existence to
God — that alone gives its intolerable odium and
poignancy to men's otherwise healthful and restora-
tive conscience of sin.   That man's personality should
utterly alienate him from God — that is to say, make
him infinitely other and opposite to God — this I
grant you with all my heart, since if God were the
least like me personally all my hope in Him would

perish. Nothing indeed can be more welcome to me than that impartial truth, for all my chances either of present happiness or future blessedness appear to me rigidly conditioned upon it. But that God should be also an infinitely alien *substance* to me — an infinitely other or foreign *nature* — this wounds my spontaneous faith in Him to its core, or leaves it a mere mercenary and servile homage. I perfectly understand how He should disown all private or personal relation to me, because personally I am anything but innocent, being to all the extent of my personal pretension — to all the extent of my distinctively personal interests and ambitions — the impassioned foe and rival of universal man. This is one thing. But it is quite a different and most odious thing that He should feel an envenomed animosity also to my innocent nature, or what binds me in indissoluble unity with every man of woman born. It is blasphemy indeed to conceive or entertain such a thought, for it makes God a wantonly inhuman being, unworthy the homage of every man who reverences his own nature, or is not spiritually a sot. I can only repeat accordingly that our inherited theology must infallibly have ended by suffocating me in my intellectual swaddling-clothes, had not my heart been providentially inspired by the many sensible tokens I enjoyed of God's vital presence

in our nature, even while undergoing the utmost personal mortification and abasement at His hands, to
reject the falsities which a perverse education had
temporarily imposed upon it.

Can you wonder then that with this intellectual
experience on my part, and holding these convictions,
I cleave for very life to the truth of God's *natural*
humanity? I do not say, mind you, the truth of His
spiritual or essential manhood: for, as I have already
said, that is a truth which no unsophisticated mind
that acknowledges the Divine existence at all can
help acknowledging: but of His natural, adventitious,
or acquired manhood, a manhood which is forced
upon Him, so to speak, by that constitutional limitation of the created consciousness to which men give
the name of *proprium* in Latin, of *selfhood, freedom,*
and so forth, in the vernacular. The Divine celestial
and spiritual manhood, according to Swedenborg, is
that which exists in the heavens, and constitutes the
heavens; being the reality of that goodness and truth
in which good spirits and angels are principled, and
of which they are appearances, consequently, and
nothing but appearances. But the natural sphere of
the mind is a universal sphere, embracing the hells as
well as the heavens, and the Divine NATURAL humanity, accordingly, is a far more comprehensive truth
than the Divine spiritual humanity, meeting the needs

of diabolical existences no less than those of angelic, and guaranteeing therefore a permanent order of human life on the earth which all the wit of man has been unable to forecast. The miracle of this order is that being natural it is spontaneous, and will accordingly dispense erelong with that indolent and imbecile array of merely professional or reflected life which constitutes the existing civilized order of the world, and hides the great body of humanity from the enjoyment of the common sun and air.* But you don't want prophecy, you want light. This however is a demand that you can expect me to supply only in very limited form and measure ; but the bare attempt on my part to supply it will, I hope, evince my abundant good-will towards you in the premises.

The creative love, because it is infinite or knows no

---

* It is curious, in fact, how blindly content the most respectable life of the world is to identify itself with "professing" or seeming to do, instead of practice or really doing. The physician does not teach men how to live in harmony with physical laws, but only "professes" to do so. The lawyer does not teach men how to live in harmony with moral laws, but only "professes" to do so. The clergyman does not teach men how to live in harmony with Divine laws, but only "professes" to do so. And yet it is in deference to the interests of this sham professional life of the world, that men are expected to forego their most veridical instincts of a really Divine life latent in men, and indeed practically acknowledge the great God himself a sham rather than question its vulgar but conventional manners and customs.

alloy of self-love, abandons itself without reserve to whatsoever is not itself, to whatsoever is most distinctly other and opposite to itself. We may indeed call this the law of the creative perfection, the necessity of perfect love : to delight in communicating itself, or making itself unstintedly over, to whatsoever is intrinsically worthless or void of substance. *Our* delight, at all events, is not of this disinterested character. Our activity craves remuneration. We delight to find a *plenum* of existence made ready to our hand. We go forth with joy only when we encounter a fulness of life and energy ; because feeling ourselves inwardly poor and needy we covet the most abounding outward satisfactions. But the creative love being infinite or free of all subjective bias, is so essentially exuberant that it cannot help constituting itself a force of boundless subjective life, a force of unitary and universal selfhood, in *others* created from itself. Its essential life or delight is to find void and desolate ground whereinto it may forever inflow and abide ; to find or rather invent in its creature so genuine an otherness to itself, so vivid an opposition or oppugnancy to its own perfection, that it may eternally inflow and indwell in the creature *as in its very self*. In truth and of necessity the creature constitutes the only selfhood known to the creative love ; for the latter being purely infinite or objective, that is, destitute of all subjective aims or quality, it is of course incapable of *realizing* itself save in what is not itself, that is, in its creature. Selfhood then, or felt freedom in the creature, is his natural birthmark, or congenital stigma, without which he would be, not creature, but creator.

Manifestly then creation imposes a certain natural limitation or stigma upon the creature which we call selfhood, and which requires to be Divinely rectified or overcome before the creature can be worthy of his creator. Creation, I say, *imposes* this obligation upon the creature : for what does creation mean ? It means, briefly but fully stated, *the communication of the creator's being or substance to the creature*. But now mark : the creator's being or substance is not material, physical, outward, it is exclusively spiritual, metaphysical, inward. That is to say, it is altogether qualitative not quantitative, being identical with the creator Himself, therefore infinite as devoid of space, and eternal as devoid of time. But how in this state of things shall we conceive the creator creating — that is, communicating Himself to — others, unless these others be made to feel themselves first of all void both of spiritual being (or being *in themselves*), and natural existence (that is, existence *in their race*) ; unless in other words both their being and their existence confess themselves purely personal or con-

scious, purely apparitional or phenomenal, as made up
of space and time? The creature in literal truth can
only be *in himself*, both spiritually and naturally, a
purely formal or supposititious existence; and the
whole gist accordingly of the creative travail with
him is to eviscerate him of his pretension to be anything else: that is, his pretension to constitute in
himself his own being or substance.

The creature of course resists the Divine teaching
with all his spiritual *vis inertiæ*. New even to existence, and utterly ignorant therefore of life, he fancies
that he embraces it all in himself, nor ever doubts
that he weaves from out that gossamer consciousness
the stupendous realities of goodness and truth. But
this consciousness of ours — this feeling we have of
our life or being as inherent in ourselves, and as absolutely our own therefore — is in truth and all the
while a bottomless cheat or illusion, unworthy of our
slightest care or affection. And to suppose accordingly that selfhood, however relatively cultivated,
refined, and exalted it may appear to our own eyes,
is the true end of our creation, is the stupidest of
absurdities. It exists in us in fact only as a most
ignorant misappropriation of the creative substance;
only as the fruit of an idiot tale told us by our
senses (known in sacred or symbolic speech as —
the serpent) to the effect, that inasmuch as we are the

subjects of organized or finite knowledge : namely, the knowledge of *good* limited by evil, and of *evil* limited by good : we must be therefore like God, and partakers of His infinitude.   It is in other words a pure misconception and offshoot of our native spiritual stupidity and immodesty ; and the best word we can say of it accordingly is, that it is a mere constitutional implication, and therefore by no means a living explication, of the great mystery of the spiritual creation. For God, the creator, being spiritual or infinite, must be inscrutable to outward, material, or finite apprehension, and can only become known to the creature therefore in so far as He Himself manages spiritually to exist or go forth *in created form*.   Now the created form — in order that it may fitly symbolize or respond to the creative being or substance — must be above all things a unitary form, as expressing the unity of each and all creatures.   But this unity of the created form is not an arbitrary or base outside result mechanically imposed upon the creature by the creator. On the contrary it is the outgrowth exclusively of the creature's nature, which to the creature's own eyes seems to belong only to himself, or possess only one element, that namely of individuality, but apart from his own eyes is seen to belong to *all* men primarily, or to claim the much more important element of universality, and to allow the individual or private element indeed only as included in that. The created form, consequently, as being a development of the creature's nature, is a strictly *regenerate* or *social* form : that is to say, presupposes a most bitter experience on the creature's part of *himself*, and a most toilsome conflict with that self : an experience and conflict through which he is finally led to renounce his cherished personal independence, his diabolic pride of individuality, with all the ungodly lusts bred of it, and to esteem himself henceforth in God's sight and with all his heart as a race only, or Divinely natural and united man. Now remember always, that this regeneration of human nature, this bitter experience and conflict of man with himself, is confined of course to the human bosom, has no existence out of consciousness, or reflects itself in space and time only as space and time are themselves embraced in man's finite consciousness; and that so long as our natural regeneration is in abeyance or immature, the Divine providence is obliged to deal with men's flimsy and fraudulent consciousness, their pretentious private selfhood or personality, as if it were a most vital spiritual reality, and not alone the intense and immeasurable counterfeit of the truth it will one day appear to itself to be.

Thus the creative power, if it would be regarded as real, is bound above all things else to avouch or ulti-

mate itself in the natural form of the creature, a form
which shall be past all dispute the creature's own
form, and not the creator's merely in him, because it
is a form of finite or imperfect knowledge, namely : a
knowledge of good in evil and of evil in good.   For
until the creature thus veritably appears to himself,
he can have no inward certainty that his creator is.
As long as the creature attributes to himself the least
reality inward or outward, spiritual or natural, he
must honestly deny the creative power.   That power
vindicates its existence to the creature past all dispute,
only by avouching itself the all of the created life
both inward and outward, both spiritual and natural:
for so long as the creature is left a particle of life or
being *in himself*, he is honestly bound to atheism.
And what most ideal nonsense it is to think and talk
of the omnipotent God leaving us free to acknowledge or reject Him !   Or imputing to us forlorn luna-
tics of time and space a sufficient degree of reason
wherewith to measure our rightful dependence or
independence upon His unknown perfection !   I can
conceive of some intolerable goose of a man, inflated
past all bounds of sanity by a conceit of his own personal consequence, posing to attract or compel my
homage.   But the great and sincere creator of men,
never !   He is infinitely free from such posturing and
trickery.   He has no finite selfhood or personality of

His own to render Him frivolous and vain, nor any
finite memory consequently of His own to render
Him susceptible to our praises and affronts. He
does not ask us therefore to take His creative name
for granted, and stifle any reasonable doubts we may
feel on the subject in an unintelligent, hypocritical
faith, for He makes our despised and degraded nature
the miraculous mother-substance of all His creative
effects, and the eternal witness accordingly of His
creative name. Thus He is at once our spiritual
being and our natural existence, our individual substance and our universal form : the sentiment of selfhood in us, or our personal consciousness, being only
the dense and unsuspected mask under which He conciliates our instincts of freedom, and gradually accommodates the great truth to our rational recognition.

Do I not well, then, to call selfhood or personality
a stigma or limitation of the created nature instead
of an endowment of it? It infers in the creature
a purely subjective or conscious existence, and this
style of existence is simply lawless, as being without
any sacred tie of nature or race unconsciously to control it. A conscious subject, indeed, without any
real or unconscious object to control him, furnishes
our conception of the devil. And if therefore we persist in referring our selfhood or personality to the
direct hand of God, we affiliate the devil to Him.

That selfhood utterly lacks this real or objective and unconscious worth, seems to me wholly undeniable. For by the hypothesis of creation, which stamps the creator the all of life, there is and can be no absolute *other* than He. He is being or life itself, and whatsoever exists consequently exists only by Him. Evidently then the only otherness we can conceive in the creature to the creator as bottoming his selfhood or felt freedom, must be purely phenomenal, conscious, or subjective, without a grain of absolute truth, without a fibre of outward or objective reality. We cannot help characterizing our felt finiteness accordingly —that is, that conscious otherness or oppugnancy in us to the infinite which we call our *selves*—as essentially unreal: which means purely personal, phenomenal, fallacious. And an existence of this shadowy sort in the creature, except as incidentally involved in some higher creative end, is of course fatal to our acknowledgment of the creative perfection.

But we have not the least right to regard the existence in question as created. Our only obligation to do so would arise from our considering creation to be an absolute work on God's part, to constitute His proper glory in short, and subserve no ulterior spiritual ends. But this would be supremely silly, for although God *creates* He does so only in order to *redeem* or *make*. He is infinitely more than a loving

or passionate creator ; He is a wise and faithful
maker or redeemer as well. It is in fact, as we have
already seen, a mere scientific or rationalistic conception of creation, to regard it as a simplistic process
or one of natural evolution by simple generation. It
is no such thing. Human nature, humanity, is the
fruit not of an orderly *evolution* of the world's force,
but rather of a stupendous historic *revolution* whereby the world's force is converted from a wholly outward relation to man to a wholly inward power in
his own bosom, a power of enlightened affection and
obedient thought. Human nature is the fruit of no
simple or generative but of a profoundly composite
or *re*generative process, implying the creature's final
or natural and objective evolution only by means of a
previous complete spiritual immersion, or subjective
involution, of the creative substance in created person
or form, and its subsequent resurrection or emergence
thence in a new or *Divine-Human* NATURE fit to confer
any amount of objective substance or formal reality
upon the creature. The scientific or rationalistic
view of creation which no doubt served a good purpose in the infancy of the mind strikes one now as
so childish and inane, that one no longer wonders at
the horde of thoughtless and flippant young persons
who give up creation altogether as an impossible conception, and are not slow even to avow themselves

atheists or nihilists : exactly as if the Divine existence
and power were truths which men had always arrived
at by .reasoning instead of revelation, or were prob-
lems which addressed themselves primarily not to the
heart but to the understanding.

But it is perfectly safe to say that the religious
instinct in men, as it never *has* sought or accepted
scientific guidance upon religious questions, so it
never will seek or accept it in the future.   It is the
inappeasable craving of that instinct in the soul,
whenever it comes to the discernment of its own
spiritual nature, that the creative perfection prove
above all things of an *active* quality ; that is, that the
creator not only *be* in Himself of an infinite and eternal worth or majesty, but that He livingly avouch
such transcendent worth and majesty by some immortal work of justice or righteousness accomplished
in the nature of His creature, which shall forever
transfigure that nature or make it serve as an all-
sufficient revelation and perpetual memento of His
otherwise inscrutable name.   We none of us, you
know, are apt to have anything but a prudential regard for a great capitalist merely, or a man buried
up to his head and ears in money ; while we feel a
disinterested respect for every man of inventive or
productive genius whose work enhances the wealth
of the race or enlarges the bonds of human inter-

course. Just so we should feel no respect for an
idle or luxurious deity, a deity for example who
though himself armed with all might, and garlanded
with the obsequious homage of heaven, could yet
be content to see his earthly creatures wallowing in
natural ignorance, indigence, and infamy, without
even for a moment sacrificing or postponing the al-
lurements of his voluptuous indolence to their effectual
relief. It is not enough to say that we should feel
no sincere respect for such a deity: our hearts would
prompt us indeed to abhor his unworthy name, and
reverence many an undistinguished man as of far
diviner credentials.

But it is high time to close this unduly long letter,
though I have by no means begun to exhaust its
superb theme, nor can ever grow tired of denouncing
the heathenish superstitions of our infidel church and
state, which utterly dehumanize the Divine perfection,
and permanently defecate its claims to our homage, by
stupidly representing it as of a rigidly *super*natural
quality. Even the literal Christian verity, in fact,
binds us to say that God's spiritual perfection whether
of love or wisdom finds its sole permanent purchase
upon our regard *in a redemptive work wrought by
Him in our nature*, which justifies us in ascribing to
Him henceforth a distinctly NATURAL or impersonal
infinitude, and so forever rids us both of the baleful

intellectual falsities inherent in the conception of His
supernatural personality, and of the enforced personal homage, precatory and deprecatory, engendered
by that conception in the sphere of our sentimental
piety.   The principle involved in this dogmatic transaction is that of the hierarchical subjection of passion
to action, of root to stem, stem to flower, and flower
to fruit.   And the practical lesson to be derived from
it is that God is not willing to be had in reverence of
men for His absoluteness and infinity, but only for
His relative perfection : in that being rich and of in-
comparable renown He yet makes Himself poor and
of no repute that we through His destitution may
become rich and powerful.   And when He who is the
acknowledged top of all perfection — the crown of
every excellency which the foolish heart of man covets,
the excellency of will, of knowledge, of power — thus
renounces His absoluteness, renounces every patent-
right He has to our regard, every conceded or unconditional advantage borrowed from our servile traditions, and consents like any unprivileged person, like
any honest workingman, diligently to sue out His title
to our allegiance in the court of every man's equitable
judgment, it is high time for us to learn that a man
is in the long run only so much as he *does*, that there
is no such thing as a chronic excellency — as an absolute or fossil perfection — ever practicable either to

man or God, and that our only chance therefore for
immortality lies in no stored-up capital of goodness
and truth we possess, but in the acute life or character we daily witness in putting all our accumulations
of goodness and truth out to active use.

We laugh, as I said awhile ago, at an inventor who
should ask us to take his genius on trust, or without any evidence of its reality. And there can be
no more offensive tribute to the Divine name than to
show Him a deference we deny to the rankest charlatan. How infinitely unworthy of God it would be
to exact or expect of the absolute and unintelligent
creatures of His power a belief out of all proportion
to their sensible knowledge, or unbacked by anything
but tradition ! In the absence of sensible knowledge
tradition is no doubt the next best thing ; but that
the deputy should be allowed permanently to supplant its principal is a monstrous absurdity. I am
free to confess for my own part that I have no belief
in God's absolute or irrelative and unconditional perfection. I have not the least sentiment of worship
for His name, the least sentiment of awe or reverence
towards Him, considered as a perfect person sufficient
unto Himself. That style of deity exerts no attraction either upon my heart or understanding. Any
mother who suckles her babe upon her own breast,
any bitch in fact who litters her periodical brood of

pups, presents to my imagination a vastly nearer and sweeter Divine charm. ·What do I care for a goodness which boasts of a hopeless aloofness from my own nature — except to hate it with a manly inward hatred? And what do I care for a truth which professes to be eternally incommunicable to its own starving progeny — but to avert myself from it with a manly outward contempt? Let men go on to cherish under whatever name of virtue, or wisdom, or power they will, the idol of Self-Sufficiency : I for my part will cherish the name of Him alone whose insufficiency to Himself is so abject that He is incapable *of realizing Himself except in others.* In short I neither can nor will spiritually confess any deity who is not essentially *human*, and existentially thence exclusively *natural,* that is to say, devoid of all distinctively personal or limitary pretensions.

LETTER XXIII.

MY DEAR FRIEND : — Doubtless you are able to discern by this time why neither my faith nor my reason is at all disconcerted by the current rationalistic criticism of the gospels. It is because I have never valued the gospels for their own sake, but exclusively for the revelation they offer of the Divine name in connection with man's nature and history. To say: that *a certain man was born of a virgin,* and that after enduring a life of great ignominy and suffering at the hands of his countrymen, he was put to a violent and opprobrious death, *from which however after three days' sepulture he rose again, and presented himself in bona fide recognizable form to his amazed disciples :* is clearly anything but a scientific statement, and arrests men's attention only because it appeals to a grander and more universal instinct in them than that of science, namely: the instinct of conscience, or the interests of their immortal life. It is strictly fair to say, moreover, that the statement never purported itself to have any scientific validity except in the hands of unintelligent and incompetent partisans. It was originally intended to furnish a purely doctrinal footing to men's intellectual and spiritual life, by connecting their nature with God in the highly exceptional and representative personality of Christ. A certain obvious antagonism has always announced itself between religion and science, growing out of the circumstance that they both make their appeal to the human intelligence, but one to a higher intelligence, the other to a lower: the only dispute being which intelligence is the higher, that represented by science, or that represented by faith. Science comprises the field of our distinctively finite knowledge, while religion has always had the pretension to connect us with the infinite. There ought to be no contrariety between the two pursuits in themselves, any more than there is contrariety between soul and body; for the interests of religion are emphatically and exclusively those of soul, and the interests of science as emphatically and exclusively those of body. Their only apparent quarrel is owing to the existence of foolish adherents and advocates on either side: many men of science being narrow enough to have no broadly human sympathies, and therefore very apt to grow indignant at having their chosen pursuit charac-

terized as a low order of knowledge compared with
any other order; and religious men being, as a general thing, not so devoted to the interests of spiritual
truth, primarily, as to feel reluctant in season and out
of season to press this humiliating conviction home
upon them.

Distribute the blame of the quarrel where you
will, however, this difference of a higher and lower
order of knowledge in man does unquestionably attach to the relations of religion or philosophy (for
the two things are sufficiently near to be regarded
for our present purpose as almost identical) and science: religion being concerned with man's direct
relations to God, and science with his indirect ones.
Science admits no conclusion within her own sphere
which is not *verifiable* by sense. And religion in
her sphere disowns and distrusts every conclusion not
distinctly and persistently *falsified* by sense. Surely
a difference more vital or practical than this, can
scarcely be imagined; and there can be no more
fatal folly with reference to man's intellectual interests, than to make light of it. On one side we
have the human soul, and the spiritual world, which
is the soul's "real habitation and native country," as
Swedenborg finely phrases it. On the other, we have
the human body, and the material world, which at
most is that body's temporary dwelling-place. The

difference between these realms is vast to be sure, unimaginably vast: but there is no fibre of conflict between them, save what is borrowed on one side or the other from men's ignorance and perversity. If men of science are content to consider man's phenomenal existence his true life or being, because it is the only life or being in him which reports itself to sense, I do not see what right religious men have to complain: *they surely are not compelled to think as men of science think.* And if religious men in their turn are content to consider man's highest life or being made up of his relations to any person or persons outside the pale of human nature, I don't see what right men of science have to complain: *they surely are not compelled to believe as the men of faith do.* For neither side has any just claim to the monopoly of error; and each therefore should diligently refrain from pressing his own characteristic nonsense upon the respect of the other.

The weakness of scientific men, as I have shown in former letters, consists in their attempting to philosophize upon strictly scientific *data.* The fundamental postulate of science is that all known existence is conditioned in space and time, and all her distinctive achievements imply the truth of that postulate. But when one seeks to get no longer a scientific, but a purely philosophic, result from that barren

premiss, his labor necessarily turns out negative and
fruitless, because it proceeds upon a mere unrighteous
confounding of being with existence. Of course philosophy has no objection to admit with science that
all known existence is conditioned in space and time.
It only denies that the unknown being from which
this known existence is derived, and of which it is
a manifestation, is itself so conditioned; and consequently it affirms that any philosophic research, or
research of being infinite and eternal, conducted upon
the mere data of existence, or space and time principles, can have no other than a negative and sceptical
result. In other words: philosophy maintains that
our time and space knowledge, or the estimate we
put upon finite existence, is the exact measure of our
ignorance of true being: and so disqualifies science
as a philosophic discipline from the start. And manifestly the only effectual thing that science can do
in rebuttal of this criticism is in its turn to invalidate the peculiar notion of religion or philosophy in
regard to man's true life or being. And this it has
never yet attempted to do, for Swedenborg is the only
man in the intellectual history of the race that has
ever intelligently formulated the axioms of religion
or philosophy in regard to man's true life or being:
and scientific men not only, but even our *soi-disant*
philosophers as well, who are, the bulk of them, mere

unaffiliated bantlings of science, are in the habit of practically ignoring Swedenborg's labors, for the cheap and easy reason that any man who claims an insight of the spiritual or living world, is *ipso facto* a self-pronounced lunatic.

The being of things, according to philosophy, is never constituted by their existence, for in order that things should be able to exist, or go forth in sensible or phenomenal form, that is, their own form, they must first have being in their creator; and it is worse than idle, accordingly, it is misleading, in science to attempt accounting for the being of things by alleging the laws or conditions of their visible existence. This is both unscientific and unphilosophic. In the first place the laws of existence are never used by scientific men to express what originates or *creates* existence, by giving it life or soul; but only to express what *constitutes* existence, by giving it body. And in the second place the being of things to philosophy never falls outside the things themselves, or in nature, but is always intensely inward and spiritual. Thus the Christian religion would grossly violate philosophy and science both, if it attempted to make the being of men convertible with their base natural existence; but it actually offends neither of them, and on the contrary accords with them both, by making it identical with Divine or creative Love. For God, the

creator of man, it says, is Love: and we men, His
creatures, must be in ourselves — not love of course,
because this would be to make creature creator — but
only *forms, phenomena, appearances, images,* of love.
That is, our fundamental natural quality, or distinctive human identity, must be constituted of affection,
and of thought thence derived; and only to a superficial or fatuous regard will it seem to affiliate itself
to the elements of space and time.

Now it is essential to our conception of Divine and
creative Love, that it be perfect or infinite. And
perfect or infinite love is altogether objectively, not
subjectively, constituted. That is to say, it *is* only
what it *does;* or reveals itself to us only by reproducing its potencies and felicities *in others, created
from itself.* It is not subjectively cognizable, or self-
cognizable: for if it were thus cognizable — cognizable
in itself — it would be differentially related to other
being than itself, and hence confess itself uncreative
and finite. In short it must essentially be, and phenomenally exist, only in communicating its being and
existence to others, so endowing them with its own
infinitude or perfection. Such is our inevitable conception of Divine or creative Love, as being infinite
or perfect.

But now observe. It follows from this conception
of creative Love, that its creatures, in order to avouch

their dependence upon it, or prove themselves proper and adequate phenomenal types, forms, or images of it, should as such typical forms or images be *objectively* rather than subjectively pronounced: that is, should be primarily forms of use to others, and only subordinately to such use forms of life or delight in themselves. In other words: it is a law of all created existence — such is the dazzling perfection or infinitude of its creator! — that it realize its peculiar potencies and felicities only in loving what is not itself, or more briefly still, in unloving itself. For it is obvious that the creature of an infinite power cannot realize life in an absolute or infinite manner: that is, by loving others *without* unloving himself; simply because a potency of this sort in the creature would argue him to be uncreated, or identify him with the creator, making *him* also to be infinite Love. And if he cannot love in an infinite or absolute manner, he can only do so in a finite, contingent, or relative manner, that is, by ceasing to love himself. For you must in the interest of philosophy perfectly understand that the only principle of evil in God's universe, — or what is equivalent, the only thing that separates between creature and creator — is the selfhood or identity of the creature:* so that there would have been no other way possible to the creative Love of

* See Appendix B.

avoiding the existing evil of the universe but by void-
ing the creature's personal identity, or leaving him
without natural selfhood: thus without the remot-
est possibility of spiritual conjunction with God: in
short, both literally and spiritually uncreated. Thus
in loving myself supremely, or in prizing above all
things else the interests of my personal identity, I
spiritually separate myself from God, and all the true
and living and lovely things the Divine name stands
for in the creature; for in so doing I make my bosom
the very *fons et origo malorum*, and consequently fill
my daily life with a spirit of hatred and intolerance
towards all other men. Accordingly it is only by
contriving to *un*love myself that I can effectually do
my part in the extinction of the hells bound up in
my nature, or ever practically succeed like Jesus
Christ in loving my fellow-men.

We are now in a position to understand what
Swedenborg says of the tendency of creative order
to *ultimate itself*, or descend to extremes, in the
nature of the creature. "By creation is signified
what is Divine inwardly and outwardly, or in first
things and last: for everything created by God has
its beginning in Him, and from that beginning proceeds according to order even to the ultimate end,
thus through the heavens into the world, *and there
rests as in its ultimate*, for the *ultimate of Divine order*

is realized in mundane nature."*   " The ultimate of Divine order is in Man; and because man is the ultimate of Divine order he is also its *basis* or *foundation.*   Since the Lord's influx does not stop in the middle, but proceeds to its ultimates, as was just said; since this middle through which the influx passes is the angelic heaven, and the ultimate to which it tends is man or the human race; and since nothing independent or disconnected with other things can exist: it follows that heaven and the human race are so intimately conjoined that each subsists by the other.   So that the human race without heaven would be like a chain which had lost a link, and heaven without the human race would be like a house without a foundation." †   " Divine order never stops in an intermediate point " (as the angel or heaven) " and there forms a thing without its ultimate, for then it would not have perfectly expressed itself: but goes straight on to its ultimate and when there it begins formation, and also by mediums there brought together it redintegrates itself, and produces ulterior things by procreations: whence the ultimate is called the seminary or seed-place of heaven." ‡   And so on.

What now is the plain meaning of these and a thousand similar passages?

---

* Swedenborg's *Arcana*, 10634.   ‡ Ibid. 315.
† *Heaven and Hell*, 304.

They express to my judgment the purpose of the creative wisdom to make its work thoroughly real to the understanding of the creature, by giving it a fixed or stable anchorage in his nature, or absolutely welding it to his self-consciousness. It is idle to suppose that a creature can ever come to consciousness, or what is the same thing, can ever realize life, or even existence, save upon a natural basis. For his nature as a creature cuts him off from life or being *in himself*, and stamps him utterly dependent for all his subjective experience upon a life or being infinitely remote from himself — viz. his creator. And unless therefore his very nature as thus subjectively imbecile and impotent be creatively organized, he can never come to self-consciousness, much less to any of the providential spiritual issues of such consciousness.* His nature as a creature is his sole reality in time or eternity, and unless he be endowed with natural reality therefore, he must forfeit his chances both of spiritual and personal, or of real

---

* There is and can be no such thing in the universe as an unrelated or disconnected existence, and Swedenborg is perfectly philosophical in denouncing such a pretension. Indeed, if it were otherwise, the natural or universal element would be wholly lacking to our sentient experience. That is to say, there would be no nature and no universe, but the entire realm of existence would dwindle into a logical poliverse, every forlorn and disastrous fragment of it fatally bumping the head of every other, or nullifying instead of adding to the sum of the other's well-being.

and seeming, life forever. His nature is abundantly real by virtue of its implicit logical contrariety to that of the creator; and all his own reality, which he ignorantly and foolishly supposes to inhere in his conscious self, derives exclusively from it. So that provided only the creator's resources be actually great enough to vivify the creature's nature, and thereby avouch His own spiritual infinitude in making the creature's intrinsic evil the eternal witness of His power, creation will always have a fixed or stable basis of reality to the creature's imagination, and in that secure anchorage the creative wisdom may ever after freely work out whatever proper and perfect spiritual issues its own infinite love may inwardly inspire.

To say, then, that creative order never halts in an intermediate spiritual plane, as heaven or the angel, but goes straight on to its natural ultimate, or resting-place, in the world or man, and there redintegrates itself, or gathers itself up anew, for spiritual procreation: is simply to say in other words that creative order is not the wilful, arbitrary, unreal thing it is generally thought among men to be, as based upon the sovereign license of the creator, but is a most tender, reasonable, and real thing, as based in the creature's own nature, which alone accordingly makes it obligatory upon him to observe it.

Let us now repeat the substance of what we have just said, in order the better to impress it on our intelligence.

The intellectual secret of creation, then, very briefly stated, is that the creator is bound by His own perfection — in order to give His creature spiritual or immortal conjunction with Himself — first of all to endow him with natural reality, or conscious projection to himself; and then spiritually to vivify this natural consciousness of his by giving it social form or quality : so enabling the creature to slough off, of himself as it were, the selfish and monstrous growths which have signalized his natural immaturity.

And now if these things be true we see at once how crudely literal — that is to say, how thoroughly destitute of living or spiritual truth — the current ecclesiastical conceptions of creative order are. Indeed the word " order " is totally inapplicable to the ordinary church dogma of creation, as this dogma makes it a mere brute work of omnipotence, resulting in the production of outward Nature, or the endless chaos of mineral, vegetable, and animal existence. It is a creation in other words with neither beginning, nor middle, nor end, and so is exquisitely unadapted to rational recognition. As Swedenborg describes creation on the other hand, it is a house of three stories or degrees ; the highest or inmost degree corresponding to the private or bedroom floor of our houses, in which the inmate dwells secure from all intrusion ; the second or midmost degree corresponding to the public or drawing room floor of modern houses, in which the inmate receives and entertains his friends; and the first or lowest story corresponding to the basement or kitchen floor of our houses, in which the merely animal or material needs of the inmates are provided for : and he names these successive stories, accordingly, the first: Natural; the second : Spiritual; the third : Celestial. But the church dogma makes creation a house of one story only, and that story the lowest, or basement ; so that he who follows ecclesiastical guidance, is left without intellectual growth, and is kept consequently in the dark as to the future fortunes of his race, and of himself, both alike. Indeed the religionist by profession has no right to know whether the dæmonic object of his worship — being totally unidentified as he putatively is by the assumption of his creature's nature — may not leave the latter at any moment in the lurch, with every tender yearning of his heart after good forever unsatisfied, as now, and every restless desire of his intellect after truth turned to rayless night.

But I concede too much to the church in saying that it makes creation a work of " omnipotence."

For omnipotence being Divine is not recognizable by sense, and creation as the church understands it pertains wholly to the sphere of sense. Omnipotence is recognizable only by man's rational mind, and in order to be so recognized, must avouch itself in a work of infinite love carried out by infinite wisdom to a result of infinite practical benignity. Accordingly wherever man's rational mind recognizes a work of this complex infinitude or perfection, there and there alone it sees revealed to its *adoring* recognition the omnipotent creator, and on bended knees gives Him the name of Jehovah God forever. It is sheer folly to make the senses a standard of judgment in relation to omnipotence or anything else Divine; because the senses are finite or organic and discern appearances only, while Divine things are infinite and inorganic, that is, the exact inversion of whatsoever finitely exists, or sensibly appears to be.

But the professional church, heeding the bare letter of revelation only, that is, restricting its intellectual interests to the domain of fact exclusively, puts itself out of all sympathetic relation to man's nascent and kindling spiritual intelligence, and proves itself in every point of view a mere cumberer of the ground which it was appointed to cultivate. For example: all the active intellect of the church at present is expended in the defence of miracles, as if God's honor

were specially imperilled by the current scientific
scepticism on that subject. But scientific men simply declare that miracle is contrary to the observed
course of nature, and that however men may have
been content to believe in it in times past, they are
no longer able to do so; churchmen themselves, if the
question were put to the test, being no more able to
do so than any other people. And it is evident that
the church can say nothing to the purpose in reply
to this criticism. And this simply because it is so
habitually indifferent to the distinction between fact
and truth, as practically to believe them identical or of
like sacredness; so that when science condemns miracle as an irrational or intellectually immoral pretension, the church feels its very existence threatened,
and its sole *raison d'être* denied. Whereas it should
say, if it were any longer Divinely empowered to say
anything: " True, miracle is irrational, and I equally
with you condemn it as unworthy of men's present
belief. But it was once the only form under which
human stupidity allowed the truth of God's infinitude
to become realized by human thought, and I prize
that truth of truths so highly that I can scarcely feel,
as you do, like taking vengeance upon the expressive
symbol which alone preserved it to my apprehension.
A sentimental mother sometimes tenderly preserves
the cradle in which her first-born was rocked asleep.

I don't know that one can justify this proceeding absolutely; but it is at least a pleasanter sight than to see her attacking it with an axe and chopping it up for firewood."

LETTER XXIV.

MY DEAR FRIEND:—If the considerations advanced in the last letter have half the force to your mind that they have to mine, you will be in no danger of depending upon science for the supply of your intellectual nutriment. The tether of science is the field of sense; and an intellect which is inwardly quickened therefore: i. e. freed henceforth from sensual limitation, since it now views the whole world of sense only in the light of an outward imagery or correspondence of man's inward being: is scientifically inappreciable. Properly speaking, the senses are completely subterranean to the sphere of our characteristic human life, the sphere of our characteristic human — as distinguished from our animal — affections and thoughts. And one would as soon think therefore of consulting a grubbing mole about the approaching occultation of Jupiter, as of consulting our best scientific men (purely as such) in regard to the

existence of spiritual or celestial realities. Men become acquainted with these realities, as it seems to
me, not through any docile hearing of the ear merely,
still less through any wearisome ratiocinative balan-
cing of probabilities, but purely in the way of an
exquisitely inward or æsthetic craving, that is, in the
way of a gradual expansion or education of the heart
to them.   And in my opinion consequently any man
must be still unacquainted with them who needs the
testimony of his senses to assure him of their existence.   For this would imply that they were not spiritual but material realities, existing in space and time.
Tell me, my friend, you who admit the existence of
a legitimate object of adoration to the human heart,
that is, of an infinite goodness and truth, what part
do your senses play in promoting your belief of that
wholesome truth?   Do they steadfastly lead you to
love your neighbor, or the human race, by practically
postponing the demands of your self-love?   Have
they ever, in fact, prompted you to make the acquaintance of good by renouncing your own habitual and
familiar evil?   Yet respond as you may to these interrogations, I am persuaded there is literally no other
way for us to do, and attain to the life of God in
nature.   Anything short of this leaves us in the mere
mud of animality, out of which we originally sprung.
And though we may all our lives reason with the

unction of self-styled seraphs, or devils, we shall only the more effectually succeed in duping ourselves : we shall never either of us add one to the ranks of true — or effulgent Divine-natural — manhood.   .

The essential or spiritual Divine manhood consists in this : that it is wholly creative, or communicative of itself to others created from itself, in which others it may forever indwell consequently as a perpetual fountain of life or being.   In other words, it consists in a power of loving infinitely : that is, without regard to self.   Such doubtless is the tide of creative life or being taken at its flood, or viewed in itself : what now is it taken at its ebb, or viewed in its results?

The answer to this question is very simple.   The *existential* or natural Divine manhood consequent upon this essential or spiritual infinitude in God — for we can no more conceive of an Esse or being without a corresponding Existere or going forth, than we can conceive of spirit without the implication of nature — consists in a most real and adoring response on the part of the creature thus miraculously endowed with being. What is this response?   It consists exclusively in the power which the creature has to love finitely : for finite love, so it be genuine and unaffected, is spiritually one or harmonic with infinite love.   Now, the only way in which finite love can guarantee its own genuineness, or its spiritual and intimate unity with infinite love, is by subordinating self-love to it : that is, by loving others at the expense of itself. For as to " love infinitely," that is, creatively, means to exert a wholly *objective* love, or one which encounters no obstacle or impediment in the subjectivity of the creator, but leaves the creature alone conscious, so the creature, or finite lover, on his part, is bound to signalize *his* love, or avouch its truth, by overcoming whatever impediment his subjectivity or selfhood offers to its exercise. And in no way short of this will he ever succeed in manifesting his own true quality. For if he should love by the direct force of selfhood, that is, without pungent self-denial, or the constraint of his own subjective tendencies, he would love not finitely, but infinitely : that is, he would be no longer creature, but creator.

This seems plain enough, and we need not attempt to make it more so. But it is logically incumbent upon me to point out the philosophic inference with which this most benign truth is fraught : an inference which leaves the philosophy of incredulity, or the science of mere rationalistic negation which we are combating, no honest leg to go upon. Bear in mind all the while, however, that I say no word in disparagement of the legitimate activity of science. I only arraign the wisdom of those of her particular votaries who are not content with this legitimate activity of their mistress, but incessantly attempt to pervert it into a power eminently if not absolutely hostile to the race's spiritual welfare.

If then it be the law of the finite intelligence to realize a life or being in harmony with that of its creator only by postponing itself to others, or inwardly dying to its own subjective tendencies, it follows that the subjective element in existence is an evil element, and is obliged to be definitely overcome or set at nought in the creature's experience, before he can have any taste of true being. He may indeed have conscious existence to any extent you please, that is, may compass the fullest possible acquaintance both with physical pleasure and pain, and moral good and evil: but his physical and moral existence do not constitute his being, they merely give him self-consciousness, which is the opposite of being. These physical and moral experiences of his are providentially in his way to being, I admit, but they are in the way as an obstacle and not as a help if he be inclined to rest in them, just as New York to an inhabitant of Boston is in his way to Washington, if he be disinclined to stay in New York: but they are not his being any more than New York is Washington. They doubtless seem to himself, while he is spiritually ignorant or unconscious of what true being is, to be the veritable thing itself; and doubtless also this

seeming life or being of his negatively promotes his
eventual experience of the reality, inasmuch as by misleading him into the gravest practical mistakes of judgment and errors of conduct, it gradually stimulates reflection upon himself, and ends by convincing him that
the reliance he has hitherto had on selfhood as a basis
of true being, has been grossly misplaced.   All this
is true, but only confirms what I have been saying,
namely : that the life a man is subjectively conscious
of, whatever providential uses may incidentally sanctify it to his true life, is yet all unworthy to be his
true life ; nor does it ever of itself exert any other
than a strictly negative bearing upon such true life.

The subjective element in experience, then, is an
evil element, especially in human life, where it attains
to really devilish dimensions, or becomes every particular man's private and most sacred selfhood,
organizing him into the fiercest and most jealous
antagonism with every other man, his natural fellow.
What makes it evil?   Because being a purely
supposititious or fantastic life, it puts a man, so
far as he comes under its influence, out of true relation to God who is his only source of being, and
so turns him into a more and more finite or organic
existence merely, with no chances of mental expansion or enlargement accordingly but in the way
of imagination or insane illusion.   The happiness

of a conscious or created being *must* consist in the peaceful or harmonious relations that bind it to its creator. And if these relations are falsified at their very core, by the creature coming to refer his being to himself, or to put himself practically in the place of God with respect to every important interest and responsibility of life, disease, disaster, and death are bound, of course, *in the interest of his own eventual spiritual sanity*, to ensue : and meanwhile the human family goes on to realize life as best it can in the discordant, disgusting, and wellnigh intolerable, form under which we at present know it.

Now science cannot go behind the senses. She is the first dry land bred of their watery and wide-weltering chaos, and her obvious *raison d'être* is to furnish a kindly fixed earth to men's feet, while they are trying to realize a worthier life for themselves than sense and science both are capable of ministering. She is not, and never will be, the beckoning heaven of men's eternal hope and aspiration; she is but the necessary illustrative earth of their peaceful and orderly enjoyment, until that heaven yields itself to their solicitations. And she cannot go beyond her foundations. Beginning in sense and its necessities, she must always report herself to the guardianship of sense to have her labors identified and acknowledged. And as the senses are too dull and blunt to recognize truth save in the lifeless form of fact, so science consequently, the child of sense on the maternal side, is nothing more than a living *memory* of the race, organizing the facts of universal experience and observation which are requisite to base its future intellectual and spiritual unity. And being thus tethered as she is to sense or the realm of mere appearance in man, it is grotesquely impudent in her to pretend to have a speculation to offer, or a word to say, in reference to any deeper question of man's being. His being is essentially immortal, and the bare shadow of it therefore at most falls within the realm of time and space, or reports itself to sense; and what should we think of a blockhead who offered to give us a knowledge of the physiology of the human body, upon no other basis than that supplied by a man's occasional shadow in a looking-glass?

Let us expect no help from science then, and *à fortiori* none from sense, in respect to our participation in God's living or spiritual creation. It is very true that the spiritual creation is eternally anchored in sense, because man's rudimental conception of Divine existence or order is exclusively organic or outward; but sense has no perception of the honor done it in this creative anchorage, persuading itself indeed that creation is altogether physical, and that its own function is simply to look on and reason

about the spectacle, and in the long run end possibly — who knows? — by enjoying it. In the earliest literature of the race, which is always symbolic
or sacred, sense is denominated the *serpent*, because
cradling as it does man's infant intelligence it takes
him captive unawares, and makes him think that
its own good and evil, its own true and false, its
own pleasure and pain, are the measure of all Divine
or spiritual reality. There is not much danger of
this effect now, for owing to the race's long experience sense is pretty well unmasked, and has had
its poor rampant and innocent head quite sufficiently
bruised indeed under the heel of men. That is to
say: the humbuggery of sense and its promises is
now perfectly understood in theory, and the human
race once having learned is not likely soon to un-
learn the lesson, however indifferent to it any number of individuals may continue to show themselves
in practice. Man is vastly more liable to harm
nowadays from the feeblest whispers of his own
inmost and unsuspected Eve or selfhood, than from
the loudest outward vociferation of his senses. And
this is a liability which all his science based on
sense is noway competent to shield him from, but
only to deepen his experience of: which remark
brings me, by a somewhat loitering *détour* I admit,
to what I left so incompletely said about the church

and its history in my sixteenth Letter. But before
resuming the thread of our discourse there interrupted let us bring the present letter to a close.

All the science or knowledge of life to which I am
begotten, born, and bred by our existing civilization,
tells me with an undeviating persistency, that there is
nothing so Divinely true, because so Divinely sweet
and sufficing, as selfhood: and the consequence is
that I actually succeed in giving the real Divinity
in my great race or nature only a scant and drowsy
recognition. Indeed if I should freely yield to the
scientific instinct within me, or abandon myself to
the current inspiration of culture about me, I doubt
not I should end by altogether sacrificing that patient
Divinity to the unscrupulous idol and counterfeit
enshrined in myself. For then my senses authenticated by science, and unchecked by conscience, would
be free to tell me that my life or being is strictly
identical with my finite personality, and that the
only death and hell I shall ever have to dread is
one which menaces that personality with desolation:
namely, the death and hell wrapped up in my most
intimate or Divine-natural innocence, truth, and chas-
tity. I confess though that having had one's eyes
once opened to a glimmer of eternal truth on the
subject, one has no hesitation in hoping that before
he is caught hearkening to this gospel of an atheistic

and drunken self-conceit, he may actually perish out
of life, and the great lord of life know him no more
forever. I for one should distinctly prefer forfeiting my self-consciousness altogether, to being found
capable, in ever so feeble a degree, of identifying
my being with it. My being lies utterly outside of
my*self*, lies in utterly forgetting my*self*, lies in utterly unlearning and disusing all its elaborately petty
schemes and dodges now grown so transparent that
a child is not deceived by them : lies in fact *in honestly identifying myself with others.* I know it will
never be possible for me to do this perfectly, that
is, attain to self-extinction, because being created, I
can never hope actually to become Divine; but at
all events I shall become through eternal years more
and more intimately one in nature, and I hope in
spirit, with a being who *is* thoroughly destitute of
this finiting principle, that is, a being who is without
selfhood save in His creatures. And certainly the
next best thing to being God, is to know Him, for
this knowledge makes one content with any burden
of personal limitation. I all along admit of course
that I, like every other man, have a natural capacity
in myself for that harmless ruminant or reflective
life, which to the sceptical or scientific mind is the
very ideal human life. But I would have you most
distinctly to understand that this respectable bovine

style of existence, with the whole Divine-human aroma, or miraculous quality, of life left out of it, is not in the least *my* ideal. The idea of the life I myself covet or aspire to, is *that of free, unforced, irreflective, spontaneous goodness*, realizable *only through a Divine reconstruction of my nature*. And I would infinitely rather die outright, accordingly, with no chance of any lesser resurrection, than yield one iota of this most lovely human hope and aspiration to the flimsy reasoners who lead our present intellectual *décadence*, and pitch the tune for the base unwholesome crew to dance to, which with lower aims than theirs yet vaticinates in the same strain.

I rejoice, then, with unspeakable joy in the gospel legend, or the fact of Christ's birth from a virgin, and of his resurrection from death: certainly not because of any literal or absolute worth the facts bear to my imagination, for in themselves they leave my imagination wholly unimpressed, as they leave my reason baffled; but because they alone suggest to my heart and mind the spiritual truth of God's infinitude. Ah! the marvellous truth which is avouched for us in the Christian legend! The simply adorable and ineffable truth of God's *natural* manhood, of the Divine nature made human down to the veriest flesh and bones of humanity, and of our nature consequently exalted into the sole vehicle thenceforth of

God's spiritual perfection! To think hereupon what a stupid dreary thing the human soul is reduced to after it has undergone scientific manipulation, and been run into a mere *pruritus* of the senses! Hamlet the play with Hamlet the person left out is nothing in comparison. The melancholy thing in this case is — not that one's bread of life becomes mere unleavened dough, for one can exist well enough, if bare existence contents him, on unleavened bread; but that any considerable number of men should be so lacking in the sentiment of infinitude within their proper nature, as willingly to make sense, in which all animals are superior to them, the sovereign arbiter of truth in intellectual things! I beg however that you will not think that it seems to me vitally important in what sense the existing battle between religious faith and science is settled. Neither party is contending for the interests of the living God, so spiritually active at present within the precincts of human nature, but only and at best for those of some traditional deity now deceased; the deity, for example, of orthodox ecclesiastical culture. The worship of this time-and-space deity at this day, and especially in this land, where human nature is vindicating with startling emphasis and iteration its immaculate Divine dignity against all manner of finite private or personal pretension in men, seems to me a grievous anachronism, and is clearly not worth contending for. Take any chance dozen reputable men of the world (so-called) who practically deny the existence of any deity outside of our own nature; and then take any similar dozen of reputable religious men (so-called) who practically affirm the existence of a deity with distinctively supernatural and superhuman attributes: and I defy you to discover any other and deeper practical difference between them. No, their sole visible difference is constituted by the presence or absence of the religious profession, together with a certain stifling pious decorum which that profession imposes: not in the least by any characteristic spiritual superiority of either class to the other. So far as the interests and intercourse of this humdrum moral or superficial life are in question, I venture to say you would confide in one class quite as readily as in the other. But, unless I am greatly mistaken, you would intelligently confide in neither class, so far as their relations to man's unseen and veracious spiritual being are concerned.

I said a moment since that the gospel facts, the miraculous facts alleged in connection with Christ Jesus, did not in themselves pique either my æsthetic or rational interest. The reason doubtless is that the Christian facts are creative facts, ultimate facts of man's universal being, and make no appeal to my in-

dividual self-love, save in a reflex way. I am not
spiritually a creature of God in my own right, or in
my individual capacity, but only in so far as I become
identified in affection and thought with universal man,
or the interests of the Divine righteousness upon
earth. The Christian facts must always be regarded,
when regarded intelligently, as a rigid accommodation of spiritual or supersensuous truth to man's
natural or sensuous understanding: the truth accommodated being that of God's infinitude, which makes
Him a spiritual or living creator of men and by
no means a natural or dead creator; which, in fact,
stamps the whole realm of nature as void of absolute significance, or turns it, solid foundation as it is
for our senses, into a boundless *mirage* whenever
we seek to get any direct spiritual instruction from
it. In short the facts pointedly refuse to be interpreted by any scientific or ontologic hypothesis of
creation, which identifies the being of things with
their existence in space and time, and thus quietly
eliminates from the problem a spiritual or living
and infinite creator. There is no more vicious
habit of mind accordingly in the point of view of
philosophy than that which drives us to speculate
an ontologic basis to the spiritual creation, in thinking it to be really or objectively identical with outward nature. Man is not naturally immortal, and

only harm is done by leading him to think himself
so. By natural birth, or in himself, he is to the last
degree corrupt and perishable, and though his science
demonstrates any amount of order, peace, and productive power in his animal and vegetable and mineral connections, it is utterly powerless to promise
himself any resurrection from the death which is latent in his own flesh and bones. To be sure science
is just as impotent to menace him with a contrary
fate, because as science is functionally confined to
the realm of mortal existence, it must needs confess
itself a mere idiotic guesser in relation to every
interest of his unseen and immortal being.

I do not say, then, that Jesus Christ is of any private consequence to me more than any other man is,
or that I derive the least hope or comfort from his
recorded life and conversation to my personal or selfish desire of immortality. I have no doubt indeed
that I shall live after death, with perhaps unhappily a greatly enhanced force of selfhood moreover,
and quite independently of my inherited or cultivated religious faith. But any amount of mere post-
mortem consciousness would prove a sorry equivalent
for immortality. Man realizes immortal life, I infer
from the Christian facts, and somewhat from my own
observation of human life as well, only under his
own spiritual midwifery; that is, only by voluntarily

compelling himself against the inspiration of his self-hood, and frankly obeying the inflowing instincts of fellowship or society which alone unite him with his kind, or out of a very disgusting animal make him for the first time a man. In short, a man realizes life Divine and immortal only by coming to view himself as so much mere rubbish in comparison with his fellows, and clinging with renewed affections to his Divinely redeemed race or nature. It is astonishing what force and expansion this new and Divine love of one's kind imports into our ordinarily graceless consciousness, or the unrelieved tenor of our daily life. How it enlarges the objective element in consciousness, and annihilates the subjective element comparatively, till at last every commonest natural form of use seems aromatic with Divinity, and all men who are not vowed to idleness or pleasure grow Divinely chaste, as all women are Divinely fair and modest. But I only want to say that incarnation avouches itself to the heart the sole philosophic secret of creation, and the Christian facts in embodying this secret in a cypher as it were until such time as the human mind had grown wise enough by experience to unriddle it, impose a definite end to men's crude speculations in seeking a scientific or ontological clew to the mysteries of creative and created being.

Perhaps it will not be amiss to close this letter

by a personal reminiscence having some relation to its theme.

A good many years ago in Paris I lived in the same house with Mrs. ——, a most charming and amiable old lady, who was the mother by a former marriage of a very distinguished son, with whom I had been for several years on terms of friendly acquaintance, and who was polite enough to insist on my making his mother's acquaintance also. The mother was a remarkably handsome woman, of the gentlest address and manners, but she very soon revealed to me that her peace of mind had been very much disturbed by doubts of the religious dogmas in which she was bred, and to which she tried to continue faithful. I usually endeavored to relieve her depressed spirits by talk about her son, whom she almost idolized, and about the very remarkable lectures he had given in New York, and other cheerful topics, but somehow our conference always reverted to a discussion of her religious perplexities, which were indeed sufficiently sombre and menacing. Her husband, who seemed a very amiable man, was a half-pay officer in the English army, altogether vowed to reading, and not much disposed to interest himself in drawing-room gossip. One evening I had mounted to their apartment, and found there an Irish lady, of extremely prepossessing appearance, who was the wife of the Paris correspondent of one of the London daily papers, and who apparently was entertaining our hostess with some account of Swedenborg's books. She seemed to know something of what she talked about, and had evidently read Swedenborg's writings with a certain interest and instruction. But I thought upon the whole that she presented her subject in too sentimental a light to attract her friend's serious attention, and it occurred to me to tell a story which might give a somewhat grimmer and more realistic impression of his lore. It was a narrative I had lately found in one of Swedenborg's private diaries, if I am not mistaken, of a murderer's entrance into the spiritual world, whose execution took place in Stockholm, and whose courage had evidently been buoyed by a very strong confidence that the rope would break, and the hour appointed for his execution elapse before it could be repaired or readjusted. Accordingly when the drop fell, and set the criminal free for his spiritual career, Swedenborg, who watched all the details of the incident through the eyes of his attendant spirits, saw him pick himself up in the other world with great alacrity, and betake himself to running towards the open country as if to put the greatest possible space between himself and the Stockholm rabble. His zeal in running became so furious as to attract attention, and some good spirits at length put after him to chase him down, and ascertain what fly had bitten him that he ran with such reckless speed. He was not long in yielding to their friendly overtures, but insisted that he should not be taken back to Stockholm, saying that the rope had broken, and the time was now past that had been appointed for his execution. The good people who had interested themselves in him perceived at once that he had taken a longer leap than he himself was at all aware of, and very soon left him in the hands of certain spirits of his own kidney to whose company he betrayed a much stronger liking.

The story was not perhaps exhilarating as a story, but I had no sooner begun it than I observed the husband of our hostess lift his eyes from the open book before him, and sit in an attitude of great expectancy till I had ended. Then he rose and shut his book, at the same time saying to me, that if he could believe the incident I had related, it would be all over with his doubts about immortality, for the incident in question bore very strongly upon the only two points on which his doubts pivoted: first, that of the persistence of man's personal identity beyond the grave; and, second, the persistence of his conscious freedom. If, therefore, he could only believe that Swedenborg had actually witnessed the occurrence I related, he would be extremely happy; but ah! the way to believe Swedenborg!

I told him that I had not reckoned upon interesting him in my poor little anecdote, but that it was intended to placate the anxieties of his wife which were always the effect of an influx of evil spirits, by suggesting to her mind the fact of the death-process being in every case so very humane and natural as to leave even a criminal like this vile murderer utterly undisturbed as to his habitual thought and consciousness, and intent still only upon cheating the hangman. I furthermore remarked that I had myself no doubt of the absolute reality of this incident to Swedenborg's experience, because I could not conceive of the creator of men once endowing them with conscious life or freedom, and then conceive of Him as again under any possible circumstances revoking His gift. But I also told him that I had been not a little interested to discover that so intelligent a person as he should be prepared to say that all his desires after immortality would be met in his experience of the indefinite persistence of the natural life. Doubtless Swedenborg's *Arcana Cælestia* were apt to breed a pretty firm conviction in the mind of the reader that an orderly conscious existence, however variously motived on the part of the subject, is the assured providential destiny of all men after death. But I should never think of recommending a course of Swedenborg in order to produce that conviction simply, under the impression that it was at all equivalent to a belief in eternal life. Swedenborg never by any chance represents one's *post-mortem* existence, however circumstantially defined it may be, as guaranteeing him against the chances of *the second death*, or as being by any means the same thing with his immortal life. Indeed our immortal interests, according to Swedenborg's showing, are much more nearly dependent upon our *cis-mortem* ideas and practices, than they are upon any imaginable amount of *trans-mortem* experience, were it the very happiest. For immortal life, to every one who experiences it, is the realization of his true or spiritual and God-given individuality, that which has been at most merely symbolized by his natural selfhood, but never in the faintest degree constituted by it. So that whatever a man's natural selfhood may be in a moral or outward aspect, determining him possibly in one case straight to heaven, in the other straight to hell, it will be utterly without any power to determine his relation to God, or his chances of immortality.

Immortal life to Swedenborg always means one definite thing, and that is — soul-power, or the prevalence of a man's inward life over his outward one. It means: *the soul's exclusive power to regulate a*

man's outward, that is, his physical and moral, rela-
tions, and so produce an ever-growing inward and
ineffable harmony between him and his creative source:
so that any man in whom this result in any sincere
degree however slight is freely achieved, or his soul
has learned to rule and his body to obey, has *ipso*
facto entered upon immortal life; and this man only.
How then shall one attain to this soul-power?

Certainly not through the exhibition of any vicious
personal favour on God's part towards him: for in
the first place God has no such personal favour to
bestow on any man, were he in all moral regards the
pattern man of his race; and in the second place if
He had any such personal favour to bestow, the
exhibition of it toward His favourite would only result in more effectually damning the unhappy wretch
to hell, by infallibly engendering within him a *meri-*
torious spirit or *self*-righteous estimate of himself
in comparison with other less favoured men. I hope
we may be careful each of us never to flatter himself accordingly that he is the beloved of God,
and the favourite of heaven: it were better for our
spiritual sanity in that case that a millstone were
hung about our necks, and we ourselves sunk in
the bottom of the sea. The only man who was
ever born to such an ominous unhallowed *prestige*
was Jesus Christ; and he worked himself clear of

the deep spiritual damnation that inhered in it, only
by making his life from the cradle to the grave one
of exquisite *self*-denial, or of earnest and assiduous
contention — contention even to death — against the
rank personal homage and consecrated self-esteem
which the fanatical Jews endeavoured to thrust upon
him. He was born apparently for nothing else than
to flatter the God-ward hopes of the most devout and
diabolical people that ever lived: that is, to give
them their long-promised, at all events their long-
expected, dominion over all other people. His birth
had been so marvellous, and had been welcomed by
such a famished expectation on the part of his self-
righteous nation, that if his fidelity to truth had only
left him free to forego his denunciations of their
national pretension to be God's saints, and defer to
the obvious voice of prophecy in their behalf, taking
the literal text of their sacred books for his guidance,
he might doubtless have been lifted to an unparalleled
height of empire. And no doubt the devil of his
secret thoughts, the devil born with his Jewish blood,
often tempted him to listen to these fleshly ambitions,
often took him up into an exceedingly high mountain,
the mountain of his inherited personal pride and lust
of dominion, and showing him thence all the kingdoms of the world and the glory of them, said unto
him: *All these will I give thee, if thou wilt be guided*

by me. But although these things must have tried
him as never man before or since was tried (for
only think what a nation of devout and selfish zealots
— the worst possible combination of the elements of
human character conceivable, breeding by their conjunction the most genuine diabolism — he had to
back him, if he would only consent to follow their
sacred oracles, and fulfil the literal Divine promises
which had been made to them), he never flinched,
but knowing his tormentors, who they were, and that
they were pre-eminently of his own filthy race, invariably replied to them: *Get thee behind me, Satan,
for it is written thus and so; and I came to do the
will of Him that sent me, and not at all my own will.*

This was the merit of Christ, that he found the
most assured religious hope and aspiration of his
people, based upon their sacred scriptures, found all
his instincts of patriotism, all his family instincts, all
his instincts of neighborhood and friendship, to be on
the side of his unlimited self-love and love of the
world, on the devil's side in short, and yet his truth
of soul was so single and spotless, his perspicacity so
unerring, that he never for a moment faltered, but
threw religion, country, family, friends, incontinently
overboard, or rather gave them each a new and spiritual Divine reproduction, that so in solitude, in suffering, in ceaseless anguish of soul, he might obey his

inward instinct of the Divine name, and bequeath his immortal sorrows alone to mankind as the only fit interpretation and remembrancer of that name. If he had, but once barely, clasped joy instead of sorrow to his bosom, if he had only once preferred Jew to Gentile, self to neighbour, truth to goodness, where should we ever again have looked for a revelation of God's true or spiritual infinitude? and without such a revelation where would be the intellect and heart of man at this day? I do not hesitate to reply, for myself: *In the grave of his burnt-out natural appetites and passions.*

But you may be in the habit of intellectually appreciating the Christian truth differently from me, and I will at once, therefore, answer your question, namely: How does a man attain to that soul-power, which, and nothing else, is immortal life?

It is by the inward perception of himself as a person *whose nature has been hopelessly depraved or corrupted before it came to his hands,* by its individual subjects in the first place having the presumption to conceive themselves to be in their own right creatures of the most high God; and then in the second place by these individual subjects having the presumption to live a life of serene and total spiritual indifference to the obligations of such creatureship. For this is the only real atheism, or vital profligacy, of the human heart: to be ready to acknowledge oneself *in-oneself* a creature of God, and yet not to be infinitely chagrined and distressed by the acknowledgment. I can imagine no more revolting idea to my own mind than that of my individual creatureship; of my having a creative right to be or exist in myself, that is, independently of other men, and independently besides of mineral and vegetable and animal: because the prime and instant logical implication of such an idea would plainly be to eviscerate myself of selfhood, that is, both of physical and moral life, for a created being has no right either to one or the other. A created being, if any such could exist, would be a being so dead in himself that the very stones of the street would hiss their contempt at him; a being of such essential dependence from stem to stern, or through and through, that the bare conception of his real existence either to sense or consciousness would be intellectual delirium or fatuity. The only thing that makes the acknowledgment of my own creatureship tolerable or excusable to myself in thought, is that I am myself a wholly unreal or insubstantial phenomenon, whose unreality moreover is shared and intensified not only by every partaker of human nature, but by every beast of the field, and every fowl of the air, and every fish of the sea. For the conception of anything as Divinely

created involves for its interpretation that posterior
and more spiritual conception of Divine power which
we call redemption, and which perfects the former
conception by showing the creator intent upon ex-
tricating His creatures from the base animal investi-
ture or deciduous mother-substance in which their
mere creation leaves them. Both terms are derived
from the limitations of man's subjective consciousness,
and are both accommodations of spiritual truth to
that consciousness, without the slightest literal or
objective reality in them; being both intended to
induct the mind into the conception of the Divine-
human infinitude which underlies our nature, and
of the irresistible power which is spiritually mould-
ing it into social and orderly form.

I cling to my selfhood then, not in the least as
affording any sign of my own reality to myself, but
simply as the sole evidence and guarantee of Divinity or infinitude within my nature; and in this point
of view I cling to it as tenaciously as ever my fa-
bled progenitor in the garden of Eden clung to
his Divinely-given Eve. For in this point of view
a man's selfhood is always a common possession of
his nature in him, and no way his own spiritual or
private and particular possession; a mere outgrowth
and necessity of his mortal consciousness or apparition, and by no means an appanage of his Divine or

immortal being. And this is why I say that it is only by the honest and sincere handling of himself as a *naturally depraved subject*, that a man ever practically attains to immortal life. For only in this way can he ever be led to disesteem and disregard that shabby self-righteous or mingled moralistic and pietistic culture which the church commends to his regard as the aim and end of his being, and which the church's necessities alone keep alive in the earth; and fix his thought upon the spiritual evils which inhere in his fallacious natural selfhood, especially after this selfhood has undergone regeneration by the church : which are in truth the only things that stand between him and the full fruition of immortal life.

Mr. —— listened to what I said with grave politeness outwardly, but with the inward air, I must say, of listening to one talking downright nonsense ; but the lovely person who sat beside his wife on the sofa took occasion to say that she had not entered so deeply as I seemed to have done into the philosophic purport of the Swedenborgian literature, but that she would ponder what she had heard. I thanked her most unaffectedly, but took the liberty of cautioning her at the same time to be more solicitous in all her readings of Swedenborg to read with free open insight or understanding than with zealous literal apprehensiveness, for if we came to Sweden-

borg with any idea that he addressed a single word
to our natural ears, and not exclusively to our spirit-
ual-rational senses, we were assuredly done for before
we began.   And I had accordingly discovered that
among the very few persons I knew who unblush-
ingly called themselves literal adherents of Swedenborg there was not one, singularly enough, who, so
far as I perceived, manifested the slightest spiritual
discernment of that author's meaning.   And thereupon I wished my friends good-night.

LETTER XXV.

MY DEAR FRIEND:—The subject of my sixteenth letter was the church in antagonism with the prevalent tendencies of human nature, which are selfishness and worldliness. And the tenor of the letter was to show that whereas the church combats and supplants these purely natural evils in man, all its ability to do so comes from its quietly and unconsciously originating a far deeper spiritual evil in him, infinitely worse than the other two: the evil of *proprium*, that is, of private selfhood or unrelated, independent character. Men do not get their private selfhood (that is, what gives to every man his distinctive worth or reality from every other) from their nature, because their nature is what they all possess in common, and therefore distinguishes none. In fact human nature is merely the principle of identity or community among men, and so intense, all-pervading, and exacting is it that whatever be man's

private, individual, or spiritual pretensions it will
insist first of all upon holding him to a perfectly
rigid accountability to itself, allowing no one a spiritual passport until he has paid every jot or tittle
of his just dues to men's natural brotherhood.* If
then men possess a distinctive selfhood or *proprium*,
that is, a private substance or reality individualizing
or differencing them one from another, now in a
favorable sense, now in an unfavorable, it is clear
that the possession cannot be in any case an original
fruit of their nature, but of some subsequent Divine
or authoritative modification of their nature. Now
the only claim to be such modification of human
nature is that put forward by the church. The
church unquestionably and plausibly claims to be a
Divine institution, engineered in the express intention of modifying human nature or abating its influence over its subjects with a view to their spiritual enfranchisement; and there is accordingly no
shadow of a reason possible why we should not
hold the church liable by its own showing for the
origination of private selfhood or personality among

---

* That is to say: nature is a dread unfaltering *nemesis* to those
who are in any way ambitious to achieve an exceptional *personal* holiness, or aspire to compass *direct* spiritual relations with God: relations
independent of, and uncontrolled by, their previous natural obligations
to human society, fellowship, or equality.

men; that is, for their pretension to enjoy an individual character, standing, and responsibility before God.

Now I will not attempt to disguise my conviction that this statement will prove very offensive to two large and influential classes of persons among us; nor will I affect a cynical indifference to such a result. For the classes I shall most offend embrace all the conventionally respectable people of the earth, my own humble friends and brethren among the rest; and it is idle to pretend that one's own blood, that is, one's conventional standing, is not dear to him, or is not very costly to lose. But my humiliation on this account admits of a striking alleviation: *it is directly in the line of Christian tradition.* We know from the gospels that the fight of Jesus Christ —*parva componere magnis*— was with the scribes and Pharisees, that is, the leaders of his people, or those particularly identified with the Jewish church and state. Now that these were the most respectable persons of his nation, and naturally therefore the most remunerative to any ordinary man's self-love, is perhaps sufficiently indicated by the fact of his provoking their incurable pride and resentment in professing to be the special friend of publicans and sinners. But we have more direct evidence of their untarnished conventional respectability. For Jesus

Christ himself testified that the righteousness of
these men was the highest righteousness conventionally recognized on earth, when he said that even
that would not qualify a man for the skies. *Verily,
verily, I say unto you that unless your righteousness*
EXCEED *that of the scribes and Pharisees, ye shall
in no wise enter into the kingdom of heaven.* Now
I am by no means so presumptuous as to aspire to
following Christ literally; but I will allow no man
— especially no respectable or conventionally righteous man — to deny me the praise of following him
spiritually.   There is no such thing possible to men
nowadays as a literal following of Christ. This pretension had a semblance of possibility only while
Christ was in the flesh, or lent himself in finite
visible form to the tentative faith of his bewildered
disciples.   But even then how continually did he
feel himself called upon to buffet their carnal ideas
of his kingdom and authority, by summoning them
to a spiritual following!   But at this day the vocation of following Christ literally has become absolutely too absurd.   I think even that it has grown
to all modest minds a revolting and disreputable
cant.   For his friends and his foes are now both
alike spiritual; being in no wise friends or foes of
his proper person, but only of that Divine or infinite
love towards the human race which he first livingly

exhibited in such adequate or self-sacrificing lineaments as to constitute him an eternal symbol or
revelation of God's name.

Who then are Christ's spiritual foes, the only foes
possible to him at this day? They are *friends* —
in varying sort, some respectful and distant, others
attached and obsequious — *to his carnal or historic
personality.* The first class may for convenience'
sake be called moralistic: being made up of that
very large number of persons who live and thrive
in contentment with the existing very infirm constitution of society: poets, literary essayists, scholars,
artists, transcendental aspirants or idealists, men of
science, men of merchandise and trade, men of uncontrolled wealth, of idle lives, voluptuaries, in short
men of whatever commonplace habitual and enforced
routine: all of whom blindly regard morality as the
absolute law of human life, and look upon duty as
the highest expression of human character, especially
for other people.

The second class is mainly ecclesiastical, of course,
and lives and thrives in sage contentment, not with
this world to be sure, but with another one which
by all accounts is greatly more unequal or undivine
and vicious even than this. It comprises all those
of every sect who regard the traditional church as
directly in the line of man's spiritual welfare, or as

supplying by Divine appointment a literal pathway to heaven.

I offend men of the former category in maintaining that morality is not absolute; that is, that it does not constitute its own end in the existing constitution of things, but is rigidly subservient to a higher style of life in man in which spontaneity displaces will, and duty succumbs to delight.

I offend men of the latter category in maintaining that the church is not in a spiritual point of view (however much it may be in a moral) directly ministerial to human welfare, but only indirectly so. I hold that the church indirectly promotes human welfare in the highest degree, indeed, by ultimating or bringing to a head in her own vicious personality the deepest spiritual evils of our nature, and so affording the Divine providence an opportunity to deal summarily with the evils in her *representative* personality alone, instead of vaguely and indefinitely combating them in the endless forms of our individual manhood. But this notion is of course of deadly augury to the ecclesiastical mind.

You see then that the opposition between these two categories of thought and feeling and my own thought and feeling could hardly be more pronounced than it is; and if my reliance were not solely in the omnipotence of truth I could easily

despair of ever being able by any efforts of mine
to bring our discords into harmony.

First let us endeavor in an amicable spirit to
correct the error of the moralist, who may be called
this-world's worldling; after which we shall see what
can be done to dispose of the churchman, who in
like manner may be styled the *other-world's* worldling. I deal with the first of these errorists first,
because he is altogether the easiest to deal with;
inasmuch as moralism is a mere parasitic disease
of the mind, or has absolutely nothing to account
for its existence or give it an intellectual *locus standi*,
but the development of the church in our nature
and history. That is to say, the church historically
breeds, sweats, or throws off from its own flanks,
the civilized state of man; and morality is the unquestionable law of civilization, the absolute substance, condition, and measure of all our civic righteousness. It is only in recent years comparatively,
while the church as an institution has been providentially declining in men's estimation, or ceasing
spiritually to function, that morality has been promoted to the guardianship of men's spiritual interests
no less than their natural. The whole Unitarian
movement in the church was a development of the
church's latent spiritual stupidity and senility, no
longer able indeed spiritually to discern between

its right hand and its left; for what can be more hugely preposterous than the logic upon which that movement was founded, namely: that one and the same law operated man's spiritual and material life?

But this is not our immediate theme. Our theme at present is the civic state of man which the Christian church has bred and nurtured, and of which morality is the unchangeable fundamental law; and we must rigidly cleave to it as time and space are failing us, and both my nerves and your patience doubtless are seriously pleading for a good long holiday.

No evil attaches to man in God's sight but the evil of a finite or infirm nature, and this is an evil which being natural attaches to all men alike without distinction of persons. This natural or generic evil of man has various specific forms of manifestation, such as false-witness, theft, adultery, murder, and covetousness. But under none of these forms does the evil out of natural become spiritual in the Divine sight, and attach to its individual subject, unless the individual subject himself really and unmistakably avouch his love for it: that is, make it his own in heart as well as in act, or inwardly no less than outwardly. In that case a man's adultery, or untruth, or what not, signalizes a deeper evil in him than any which is imposed by his na-

ture, namely, a spiritual evil, which is the evil of
a confirmed selfhood or *proprium*. For no man is
spiritually hurt or degraded by subjection to any
form of natural evil, unless he remain impenitent
for it: that is, so love the particular evil as to make
it his own or identify himself with it.

But with spiritual evil in man we are not called
upon to busy ourselves just here. We shall say
what we have to say about it farther on when we
address ourselves to understanding the error of the
churchman.   Just now I have to do with the moralist alone, who vehemently distrusts me because I
maintain that what we call moral evil (say the evil
of false witness, theft, adultery, or murder) does not
attach to the moral subject in God's sight, unless
he be spiritually depraved as well: that is, make
self the end of his activity in preference to God and
the neighbor: but attaches to human nature itself.

The reason why the man of the world condemns
this doctrine is that it makes intellectual havoc, if
it be accepted, with the claims of our existing civilization to be a finality of the Divine administration in human nature.   Our civilization is based he
thinks upon the absoluteness of morality, that is,
upon the truth that a man's moral, or outward and
actual, relations to his fellow-man are of paramount
Divine obligation upon him, and that any contrary

idea to this in weakening the foundations of civic order would expose us to the Divine judgment. No one can doubt that a man's moral character as good or evil is based, and based exclusively, upon the outward and actual relations he sustains to society or his fellow-man: the man being characteristically *good* if he actually or outwardly abstain in his intercourse with his kind from the evils of lying, theft, adultery, murder, and covetousness, and characteristically *bad* if he does not so abstain. But this does not prove by any means that our civilization is based upon the absoluteness of morality, or upon the idea that duty is the Divine ideal of human action.

In the first place, if morality were absolute in its demands upon human nature, and duty constituted the Divine ideal of human action, then the teaching of the church, and the soothing ministry of its clergy at our death-beds, would be wholly out of place in civilized life. For civilization being based upon the absoluteness of the moral sentiment the instinct of self-defence or its own preservation would keep it from tolerating any influence which went to the weakening of this sentiment. But the church, at least the church in its orthodox aspect, is practically the sworn foe of the moral pretension in men. The church, so long at all events as it witnessed to man's *spiritual* life, allowed no moral differences among men to intervene between the soul and God, or complicate the gospel blessings to universal man. Its founder earned the odium of all the morally righteous men of his nation by proclaiming himself the friend of publicans and sinners, and it would be indeed difficult, nay impossible to discover why his gospel was called a gospel, if it had not been addressed primarily to the special relief of those who had a conscience of sin towards God only because they had violated the law upon which their national dignity was founded.   And the apostles of Christ emulating the teaching of their master, and inspired by him, everywhere instructed the awakened conscience of their Jewish converts that what the law notoriously could not do *in that it was weak through the flesh :* namely, beget a man to spiritual peace and hope in God: this the gospel infallibly did, and thereby avouched its eternal supremacy to the law as a mode of intercourse between man and God.   It is idle then for the moralist to appeal to the church for confirmation to his doctrine that morality is the absolute law of human life, or furnishes an adequate rule to the soul in its aspirations after spiritual life.   For the church, so long as it continued to be worthy of its name in the Divine sight, and evinced such worthi-

ness by providentially succeeding to the inheritance
of the Roman empire, always persisted in stigmatizing that doctrine as of especially treacherous augury to the Christian tradition upon which its own
fortunes were founded.

The truth is that the theoretic moralist is totally
out of place in this spiritual day and generation:
as much out of place as an owl or a bat would be
after natural daybreak. His visual organs served
him excellently well during the spiritual night of
the mind to discriminate between moonlight or star-
light and shade; but now that the full splendor
of spiritual daylight is inwardly bursting upon the
soul they are of no avail but to make him a
laughing-stock to the unsympathetic or unfeeling.
He insists upon holding natural daylight and spiritual to be one and the same thing, or of one and
the same essential quality though admitting of quantitative differences; and consequently does not see
that they require different visual organs for their
discernment: one exclusively outward or material,
the other exclusively inward or rational. What
originally stultifies our belated critic and friend,
and makes him spiritually so owlish or bat-like in
appearance, is the fixed idea with him that creation
is primarily natural, and spiritual only by derivation
from that. Whereas, the spiritual truth would teach

him, if he were only willing to receive it, that our *being* is altogether spiritual or real, while it is our mere superficial or supposititious *existence* alone which is natural or phenomenal. Still it is vastly better for the moralist to cling to his fixed idea of creation being originally natural, than it would be for him to abandon it save at the instance of the spiritual truth upon the subject. For in that case he would be left destitute of all reverence for the Divine name even as an outward power, and sink rapidly into the condition of a mere spiritual tramp and vagabond preying remorselessly upon the peace, order, and innocence of civilized mankind.

But all men in this day of the church's spiritual imbecility are more or less moralistic. The Unitarian or latest form of church development which represents the church in its vastated spiritual plight more faithfully than is at all agreeable to the orthodox imagination, has pushed moralism so far as to have almost openly declined, itself, into a mere school of good manners, while the orthodox congregations by a necessary reaction have been driven to contra-distinguish themselves by a gospel of fervent but puerile ritualism. Thus between the "world" and the "church" the only discernible spiritual difference is that while the former continues to be seriously moralistic in its doctrinal beliefs as to

another life, the latter grows more and more frivo-
lously so. The consequence is that the church tradition of God's spiritual or creative infinitude is
now practically discredited and as it were discarded
among men, and the great creator of men has
accordingly sunk into a mere moral pedagogue or
schoolmaster intent upon publicly vindicating his
own paltry self-consequence by rewarding his friends
and punishing his enemies. It is rare indeed to
meet with any one who, speculatively at least, does
not look upon our shabby moral history as a source
of legitimate pride to us rather than humility;
who does not regard conscience as designedly a
ministry of righteousness rather than sin, of justification not of condemnation, of life not death; and
who is not unfeignedly surprised therefore when
any sincere votary of it is found incurring death
at its hands. There is doubtless good ground for
surprise, and even shock, when any one of assured
civic standing, enjoying the esteem of his fellow-citi-
zens, turns out so wantonly imprudent as to violate
the moral law, and expose himself to men's reproach.
Imprudent, I allow, even to the pitch of insanity
every such man must be; but there is no need
of imputing the least spiritual turpitude to him.
Falsehood, fraud, adultery, murder, covetousness, are
vices exclusively of our moral or voluntary constitu-

tion ; and a liability to them therefore does not any more argue spiritual depravity in a man, than a liability to small-pox, which is a vice of our physical constitution, argues moral depravity. Many a violator of the law moreover suffers so poignant a sense of guilt as to be willing even — if that were possible — to give his life a ransom for his offence. And clearly the spiritual state of such a man is infinitely more hopeful than that of any person, who himself as yet undrilled or inexperienced in the deadly letter of the law, and grossly ignorant therefore of its redeeming spirit, triumphs over him, or withdraws his fellowship from him.

In fact human nature has so inward, so spiritual, so living a root in the infinite mercy of God, that the average man does not find it easy to obey an outward law, a law which aims to regulate his intercourse with others. No one seems able to do so sincerely who does not do it on religious grounds ; that is, who does not put a great deal of conscience towards God into his conformity, and obey chiefly for his soul's sake. Other people do not necessarily disobey it by any means, but their apparent conformity to it is in reality a conformity to something else. We all of us well-to-do-people for example habitually maintain a good moral repute in the community, but then it is by virtue of the prudential instinct

in us, or an ever active self-love. We are kept, the
mass of us, honest, chaste, and gentle because it is
our interest to be well-esteemed by our fellow-men.
The esteem of others is so dear to me, for instance,
that I could almost die rather than do anything voluntarily to impair my conventional standing; at all
events my children's. But what I mean when I say
that no one sincerely obeys the moral law but by the
grace of God, is that no one is capable of giving it
a hearty allegiance, a spontaneous or disinterested
obedience, until the force of selfhood in him is effectually broken and routed. And this consideration
ought by the way to be allowed much more weight
in all questions of practical casuistry than we usually
concede to it. It is not enough to stamp a man a
liar to a spiritual regard that he should have told
a lie on a certain occasion ; nor a thief, an adulterer, a
murderer that he should have committed the offences
designated by those names. For these offences are
for the most part committed inadvertently, that is,
in utter ignorance of their spiritual quality ; what
is really false in them, or fraudulent, or adulterous,
or murderous, being so obscured and swallowed up
for the time by their subtle and extreme agreeable-
ness to sense, as to seem an actual good. And surely
men will forgive any weakness to the average human
will, when it is thus placed in hand-to-hand conflict

with the tremendous force of the physical organization on the one side, and is unbacked on the other
by a living faith in God. For my own part, and I
do not know that I fall below the moral average of
men, I have always found myself thoroughly impotent,
when tempted, to overcome evil simply as *evil;* and
for this excellent reason, that when I have been
tempted by evil it was never under its own lineaments, but always in the counterfeit guise of good:
so that my only chance to avoid it lay at last in giving
submissive heed to the voice of my religious conscience, which tells me that whatsoever the flesh
reckons to be supremely good is *ipso facto* spiritually
evil.

I say emphatically: *when tempted;* observe that.
There are very many persons who will not understand
this limitation — their number seems indeed to be
growing; at least I think it could never have been
so great as now — inasmuch as they themselves are
exempt from moral conflict, and do not know except
from hearsay what false-witness, or theft, or adultery,
or murder is. These persons exhibit a great natural
advance upon the average man, being of an almost
purely æsthetic turn, with the ordinary moral virus
all left out. Of course they know very well what is
signified to the ear by the offences in question, but
they have no idea of the spiritual substance which

is covered by them. They suppose that false-witness and theft and adultery and murder are not only so many literal words but so many veritable *things* as well, physically determined; which a vulgar sort of people are prone to do, but to which they themselves have not only no leaning, but a marked distaste and repugnance.

But this in my opinion is a very superficial judgment. *N'est pas pécheur qui veut.* No such thing is known to nature as false-witness, as theft, as adultery, or murder; otherwise of course animals might incur guilt. And surely no well-wisher of these could desire to see their innocent life converted into a moral and rational one. The offences in question are not the least physical, as against nature, but strictly moral, as against culture. They characterize man not as he stands inwardly affected to the interests of Divine justice in the earth, or the evolution of human society; but as he stands *outwardly related to a strictly factitious or conventional order of human life which is called the State, and to which he is born subject:* and they have no shadow of philosophic pertinency but in application to such subjection on his part. In other words the terms indicate so many strictly *instituted* or *legal* offences of men : the temporary order of which they confess themselves violations having been providentially instituted, not with

any view to bound men's aspirations, or define their
just hopes and expectations towards God, but rather
with a view to foreshadow a permanent or DIVINE-
NATURAL order of human life one day to appear in
the earth, and by the insufficiences of the present
order gradually prepare them for it.   In short the
existing order of human life is essentially educative
or disciplinary: its whole practical purpose being to
lead the mind out of carnal into spiritual ideas of
justice or righteousness; or what is the same thing
out of selfish into social conceptions of human life.

I repeat then that false-witness, theft, adultery,
murder, and covetousness are not the least physical
offences, or offences against nature, but purely moral
offences, or offences against law.   They are vices of
our civic constitution exclusively, and therefore belong quite equally to all the subjects of that constitution, if not actually yet potentially: in which case
of course we have none of us any more right to boast
ourselves inwardly over our neighbor in respect to
moral purity, than we have a right to boast ourselves
outwardly over him in respect to physical health.
And if you, dear friend, ask me hereupon to state
more explicitly what I mean by our civic constitution, I will do so with all necessary fulness and dis-
patch.

By our civic constitution I mean the form of public

order under which you and I have always lived, and
which is called civilization, because it suspends every
man's consideration upon the relation he voluntarily
sustains to the State, regarded as the power of a
present Divine life in the world, in opposition to the
Church, which claims to be the power of a *future*
Divine life. This antagonism between Church and
State was never indeed overt or pronounced till after
the Reformation; but it was always latent, because
the Church in spite of her pedigree always bore the
State in her flanks, and nursed it to maturity; and
the child is bound to inherit of the parent, or thrive
by the latter's decline and decease. It is only now
in our own day accordingly when they both feel the
hand of doom upon them, and are reluctantly preparing to be swallowed up in the long-promised reign
of God's JUSTICE upon earth, that they abandon themselves to unlovely but well-merited mutual recrimi-
nation, and would literally fly — if they were not all
the while mere shadows devoid of human substance
— at each other's vicious throat. But the ideal of
the State however faithless the State itself has been
to it, is to make men good citizens, or reproduce
upon an enduring basis their lost paradise; while
that of the church, however little she herself has
practically exemplified the influence of her ideal, has
always been to make men saints, or show them para-

disc well lost for heaven. And there can be no doubt as to which of these ideals is most likely in the long run to captivate men's imagination, especially as the church's practice has always supplied so exquisitely inverse a commentary upon its preaching.

Understand then : civilization all unconsciously to itself yet *aims at the practical secularization of man's religious conscience, or his hope towards God.* But its method is hopelessly infirm and imbecile because it has, to begin with, no adequate conception of human nature and human destiny. It is in truth a mere steward of humanity, and has never had the least pretension to be taken into its counsels or to direct its fortunes. Thus it assumes without misgiving that man is by nature or creation a moral and rational force, not at all perceiving that it thereby denies him all generic or race quality. If man be an *essentially* moral and rational existence, that is to say, a subject primarily of truth in his understanding, then it is plainly impossible that he should ever attain to universal form or realize his social destiny : inasmuch as that is to be led primarily by good in his heart, and only derivatively by truth in his understanding. And to make a universal consciousness impossible on man's part, is really to deny the creative infinitude and heap practical contempt upon it. The truth is we are moral and rational only because we have not

yet intellectually realized our nature or spiritual creation, but stupidly insist on the contrary upon identifying it with our vulgar and pragmatical selves.
Undoubtedly we are the creation of infinite love and
wisdom, but we are this only in our generic or universal, and not the least in our specific or private,
capacity. But there is just as little doubt that to
be the creature of infinitude is *existentially* to be a
finite form of will and understanding; because without such limitation the infinite substance could have
no fulcrum or *point d'appui* in the created consciousness whereby to operate its universal results. Nevertheless we are not authorized to confound what is
strictly existential to a thing with what is properly
essential to it. And yet this is what civilization
habitually does. For what is properly *essential* to
man is his nature as a creature of infinitude, since
without it he could not as a race, or absolutely, *be :*
and what is strictly *existential* to him is his private
selfhood or conscious distinction from all other existence, since without this he could not contingently
exist or appear. Now civilization confounds this
merely personal or existential element in human experience with its natural or essential element; and
consequently makes our nature, which in its last
analysis is Divine and immaculate, the stalking-horse
of all our immeasurable personal folly and corruption.

Starting with this monstrously inadequate conception of what man is by nature or creation, the method
which civilization employs to effect its own comparatively low ends, or make men good citizens, cannot
help proving signally inefficient.   For regarding man
as an essentially rational and moral force, whose heart
is firmly bound to the allegiance of his head, and
whose normal activity consequently is voluntary not
spontaneous, calculated not free, it seeks to accomplish
its ends with men by an appeal to their prudence
mainly : that is, through the pressure of an *instituted*
order and decency, or one which is guaranteed in
the last resort not by the inward consent of the
subject, but by the outward force of the community.
In other words, it utterly excludes from its horizon
any social or distinctively *race*-destiny for man, and
would doubtless freely commute that heavenly birthright any day for whatever steaming and savory
mess of pottage might be complacently proffered us
by political economy.   Thus civilization is organized
upon the truth of an absolute or unconditioned selfhood in man, instead of a rigidly phenomenal or
provisional one ; and hence it regards him not as a
typical or shadowy and unsubstantial *person*, literally
masking an infinite reality, but as a strictly real or
secular and finite *thing*, rightly and rigidly amenable
to all other things for the good and evil consequences

which inhere in his actions. I am sure then that
you, good friend, will justify the indictment I bring
against our existing order — the merely *instituted*
decency, the merely *legal* justice or righteousness
under which we have been sheltered all these centuries — when I say that it stays itself mainly upon
self-love and worldly prudence in its votary as his
ruling principles of action, and hence not only speculatively ignores his spiritual nature or social destiny,
but systematically obstructs and resists its providential evolution, by practically authenticating all the
baser, and outlawing all the more generous, attributes
of humanity.

The mistake has been unavoidable. Men do not
know their own nature as determined primarily by
their creator, that is, as pre-eminently spiritual or
social; but only as determined by themselves, that
is, as pre-eminently personal or selfish; and hence
they lend themselves without scruple to the enforced
conventional order of human life represented by priest
and king, and embodied in the institutions of Church
and State. And the reason why we thus inevitably
conceive our nature to be determined by ourselves
and not by our creator is, that creation itself, spiritually viewed, means the actual transfiguration of the
created *nature* by the plenary creative perfection,
neither more nor less; and hence can only report

itself intelligibly or credibly to the creature in so far as he feels *within himself* a life or spirit truly Divine: and notoriously we as a general thing have been utterly void of such life or spirit. The nearest approach we have ever made to it has been purely formal and picturesque, consisting in the unaffected reverence we have hitherto paid — *a reverence which at this day, and especially in this land, has become purely wilful and superstitious* — to certain traditional institutions, such as the altar and the throne, under which the creative energy has always masked or accommodated itself to our carnal and stupid recognition. And now that a bumptious but providential and inexorable science is fast robbing these hoary institutions of their absolute sanctity, and reducing them to a relative or representative worth at most, all those of us who are intellectually honest will be obliged, henceforth, either to accept creation exclusively as a living or spiritual truth falling primarily within the compass of our generic or race consciousness, and only derivatively thence within that of the private consciousness : or else to reject it altogether.

The spiritual form of nature or creation — its form as determined by God, is constituted by what we call SOCIETY; meaning by that word not any merely empirical or tentative order of human life, such as we are now groaning and stifling under, but the *essential*

brotherhood, fellowship, equality of each man with all
men, and all men with each, *in God*. For inasmuch
as by the exigency of His perfect love God is *essen-*
tially creative, or finds His proper life only in communicating Himself to what is not Himself, to whatsoever in fact is *in se* most opposite and repugnant
to Himself, the nature of His creature in order to
reflect such love must be supremely social; since
society alone enables us naturally to love others as
we love ourselves, and even more than we love ourselves. If God's love be essentially creative as freely
endowing others created from itself with its own life
or being, then it must also be essentially *social* — as
finding all its own felicity in the creature's receptivity
to its advances. And if the absolute life or being
we have in our creator be social, then it follows that
the mere contingent or incidental existence we have
in ourselves, however egregiously unsocial it may for
a time appear, is necessarily tributary to that being,
and must infallibly tend in the long run to avouch
and reproduce it.

But obviously this social or regenerate tendency
in our nature cannot be fully constituted, cannot be
livingly or spiritually realized by us, save in so far
as we shall have practically renounced — save in so
far as we shall have cordially *lived down*, so to speak
— our selfish or gregarious instincts. This renun-

ciation accordingly has been the one great lesson of God's providence to us in all the dreary past. To this end alone prophets have taught, priests ministered, and magistrates borne rule. We have been extremely slow to learn no doubt, yet millions of men see to-day what but a handful saw a century ago, namely: that civilization has had no other providential mission than gradually to socialize the human consciousness, by thoroughly demonstrating the vanity of all human pretension, the vice that is latent in all our virtue, the selfseeking that underlies and arms our fiercest piety, the love of dominion that animates our loving-kindness even, and turns it often to cruel tyranny. In fact our historic past has apparently existed for no higher providential end than to *make manifest the evil* which is latent in the finite selfhood, and so prepare a permanent foundation in experience for human society. The evil thus latent is commensurate in quantity and quality with the infinite Divine goodness: because it is really that in substance, though formally perverted by a finite recipiency; and no diviner mercy could befall us consequently than to allow it to be played out betimes in all its hideous malignity. Every thoughtful parent knows the philosophic value of this principle of *the manifestation of evil* in the education of his children. For every child upon earth is liable to inherit evil dispositions with his blood; and nothing could be more impoverishing and indeed fatal to his manhood, in so far as his manhood is contingent upon a true self-knowledge, than that these dispositions should be violently suppressed by parental rigor, instead of being allowed to manifest themselves in the gristle, and so become tenderly corrected.

This letter outrages all bounds, I know, my friend, but I must make it still more tedious by a word of additional appeal to you. I want you definitely to understand, then, as the upshot substantially of all I have said, that selfhood or personal consciousness, though it is doubtless perfectly *implied* in our spiritual creation as stem is implied in rose, is yet not our creation any more than stem is rose — any more even than the base earth out of which the stem itself grows, is the stem. It has always been our supreme infatuation to regard it in that deceptive light; to look upon it as an all-sufficient *explication* of creation, and not as a mere abject *implication* of it. By thus systematically identifying our spiritual creation with our preposterous and idiotic selves, the personal pretension within us becomes so inflamed and inflated out of its normal provisional dimensions, as to insist upon being no longer base but superstructure to our nature, and to require accordingly the most deadly machinery of morality to keep us each from turning out a flagrant nuisance to every other. We have been taught from time immemorial by our pastors and governors, that we are each of us a direct creature of God, a valid creation in our own personal or private right, and not by virtue exclusively of our natural solidarity with our kind. And this illusion breeds such unwholesome mists of vanity in our breasts, and such dense clouds of error in our understanding, that the heat of God's love and the light of His truth have at last lost all power to penetrate our indurated moral hides; and the entire spiritual world consequently — the world of our true being, of what ought to be our undefiled and unshackled commerce with God and man — necessarily takes on a divided aspect, or resolves itself as it were in spite of the creative unity, and by a sheer instinct of self-preservation, into two hemispheres of good and evil respectively, or heaven and hell: the former a realm of ever active inward association or assimilation between the Divine and human natures; the latter a realm of ever active outward waste or elimination, by which all things permanently incommensurate with the created form, because alien to the creative substance, may be gradually brought to the surface of consciousness, and so definitively sloughed off. And I for my part am perfectly persuaded that if the stupendous illusion of moral responsibility, or a private selfhood in man adequate to the highest wants of his nature, had not been thus utilized spiritually, by being made the base of a *quasi* Divine life in the earth, or a *provisional* kingdom of God in human affairs, *which might at least correspondentially reflect and inaugurate the true and permanent things of creative order*, our minds could never have become — as they have now become — enlarged and disciplined to the discernment of spiritual truth.

The moralist then, as it seems to me, is very fairly answered. His error consists in maintaining the absoluteness of our moral judgments, and this error I think I have sufficiently demonstrated by showing that our moral experience, in place of being absolute, has been rigidly subservient in the miraculous wisdom of God to a superior providential end: which is, first, the manifestation through the church of living or spiritual evil, the evil of confirmed self-hood or self-righteousness, in men's natural personality; and then through that again, the definite rescue of our race-consciousness from the dominion of such evil, in its own reduction to social form and order. Let us then leave the moralist, and hasten with what speed we may to consider the opposition of the churchman: so bringing our somewhat protracted labor to its natural close.

LETTER XXVI.

Y DEAR FRIEND: It is the idea of the moralist, as we saw in our last letter, that civilization is an absolute end of God's earthly providence. But I have endeavored to show you that it is a wholly mediate and subordinate end, being strictly contingent for its own development upon the manifestation of the Divine good-will to universal man, or, what is the same thing, the revelation of the Divine infinitude or omnipotence in our nature, and bound therefore to disappear whenever the necessary machinery of such manifestation allows the Divine omnipotence to become visibly or actively efficient in human affairs.

The misconception of the churchman with respect to God's heavenly counsels is strikingly analogous in point of form to this of the moralist with respect to His earthly counsels; but it is vastly more serious and alarming in point of substance, since a mistake in earthly things is of comparatively no moment beside a mistake in heavenly or Divine things. The churchman conceives that the Divine love for man is *fitly or perfectly expressed in the regeneration of individuals :* and this although it is evident that every case of individual regeneration is effected at the cost of a proportionate *de*generation and degradation to other individuals.

The moralist, stupid soul that he is! foolishly assumes that because he himself is inwardly content with our existing order, although that order be stayed upon any amount of force, or necessarily involve in itself a huge infernal enginery of bayonets, prisons, dungeons, and scaffolds to give it permanence, therefore God most high must be inwardly content with it also.

In like manner precisely the churchman — because his own social sympathy, or sense of fellowship with his kind, is so shallow as not to be scandalized by the thought of himself being declared righteous and blessed, while other men exactly as good as he by nature, and very much better perhaps than he by actual culture, are remorselessly cast out of the Divine favor — just as foolishly assumes, self-righteous soul that he at heart is! that a state of things so flagrantly irrational and inequitable cannot be otherwise than eternally grateful to the pure heart of God also.

It is plain then that the error of both these men has one and the same root: the infatuation of *proprium* or selfhood; only with the moralist the infatuation is venial, as being addressed to the selfhood naturally regarded; while with the churchman it is fatal, as having reference to the selfhood spiritually regarded. Both men have an insane belief that one man has a capacity to be better *in himself* than another; but this belief is much more insane in one than the other, as the moralist thinks such capacity due to the man's nature merely, while the churchman thinks it due in every case to the man's spiritual culture or regeneration, that is at bottom, to the man himself: and this latter persuasion is far more inveterate than the former. Thus the men are alike blind, only one superficially, the other substantially, so; the moralist being outwardly blind, blind to the light of natural fact, and the churchman inwardly or spiritually blind, blind to the light of Divine truth. You see then that the outlook of the moralist, who is this world's worldling, is not half so gloomy spiritually as that of the churchman, who is the worldling of another and a better world, as it is called: for the former is simply unintelligent or errs by defect, while the latter's lack of intelligence is handicapped by a wholly fatuous or misleading light, which is that of self-righteousness.

There seems accordingly but little hope for the churchman. The moralist may be safely left for correction to the course of events, which seems to be fast ushering in a more stable order than that he is wont to delight in. For the moralist's judgment follows the guidance of sense exclusively, and when sense itself attests the spiritual truth of things he will no longer be victimized by error. But the churchman has not this agreeable prospect before him. *His inward light has itself become darkness,* and when that is the case the darkness is utter and absolute: for it is no longer the subject eye that is in fault (as with the moralist), but *the objective light itself, which alone empowers any eye to see, has undergone eclipse.* The churchman as such * accordingly is without a future, his lot being to decrease as the substance he has always spiritually symbolized or stood for increases: this substance being the Lord, of Divine Natural man, that is, Society.

---

* For I hope no reader of these letters will deem me so presumptuous as to think of pronouncing judgment upon the future of concrete flesh-and-blood men — whether they be churchmen or statesmen — for I venture to say that these in common with us much happier nameless men will have a greatly better personal fortune at the Divine hands than any of them ecclesiastically or politically deserve, whether that fortune consign them to heaven or hell. It is only the abstract churchman and statesman (as alone representatively existing to the Divine mind) whom my strictures have to do with, and by no means any literal person so named.

Doubtless the reason why the evil which the churchman formally embodies, or with which he is representatively identified, is so much more hopeless than that which the moralist propagates and perpetuates, is, as I have perhaps already said, that it is spiritual or central, involving the heart, while the other is merely natural or circumferential, involving the senses. False witness, fraud, adultery, murder, and covetousness are natural to man, that is, are inevitable to his nature as a creature of infinitude so long as he is intellectually unaware of the spiritual or inward and impersonal quality of such infinitude, and instinctively seeks to realize it in this absurd personal way : as if the bonds of his personality (which are so useful and necessary in giving him fixity or standing-ground to his own consciousness) had only to be thrown off, and not reverently taken up into his own spiritual substance, in order to achieve the freedom he thus instinctively or humanly craves.   It always seems to flesh and blood that freedom is one with emancipation from law, and it is nothing but this false persuasion that makes all our clandestine ways appear so sweet to the ordinary flesh-and-blood mind.   The moment a thing is forbidden to that mind, however indifferent to it the man may have been the moment before, he becomes eager to do it.   The reason is that he mistakes the

purpose of law, which is by no means to suppress
our outward freedom, but by moderating its wanton and suicidal extravagance, or guarding it from
license, to educate us to inward, spiritual, or Divine freedom.   The flesh-and-blood mind is not the
true or distinctively human mind, but merely the
mind of the animal in us.   And the animal mind is
bound of its own nature to be servile to the human
mind, and realize its only chance of freedom by
acquiescing in such servitude.   Of course the man
himself has got to be de-animalized, that is, to
become spiritual and human before the animal in
him can be placated or subdued.   The State prison
convict no doubt finds it very hard to imagine *while
he is in prison* that his nature entitles him to any
truer freedom than that which the opening of the
prison doors would give him.   But this is only because his misconduct in depriving himself of outward
freedom has enhanced and inflamed the animal consciousness in him, and thereby deadened him for the
time to all inward and higher manifestations of
freedom.   When one is incarcerated *by his own mis-
deeds* I defy him to entertain anything but a most
unmanly conception of freedom, being sure to make
it outward solely, or to lie in the power of doing
evil with impunity.   If his folly had left him free
to conceive of it in its human aspect, as the power

of doing good, and good alone, at the instance of one's heart, he would be instantly reconciled to his fetters, nay, would pray for additional bolts and stronger bars.

But this *natural* ignorance of man, profound as it unquestionably is, is altogether excusable and transient, and by no means leaves him without hope; for any possible subsequent Divine enlargement of his nature will be sure to enlarge and improve his moral temper. Thus we may say that the slanderer, the swindler, the adulterer, the murderer, the covetous man universally in short, whatever be his spiritual ignorance or superstition, never finds it excluding him from immortal life, if indeed he himself have happily any aspiration towards such a thing. For, as Christ taught, "*all manner of sin and blasphemy shall be forgiven unto men, except the sin or blasphemy against the holy spirit, which has no forgiveness either in this world or that which is to come.*" That is to say: our moral evils are natural, and spring from the circumstance that our nature is not yet Divinely redeemed or recovered from the influence of man's finite personality and reduced to permanent order; hence they have only an actual force and will altogether disappear when human nature comes to spiritual or social out of material or selfish form. But self-righteousness is an inward or spiritual condition of the subject laying hold upon a man not through his body, or what relates him to the outward world, but through his soul, or what relates him to God: so vitiating or falsifying him at the very core of his being. For a man's being is spiritually determined solely by the idea he entertains at heart of God as a being of really infinite goodness, towards whom his only logical or proper attitude therefore is one of prostrate adoration or humility. Now it is evident that no man who is at all satisfied with himself — much less a man whose self-satisfaction is motived upon a persuasion of his own exceptional private regeneration — is capable of feeling adoration towards the infinite goodness: or, to say the same thing in other words, is capable of a humble or deprecatory judgment in relation to himself. How shall a man dare to think meanly of himself when he looks upon that self as a piece of exquisite Divine or regenerative workmanship? This would be to think meanly of God, so that even the churchman's piety is a snare to him and constrains him to self-delusion. In fact the devil arms his hooks nowadays with no subtler or more specious bait than that of piety, and people who are so unfortunate as to have it in their blood, inheriting a more or less devout temperament from their ancestors, cannot be too thankful to the frosty providence that so often kindly nips in the bud their nascent aspirations after personal holiness, and so if need be compels them personally into the safer spiritual paths of a frank and utter worldliness.

Certainly then self-righteousness — which is a satisfactory estimate of one's own selfhood, character, or standing as compared with that of the vast majority of men, those embraced in the "world" for example — is spiritually the only fatal form of ungodliness. And just as certainly it is a plant requiring for its development a church-soil; so that if the church had never existed as an integral or representative factor in the development of human nature, we should have been at a loss to imagine any soil rank enough or tropical enough to produce it; and men accordingly would have been left to the much less harmful dominion and devices of their merely selfish and worldly loves. This at any rate is my own thorough intellectual conviction, and I am bound to show you the grounds of it.

Do me the justice however not to imagine that I am going to overwhelm you with any scientific evidence of the truth of my conviction, such evidence as will compel your assent, or deprive you of freedom to think differently from me. For such evidence is out of place in reference to intellectual things or truths of perception. My conviction, for example, in relation to the intimate connection between a self-

righteous temper in man and the atmosphere of the
church institution, is not the fruit of any scientific
observation or inductive reasoning on my part, though
these things aptly enough come in to enforce it.
And a parade therefore of the scientific grounds of
such a conviction would not only be uncalled for
or inappropriate, but would prove derogatory to the
interests of a much larger and Diviner life in man
than that of science, to which I at all events feel
my sympathies primarily due: I mean of course our
distinctively intellectual life, or the life which is
authenticated by our affections, and not by our senses.
Neither is the conviction in question the fruit primarily of any private spiritual regeneration on my
part, but is such fruit only in a rigidly secondary
sense, that is, only in so far as my private spiritual
regeneration is itself the fruit altogether of a Divine
redemption of our common nature. In short, you
must all along assiduously remember that we are not
now talking of any paltry fact of organic experience,
or fact of sense, which can be scientifically probed
or proved: proved, that is, to men's senses: but of
a truth of men's inward or regenerate nature exclusively, of their *living* or spiritual experience, of their
soul-history as it were; a truth which has slowly
flowered out of the suffering human heart, and which
therefore appeals for its ratification in every mind

solely to the man's cultivated or disciplined affections. It is a truth which no amount of merely scientific culture, nor any ardor of ratiocinative acumen, will ever qualify a man to do justice to. In fact these things are very apt to *dis*qualify men for the acknowledgment of spiritual or living truth, since the method of science and that of intellectual cognition are directly opposed: the one proceeding from without inwards, or from sense to soul; the other from within outwards, or from soul to sense.*

But let me at least present some orderly considerations to you which may throw light upon the grounds of my conviction that all our spiritual evil — evil of self-righteousness — is intimately connected with the outgrowth and development of the church in human nature.

For the "church" is just as much a natural fact, or outgrowth of human nature as the "world" is. In casting our eyes back to the beginnings of man's earthly genesis we find his consciousness almost com-

---

* A man shaving himself before a looking-glass always appears, to one whose eye is fixed upon the glass, to be shaving himself with his left hand. This illustrates the immature judgment of science in making sense the supreme arbiter of truth as well as of fact. Of course the man's living or intellectual judgment of the truth of the case is sure to correct this scientific judgment, inasmuch as, to the intellect or life, the sensible form or appearance of things is never in direct but always in inverse accord with their spiritual substance or being.

pletely submerged by his senses. The needs of their visible subsistence are at first imperative upon men, and they know little more than the instincts and the arts that relate them to the satisfaction of their bodily appetites. Some men are endowed with quicker senses, with greater physical force and endurance, with subtler inventive ingenuity and alertness, than others, and these qualities insure their subjects an exceptionally successful career. Men of a slower nature on the other hand, men of a defective wit and sagacity, men of a sluggish individual genius with perhaps a greater tendency to sociability or companionship than others, constitute a comparatively unfortunate or inferior and dependent class. The former no doubt in every community are a small minority of men, and " keep the world going," as we say, for their superior practical or productive energy soon throws the government of the community into their hands. The latter are a very large majority of the human family, and are doomed to gravitate erelong into the condition of mere proletaries, keeping up the fecundity of the race. All which is only saying, in other words, that the former constitute a select or distinguished class of men, while their brethren as a class are totally without distinction.

Now to the devout imagination: for it is almost needless to say, that in face of this great and formidable reality of a fixed outward world, and before the world has betrayed its latent humanity, or subserviency to Divine uses, all men are helplessly, or as we say instinctively, devout, even to the pitch of superstition or fetichism : to the devout imagination of men, I repeat, there is in this obvious characteristic division of men into two classes a natural basis for the church, or for the acknowledgment of a Divinely providential order in the earth. There is as yet of course no such thing as the church *in name*, or as a corporate organization fenced in from the outlying world of mankind by ritual ceremonies or observances ; but it is there practically or *in substance* all the while, inwardly recognizable to every one in whom a strong virus of personality, or selfhood, or character has had opportunity to assert itself, and it only awaits the imposition of its name to be submissively recognized or acquiesced in by the vulgar intelligence as well. For the fundamental idea of the church as a corporate or visible institution is that of a select or chosen few of mankind Divinely culled, or called out, from the undistinguished, chaotic or monotonous mass of men, and set apart to the Divine service and honor. And where to the eye of our innocent or unsophisticated carnal intelligence is this idea better embodied than it is in those who either by their productive genius and

energy first make the earth fruitful, and introduce
the community to the acquaintance of wealth and its
resources, or else by their manifest military skill and
prowess teach the community how to defend and protect their life and property from the cupidity of in-
vaders? These men by their inventive sagacity and
enterprise, by their heroism, by their administrative
skill and ability, are for the time a true Divine seed
in human nature, and mark or constitute the distinctively providential movement in humanity. They
are the astute Abrams, and Isaacs, and Jacobs who
all unknown to themselves marshal the otherwise
imbecile masses of men into line with man's Divine-natural destiny. And they constitute accordingly
God's true church in the earth so long as the church
is at all a puissant reality : that is to say, long before
it has attained to the outward name or consciousness of being a church, and sunk into the unwholesome and emasculate spiritual dilettantism which
that unfortunate name or consciousness connotes.

Here then is my first point made : the church
and — by virtue of its inclusion in that — the world
are both alike rigidly *natural* facts, are both alike
indubitable *historic powers or functions of human nature*, and represent nothing more than the alternate spiritual and material aspect which human
history derives from its undoubted natural factors.

And the second point which I intended to establish
was that our existing self-righteous tendencies, which
spiritually viewed are the only reprehensible tendencies of human nature, come from the church, and
are a wholly proper development or expression of
her spirit in us.   That is to say, my general purpose
in establishing this point is to show that the sacred
element in human life, *in so far as it has come to the
surface of consciousness in institutions, or can be in
any way literally identified,* is infinitely less innocent
than the rival secular element, and does infinitely
more harm to the spiritual life of man.

—— But this proposition, because it involves a
much more spiritual apprehension of the meaning
of human nature, and a much closer insight into
its metaphysical principles, had better be left for its
working out to another letter.

LETTER XXVII.

MY DEAR FRIEND: We saw in the last letter that the church and the world are both alike facts of human nature, and express nothing but her composite parentage, her mixed Divine and human genius. Human nature has an equal aspect towards God and man, for it is confessedly the nature of a creature, and a creature is nothing in itself but the existence or going forth of its creator. Thus we may say it has both a Divine side by virtue of God alone being a creator, and a human side by virtue of this creator being essential man. For we must always bear in mind that the human side of our nature is not in the least constituted by us phenomenal men (by you and me, for instance, and others like you and me, who call ourselves men) but solely by God the Lord who alone is Man both spiritually and naturally. You and I, you know, are merely *conscious* men; that is, we seem to ourselves to be a human reality, but in truth we are mere shadows of such reality, having no more of human substance in ourselves, no more pretension either of us actually to be the man we seem, than our shadow in a looking-glass has to be our personal substance. We are just the same seeming or semblance in the natural sphere, or sphere of consciousness, which that phenomenon is in the scientific sphere, or sphere of sense, with precisely the same claim to objective reality or spiritual being, as *it* has to subjective reality or moral consciousness, not a particle more or less. Besides you know that nature is one and universal, while we are nothing if we are not many and particular. You know moreover, at least I have no doubt you do, I do at all events, that though we all the while flatter ourselves that we possess this universal substance, and are wont to claim human nature as our own, what a struggle it always costs us to arrive at the least inward realization of it, or *universalize* ourselves in our affections one jot. And then, after all our struggles, we are compelled to lay aside our familiar flesh and bones in the grave, as if we had been confessedly animals all along and not men. Thus I admit that you and I and all other men are phenomenal or conscious forms of humanity, and give forth or reproduce in our petty persons some faint shadow of her stupendous substance. But this is a totally distinct thing from saying that we

ourselves constitute humanity, unless indeed we are
willing to reckon the shadow of a thing identical with
its substance.   For if we are veritable phenomena,
manifestations, products of human nature, unquestionable deliverances of her miraculous womb, it is
simply preposterous to suppose that she can feel her
existence contingent for a moment upon ours, however much indeed the *consciousness* of such existence
may be confined to us.

Remember then, my friend, that you and I and all
the other minim personalities of the universe are so
far from constituting the human side of our nature
that we are full surely constituted by it, deriving all
our power consciously to exist and act from it, and it
alone.   Nor can any of us atomic men, however much
we may claim to be children of nature, ever boast
himself of being in any sense her favorite child.   She
makes small account of persons at any time, allowing
us to be cut down in myriads whenever she feels herself impelled to a fuller manifestation of herself, and
she drenches us with a perpetual shower of personal
disasters, which rob us of assured health or fortune
or of stable domestic felicity in a way to prove even
to the dullest imagination, that she is at deadly and
deliberate war with our private welfare save in so far
as it is a mere reflection of our public worth.   The
undeniable reason of this inveterate hostility on the

part of nature to men's private consequence when unconditioned upon their public desert, is that being human *au fond* her form is necessarily social, being the intense marriage unity of its particular and universal interests, or its private and public elements : and so long therefore as this natural marriage unity lacks its literal or ritual consecration in our outward or phenomenal personalities, this social form of humanity will never come to men's knowledge, and every man accordingly must be left to perish in his selfishness.

Our natural history in fact is providentially designed for no other purpose than to exemplify the vanity or nothingness of human individuality when underived from race or nature, and the gospel it proclaims to every man as the only gospel of immortality, as at least the only one he can *inwardly* live by, is that of a thoroughly righteous self-contempt, or a just disdain of his own interests whenever they bring him into collision with those of society or his fellow-man. For the only real fellow that the individual man has in nature, is by no means some other individual man (for this would be not fellowship or equality but identity) but the complex or composite man, society. Society is the only real or Divine natural man, and we individual men (falsely so-called) attain to a real or Divinely recognizable individuality only in identifying ourselves with him : that is, *in losing our life in ourselves and finding it again, resurgent, in society.* The intellectual meaning with which this great fact of experience is fraught is, that what we call nature, meaning thereby the outward world, the world apprehended by sense, and in spite of its overwhelming reality to sense, is at bottom a profound Divine imposture or cheat which is most providentially engineered all the while in the interest of ineffable (that is to say, infinite and eternal) spiritual realities of which it is the exact counterpart and correspondence, and which therefore we should always remain ignorant of unless we were thus figuratively or experimentally taught. These ineffable and (unless they be revealed) unthinkable spiritual realities are God : as He is called by those who recognize Him mainly as he is outwardly revealed to the understanding under the form of Truth : and Man : as he is named by those who recognize Him mainly as he is inwardly revealed to the heart under the form of Good : but God-man, or the Lord, as He is more comprehensively designated by those who recognize him as a practical providence in history, that is, as He becomes revealed to sense under the form of power, or goodness and truth *united*, in order to effect the actual redemption of human nature or the human race from death.

What then finally *is* nature in herself regarded ? I don't mean what is commonly called nature, being the external world, which is a mere chaos of mineral, vegetable, and animal existence without rhythm or law in itself to make it intelligible, for this in truth is not nature but merely that necessary background or basis of specific existence which nature requires to emphasize or set off her own universality. No, I mean by nature human nature, the nature of man, for this is the only nature that objectively exists to its own subjects, and so is capable of giving them elevation out of themselves. And if we ask what human nature, or the nature of man, is, we have a sure index to the answer in ascertaining what man himself is : for the nature of a thing is merely the development of its being to its own consciousness.

Now man is a purely personal, unreal, or phenomenal subject, existing only to consciousness, not to sense, but firmly related to lower or outward things by his bodily organization or senses which give him fixity or finiteness, and to higher or inward things by his inorganic, percipient soul which gives him freedom or rational enlargement. And human nature, then, being the nature of man, must be the sphere of consciousness in him, the sphere of his conscious life, outside of which he does not exist. How then does it differ from the man himself ? If human nature be the sphere of consciousness in men, and man have no existence out of consciousness, what hinders me identifying myself with my nature? This fact alone: that I being a person am a finite or particular form of consciousness, without universal quality, whereas nature not being a person is not a finite or particular form of consciousness, but a most indefinite or universal one, without particular quality. Accordingly nature is to be logically defined as the realm of consciousness in man, the peculiarly *human* realm, inasmuch as it separates him from the realm of sense which he shares in common with animal and vegetable and mineral. It is no *thing*, nor yet any congeries of things save to sense and the judgment begotten of it, but a certain undefined or purely potential and promissory existence which subjectively never *is* but is always *becoming* or *to be*, and on its sensibly objective side images or reflects the intercourse of infinite and finite, God and man, spirit and flesh, constituting indeed to our sensuous imagination the eternal link or *liaison* of the two. For as God being creative is infinite *in himself*, that is, spirit or life, and therefore essentially inward, and as man being created is finite *in himself*, that is, matter or death, and therefore essentially outward, there must be spiritually an endless and fatal subjective disagreement between the two creative factors: so that if some middle term did not exist to

fuse or reconcile these discordant factors in her own
commanding objectivity, creation would be a failure
in first principles.   Now nature is this actual middle
term.   She offers her effectual mediation to the rival
or opposite creative factors, and by her strictly undefined or universal objectivity covers up or makes
amends for their subjective disagreement by allowing
them to become objectively one or united, *within her
own strict limits* mind you, or mutually to change
places, infinite becoming finite and finite infinite, in a
new and immortal human individuality.

Nature accordingly is not creation, nor any part
of creation (though she is included in it as the creature's constitutional or mother-substance), for creation
is wholly spiritual, living, or subjective, being the
work of omnipotence, or of God's infinity and eternity,
and is therefore inscrutable to mortal ken.   But though
nature is not either in whole or in part God's spiritual creation, she nevertheless most truly REVEALS or
accommodates it to our nascent and obstinate intelligence, and is herself frankly unintelligible and
misleading save as such revelation.   We should never
have been able even to dream of creation as a living
and spiritual or miraculous work of God, nor of God
himself consequently as a being infinite and eternal
in love, wisdom, and power, if nature were a fixed
physical existence or quantity shut up to the dimen-

sions of space and time. But this is just what she is
not — a fixed physical existence, but a wholly unfixed
or metaphysical one, forever enlarging to men's affection and thought as their affection and thought themselves become penetrated and interfused by the Divine
infinitude, or moulded to the inspiration of the creative
goodness and truth. It is true that being the abjectly
helpless and dependent intelligences we are, we are
indebted for our earliest recognition of nature's presence and power to the gross sensible forms of mineral, vegetable, and animal existence, and for a long
time indeed do not scruple to identify her personality
with such forms. But it is not long before we begin
to divine her intensely human quality, and thenceforth
we come to acknowledge her only as the perfect marriage fusion or unity of the Divine and human natures.
Remember then that nature in herself or subjectively
is neither God nor man, but the rigid neutrality or
indifference of the two, while on her objective side, or
viewed from the maternal uses she contributes to the
spiritual creation, she reflects each to the knowledge
of the other, and so enables them each to reap the
transcendent spiritual or subjective fruits of such
knowledge. Or, to say the same thing in other
words, remember that nature is neither a spiritual nor
yet a physical existence, but a most strictly metaphysical or empirical one, provisionally mediating between

the two, since while it owes its base or fixed body to physics, it owes its superstructure or free expansive soul entirely to spirit.

But although nature is a purely metaphysic realm, it will not do to infer that she is therefore without cognizable form. Existence is not possible without cognizable form, nor even conceivable without think-able form, because distinctive form is the essence of a thing or what it derives from the creative Esse. It is true that nature being metaphysic substance is with-out material form *in se*, form discernible to sense ; but the entire realm of personality is hers, and the material world exists only to furnish a basis to person-ality. Thus though nature herself is not material she yet holds the whole realm of physics subject to her metaphysic will. Sense in fact is simply con-sciousness in solution. And the reason doubtless therefore why personality is never discernible to sense but only to consciousness, is because sense is included in consciousness as the marble in the statue, or what-ever mere *materies* in whatever *opus*. And surely you would not expect the dead matter of a thing to be able to judge of the living form to which it is subservient.

It is very much the fashion just now with scientific fledglings and unintellectual people generally to decry metaphysics, or sneer at them in fact, as though metaphysical existence were confessedly no existence, or as if all existence were bound to be real or impersonal, and confess itself in the last analysis a *thing*. I don't mean to profess any contempt for *things*, for at times I feel a very considerable relish for them, and derive much comfort from them. But at the same time I should be wretched to think all existence confined to them. My affections are very apt to go out towards persons, and if I could be persuaded therefore that persons had no souls, but only bodies, my proper human life would be very much diminished. Instead of being as I had thought it a house of three stories at the very least, I should find it reduced to a house of one story, and that a squalid basement sunk in earth. These persons to be sure are but finite forms, imperfect images, of goodness and truth. But in consequence of that very fact they exert a most benignant power or influence upon my life : for I cannot know goodness and truth in themselves, but only as they approximate themselves to my feeble understanding in finite types. I am much impressed also with the beauty of certain persons, with their artistic genius or their executive talent and skill, and if the persons did not exist who betrayed these attractive qualities to me, I should feel myself sadly mystified or trifled with. But if these persons exist at all, they exist one and all only metaphysically. That is to say, their existence — while it acknowledges a physical *basis*, imperatively claims at the same time *a free or spiritual superstructure*. And it is only a priggish or pedantic person who is liable to the gross mistake alike in science as in art of making base dominate superstructure, or body govern soul.

Now by what signs is metaphysical existence characterized that it shall not be swamped in physics? In other words, how do we recognize the natural force in things, and recognize it so infallibly as to be in no danger of ever confounding it in thought with their material force? I think this question admits of a satisfactory answer.

The natural force in things then signalizes itself by this infallible earmark, namely: it is a force of law or order, constraining our allegiance under pain of death. This is the invariable distinction of natural law: its strictly *negative or death-bearing quality towards its finite subject*. It has on its face no positive or life-bearing quality whatever for its subject, absolutely none, but remorselessly shuts him up to despair and death *in himself*, as if to warn him past all possibility of mistake that nature disowns a finite subjectivity, and will never therefore under any circumstances justify his private pretension to be her proper offspring. It chases the subject out of every hidden nook and corner of his personal conscious-

ness, and makes even his most innocent and transient
animal delights perilous to his freedom, or dangerous to his soul's peace. Thus when I eat and drink
and sleep, or enact any other automatic function pre-
scribed by my animal organization, I am constrained
to be very prudent lest I suddenly find myself in
undesigned conflict with my nature; and this is the
only way that I gradually come to natural consciousness, or learn to separate myself from the animal
chained up in my body. For I never eat and drink
and sleep, you will observe, at the instance of my
proper nature, which is exclusively human, and therefore Divine and infinite, or free from all want, but
at the prompting of those gross animal, vegetable,
and mineral wants or appetites which are necessarily
bound up or involved in my nature by way of affording it a ground of evolution to the consciousness of
its subject. For human nature has no outward or
objective evolution, that is, no evolution in itself,
but only to its conscious subject, and as the true or
metaphysic form of such subjectivity. Thus it has no
existence to sense, but only to consciousness. And
no man who does n't come to his consciousness of it
in the purely inward or metaphysic way I have described, that is, *only in a way of hearty resistance to
his tyrannous animal appetites and tendencies,* has any
consciousness of it at all, but remains at his very

best a mere conscious animal in human form. Accordingly let me eat or drink to excess, and sleep without regard to time and place, or perform any other of my automatic or animal functions with a full animal absorption in it, that is, without a primary respect to the superior human *convenances* which qualify such functions to men, and I am instantly sure to hear an inward Divine voice arraigning me as a culprit to my own nature, and compelling me perhaps to walk humbly many days afterwards.*

---

* *Sic itur ad astra :* there is no way of getting to heaven but the way of *self*-denial, which is inward or spiritual humility. There are but few who are content to walk in this heavenly way, I know, because it is not half so sweet and alluring to carnal thought as the way of self-indulgence, which is that of saintly asceticism. There is nothing so inwardly nourishing to SELF-hood in man as the culture of asceticism, or the practice of needlessly snubbing one's innocent and unconscious flesh : for of course the more that is done of this unrequired or gratuitous work, the more the subject's complacency in himself abounds, and the greater grows his sense of merit, which is the source of all our spiritual defilement. Our nature never prompts any mortification to the flesh in us : for the flesh is always Divinely sweet and modest until it has been bedevilled by our ascetic efforts to worry some comfort out of it to our *self*-righteous pretensions : but only to *the fleshly mind*, which is *the exact mind of the ascetic or church-saint.* If accordingly you want to see how exquisitely filthy a man may inwardly be who is outwardly expert and cultivated in the spirit and methods of ascetic piety, you have only to look up some of Swedenborg's *Memorable Relations,* describing certain of the Romish saints as they appear in their spiritual undress, when stripped of their decent and honorable natural clothing, and if I mistake not you will find yourself agreeably edified. To judge from Sweden-

Such is human nature, and its adverse bearing
upon men's animal or finite and outward personalities.   But this inauspicious bearing of it seems
very much heightened when it assumes moral form,
and is seen no longer simply controlling the relations
that bind a man to his own body, or to the animal
force in his own body, but much more the inward or
metaphysic relations of man to man.   For now its
death-bearing *animus* becomes vividly enhanced in
its stamping men no longer vicious merely, with the
hospital and lunatic asylum in prospect, but criminal
as well, with the jail and the scaffold in the distance
to emphasize or give force to the verdict.   It now
practically says in fact that men are not only corrupt

---

borg's remarkable daguerreotypes (for they have all the softness of the
daguerreotype, betraying the warmth of love in their production, no less
than the light of intelligence) I should say that this class of persons,
the church-saint, of all our spiritual *mauvais sujets*, displays the most
inveterately subterranean proclivities or shows men's evil possibilities at
their *ne plus ultra* of development, their utmost refinement of natural
degeneracy.   I say this of course not because the saints in question
happen to be Romish (though the Romish church unquestionably deals
with a lower order of heart and mind than the Protestant does, and is
very apt to breed therefore much more coarse and brutal conceptions of
sanctity when it breeds any), but simply because the aspiration after
personal holiness, whether in Protestant or Catholic, is the most depraved spiritual tendency of the human heart, and is *utterly* fatal therefore to God's love in the human soul.   For the infallible law of spiritual life is that *he who exalts himself shall be abased, and he who abases
himself* (not *his flesh*, mind you !) *shall be exalted.*

or worthless on their passive physical side, which is the mother's side in them, but also and much more on their active, voluntary, or moral side, which they inherit from the father. Thus my nature finally reveals itself in its moral form of evolution not merely as the organ of my instincts, but as the true and sole organic power behind my will or personality : so assailing my moral or self-righteous power, my pride of freedom or selfhood, in the most secret fastnesses of its strength, and asserting its death-bearing energy over my human person with new emphasis in making my fellow-man henceforth the register and vindicator of its decrees, in addition to or in place of my own less faithful private conscience.

I have now at length, I hope, succeeded in making two points of first-rate philosophic moment perfectly clear to you. 1. We have seen what human nature is in itself, namely : a middle-ground, or transition-point, between creator and creature, God and man, infinite and finite, spirit and flesh, making the two freely interchangeable. 2. We have seen also by what infallible tokens it reveals itself in men's finite or private consciousness, namely : as a free or regenerative spiritual force in them aiming to give them life out of death by releasing them from their finite limitations, or the bondage of their animal, vegetable, and mineral ties (which merely give men visible constitution or make them phenomenal to themselves), so allying them at last in conscious fellowship with God's spiritual infinitude.

But a third point remains to be considered, not perhaps of equal speculative importance with these, but of even greater practical consequence, and that is, briefly stated : What is the machinery by which our Divinized human nature vindicates itself, or avouches its existence, to the *public* conscience of mankind, so inaugurating the reign of God's justice or righteousness upon earth ?

—The answer to this question, however, will require a letter to itself, but I hope this letter will be a final one, and gather up all that yet remains to be understood between us.

LETTER XXVIII.

MY DEAR FRIEND:—In my last letter I answered, or tried to answer, two questions each of sovereign import to the speculative welfare of philosophy. The first question was about human nature itself, its origin and quality. The second led us to consider its method of actual development to the consciousness of its carnal votary, as *conscience,* or *the negative law of human freedom.* If you will allow me now briefly to resume or recapitulate the answers I gave to these questions, bearing as they do so profoundly on the speculative interests of religion and philosophy, we shall both of us be better able to do justice to a third question which we are more particularly bound to consider in the present letter, and which is of transcendent practical importance to the interests, not of any special science perhaps, but certainly to the general science of human life.

We saw then in our last letter that human nature

is a strictly metaphysic existence, postulating the entire realm of physics beneath it or under it precisely as the pedestal is postulated in the statue, or the body in the soul: in order adequately to base it, that is, to finite it, or give it on its objective side permanent fixity or isolation. Human nature originates spiritually in God who is real or essential man, and it merely expresses on its inward or spiritual side the ceaseless effort of His providence to manifest itself creatively, that is, to attain to adequate actual or existential form in His creature. The creature of course *ex vi termini* is in himself, or *quâ* creature, utterly "without form, and void" of distinctive quality, and any form or quality he may exhibit therefore is not attributable to himself but to the creator in him : unless indeed it be a purely evil and fallacious form or quality, in which case it exists only to consciousness, and has no fibre of reality outside of it.

But although God is in truth most real or essential man it will not do to infer that He is, *ipso facto* merely, formal or existential man as well. Of course He who alone is real or essential man is *ipso facto* also *virtually* formal or existential man, since there can be no such thing as an absolute divorce between substance and form : but only virtually, or in potency, not actually. His becoming actually what He is potentially, or outwardly what He is in-

wardly, depends entirely upon His being creative
and thus having a sphere of actual or outward manifestation put within His grasp. For the creator who
is real or inward and essential man becomes actual
or outward and existential man only through His
creature, or by virtue of His first giving spiritual
or inward being to the creature. The creature no
doubt, unapprised as yet save by revelation of his
being spiritually created, or of his having any *inward*
potency of life, *seems* to himself to be a most veridical actual man. But this is all a seeming. For
he being created is of necessity in himself a mere
finite form or image of humanity; and even as
such form or image can only reproduce the human
type in so far as he is freely united to his brethren :
which he can never be, which in fact he selfishly
loathes to be, until his proper interest tardily constrains him to that mercenary policy. Besides, as
I have already intimated, it is illogical and stupid
to suppose that any one can be actual or formal
man but He who is first real or substantial man.
For if substance and form differed in themselves,
and not simply in relation to a finite intelligence,
creation would be at a *nonplus*. In truth then God
alone is both real, or inward and essential man, and
actual, or outward and existential man. In short, He
alone is man in substance, and man in form.

Be it understood then between us that we ourselves, however truly we may be said to symbolize
actual human nature, or typify formal manhood, have
yet no shadow of a claim to constitute such manhood, any more than we have a shadow of claim to
constitute Divinity, or real and essential manhood.
For we are only at our best finite phenomenal men,
and neither singly nor in mass therefore can we ever
hope to be that actual and unitary *form* of man,
which as being correlative to its real or essential
Divine substance, must be every way proportionate
to such substance, and therefore itself Divine and
infinite. But though we have no shadow of justification in so doing, we do nevertheless all the while
betray our spiritual ignorance in assuming *bona fide*
to constitute *the whole of the formal and actual humanity which exists on earth*, and which in theory
reflects the inward and essential humanity of God:
thus and thereby baffling or indefinitely retarding
the Divine purpose (and indeed the Divine ability)
eventually to show us the spiritual truth of the case.
For God is too wise and good a being (since He is
real or essential man) practically to contemn or over-
ride His creature's natural prejudices, and very much
prefers to make His creature also, like Himself, wise
and good by gradually illumining those natural prejudices, and bending them to the truth.

Allow me then to repeat to you a truth which we have as yet barely glanced at, but which is calculated yet to shed an infinite amount of light upon the philosophy of human nature and human history. That truth is as follows, and I conjure you to ponder it well if you would ever hope to master the true secret of the spiritual creation: Although God our creator is real or spiritual and inward man, and *by that fact stands pledged eventually to show Himself sole actual or natural and outward man also*, nevertheless His entire ability to do this is in strict abeyance to His creature's good pleasure in the premisses, or depends upon the human race giving Him a chance to accomplish the task. For He is the absolute creator of men, and by that very fact bound in such intimate solidarity with them, that He cannot bestow any of His own potencies and felicities upon them without their own free consent and concurrence. Much less therefore can He bestow upon them that knowledge of Himself as the only true subject of their nature which is immortal life, so long as they each stupidly persist in maintaining that they themselves are its sole true subjects, and He himself consequently its sole undeniable object. We cannot hope then to see God avouching himself both inwardly and outwardly, both really and actually, both spiritually and naturally, true man, and

alone fit to bear the untarnished name of Man, until
the human race becomes so fused *within itself* —
that is, so constituted in felt or conscious unity with
itself — as to form a perfect society, brotherhood, or
fellowship of its particular and universal elements,
each of its members spontaneously devoting himself
to the welfare of all, and all the members in their
turn freely espousing the welfare of each.

Then doubtless, and not before, the creator of men
will have become formal, existential, or natural man
as well as substantial, essential, or spiritual man, and
you and I will never again be such arrant idiots
spiritually as to deem ourselves God's true creatures
in our own private right, or out of social solidarity
with all other men.   For the great phenomenon of
human society — *of men made social out of, and* so
to speak *by virtue of, their extreme and inveterate
selfishness* — will then strike every eye as the consummate miracle of God's spiritual perfection in our
nature, and the eternally sufficing manifestation of
His matchless adorable name.   But until the human
race attains to plenary social form we may be very
sure that as the end of God's spiritual creation in
human nature meanwhile must be perfectly obscured
or overlaid by men's prevalent ignorance and superstition, so, much more, the origin of that nature in
God's infinite love and wisdom will be completely

misapprehended, as we see in point of fact it has
been. For men have always been wont to attribute
any thing but a Divine genesis to their nature, assigning a purely *à posteriori* origin to it in place of
an *à priori* one. That is to say, they make it originate in a gradual evolution of humanity from precedent mineral, vegetable, and animal forms: thus
in effect or figuratively making the head of creation
take the place of its heels, or subjecting soul to
body, statue to pedestal, oyster to shell, ship to
sails, church to steeple, house to foundation, man
to clothing.

Now let me say that it is nothing but this helplessly *carnal* habit of mind in us — this instinctive
and inveterate tendency on our part to envisage creation, not as a spiritual Divine life or truth in man,
but only as a dead material fact or thing — which
forever condemns us *in ourselves* to a purely natural
or metaphysic and phenomenal existence; that is
to say, to an existence which is as remote in itself
from spiritual truth as it is from material fact, being
equidistant from, and inaccessible to, the inward
life of the angel on the one hand, and the purely outward or sensuous life of the devil on the other. And
the obvious reason of this state of things: that is
to say, the reason why nature exhibits this strictly
neutral or equatorial quality — making the divided

hemispheres of good and evil, heaven and hell, spirit
and flesh, eternally spherical in itself, that is, making
them one and equal as the two opposing abutments
of a bridge are made one and equal in the bridge
—is that the problem of creation to the Divine
mind, being how eternally to reconcile two factors,
creator and creature, which are totally irreconcilable
in themselves, one being all fulness, the other all
want, one all spirit or life, the other all flesh or
death, inexorably demands therefore for its solution a third or middle term which shall be neutral
or indifferent to either factor, infinite or finite, by
avouching itself a rigidly indefinite or universal quantity as the unity of each and all. Accordingly this
requisite and accommodating middle term which
actually solves the creative problem is supplied
by human nature. Human nature impartially solves
the creative problem, because while it is absolutely
neutral or rather altogether negative with respect to
either interest, creative or created, *in se*, it is therefore most positive or affirmative with respect to
both as they become conjoined in living unity. The
method of this conjunction, from which the spiritual creation results, arises from the gradual experi-
mental conversion of the principle of self in man,
the evil principle, which represents the finite man,
into the principle of society or fellowship, the good

principle, which represents the infinite humanity, so making God and man naturally, as they always have been spiritually, one.

This then is an explicit statement of what I implicitly said about nature in the last letter; but after all it is an account of nature on its theoretic rather than its practical side, or as it exists to the mind of its author only and not as it appears to a finite dependent intelligence. Practically then, or to the finite mind, nature, as I went on to say in that letter, reveals itself not, to be sure, in its own perfect or consummate spiritual way, as an undefined or universal form, being the unity of the whole and its parts, but in the specific form of *conscience*, or the law upon which man's natural freedom is negatively conditioned, the purpose of conscience being to redeem him out of the bondage he is under by birth to his physical organization, and so qualify him for social or distinctively human form, which is the only form commensurate with the spiritual Divine perfection or infinitude. In other words creation in its finite natural aspect, its aspect towards the carnal creature, necessarily wears the appearance of an emancipating, spiritualizing, or redemptive operation, divorcing the creature from the organic bondage to which he is born subject, and investing him instead with moral and rational freedom.

But here I must beg you to note with most minute attention one thing, which is: that *morality and rationality, although they separate man from animal, and thereby qualify him to take the name of man, yet they do this only provisionally.* They do not invest him with absolute, but only with phenomenal, manhood, making his real participation of human nature altogether contingent upon his personal humility, or the degree in which he freely admits the neighbor to a first place in his habitual regard, and limits himself to the second place. Freedom and rationality by no means give any of us a title to the Divine potencies and felicities which inhere in human nature; they only make him, or inscribe him as, a candidate for such title. In short they give man a *quasi* or mere negative and seeming natural consciousness, by no means a real or positive one, and hence they do not guarantee him the spiritual Divine being of which human nature is the sole possible vehicle whether to man or angel.

For example. My moral manhood, which stands in my felt freedom of will to choose between good and evil, is not absolute but contingent or conditional: being rigidly conditioned *upon my actually choosing good.* If, as some persons not very clearsighted are wont to pretend, my will cannot feel itself free to do one thing unless it feel itself also free at the same time to do the exact contrary thing, I would not call this latter faculty by the sacred name of freedom, but by that of bondage, since it can be exercised only at the expense of renouncing one's manhood. *My moral manhood depends*, and depends absolutely, *upon my felt freedom always to take the side of good in preference to evil whenever and wherever I find them conflicting, and never the side of evil in preference to good.* Thus if in case of conflict I actually choose evil, or prefer it to good, my moral or provisional manhood not only turns out an actual sham, but *by the foreclosure of the condition on which its entire possibility was based*, sinks below animality even, and becomes frankly evil or diabolic. It is true, I may not in so doing recognize that I am incurring a forfeiture of all human possibilities, and probably shall not, going on indeed to prate of my superb and lustrous manhood even after I have shut myself up in hell. But this will be simply because manhood is an inward not an outward form or quality, and therefore only to be inwardly discerned, whereas I in the circumstances supposed am really or inwardly knavish not human, and recognize manhood therefore only as accomplished knavery.

In like manner precisely my rational manhood, which stands in the freedom of my understanding to discriminate the true from the false, proves itself no manhood at all, but the veriest monkeyhood and mockery of humanity, if I forbear to exert it, or devoutly exercise myself in it, *by actually loving the true and rejecting the false.* To be sure, as some of our egregious logic-choppers counsel me to do, I may interpret my moral and rational manhood into a state of utter serene indifference with respect to the rival claims of good and evil upon my heart, and the rival claims of truth and falsity upon my understanding. But in that event my vaunted moral and rational manhood turns out a mere faculty to prefer good *or* evil, truth *or* falsity, at my own ungodly pleasure. In which case my moral manhood is my right to do just as I please, without regard to any holier or higher law. In other words it expresses my actual independence both of God and man. But this is a manhood which can never come from God, for there is no fibre of foundation for it in the whole range of His perfection. He himself has no independence of action, and He could never impart to His creature therefore what He did not Himself possess. His inmost life is dependent upon His actually equalizing His creature with Himself, or making Himself over to the latter in all the plenitude of His resources. And all His action is constrained by this unselfish end, and addressed unfalteringly to its promotion. Any freedom or manhood therefore which looks towards independence, or makes the moral and rational subject his own law, should be indignantly spurned by him as a base infernal counterfeit of the true Divine manhood. That a man in loving good should feel himself free to love its opposite can only be possible on one of two conditions: Either good and evil must be at bottom identical, and differ only in name; which is an hypothesis too obviously stupid to invite consideration: or else the man does not honestly love good but for some temporary motive is willing to make a pretence of loving it: and this hypothesis thoroughly vitiates the problem, or reduces it to actual insignificance, by changing its terms. I do not deny of course that a man may actually or outwardly *take* tea, when he really or inwardly *prefers* coffee. But that while he prefers coffee he should also feel himself free to prefer tea, is plainly a phenomenon referring itself to that grotesque world imagined by the late hard-headed but warm-hearted Mr. Mill, which no sun enlightens, but where a mild moonshine reigns supreme, and even the virtuous multiplication table grows wanton and indulgent, permitting all its tender mathematical nurslings to say twice two are five, and if five, why not fifty?

At any rate there is no such freedom as that here combated in God, and there can be no appearance of it in man His creature save as a diabolic illusion.* Whatever his silly creature may do in the premisses,

---

* Swedenborg accordingly traces the existence of the hells to the strength of this illusion in men, and this undeniably is a sufficient foundation for them. That is to say, the hells simply mean — nothing more and nothing less — the enforced or obligatory companionship of all those among men who feel no inward *liaison*, or Divine-human bond of cohesion, drawing them to unity, and hence depend for their highest happiness upon the activity of the prudential instinct in them, or a life involving the perpetual balance of hope and fear. And if men really persuade themselves that their Divinely given manhood or freedom involves the power of being good or evil at their own pleasure, I cannot for my part see that the hells are not the logical spontaneous outcome of such a persuasion. In fact their existence at once ceases to be a mystery, and becomes an open exigency of human welfare, an obvious inevitable necessity of man's natural development. For human nature, or the human race, is absolutely conditioned for its development upon man's power to love God (that is, infinite goodness and truth) *apparently*, but not really, of himself; or as Swedenborg writing in Latin prefers to say, *as* of himself, but not *of* himself. For if man spontaneously loved goodness, loved it of his own natural force, he would be God, and no longer a creature of God; and yet, so long as he does not love God or goodness of himself, if he did not at the same time love Him *apparently* of himself, or *as* of himself, he would not even have a negative approximation to his creative source, much less furnish a background or basis to the Divine being for the development of human nature. And failing both a positive and negative relation to God, of course the man can have no reality in him, spiritual or natural, and must remain the subject of a mere illusory or fantastic existence: and to be such a subject is to be a hell in least or miniature form.

or rather boast himself of doing, God at least has no privilege of arbitrary or capricious action, because He has not the slightest power to do as *He* pleases, or make Himself into His own end of action. For God, as I have often enough said already, is *essentially* creative, creative by the whole force of His being; and His action therefore is inexorably under law to the welfare of His creature. He is not creative from any inspiration of the head merely, that is, morally or voluntarily creative, as either from a sense of duty to His creatures, or from a sense of what is expedient with a view to enliven His own solitude, or better His own condition in any way; for His creatures have their being wholly in Him, and consequently can impose no outward obligation upon Him, and He himself consequently has no existence save in His creatures, and can therefore feel no obligation to act with a view to the improvement of His own independent circumstances. Neither is He æsthetically creative, like the artist, that is, creative from the hand, through taste or overpowering attraction: for His taste would utterly revolt from producing such loathsome vermin as His creatures are bound to be in their finite *selves*, if like the artist's creations those finite selves were unhappily to know no natural renewing. He is creative therefore only from the heart, that is, freely or spontaneously

creative, creative in Himself, or with His whole vital
energy: which insures in the first place that His
inmost life lies in communicating His own deathless
being to the creature, that is, His own infinite and
eternal potencies, felicities, and beatitudes, and then
that all His innocent wisdom will go to supplant or
render superfluous the wretched *self*-righteousness of
the creature, in endowing him first of all with a
righteous nature, or stable constitutional basis of existence, whence he in his turn may every way freely
or spontaneously react to the interior creative impulsion.

We see then that the creator does not, and absolutely cannot, spiritually exist save in His creature.
A fortiori therefore He has no power to make His
own pleasure the law of His action, unless the blessedness of his creature be always subsumed in that
pleasure as its total substance and root. Thus He
is absolutely inhibited by His *essential* infinitude or
freedom from making self the end of His action, or
ever doing under any circumstances as *He* pleases,
without reference indeed to everybody else's welfare.
He cheerfully allows us a monopoly of that saddest
and most vulgar delight. For he who is essentially
free or infinite as being creative, abjures all empirical,
or felt conscious and phenomenal, freedom, because
He is absolutely without selfhood, and has no contact

with the unclean thing save in His creatures. All
His infinitude or freedom is mortgaged to the necessity of bringing His creature to ripe natural or
spontaneous manhood, and only when that burden is
accomplished and that most Divine pleasure realized
will He enjoy His first faint chance of seeing *Himself* reflected — *in the happiness of His creature.*

Very well then : our moral and rational manhood
is not our natural manhood, but only a distorted and
diffracted image of that unitary substance as seen in
the mirror of our divided and discordant personalities.
It is a similitude of our natural manhood, a sort of
photographic negative of it, by whose constant school-
ing the Divine Artist prepares and leads us eventually
to descry and detect the positive truth upon the subject. It is a similitude or semblance which we indeed are long content to mistake for the reality, but
this comes of our never having yet known the reality
by living contact, but only by hearsay. It is true
that the reality once made itself known to men in
a general prophetic way through a very remarkable
historic person, miraculously born at a great crisis
of the church's history, when the church itself was
putting off her ritual or ceremonial dress, and taking
on actual flesh-and-blood substance. But the great
and merciful truth at that time clothed itself in such
weak, dejected, dying literal form, that though its

perfect humanity was seen, men have always been
afraid to argue from that to its equally perfect divinity, and have been content instead simply to cherish
the ecclesiastical tradition on that subject.* On his

---

* This tradition does not appear to have profited men much intellectually, but doubtless it has kept their memory, which is the porch of the
mind, open to the admission of the spiritual truth on the subject. I
remember a good many years ago conversing on this topic with a highly
valued friend, who was besides a very distinguished name in literature.
And he said in reply to an account I had been giving him of Swedenborg's intellectual position with respect to the Christian revelation:
*The fatal criticism upon Christ's pretension to Divinity will always be the
fact of his having ignominiously succumbed to his persecutors, when if his
personal pretension were well founded he ought to have annihilated them.
If Christ had ever authentically revealed Deity, he would have flashed
home the conviction of his truth to every man that saw him, in sheer
despite too of the man's strongest rational prepossessions to the contrary.*
I ventured to rejoin, that my friend's own notion upon the subject seemed
to reduce poor deity to what the French would call an *impasse* within
his own creation, or what our own rustics would call "a very hard fix,"
inasmuch as it neither allows him to become known in himself, nor yet
permits him to reveal himself to men's knowledge in the nature of his
creature, without effectually blighting at the same time all that makes
that nature respectable, namely, the creature's freedom and rationality.
This freedom and rationality, which alone give the creature a consciousness of manhood, are however what actually prevent his ever truly
knowing God, for he both instinctively and deliberately claims these
superb attributes as proper to himself or *his own* absolutely, and not
exclusively as *God's attributes in his common nature.* A revelation from
God accordingly which should involve the least practical dishonor to
these attributes in man, is not to be thought of as possible. In fact
the only revelation at all possible or thinkable from God to man, is
one which conciliates every man's private freedom and rationality to it,

Jewish side of course, which related him to a purely typical or figurative economy, Christ was bound to be accursed both of God and man; for his personal pretension as the Jewish Messiah, sent to deliver his brethren according to the flesh from bondage, and exalt *them* to the supremacy of the nations, was as full of inward blasphemy towards the Divine name, as it was full of outward contempt towards the human race. It was only in his *crucified* aspect accordingly that he vindicates the spiritual truth of his mission, or allows any trace of his divinity to appear; for here he is seen, in open contempt of every most sacred national tradition, sternly rejecting from himself a Jewish humanity, and putting on a universal one, that is, one which should be neither Jewish nor Gentile, but broadly unitary or universal, to the effacing of all literal discriminations whatever among men.

But I have not taken so much pains to prove to you: that our moral and rational manhood is not a real manhood, but a *quasi* one, intended only as a preparation for our real or natural manhood when it comes: altogether for its own sake, but with a view also to get some needed light upon the answer to our third question, which it is high time we were con-

---

by showing that God himself is the sole and infinite substance of these attributes, only in natural or impersonal, that is, universal and unitary, human form.

sidering. Our actual manhood as we have seen is an altogether provisional one intended to serve as a mere scaffolding to our natural manhood, as a mere foil or set-off to it when it is ready to appear in its own infinite Divine lustre; and I have thought that by first familiarizing your imagination somewhat with this mighty truth I might assist you to a fuller comprehension of the answer I am about to give to the question now before us. That question may be formulated thus: *What precise machinery does human nature require in order historically to avouch itself, or authenticate itself to the public conscience of men,* AS THE WORLD'S SOLE LIFE: so at long last harmonizing the finite, phenomenal, or merely conscious man with God's spiritual infinitude or freedom?

The machinery of human nature by which it ultimates its proper life, turning all history into its obedient vehicle, and filling the entire public consciousness of men with its renown, is solely made up of what we call *the church* and *the world.* These terms, however, remember, express no objective but a purely subjective reality in man; or what is the same thing they neither of them indicate a physical or material, but on the contrary a purely metaphysical or immaterial, substance in humanity. And a purely metaphysical or immaterial substance in humanity can only be A MIND. This accordingly is what *the church* and *the world* mean, *a purely mental or subjective reality in man;* the former term being employed to designate in those to whom it is applied affections turned heaven-ward; the latter, affections turned earthward: "the church," in other words, characterizing the sphere of man's progressive mental development, "the world" the sphere of his arrested mental development. The whole of humanity is comprised in these two forms of man's mental subjectivity. A man must neces-sarily have his affections turned towards heaven, or confined to earth, and according as either is the case with him, he is a least or miniature form either of the church, or the world. The church of course tends to issue spiritually in a heaven made up of inwardly *regenerate* men, and the world in its turn to issue in a coequal hell made up of inwardly *degenerate* men, so that unless the Divine power had effectually ultimated itself in human nature, and thereby broken up this fatal spiritual equilibrium, heaven and hell must have practically forever divided the spiritual world between them, and forever have given the lie consequently to the sovereign truth of God's creative infinitude.

Nothing, I venture to say, can be imagined more re-volting to our humanitary instincts of such infinitude than the perfectly veracious or unexaggerated pictures which Swedenborg's phlegmatic genius gives us of what he witnessed among our *post-mortem* friends and cronies. If the friend or crony in question had been on earth a reverential person, and now consequently had his lot among the angels, Swedenborg invariably found that the man's natural imbecility, or insufficiency to himself, had undergone no change through the event of death, the man being all the while spiritually restrained from *the frankest profligacy solely by the providence of God exerted towards him through angelic association.* And if, on the other hand, our deceased acquaintance had been on earth an habitual votary of self and the world, and therefore inwardly a mocker of God and the neighbor, so that he now found himself to his great delight enrolled among the lowest of the low, Swedenborg nevertheless invariably discovers that the fellow's braggart selfhood is at bottom a pure hallu-cination or sham, dependent every moment for its illu-sory existence upon hellish influx and association, and tolerated only for some transient incidental use pro-moted by it to other existence.

Could any thing then well be more hideous and implacable to human pity than such a picture of men's celestial or infernal possibilities, if the picture were intended to represent an eternal reality? The picture to be sure was not intended to represent an eternal reality, but we see from it excellently well what the eternal reality must have been (only much worse),

if the true sphere of the creative infinitude had not
been realized in our nature. Now the evolution of
man's natural destiny, and with it consequently his
participation of immortal life, has been strictly identical with the growth of the civilized State, that is,
with the growth of our earthly life out of absolute
bondage to the material elements of nature into a condition of free citizenship: so that we may say with
entire truth that the advent of this (prospectively) free
State of man on earth under which we have the happiness to live, has been the fruit of a gradually fiercer
attrition between the church and the world, and of
that exclusively.

The two universally recognized elements then of
our Christian civilization, which are *the church* and
the world, make up between them that requisite machinery of human nature by whose conflicting yet con-
current play it finally avouches itself the supreme law
of man's activity. I do not say, mind you, that the
church and the world are in the least identical with
human nature, or that they have any claim to a particle of her Divine prestige and dignity. God forbid!
All I say is that they constitute the mere *machinery*
of human nature by which it gradually works itself
out to the light of day. They are *the simple machinery
of its evolution* by which it eventually succeeds in
bringing itself to men's recognition as the *conditio*

sine quâ non of their Divine and immortal life. Their
sole historic or Providential purpose has been to serve
as a platform to the development of men's *real* or
natural consciousness, as utterly distinct from and inveterately hostile to their phenomenal or personal consciousness; and when this use has been accomplished
they are bound, both of them, to tumble off into "the
condition of weeds and worn-out faces." Thus the
church and the world bear to each other the relation
of base and superstructure, or negative and positive
conditions of one and the same metaphysic result, that
result being the evolution of humanity, or of men's
natural consciousness in orderly social form. The
incessant attrition to which these base mechanical
factors of human nature are doomed by their fierce
mutual antagonism, is practically obviated in great
part by their engendering between them what we term
the civilized State of man, as a temporary compromise
between creature and creator, or a richly provisional
outcome of human destiny while the social form of our
nature is still unachieved, or its grand consummate
celestial flower is still in abeyance to the coarse earthly
necessities of leaf, and stem, and roots. And they
both appear at last so approximately humanized, or
weaned of their inveterate animosity, in their child the
State, but especially in their grandchild, which is the
free State or republic, that although they have neither

of them the least intrinsic fitness to guide or control human destiny, they have yet somehow had the art or address to perpetuate their bad empire over the human mind down to this very day.

This in fact is to-day the world-wide tragedy of human life. Human life, even now when its social ideal is so imperfectly realized even in thought, would be a tolerably clean and reputable thing, were not its honest interests so foully complicated with those of the self-righteous church and the selfish, servile world. This metaphysic machinery of human nature, instead of any longer unconsciously promoting its evolution, has consciously undertaken to stifle it by compressing its nascent activity. That is to say, the church and the world, in the persons of their more astute adepts, have begun dimly to feel that their joint offspring, the civilized State of man, was never intended by God's providence to be a finality in human history. I don't mean to say that worldly and ecclesiastical minds, however astute they may be, have the least intellectual insight of God's truth upon this subject. I have n't the slightest idea, myself, that they have any intellectual discernment of the entirely provisional or providential character of our existing civilization, in that it was intended to base a *Divine-natural* evolution of human life, and disappear bag and baggage when that end is accomplished. But these secular and ecclesi-

astical minds are at least in sensible contact with the
actual facts and leading providential tendencies of the
time, and their own inordinate self-love and love of
rule insure that none shall feel so keenly as they the
gathering clouds that are rolling up *from within* over
the technical State, erelong to descend in floods of
devouring rain, hail, and tempest upon the devoted
heads of those whose hope in God is limited to it.
Hence their present persistent efforts to perpetuate
and extend their empire, by appealing no longer to
the political or civic conscience of men for support,
but to the hopes and fears of the private or personal
consciousness.

This however is a gross usurpation. Neither church
nor world has a shadow of claim upon men's individual
respect and attention, save in so far as men first of all
have a purely superstitious regard for the State as a
finality of God's earthly providence. Nothing can be
more preposterous than this baleful superstition. The
State has no permanent or absolute rights over the
human conscience. It was never intended, as I have
already shown, for any thing else than a mere *locum
tenens*, a simple herald or lieutenant, to Society, while
Society itself was as yet wholly unrecognized, and
indeed undreamt of, as the sole intellectual truth of
man's Divine-natural destiny. And the church meanwhile as the *genitor* of this temporary civilized State

of man, has no other office in the name of the celestial or paternal providence that presides over it, than
prophetically to promise every man a *mens sana*, that
is, a sound mind. Neither has the world, as the
genitrix of the State, any other office derived from the
earthly or maternal providence involved in the State,
than prophetically to promise every man a *corpus
sanum*, that is, a sound body, wherein his *mens sana*
may house itself with comfort, and exercise its power
unimpeded. But no one has ever been such an abject
noodle as to maintain that this Divine prophecy and
promise in behalf of universal man kept up by the
church and the world, were ever intended to be fulfilled by the merely instituted State of man, that is,
by a regimen of mere citizenship, in which the conscience of men should be persistently held submissive
to tutors and governors. At all events, the actual
facts of the case must soon disenchant him. For no
fact is more notorious than that there is actually no
man within the precincts of civilization possessing an
absolutely healthy mind, or an absolutely healthy body.
In truth the church and the world, in generating civilization, have had a purely prophetic relation to the
human mind, and no pretension can be more utterly
absurd on their part than to claim any relevancy to
man's living or spiritual consciousness. They have
never had the slightest claim to human respect in

themselves, but only in producing their joint offspring, the State. They rightfully end or merge in her formation, and have no logical pretension to survive it a single instant. Above all and at this day they have no particle of right to arrogate the least control over the mind of any man who does not conscientiously identify his manhood with the State, or limit it to good citizenship, so forever rejecting the invitations of infinite goodness and truth.

For this empirical State of man, whereby he is providentially led into accurate self-knowledge, and so prepared for an immortal destiny, is with us — as our constitutional polity as a community announces — *functus officio*, or thoroughly exanimate as to the beneficent spiritual uses which once consecrated it to men's respect. Our constitutional polity as a community makes no provision for priest or king, which seem essential to the State in its merely political form, and we may not unreasonably infer accordingly that the State under these skies is casting its old political skin, and putting on one which is more decidedly flexible, and congruous with the perfected or social form of our nature. In other words: the common life of man in this hemisphere is undergoing a marked formal or providential change, in ceasing any longer to acknowledge outward sanctions, and learning more and more to acknowledge only inward ones. Of

course this improvement in the common lot involves
a corresponding demoralization in the private or personal sphere, save where men's personal life distinctly
reflects the common life, or acknowledges no law so
sacred as that of the public welfare.   For there are
it must be admitted too many fierce and avaricious
natures among us to whom the State no longer exists
as the symbol or representative of an outward order in
human life, and at the same time does not begin to reveal itself as the symbol or representative of a much
more constraining inward order, and all these necessarily look upon their fellow-men as delivered over to
their use to be fleeced *ad libitum*.   But notwithstanding these deplorable limitations I insist that the distinctively common unconscious life of these spiritual
latitudes — that is to say, the heart and mind of the
American people, uncontaminated by European and
especially sacerdotal pauperism — is one of great elevation.   And there is no way to account for the fact but
by acknowledging that the American State is really
become the vehicle of an enlarged human spirit.   I
have myself no doubt of the constant operation of this
cause.*   Living as I for many years have done

---

* It ought not to be forgotten in this connection that the form of our
polity bears on its very face, that is, in its name, an intimation of the
spiritual change it represents.   It is not America, but the UNITED
STATES *of America*, "one out of many," as its motto reads, to which the

among plain New England people, I am continually struck with the singular natural or interior refinement I encounter in persons who have obviously been all their lives without any exceptional outward advantages. They spread many of them such a humane or impersonal savor around them that they seem "native born" to the skies, and if their culture were only equal to their nature, or their manners as good as their morals, heaven would begin to be realized on earth. But we cannot have everything at once, and they give us the essential at least.

The sum of all I have been alleging is that we as a community are fully launched at length upon that metaphysic sea of being whose mystic waters float the sapphire walls of the New Jerusalem, metropolis of earth and heaven. It is not a city built of stone nor of any material rubbish, since it has no need of sun or moon to enlighten it; but its foundations are laid in the eternal wants or passions of the human heart sympathetic with God's infinitude, and its walls are the laws of man's deathless intelligence subjecting all things to his allegiance. Neither is it a city into which shall ever enter any thing that defileth, nor

---

expiring states of Europe bow, or do deepest homage, in sending over to these shores their starving populations to be nourished and clothed and otherwise nursed into citizenship, which is a condition preliminary to their being socialized.

any thing that is contrary to nature, nor yet any thing
that produceth a lie; for it is the city of God coming
down to men out of the stainless heavens, and therefore full of pure unmixed blessing to human life, and
there shall be no more curse. These things are hard
to be believed as falling within the compass of our
dishonored and bedraggled life. But this is only because our feeble-minded and narrow-hearted clergy
have been so utterly incompetent as a general thing
to divine God's infinitude, or enlighten the public
sense in His adorable ways. For do not they themselves regard our beggarly citizenship as the final
achievement of God's omnipotence in our nature?
Do they not perpetually sacrifice the patient bleeding
truth of human brotherhood or society to it? Do
they not consequently cling to their squalid and venomous little ecclesiasticisms as the last hope of humanity? These very ecclesiasticisms it is which are
the foulest stain upon humanity, and do more as
Christ alleged than all the world to make men willing
children of hell. At the bottom of every human heart,
not ecclesiastically perverted, there is, we may be sure,
a latent belief in God's spiritual omnipotence or infinitude, and a hope of seeing it eventually realized in
our natural form. But what chance have this benign
belief and hope of surviving the torrent of falsity and
unbelief which now descends from the Christian pul-

pit, orthodox and unitarian alike? Christ's own name in the church has become a synonyme for the most signal dishonor shown to God's spiritual perfection, and he who was put to his death of shame only by the righteous men of his day and generation, now finds himself in ours resuscitated to one infinitely more infamous and helpless, in being made the shibboleth of the frankest and most unconscious spiritual hypocrisy ever revealed under heaven.

The best life of the world is growing more than suspicious of the sanctity which attaches to facts or events, and insists accordingly upon finding the Christian facts and events interesting or memorable only in so far as they consent to *represent* a truth very much more universal than they literally, or on their face, constitute. And this accounts for that alleged " decease of faith," which has become among our dishonest churchmen the fashionable religious cant of our day. Men of a spiritual or humanitary culture are becoming very contemptuous of any Divine credentials that are not first of all exquisitely and intensely human. They unaffectedly resent the old dogmatic traditions of God's outward or physical activity in creation as dreams of the race's pagan infancy. They are ashamed any longer to acknowledge God as a clever charlatan or conjurer, seeking by an incongruous display of magical power and

majesty to propitiate men's inward and rational reverence. And in confirmation of this statement I
appeal to your own testimony whether, when any
noisy "evangelist" so-called, like the late collapsed
Mr. Moody, or the present distended Mr. Cook, comes
along to insult this tender, ineffable Divine-natural
renaissance in us, and menace it with the blight of
the lower regions, you have not yourself always observed that the energumenous mountebank never succeeds in doing any thing beyond inflaming his fellow-
quidnuncs of the conventicle but convert himself
into an object of quiet public contempt and derision?
This indeed is one of the most heavenly omens of our
day, when we consider the hopeless inertness of the
mass of men to the solicitations of spiritual truth, that
some untidy zealot or other should ever and anon feel
himself prompted by his irritable lusts to come forth
from his subterranean lair, and vituperate the sunshiny upper world — this sunshiny, respectable, commonplace world — until by his grotesque antics he
forces it in spite of itself to recognize the spiritual
arrogance and blasphemy which are the veritable soul
and substance of our professional religion. I don't, to
be sure, very much love this respectable, commonplace
world myself, and am very apt to feel my respiration
impeded under its decent bondage; but I easily con-
done all its shortcomings, were they twenty times

greater than they are, whenever I am thus made to see how steadfast a providential breakwater it makes to every recurrent wave of men's fanatical self-righteousness, or tyrannous love of dominion.

But it is time to bring this letter, and the whole series of which it is a part, to an end, for though many an interesting point remains to be touched upon, I have substantially finished the task I contemplated when I set out, and my bodily health is no longer good enough to make work for its own sake attractive to me. Now that my task is done, I wish I could have accomplished it more skilfully; though to have accomplished it at all, with the impoverished nerves left me, is matter of no little thanksgiving. I have had no help in writing but that of the Holy Ghost, which nowadays is no private possession, but is the common property of all spiritually upright men, being the identical spirit of their nature. And accordingly my only dread all along has been lest my inevitably private and particular accents should somehow overlay and obscure its public or universal ones. What I thought by its inspiration to say to you at the beginning was a very simple thing. I intended to show the exact harmony between the literal personal facts of Christ's life, and the spiritual or creative truth of which those facts have been our only adequate harbinger and revelation. Christ's suffering and glorified person was but a normal outcome and expression of the infinite creative love towards the human race, a love which contents itself with nothing short of the rescue of the created nature from the hands of the actual or phenomenal creature, and its exaltation to supreme dominion : and if we honor the historic type of this great transaction, much more ought we to honor the infinite and eternal spiritual substance which alone inwardly shaped it, and made it the only symbol of thoroughly perfect or Divine manhood the world has ever known, or ever will know. And having done this I thought to sing a pæan over our despised and dishonored nature, which is at last enthroned in omnipotent majesty above the spiritual world, so that the once divided but now united realms of heaven and hell fall beneath it, and equally attest its will : or if not equally, who knows whether in the miraculous providence of God, what is last in rank may not as heretofore avouch itself first in use?

This I repeat was all in effect I intended to say, and so do justice to the peaceful spiritual meaning of the Christian facts as they are reported in the gospels. But I found my pathway so beset with gainsaying not only on the part of our professional religionists, but on that also of our sectarian scientific zealots, that I was obliged to pay my respects to these several opponents as I went along, so that in spite of myself my voice grew full of tumult even in setting forth the pacific gospel truth. The sectarian religionist cleaves to the Christian facts, *but denies their subserviency to a higher order of truth.* The sectarian "scientist," as he is called, denies the authenticity of the Christian facts *in submission to a lower order of facts.* I hold the Christian facts to be authentic, because I see them to be needful ultimates or exponents of otherwise undiscoverable and inconceivable spiritual truth. Indeed I hold the life, death, and ascension of Jesus Christ to be the only facts of human history which are not in themselves illusory or fallacious, because they alone base a new creation in man to which every fibre of his nature — starved and revolted by the actual creation — eagerly responds. But viewing the facts absolutely : that is, regarding them apart from the light they reflect upon the creative infinitude and the destiny of man the creature of that infinitude, and consequently as designed merely to set off the person of Christ to the everlasting homage of mankind : they seem to me utterly flat, vapid, and contemptible. I by no means desire to apologize then for the contentious strain of my letter, but prefer to end by rehearsing a lovely bit of Swedenborg's experience.

"Once upon a time a numerous crowd of spirits was about me which I heard as a flux of something disorderly. The spirits complained, apprehending that a total destruction was at hand, for in the crowd there was no sign of association, and this made them fear destruction, which they supposed also would be total as is the case when such things [namely, the absence of mutual association] happen. But in the midst of this disorderly flux of spirits I apperceived A SOFT SOUND ANGELICALLY SWEET in which was nothing but harmony. The angelic choirs were *within*, and the crowd of spirits to whom the discord belonged was *without*. This flowing angelic strain continued a long while, and it was said that hereby was represented how the Lord rules things confused and disorderly which are without or on the surface, namely : by virtue of A CENTRAL PEACE, whereby the inharmonic things in the circumference are reduced into order, each being restored from the error of its nature."

If then you discern the central peace which is in my little book, I do not think its superficial polemics will seem out of place. And so, farewell.

APPENDIX A.

ERCY is equal whether exhibited towards heaven or hell. It is of mercy to be punished, because all the evil of punishment is made subservient unto good. — *A. C.* 587.

Equilibrium is so perfect in the spiritual world that evil always inevitably returns upon him who commits it, and so punishes him. This is called the permission of evil, and is allowed for the sake of amendment, and thus the Lord turns all the evil of punishment into good, so that nothing but good is from Him. — *A. C.* 592.

An evil spirit told me that he was in heaven when he was in the life of self-love, and that it was impossible any other heaven could be than the one he made for himself. But it was replied that his (self-made) heaven is turned into hell whenever the real heaven flows into it. — *A. C.* 6484.

By the marvellous providence of the Lord evils are continually *bent* to good : for the Divine end to good universally reigns. Hence it is that nothing in the universe is permitted except for the end that some good may result from it. But whereas man has freedom to the intent that he may be reformed, he is bent to good so far as he permits himself to be bent in freedom ; thus continually from the most grievous hell into which he strives assiduously to plunge himself, into a milder, if he absolutely cannot be led to heaven. — *A. C.* 6489 ; see also 3854.

No evil can befall any one without its being immediately counteracted, for when evil preponderates then it is chastised, by the law of equilibrium ; but solely to this end, that good may ensue. — *A. C.* 689.

When any one in hell does evil, he is punished; the Lord permitting this for the sake of his amendment, since He is essential justice. — *True Christian Religion*, 459.

God governs and disposes all things by turning the evil of punishment and temptation into good. — *A. C.* 245.

It is to be further observed that all evil inflows into man from hell, and all good from the Lord through heaven. But the reason why evil, being thus an influx into man, is appropriated to him or becomes his own, is because he believes and persuades himself that he thinks and does it of himself; whereas if he believed according to the truth of the case that it is always a veritable influx, evil would not then be appropriated to him, or become his own, but good from the Lord would be appropriated instead. For in this case when evil flowed in the man would instantly think that it came from the evil spirits attendant upon him, and when he thought this, the angels would turn it aside or reject it. *For the influx of the angels is into what a man knows and believes, and never into what he does not know and believe :* since angelic influx is nowhere fixed or permanent save in things pertaining to man. When man thus makes evil his own, by obstinately believing that he originates it, he procures to himself a sphere of that particular evil, and so conjoins himself with hell, for in spiritual life conjunction is effected by accordant spheres. Thus the spiritual sphere of man or spirit exhales from the life of his love, and advertises his quality even to those at a distance from him. — *A. C.* 6206.

They who think from an idea of space, as every one does who is in the world, perceive that hell and heaven are spatially very remote from man. But the fact is exactly contrary to their impression of it, heaven and hell being in man, and nowhere outside of him, heaven in the good man, and hell in the bad man. Furthermore every one after death floats into the exact heaven or into the exact hell with which he identifies himself in the world. — *A. C.* 8918.

Sometimes spirits recently deceased, who have been evil inwardly during their life in the world, but outwardly orderly from prudence, complain that they are not admitted into heaven, having apparently no other opinion of heaven but as a place into which admission is granted of favor. But they are told that heaven is denied to no one, and if they desire admission they may have it. But when they come into the most external and superficial of the heavenly societies, they perceive, by reason of the incongruity of the heavenly sphere with their own, what seems to them an infernal anguish and torment, and cast themselves down, saying that heaven is hell to them, and that they had no notion previously of its being such an uncomfortable place. — *A. C.* 4226.

APPENDIX B.

PROPRIUM OR SELFHOOD, THE SOURCE OF ALL EVIL.

MAN'S appearing to himself to have a proprium, or private selfhood, is a state, says Swedenborg, resembling sleep, because while he is in it he knows no otherwise than that he lives, thinks, speaks, and acts *of himself*. When, however, he begins to know that this is false he starts as it were out of sleep and wakes up. — *A. C.* 147.

Man's proprium when viewed by heavenly light appears altogether like something osseous, inanimate, and thoroughly deformed, consequently as in itself dead. But when vivified by the Lord's life it looks like flesh. Man's *proprium*, or selfhood, is indeed a mere dead nothing, although to himself it looks so real and important as even to be his all. Whatever lives in man flows in from the Lord's life, and if this influx were arrested the man would drop stone dead; for man is only an *organ receptive of life*, and according to his recipiency as an organ will be his reproduction of the life. Real *proprium*, or selfhood, belongs to the Lord alone, and from his proprium is vivified that of man. The Lord's *proprium* is indicated by his saying after death to his disciples who thought him a spirit : " a spirit hath not flesh and bones as ye see me have." — *A. C.* 149.

It has been proved to me by sensible experience that a man, a spirit, and an angel, *considered in himself*, is as the most vile and filthy excrement, and *when left to himself breathes nothing but hatred, revenge, cruelty, and the foulest adulteries: these things making up his proprium, and will.* This may appear to any person who reflects that man, when first born, is more vile than any living animal, and that when he grows up, and is left to his own devices — unless he be prevented by external restraints, such as legal penalties, and those prudential restraints which he imposes upon himself in order to become great and rich — he would rush headlong into all sorts of wickedness, and never rest until he had subdued all men to himself, and seized their property, not sparing any but those who promised to become his slaves. Such is the nature of every man [by reason, no doubt, of the infinitude of his creative source, reflected in what is so obviously unsuitable to reproduce it as the *proprium*, or private selfhood, of the creature] notwithstanding his own ignorance of it growing out of his actual inability to accomplish his latent evil purposes. But were it possible for him to accomplish them, all restraints being removed, he would rush headlong into their execution. This is by no means the case with beasts, who are *born to* a certain order of nature, and kill and devour purely to appease the cravings of hunger, and when this is satisfied they cease doing harm. — *A. C.* 987.

A man's *proprium*, or private selfhood, is actually his own particular hell, for by it he communicates with hell. Thus the selfhood of its own nature desires nothing more ardently than to precipitate itself into hell, and also to draw all others along with it. — *A. C.* 1049.